ESCAPE SEQUENCE

The Abduction

By
Michael R. Vogel

PublishAmerica
Baltimore

ISBN: 1-60813-774-0 (softcover)
ISBN: 978-1-4489-0727-4 (hardcover)
PUBLISHED BY PUBLISHAMERICA, LLLP
www.publishamerica.com
Baltimore

Printed in the United States of America

ESCAPE SEQUENCE

The Abduction

Love you
Little Sweetie!

Love, Papa ♡

CHAPTER ONE

Having been awakened once again by a recurring nightmare, Sean Daniels sprang out of bed gasping for air like he had just come up from a three hundred foot free dive but sweating like he had ran a grueling marathon.

Although he could not remember the details of the dreams that had haunted his sleep the previous weeks, he did however remember the same intense light, the unimaginable torturing heat and the soul-possessing fear of being trapped that all the dreams shared.

Prior to his recent nightmares, Sean had been an average man of forty-nine. Standing just over six feet tall, he had executive cut, jet-black hair with a little gray just starting to appear at the temples and a three-day-old beard. A man of average looks, and although he had been college educated, with a Bachelor's Degree in Engineering he received on the GI Bill after the war, he was of average intelligence.

However, while in country during the Vietnam War, Sean was anything but average. It wasn't courage that got him through the war; it was fear. The fear of capture turned an otherwise average man into an angry, vicious warrior who was bound to return home with his life and the lives of his brothers-in-arms who were put in the middle of that heinous war against their will. He wasn't convinced that his country belonged in the middle of another country's civil war. Nevertheless, he looked at his involuntary induction into the Army as his temporary duty. He wasn't about to run to another country like some coward with his tail tucked beneath his legs, regardless of whether or not he believed they belonged there. While he didn't feel good about the reception he received upon returning to the United States, he was proud to have served his country with honor.

After catching his breath and trying to calm his anxious nerves, Sean began what he thought was going to be a normal day at work in his hardware store. He stepped into the shower and let the hot water run over his head for twenty minutes. It was a small blessing that many people didn't get to share, to be able to have twenty minutes of hot water in the morning, but having the only apartment in a building and being the only one using the hot water had its distinct advantages, and this was one of them. Not to say that it wasn't lonely at times, but at this particular moment, hot water seemed to be a very good comforter.

Standing at the mirror and shaving his weekend beard away, the horror of his nightmares returned to him. The shower and shave brought some relief, but the haunting dreams were ever present in the back of Sean's mind. He dressed in his usual dress shirt, Dockers and coordinating Hush Puppies and picked up his lucky army medallion and pocketknife. American Express was always advertising, 'Never leave home without it,' referring of course to their charge card, but for Sean that meant his lucky medallion and pocketknife. General Whitie gave the medallion to him after Sean single-handedly took out an advanced VC scouting party, and the pocketknife was given by a soldier whose life he saved in a battle shortly thereafter.

The very next time Sean was in battle, his new knife saved his life. While on a recon mission, Sean stepped on a bouncing Betty land mine and had to cut his boot away and carefully replace his weight with some rocks. That knife and his quick jump behind a nearby tree saved him. He was very lucky to have survived the land mine, lucky to have been given the knife days before he went on that maneuver and lucky to have a tree close enough to jump behind. Providence had played a big role in saving his life that day for sure, and from that day to this, he'd never left home without it.

He went to the refrigerator for some breakfast but only found a half eaten, week old pizza, something that resembled a half gallon of milk mixed with large curd cottage cheese and a few grapes that looked more like hairy marbles than grapes. He decided to catch a light breakfast at a sidewalk café on the way to work.

Aside from the horrifying dreams it was a normal Monday morning in early May. Named after a Civil War general, Morgantown was the epitome of small town America. A quaint, village like town that still had cobble stone sidewalks and gas lanterns lining the central road, bordered with family owned stores and the ubiquitous soda shop. Located in the heart of the Appalachian Mountains on the western edge of North Carolina, Morgantown was a modern town but caught in the past as well. Time seemed to move slower here than in the rest of the country.

The big city didn't have much that the simple town folk that lived there wanted. What Morgantown didn't have they thought they could do without. The latest newcomer to town was the Bagel Shop. It was the latest craze and everyone seemed to stop there for breakfast. Who would have thought that boiled bread would take first place over greasy fried donuts? The old timers figured it was probably just a phase people were going through, probably just trying out the new gig in town. It would all blow over soon, they thought, and the stranger in town would pack up her fancy boiled bread machine and drive back to her fancy big city and her big city ways. Truth be told, the other business owners in Morgantown liked the Bagel Shop. They liked eating outside where the air was clean and void of the greasy smell of fried donuts and free of the old clan rhetoric. In addition, they could get a cup of coffee that hadn't been burning in the pot since five o'clock that morning. The shops didn't open until nine in the morning and most of the shop keepers didn't get there until eight thirty, so why put on the coffee at five except for the old timers and old clan types who liked to gather for old time sake at the donut shop? The Bagel Shop was here to stay.

Sean sat down under an umbrella-shaded table on the sidewalk and waiting for the owner/waitress to come out.

"Good-morning, Sean," she said cheerfully.

"Good-morning Jane," Sean replied looking up and squinting through the morning sunrise.

"What will you have this wonderful spring morning, the usual I suppose?"

"No—today I'm thinking of changing things up a bit. Instead of a bagel with jam, just bring me a bagel with cream cheese, and black coffee, please."

"Oh you, how can I keep you healthy with a breakfast like that?"

"Oh—you will, believe me it's a lot better than what I have at home in my frig."

"You're the boss," she said as she walked inside.

At that moment, the town sheriff drove up and got out. He was born and bred in the mountains, and was a sixth generation mountain man. He stood six feet, seven inches tall and probably weighted every ounce of three hundred pounds. If there ever was a man for sheriff of this area, this was the man. There wasn't a man in these parts who would stand toe to toe with Bruce. People around called him "Bruce the Spruce," because he was as tall as a tree and just about as round. They said he could push one over with his bare hands. While myth is always more colorful than truth, in this case they might have been right.

During a recent official, un-official battle of the beards, an annual event held at a local pub where the length and strength of the local's beards were measured, the battle became just that, a battle. It was more like a brawl. The pub was being destroyed, and hating to lose all the revenue he was making on the liquor sales, the pub owner waited to call the sheriff until it was almost too late. When the sheriff did arrive, all he had to do was step inside. When they all saw "Bruce the Spruce" standing in the doorway, the fighting stopped, and they all went home. There were more than fifty men fighting, drunk, and they were not all law abiding men. Some of them were ex-cons, some ran moonshine, some were bikers or clansmen, but they all just stopped fighting and left silently like a bunch of boy-scouts. In that case the myth beat them without a fight. They were just plain scared.

The sheriff got out of the car and walked up to Sean. "Mind if I join you, Sean?"

"Please," Sean said, motioning to the sheriff, "pull up a chair."

"How's business been lately?"

"I can't complain, I guess. Nuts and bolts—something everyone needs at some time or another. How about you, had any bad guys making your life crazy?"

"Oh, you got the crazy, drunk, hillbilly feud once in a while, nothin' to get up in arms about. I guess if there is a town to be sheriff of, this would be the one."

Jane came out with Sean's breakfast and said, "Well, hello, Bruce, the usual?"

"That'll do just fine, Jane."

"The usual," Sean asked. "Doesn't your wife cook?" Bruce laughed, "Yeah, she's the best cook in the county too. But man, that was more than three hours ago. Had a good breakfast casserole, six eggs, sausage, diced ham, 'tatoes, and cheese, all stirred up and baked in the oven 'bout a half hour or so. Oh! It was so good! She even served it up with her homemade sour-dough bread and fresh coffee. That's why I married her, but heck, man! Like I said, that was more than three hours ago."

"I don't get it, Bruce. How do you keep your girlish figure?"

They both laughed as Jane brought out Bruce's usual second breakfast. Then Sean realized he had been suckered.

"Coffee," Sean said.

"Yeah, coffee, black, sugar, stirred not shaken," Bruce said, laughing.

"Oh, you're a riot." Sean said, happy for the few minutes of relief from the nightmare flashbacks. If only the rest of the day can continue like this. He thought.

"Well, I better get on my way. Let me know if you need any help with those bad guys."

"Oh, I will. I'm liable to get weak, being I'm on a diet and everything," He said laughing.

Walking to his store, Sean could not shake the feelings of intense fear and despair that had come in his dreams. A sense of dread was with him every day now.

He had to stop momentarily at a cross walk while a school bus picked up children for school. He overheard two women comparing recipes for strudel and arguing over which of the sweet confections was the greater of sins, when the feeling hit him again. This time it hit him more strongly than ever before. It was as if he were reliving the most violent and horrifying battle he had experienced during the war, with mortar fire and blazing bullets all around him, watching his comrades in arms dropping like flies and not being able to do anything to stop it. On a scale of horrifying experiences it was overwhelming. There was no physical fit or tantrum, no violent convulsions, no seizures, or spiritual manifestations, he just got really sick to his stomach and started to have cramps like he never had before. A hot flash hit him hard, and he began to sweat profusely. He turned abruptly to the women standing beside him and yelled, "RUN!"

Startled, the two women jumped away from Sean and the younger woman grabbed the arm of her companion for moral support. Backing away slowly and looking around for any possible threat and finding none, they simply smiled politely, thinking, Sean a weird guy. The older woman said in a whisper, "Let's go Nancy, there's something wrong with him."

She was about fifty years old, and was wearing some kind of uniform, like a dental assistant might wear, and white tennis shoes. Her hair was cut short, barely below her collar and was extremely black, too black not to have come from a bottle. The younger woman, referred to as Nancy on the other hand was about thirty-five and wearing white shorts and a light yellow tee-shirt with "Babe" embroidered on the front in blue tread. She had shoulder length auburn hair. A soft creamy complexion together with a bright cheerful smile made her look and act more like a college cheerleader than the mature woman she was. The only thing mature looking was her glasses. She wasn't wearing the stylish retro glasses. She was wearing the oversized type that one would expect a college professor or chemist to be wearing. They made her look intellectual. They certainly didn't match her wardrobe or her bright and cheerful disposition.

She was the third bright and cheerful person that Sean had run into that morning.

He was beginning to wonder what was wrong with him. Why is everyone else so happy and I'm in so much torment. He thought. Is God punishing me for something I have done? Or does God even really exist?

The light changed and the crosswalk signal blinked, allowing them to cross, but Sean was unable to move for a brief moment. It was as though his feet were nailed to the ground, and while he desired to walk, or more likely run, he was not able to. Breaking out in a sweat again and turning pale, he felt like he was going to faint. The two women started to cross the street and Nancy looked back briefly at Sean thinking, what a strange guy. When she noticed how pale he was she stopped and turned toward him. "I'm going to check on him," she said to her friend, nodding at Sean.

"Are you sure you want to get involved? He's strange."

"Yes, I think he's having a heart attack or something."

"Ok, be careful, I've got to go or I'll be late. I'll see you later."

Nancy walked slowly back to the other side of the street. "Are you alright, sir?"

Sean grimaced, "I'm not sure; I'm scared stiff, but can't explain why. I'm—I'm not feeling so good."

"Here, let me help you." she said taking Sean by the arm. "There's a bench up ahead. Can you make it that far?"

"I think so." Sean replied. "Thank you so much."

They made it about a half a block when they came to the wooden bench outside the barbershop. At first glance it looked like any other bench. It was painted hunter green and has had so many coats of paint applied over the years, it felt plastic to the touch. With the exception of the chipped areas and ubiquitous carved hearts with initials, you couldn't' tell how long the bench had been there.

They sat down together and Sean took several deep breaths.

"Thank you for your help; I don't know what came over me. My name is Sean…Daniels," he said reaching his hand toward her. "I own the hardware store just down the road."

"Nancy Baker," she said as she took his hand. "Should I call an ambulance?" Or can I help you get somewhere?"

"No! No ambulance, I'll be alright, I think."

"Can I at least help you get where you're going? I hate to leave you here alone."

"Well, if you don't mind, you could help me get to my hardware store."

They stood and once again Nancy took his arm as they walked. Sean told her about his recurring nightmare and the feeling of dread he has not been able to shake over the past week.

"I bet you think I'm crazy or something. Honest, I've never had anything like this happen to me before. Thanks again for all your help."

"Oh, don't worry about it. It's the least I can do. I hate seeing people in trouble, but I don't mind saying that I wasn't sure if I should help or not. I was just as scared as you were, I think. Why did you tell me to run?"

"I'm not sure. A feeling of immediate danger just came over me, but I wasn't able to move."

"Are you going to be alright?"

"I think so," he said as they approached his store. "Can I get you a cup of coffee or something?"

The moment he put his key into the door time and space began to unfold and become surreal. He was conscious of everything around him and he could move his eyes, but nothing more. Then the air became stagnant and dead, still, as if he were in the eye of a hurricane. The sky turned from a softly lit, robin-egg blue with scattered fluffy white clouds, to a stormy black-gray with a fire red core. Clouds moved in from nowhere and then pain hit him and Nancy with such intensity that they both cried out in pain. Sean thought he was being pulled apart from the inside out. He couldn't even move enough to turn the key and wanted desperately to run as fast as he could to get away from whatever was haunting him. Just as he felt he would pass out, a brilliant light engulfed him with such intensity that he was blind to anything but the light. Immediately after, he was burning with a heat that challenged any other experience he had ever had. It was as if he was in the middle of a hell storm of napalm. His nostrils burned and his stomach wrenched with the unsettling smell of burning flesh and hair. Then just before he passed out, he caught a glimpse of Nancy and realized that she too was trapped. He realized for the first time that it wasn't just in his head.

Everything went black.

CHAPTER TWO

Sean and Nancy awakened inside a rectangular room some forty feet long and twenty feet wide, sterile, white and completely void of anything but themselves. The walls and floors were smooth without even so much as a joint line and as hard and cold as granite. The twenty foot high ceiling was bright white and illuminated the entire room like the inside of a stadium. They were wearing white tunics devoid of any buttons or trim and were both bare foot and cold. The room was cold to the touch, like a mortuary and no more than sixty degrees. It had a door ten feet tall by two feet wide.

"Where are we?" asked Nancy, trembling.

"I don't know, but I don't like it. I can't explain it but I feel like I've been here before somehow."

Sean got up and took Nancy's arm. "Come on, let's get out of here," he said.

They walked over to the door and Sean tried pushing on it, then tried to slide the door open and in desperation began ramming the door. On the third attempt, the light in the room became intensely bright and hot and the pain he had felt before returned to him, it was so intense that he stopped and fell to the floor. As quickly as the room lit up and got hot, it dimmed a bit and grew cold again.

"What is going on here?" He screamed at the top of his lungs. "Let us out!"

Nancy sat quietly on the floor. She was no longer the bright young cheerleader that she'd seemed to be just minutes before.

Hours passed. While they were sleeping, huddled together for warmth, the door opened and a woman stepped into the room wearing a snug fitting one piece uniform. It was dark green, almost black in color, and had an iridescent sheen. Her hair was cut exceptionally short and was a dark gray, almost black color. She was six foot tall, very lean and resembled an anorexic fashion model, but she had a very forceful and demanding presence. Sean and Nancy woke to find her standing over them in a condescending way, projecting an air of superiority with her arms crossed and standing very erect.

"My name is Karna," she began looking down at Sean. "You are here because you possess an intellect, greater than any of your kind, and we desire to study you."

"My kind," Sean asked sarcastically. "What do you mean by that? Who are you?"

While Sean was looking at her he noticed something very peculiar about her. Her body was too perfect. She had the type of body a person has that is continuously having plastic surgery in an attempt to obtain perfection, and her face was long and very lean. But there was still something about her that Sean couldn't figure out. He had never seen a woman with such distinguished facial features before. From her eyebrows to her chin, every feature appeared to not only be perfect, but each stood out. Then he noticed her eyes. They were pitch black. It was as though the color band around the iris was completely gone.

"I am your captor and you will do as I command!"

"Oh, no I won't!" Sean yelled as he jumped up and simultaneously grabbed the woman around the neck with one hand, while holding one arm behind her back with the other. "You have no right to keep us here! Let us go NOW!"

With no muscular strain at all and the strength of ten men, Karna threw Sean fifteen feet through the air and against the hard cold surface of the wall. His body made a sickening thud as he hit the wall and slid to the floor. After a moment to regain his strength, he ran and thrust himself toward Karna again but was stopped dead in his tracks by the same blinding light and intense pain as before. This time the pain was concentrated in his head and gut, taking him to the floor curled up like a baby and screaming in torment.

Nancy stood up, and facing Karna, she pleaded, "Please stop hurting him! He's only trying to get free. We don't belong to you. Please make it stop!"

As though Karna were unable to see or hear Nancy's pleading, she continued, "Your resistance is foolish. If you desire to be without pain, you will obey the commands you are given. If you do not, you will certainly die. You will soon learn our ways, and you will perform without question. You will begin soon. As far as the woman is concerned, she is now with you and as such will become part of your study."

With that she turned toward the door. It slid open and she left.

As soon as Karna left, Nancy moved over to where Sean had fallen and tried to comfort him. It was minutes before he was able to move again without pain.

"Where do you think we are Sean?" Nancy asked.

"I don't know. I just don't have any idea, but it would seem that we are about to find out. That…that whatever she was said something would start soon."

"What did she say? You have superior intelligence? What was she talking about? And what did she mean by your kind?"

"I don't have any idea. I'm just a regular guy who owns a hardware store. Trust me on this, there is nothing special about me at all. I'm sorry I got you into this Nancy. I'll do whatever it takes to get us home. I promise."

"Sean, I'm really scared. How did we get here, I don't remember anything except intense heat and pain. Do you have any idea on how we're going to get out of here and why they're doing this to us?"

"I'm sorry, but I just don't know any more than you do right now. We'll get out though. Somehow, we'll get out. I'm tired, really tired. I have to rest now."

Nancy watched him quietly as he sat still and fell asleep. Questions raced through her head as she pondered her captivity. Haunting flashes of her past, horrifying experience started to surface, thoughts she hadn't had in years and had all but forgotten. Trying to comprehend why they were there and how she got involved, Nancy's eyelids grew heavy, and she drifted off to sleep leaning against Sean. She was glad that she had someone with her, and while she didn't really know Sean, she hoped against hope that he would be strong enough to get through it.

Ten hours later...

Beginning to stir, Sean became aware that everything that was happening was not a bad dream. He had to figure out a way to escape. Without any knowledge of passing hours, night, or day, the time spent inside the room seemed like an eternity. By the signs his body was sending it must have been a long time. He was freezing, hungry, thirsty and most of all in pain from needing to relieve his bladder.

Nancy woke and said, "I have to pee really badly."

"I know what you're talking about. I was just thinking the same thing. I'll try to get someone's attention, if torture isn't the result."

With that he knocked gently on the door. There was no response.

"I'll try harder," he said.

Sean began to knock harder and longer, then banging on the door, and then began kicking and screaming. "Let us out! Please!"

He braced for the pain he felt was sure to follow but nothing happened. He finally gave up, slumped against the door and slowly slid to the floor. "It's no use. The door won't budge."

Just then he heard the sound of a door opening on the other side. The door began to open behind him and he moved away from it as quickly as he could and saw a short dark hallway not more than five feet long. On the right side of that was a smaller room. As he stepped into the room to investigate he saw a bowl shaped receptacle on the floor with a hole in the middle about eighteen inches high and the same in circumference and a similarly shaped receptacle, only smaller, on the wall. Next to the wall mounted bowl was a piece of fabric similar to the material that Karna's uniform was made of, and the same dark green, almost black color.

"I think it's a bathroom!" he yelled out to Nancy.

She came running through the door and Sean motioned and said, "You go first."

Since there was no door to close, Sean stepped back into the big room and waited for her to finish. Hearing the sound of water running and remembering his burning thirst and exploding bladder, he called to Nancy, "Can I come in now?"

"Yes, I'm sorry. Come in."

When he stepped into the room, he was surprised to see Nancy sticking her face into the very small sink and gulping water as it poured from a small hole in the wall, completely soaking her hair and the top of her tunic.

"You better take it slow, Nancy. Too much, too fast will make you sick."

Nancy stood up and without saying a word walked out of the bathroom. Sean could hardly wait until she was out of sight before he began to relieve himself. It was not a normal toilet. It was not like anything he had seen before. As he stepped up to the bowl on the floor, water began running from a small hole along the upper edge of the bowl and drained constantly. As soon as he had finished, the water stopped running at the bowl and began running at the small sink. He also began drinking but was wary of taking too much, too fast. He left the room and returned to Nancy, who was sitting in the corner of the big room with her knees pulled up against her chest, rocking back and forth slowly.

"Are you alright, Nancy?"

There was no response; she just sat there soaking wet and rocked as she stared ahead. Thinking she was going into shock, he sat down beside her and pulled her into his arms. "It will be alright, I don't think it will be long before we find out what is going on."

"Why do you say that?" she said softly.

"Well, I just think that…well we've been in here a long time and the woman, Karna, said some study would begin soon. That's all. I really don't believe it has anything to do with you at all."

No sooner had the words came out of his mouth when the outer door at the end of the short hallway slid open, and Karna stood in the doorway of the room.

"It is time to begin your study," she said.

"Would it be possible to get something to eat? We've been in here for some time and are both cold and hungry. Nancy is not well and there is not good reason to keep her here, if I am the one you wish to study. I'll so whatever you wish as long as you let her go."

"You will do whatever we say, or you will die." Karna responded, "But as you wish, you may have nutrition before we start. The woman will stay. She is now part of the study as well. If you perform as requested, your time here will be brief."

She motioned for them to follow her and she turned to leave. Sean helped Nancy to her feet and in an attempt to play down what was happening to them, he said, "Let's go get something to eat so we can get this thing over with. Then he leaned in and whispered, "We'll play along for now. It will give me a chance to get out of this room and look for a way to escape."

They left the room and Sean scanned the fantastic size of the place they were in. The doorway opened into a colossal arena that had hundreds of doorways on the sides. Each door was unmarked, and lacked any type of hardware. In the center of the great expanse was a column of brilliant light, distinctly separated from the ambient light that filled the entire expanse. Almost like a grand pillar that supported the ceiling, it was so bright and tall that you could not really distinguish where the walls stopped and the ceiling began. As they followed Karna through the great room, Sean was looking desperately for a way out. He saw no guards, no organized assembly of personnel, just the column of light and several small groups of people walking form one point to another. The first thing that he realized was that there seemed to be two distinct groups. Most of the group, including the women, was all over six foot tall. The other groups, in much smaller numbers, were giants, but he could not see any details just shadowy figures because of the bright light. They were walking toward the column of light and Sean wondered why Karna was walking so far ahead and not watching them. What would keep us from just walking away? Sean thought to himself. As if she could hear his thoughts, Karna turned abruptly towards Sean and stared at him with cold, black eyes. Sean had never seen anyone with such dark eyes before. The only thing that he could think of was the eyes of a great white shark he had seen on Animal Planet, cold, lifeless, black, unblinking eyes that seemingly starred through him and into his very soul.

They stopped at the edge of the column of light and Karna said in her monotone voice, "Step into the light."

With great anxiety, Sean led Nancy to the edge of the light and slowly reached his arm toward the light until he could feel the warmth of the light. He turned to look at Karna and asked, "What is it, what is inside?"

"Just go inside the light, you will find what you seek there." She replied.

Thinking that it was somehow a trap but not knowing what else to do Sean stepped into the light and Nancy followed. They stood in the middle of the light and were bathed in warmth. Not the agonizing heat as before, but more, he thought, like what it might feel like inside a mother's womb, soft, pleasant, calming warmth. He was beginning to feel at peace with where he and Nancy were and began to feel full. His strength was beginning to return and he saw Nancy basking in the warmth as well.

Karna reached into the light and pulled Sean from it. "You are refreshed and filled?" She asked. "It is time to return to your room now."

"No, please," Nancy pleaded. "The room is so cold, and it drains my strength."

Karna said, "Let us go now!"

They began their long walk back through the expanse of the great hall, dreading the room. Sean scanned every inch of what he could see from behind Karna. He had to find a way out before they got locked into the room again, but he feared the pain. He dropped back a few paces behind Karna, and with all his strength ran and launched himself into her back, sending her stumbling to the floor. He grabbed Nancy's hand and took off running the opposite direction. They ran as fast as they could, and Sean was shocked and surprised when he turned, expecting Karna to be hot on his trail, but no one was there. He expected the bright light and pain to hit him hard, but it too was absent. He reasoned that it only worked inside the confines of the room and thought his only recourse was to keep running. Trying several doors along the way for a passage out, he came upon another hallway and ducked into it dragging Nancy behind.

"Why did we leave the light?" Nancy asked. "It was so warm and nice in the light. Please go back, I need more."

"No, Nancy! Listen! We've got to keep going. We've got to find a way out of here! Are you listening to me?"

Sean was beginning to wonder about all the strange things going on around him, and to him. How could they cause the intense pain with a bright light and how could it only have affected me. Did they implant something inside me while I was unconscious? What could be inside that light that could cause us to feel so much better after being inside it for just a few minutes? None of this is making any sense. We've got to get out of here.

Letting go of Nancy for a brief moment to try another door at the end of a short hallway he stumbled and fell toward the door. The door automatically opened when he was a foot from the door and he fell through the doorway onto the floor of another room. He lay motionless for a few seconds scanning the room to see if anyone saw him. When he saw no movement he quickly jumped to his feet and out the door again to retrieve Nancy but she was not there.

Remembering his encounter with Karna the first time he attempted to resist, Sean had no desire to be caught and suffer again. He looked all around to make sure Karna was nowhere around and ventured back inside the great room to find Nancy.

"Nancy!" He whispered loudly. "Where are you?"

The great room grew brighter than before. It was so bright that he had some difficulty distinguishing the great pillar of light, but knowing that Nancy wanted more of whatever was in it, Sean thought that would be the best place to look for her. After searching for the pillar of light for several minutes he finally found it and stepped inside to get Nancy. He found her lying on the floor just staring up toward the light in a somewhat catatonic state almost unaware of his presence.

"Come on Nancy, it's time to get out of here. I found a door that leads someplace else. It could be the way outside."

"No, I just want to stay here. It's so peaceful and quiet." She said just above a whisper, each word dragging into the next.

"Come on! We've got to get out of here! Look what this is doing to you!" Sean said as he reached down and pulled her to her feet.

Facing her, Sean backed out of the light pulling gently on both arms.

"We're almost there Nancy, just a little bit further."

Just as they were clear of the light Sean turned toward the hallway he had found and ran right into two of the giant males he had noticed before and a shorter man, all wearing the same uniform as Karna. The one in the middle held out his arm and grabbed Sean by the shoulder with so much strength and pressure Sean immediately went down on one knee.

"Ok, ok, I give up!" Sean yelled

Speaking in very poor English, the shorter man on the left said, "Foolish is your running, you know we caught you. Go back your room now."

Sean was beginning to think they had been captured by some third world country or something by the way he was talking. He couldn't place the accent and couldn't explain how he got there or why everything was so weird, so different, but he knew he wasn't in Kansas anymore.

At many moments of Sean's life he had been placed in positions where blind fear was his only guide. He was in that position now. Fear was his worst enemy and his best friend before. Fear would be his motivation to escape and return to his uneventful life now. But he knew their lives weren't in any immediate danger because they wanted some kind of test. And now that he knew a way out, at least a way out of the huge room. If they were going to escape they would need a plan. So, he decided to pick his fights carefully, and going up against the big brutes with Nancy in her euphoric state would be a mistake, at least for now.

When they arrived back at their room they found Karna standing there as if she had just arrived from taking them to meet their needs.

"We have adjusted the lights down and supplied water for you to refresh yourselves. You will find the room warmer in a short time. You have passed your first test," she said, "Enter and rest."

Nancy and Sean stepped into the room and Karna left quietly and without any threats. The inside door was left open, and they had access to the small bathroom. Although they were dirty and had began to stink, neither of them was concerned about what they looked like and just wanted to go home.

As soon as the door closed behind them Sean pulled Nancy near a corner and looked suspiciously around the room. "Listen Nancy, I'm not exactly sure what is going on here and I'm getting more confused by the minute. One moment that Karna woman is cruel and heartless and the next, she is somewhat cordial. I can't figure her out, but at least we are still together and not in any immediate danger. Let's take advantage of it and get some rest. We're going to need all our strength to escape."

CHAPTER THREE

The moment the brilliant light appeared outside Sean's hardware store, Bruce happened to be driving down Main Street making his morning rounds. He hit the brakes so fast the car following him crashed into the back of the squad car, pushing the rear bumper into the trunk and smashing the other car's front bumper into its radiator. At that moment, amidst the chaos of the accident, with steam clouding the street, and a crowd gathering around the accident, the quiet little town was becoming the epicenter of the most critical and life threatening event in the history of mankind. Although the citizens weren't aware of it yet, Morgantown was about to become headquarters to a new type of war and Sean would be the Commander and Chief through it all.

Having just witnessed Sean and a woman he recognized as one of the flower shop employees, disappear before his eyes, the sheriff was oblivious to not only the accident, but the angry driver yelling at him and the crowd gathering around the accident.

"What in the world did you stop for?" an angry woman yelled as she examined the front of her car.

Bruce completely ignored her as he walked toward the hardware store and looking at the sky. The clouds had disappeared, and the clear blue sky returned. Bruce was in an state of shock and disbelief, and somewhat dazed, but the woman, more worried about what her husband was going to say, wasn't concerned about Bruce's health at all.

"What about my car?" the woman asked, following Bruce down the middle of Main Street.

"What?" Bruce said a little hazy, as he finally turned back toward the angry woman.

"What about my car," she repeated. "Why on earth did you stop?"

"Oh yeah, don't worry about it. I won't give you a ticket."

"You won't give me a ticket!" she yelled.

The small woman stood toe to toe with Bruce. She wasn't even five feet tall and couldn't have weighed a hundred pounds soaking wet, but she was yelling at Bruce.

"What are you going to do about my car? My husband is going to be furious!"

Finally getting his wits about him again, Bruce looked down at the lady and asked; "Can I help you ma'am?"

"What do you mean can you help me? Look what you did to my car. I'm going to sue you for everything you have! My husband knows the mayor mister and you had better take care of this right now!"

Now completely himself again, Bruce was getting upset with this little lady screaming at him in front of the people gathering around. "Calm down miss, it's just a little finder bender."

"Did you just tell me to calm down? I can't believe what is happening here!" She said, jabbing Bruce in the chest with her finger.

"Now hold on a minute!" He yelled back as he took her hand and forced it away from him. "I said Settle down and I mean it! First of all what you are doing is assaulting an officer of the law. Do you really want to add jail time to your wrecked up car lady? And what's more, you were following too closely, or you wouldn't have run into me. You were also speeding, or you wouldn't have hit me so hard. You better back off, or you will be arrested for obstructing an officer while performing his duty, assault and careless and imprudent driving! Am I getting through to you?"

The shock of what he had seen was wearing off and turning into anger. He didn't like the thought that he wasn't in control of what happened in his town, and he certainly didn't like some short little woman yelling at him after she ran into him.

"You call your husband and tell him to come and get that heap off of my street, or I'll have it towed. And you better make it quick! And another thing, if I hear another thing about it from anyone, I'll have the judge order a bench warrant and I will arrest you!"

"Yes sir," She whispered.

"What was that?" He snapped.

"Yes sir." She said louder.

"Alright, now get that heap off of my street."

Bruce walked back to his car, pulled over to the hardware store and got out. He looked out over the crowd that had gathered, and after pulling out his public address microphone from his car, he said, "People, did anyone see anything unusual just before the crash?"

He waited for a response or for someone to raise their hand but no one responded.

"Did anyone notice it get cloudy for a brief minute?" He waited for another minute and like before got no response. Everyone was just milling around whispering to one another.

"Forget it!" he said and threw the mic into the car and walked up to the front door of the hardware store, leaving his squad car parked in the middle of the street. The key was still in the keyhole on a key chain with three other keys. He turned the key and walked inside.

Silence…this was the weirdest experience Bruce had ever been in. He thought he was stuck in a 'Twilight Zone' movie or some kind of practical joke. If he hadn't seen them vanish with his own eyes, he would have never believed it. For the first time in his life, he didn't know what to do. He had been sheriff for over twenty years and had been friends with Sean since he moved there right after the war ended in 1974.

I've got to do something but at the same time if I reported this, who would I report it to? He thought. And if I do report it, it'll sound so crazy they might just lock me up and throw out the keys.

Bruce went back to the Sheriff's department. He sat at his desk for hours, just thinking about what he had seen and what to do about it. The deputies were playing cards, and a small television was playing in a corner of the squad room. A program came on introducing a new program to be televised the next evening: 'Alien Abduction in America'. Bruce's interest was piqued.

"Turn that garbage off!" One of the deputies said.

"No way," said another deputy. "This kind of stuff really happens. Didn't you hear about that case out in the forest of Washington state a few years back?"

"Oh come on, get real will you? You don't really believe that trash do you? That stuff is nothing more than crazy talk from crazy people that need to get a life! The first deputy said as he clicked the remote to wrestling. "Now this is real!"

The sheriff stood up and shouted, "Leave it alone! Put it back to the other channel!"

"Yeah sure boss," said the first deputy.

"What's up with him?" The other deputy asked.

"How am I posed to know? Just deal the cards!"

The Sheriff watched the program intently for ten minutes and immediately went to the phone and called the station to get the number of the network that was producing the program. He got the number and called the network. After holding for what seemed like hours and being transferred ten times, he finally got to talk to the host of the program.

"Hello, my name is Bruce Faulkner; I'm the Sheriff of Morgan County, North Carolina. Am I speaking to James Everett Rose, the host of the new television show on Alien Abduction in America on NBC?"

"Yes, you got me Sheriff. How can I help you?"

"Well, I don't know how to do this, so I am just going to start bang off."

"That's usually the best way to do things, Bruce. May I call you Bruce?"

"Uh—Yeah—sure, whatever you want. Well, here goes. This is going to sound really weird."

"This topic usually does, and I rarely hear a story without hearing that statement first, so feel at ease, Bruce. Go ahead. Take your time."

"Ok, I've been Sheriff here in Morgan County for more than twenty years and never seen anything out of the ordinary, but this morning, right after having breakfast with me, a friend of mine walked to work a few blocks away. I drove downtown a couple of minutes behind him to check things out like I do every day. Now, this is a very small town and nothing ever happens, but this morning I saw him standing at the door of his hardware store just getting ready to open the door, and he had a young woman on his arm with him. I remember thinking, alright Sean. That's his name, Sean Daniels. I was thinking way to go, Sean, you old dog, you finally got a lady, and the sky suddenly turned really dark and these purple rolling clouds moved in really fast. And Inside the clouds it looked like there was fire. Then this really bright white light came through the dark clouds and concentrated on the hardware store. Suddenly Sean and the lady weren't there anymore. I slammed on the brakes and jumped out, staring at the clouds and then the hardware store and back to the clouds, and the sky was clear and blue again. I've never seen anything like it in my life. I went to the store, and the keys were there in the door, so I unlocked the door and went inside. I yelled for Sean, but the place was empty, and Sean was nowhere to be found. I went back to my office and sat there for hours trying to figure out what happened, and that's when I saw your program. What do you think?"

"That certainly meets the criteria of an abduction Bruce. It sounds like other stories I've heard, only this time it comes from someone with more credentials. Can I come to Morgan County and meet with you in person and go to the place where it happened?"

"You bet!" Bruce replied. "When would you like to come?"

"How about today, I can leave in about an hour?"

"Boy, you guys don't mess around."

"In cases like what you described, there is evidence that doesn't linger. We must attempt to gather it in order to substantiate the story. I'm sure you can understand that, being in law enforcement."

"Sure, but what evidence can there be other than an eye witness?"

"I have some specialized equipment that, among other things, measures radiation. We can measure the radiation levels on the door of the hardware store and surrounding area. Where is the closest airport?"

"Well, there you're going to have a problem. The closest airport is more than two hundred miles away. We do have a small landing strip outside of town but you would have to have a pretty small plane to land there. The town's name is Morgantown."

"That settles it then. I'll leave in an hour and charter a private jet to fly directly to Morgantown. Can your landing strip handle a private jet?"

"Yeah sure, if the plane is small enough."

"Very well then, Bruce, I'll see you in about three hours."

✱✱✱

Although they had not physically eaten, Sean and Nancy were refreshed and had a full feeling. Sean for the first time was able to concentrate on what he had seen on the outside, and began to formulate a plan of escape. Not knowing how long they had been there became inconsequential. Just getting out became his only concern…survival.

"I've got a plan," Sean said. "The next time they take us out, they will not doubt return us to the column of light. When we are taken out, we will lock our arms and bolt at Karna. With any luck we'll knock her down and be able to escape to the door I found. I don't know where it leads, but it will go someplace else and may lead to a passage out of this place. At any rate we can only learn from future attempts. I expect a painful punishment for the attempt, but so far they have not caused any pain to you. Their reprisals have always been directed to me."

"Are you sure that is the smartest thing to do, Sean?"

"No I'm not, but what else would you suggest?"

"I don't know, but I'm afraid they'll kill us if we fight against them."

"Oh, I don't' think they'll go that far. They have taken me because they think I possess some exceptional knowledge of something. I think they will only punish me for attempting escape until they learn what it is they are after. Hopefully we'll find a way out long before that time comes."

They sat quietly for hours while Sean meditated on everything he has seen. Now that they at least had a bathroom of sorts, they could be somewhat comfortable while they waited for their next opportunity.

Nancy became more withdrawn as time passed. Sean noticed her portraying textbook symptoms of traumatic stress syndrome. He had seen it before in his comrades after a lengthy battle and he was acutely aware of the potential outcome.

"Nancy, are you alright?" he asked softly, knowing she was not.

There was no response. "Nancy." He said again, this time reaching out to touch her. She jumped back and looked scared.

"It's ok, Honey, it's only me. Don't be afraid."

She reached out and began hugging him so tightly he nearly lost his breath. She was trembling. "I'm so terrified." she said.

"I know you are, I am too, but I'll get you out of here. You just have to hold on and do what I tell you to do."

"I can't, Sean, I'm too terrified."

"You have to, Nancy, but I'll be right there beside you all the way. Have you been in trouble like this before?" He asked tenderly.

Nancy just sat hugging him and weeping softly. By her actions it was clear that she was not emotionally able to handle this. Who would be, he thought, but she was acting more like a small child about ten years old than a mature woman of thirty-seven. It was strange that she was more scared than mad.

She stopped crying and whispered, "When I was a little girl, I was taken from my family at a park. I was held in a small room for three days without any food or water. The man that took me was very rough and mean. I've never been able to deal with people like that from that day on. The room I was held captive in was filled with old machine parts and had a dirt floor. There weren't any windows but you could see light coming through cracks in the wall. I screamed until my voice was strained but nobody heard me or came to help me. I was only eight years old. On the third day, a lineman working nearby heard me crying and rescued me. It took years of counseling before I was over the experience, but now everything has come back as though it happened yesterday." She paused and sat quietly for a moment. Sean didn't know what to do or say, so he just held her. "I guess, sub-consciously I've never really trusted men, and that's why I remained single all these years."

"I'm so sorry." Sean said.

"I know, Sean," she replied, "I don't know why, but you are the first man I've really been able to trust and I don't even know you that well. But, when you first saw me and yelled for me to run, I thought you were crazy, and I just wanted to get away from you. I guess that for now you are the lineman who rescued me from my horrifying kidnapping experience."

Time passed and they began to get to know each other a little better. Sean shared his experience in Vietnam and his subsequent battle with fear of the unknown and the irrational fear of capture he battled with daily. He went on to detail the dreams he had been having for the previous weeks and why he felt as though he had been where they were before.

"The last thing I remember in my dream was being chased before I woke out of breath and sweating. That was the morning we met," he explained.

The outside door opened and without warning three extremely huge men, all over seven foot tall, entered running directly at them. They had no facial detail, as if they were wearing masks, and had greenish-gray skin tone. They were exceptionally strong, and one of them, at least a foot taller than the others, seemed to be the leader. They had no visible hair, black fingernails, and they stank really badly, like rotting flesh. Grabbing one arm each, two of them dragged Sean to his feet while the third one, the tallest, jabbed him in the stomach with a rod that emitted a sharp stabbing feeling that radiated through his muscle, causing extreme cramping. Sean had never experienced anything like it before. He yelled out in pain, and Nancy scurried to the nearest corner, crying. They dragged him across the room and out the door, leaving Nancy sitting alone.

"Why am I here," she whispered. "Please let me go, I need to go now. What have I done to deserve this?" As though she were pleading with someone in the room, Nancy continued her whispering questions. Once again she was alone and scared. Softly rocking with her knees drawn to her breast, tears trickled down her cheeks. "Why has God allowed this thing to happen?"

Her faith had not ever been very strong. Although her parents took her to church regularly, she never saw or felt anything that would compel her to trust in God. Her parents didn't attend with her, and maybe that was a deciding factor in her mind. If they didn't need God, why should she seek him? But in the solitude of this cold, hard and sinister room she prayed out to God, "God, if you're there, please get us out of this place."

The door slid open and expecting to see Sean, she excitedly turned toward the door. She was disappointed to see that Karna was standing in her usual pose, and presenting herself superior to Nancy. Standing there with her supercilious expression, Nancy understood why Sean had referred to her as the 'queen of contempt'.

"What are you, doing here?" asked Nancy.

"I am here to help you adjust," Karna replied, attempting to sound sympathetic.

"I don't need your help," replied Nancy. "I just need for you to release us."

"I have every intention of doing just that, as soon as we have what we need form the male."

"His name is Sean! Nancy yelled.

"Well then, Sean is going to teach us what we need to know. As soon as, Sean, gives us what we need we will let you both go."

"You said you needed both of us. What do you need of me?"

"We just need you to be yourself so, Sean, can be who he needs to be."

"That doesn't even make sense. Who are you, really? Nancy demanded. And, what if I refuse to help you?"

Karna laughed a laugh that sounded cursory, depthless and shallow, and almost mechanical. Then she said, "You are you, and there is nothing you can do to change that. You simply cannot help but to give us what we need."

Nancy's eyes started to tear again, but she wiped them away and glared at Karna.

"Don't misunderstand me. I want to help you and—Sean—become as comfortable as possible while you are with us. My role will be that of your host. Just let me know how I may be of service to you."

Nancy initially thought that she was being played but Karna was beginning to convince her. Maybe just maybe she was being sincere. Nancy thought. Expecting to encounter both good and evil, but at the same time needing a sense of normalcy in this insane place, she continued, "How do you intend on helping us, ah, adjust, as you say?"

"Ask me anything and I will comply, to the best I am able too," Karna replied.

"Well, for one thing we could use some real food to eat. We're not machines that you can just plug into your great light for food."

"Was your last experience not fulfilling?"

"I don't know what it was, but it certainly was not food!" Again answering with a grain of distain.

"I will see what I can produce for you. Is there anything else?"

"Yes, while you're at it how about providing something to sleep on other than this cold hard floor?"

"What do you require?" Karna asked.

"A bed perhaps," Nancy replied sarcastically.

Again Karna replied, "I'll see what I can produce for you. Come with me now. I will take you to the light; it will be a while for me to produce...food...for you.

Each word Karna struggled with seemed to be foreign to her. Food, bed, these words seemed to have not only little meaning to her, but abstract. Nancy got up and began to follow Karna, as before, into the colossal, expanse. They were three hundred feet or so from their room and about half way to the column of light, when someone walked quickly up to Karna and began speaking to her in a whisper. Nancy didn't get a good look at the person who Karna was talking with and could not hear them plainly, but it sounded like a foreign language mixed with some harmonious, almost digital undertone, switching pitch and mechanical in origin. Not being able to understand what was being said, she began to examine her surroundings a little more closely. The ever present light radiated so brilliantly it made it difficult to see a long distance clearly. It was though she was looking through a cloud or heavy fog. In the near distance she could make out the shape of small groups of people going to and fro like the ebb and flow of the ocean. She saw others that looked like Karna, tall, thin and almost fluid in their movement but never moving faster than a brisk walk. They were leading two or three people in and out of doorways and toward the column of light. Nancy couldn't help but wonder if there were other people, like her and Sean, who had been taken against their wills and were subject to every whim of their captors.

Once again Karna began to walk, and Nancy followed like a lamb following her shepherd. When they arrived at the great light, Karna simply stepped aside and motioned for Nancy to enter. Nancy began to warm slowly and began to lose herself to the light. She began to feel that she was in a safe place, and thoughts of terror, confusion and anger began to drift away. The light was so comforting and fulfilling, it not only gave her peace about where she was, but was lifting her body physically, mentally, and almost spiritually. She started remembering happy, joyous memories, and one memory came through more than any other. She remembered the warmth and security of her father's embrace when she had been reunited with her family after her childhood abduction. There was no safer or warmer place in her mind than that of her father's lap, with his strong, muscular arms wrapped around her. She knew she was safe and secure as long as she was being held in his arms.

Although only thirty minutes had passed in literal time it seemed like hours to Nancy but when Karna reached into the light to pull her out, Nancy resisted. "Please, just a moment longer," she pleaded.

Karna responded, "We must return now. It's been too long already."

Without any further discussion, they proceeded back to the room. Nancy was in a different place, at peace, compliant and fulfilled.

The door opened and Nancy stepped into the room. In the middle of the room was a small table that held a small spread of fresh fruit, vegetables, bread and honey. At one end of the room was a platform that resembled an enormous bed. It was a raised platform eight feet wide and ten feet long. It was two feet off the floor, with some of the foreign looking fabric covering a four-inch pad.

"I trust this will meet with your expectations," Karna said.

"Yes, yes, it will do nicely," Nancy replied. "Can we lower the light so we can sleep more comfortably?"

"It will only be lowered during the resting phase. At all other times the light must remain as it is."

Saying nothing more, nor waiting for anything more to be asked, Karna turned and exited. Nancy went over to the table and tasted a grape. It resembled a grape, it had the right texture, color and shape, but it had a peculiar flavor. It was not too sweet, nor too sour. It was just strange. Nancy went to the corner where the platform was and found a clean tunic. Although she felt unclean and would have preferred to shower first, she went into the toilet room and rinsed herself off before changing into the clean clothes. She tried some of the bread with honey and while it also had a peculiar taste, she was hungry enough to eat it. After feeling somewhat cleaner and filled, she stretched out on the bed.

Just as she was about to fall into a deep sleep she heard the swishing sound of the door sliding open. She rolled over and looked toward the door to see the three huge men come in as before. They walked slowly toward Nancy and stopped at the edge of the platform. As they advanced toward her, Nancy crept away and had her back to the wall by the time they arrived at the edge of the bed. They stopped and looked at her, studying her like she was an exhibit at the zoo. This time she was able to get a better look at them. They were huge in comparison to a normal man. Each standing very erect and seven or eight feet tall, they wore the same uniform as Karna wore, but they were different in every other way. Their skin was green with a pale gray tint resembling a corpse. When she first saw them they looked as though they had no facial features at all, but upon closer examination, she realized that their faces, although different from that of Karna's were covered with some kind of screen like material which reminded her of the safety equipment that fencers used during practice. The shape of their head was elongated, and while it was difficult to see because of the mask like shield, it appeared that their mouths extended well beyond their face. Like before, their body odor was overwhelming and repulsive that she nearly vomited before she was able to screen her nose with the cuff of her tunic.

"Where is Sean?" she asked quietly.

They looked at each other briefly then back to Nancy. One of them turned to leave the room while the other two climbed onto the platform and began reaching toward Nancy. She screamed as loud as she could, "Get away from me you creeps!"

They reached out for her as they climbed onto the bed and slowly crawled toward her. She tried to repel them by kicking at their faces, but they overpowered her and managed to grab your arms and pull her off the bed. As they pulled her off the platform, she continued kicking, punching and screaming but they were simply too strong. Just before they got to the door, Nancy reached down and dug her nails into the oily forearm of one of the men but instead of bleeding, a noxious, putrid puss, mixed with black fluid began running down his arm and onto Nancy. The smell was so revolting she purged the food she had eaten earlier all over herself. Blood curdling screams filled the room but to no avail. No matter how hard she kicked and screamed, they continued dragging her out of the room. The door slid open and she was passed to a large group of the huge men waiting outside who placed her onto a metal cart. Despite her struggling with all her strength and determination not to be taken, she finally succumbed and fainted. They strapped her down to the cart and began crossing the great abyss.

CHAPTER FOUR

Karna walks through the Piiderk, the leviathan space that the great column of light occupies. Her mission is to acquire information that has been illusive to her race thus far. Much has been learned through outside observation and some internal observation of involuntary participants, not unlike Sean and Nancy. Before her mission can be called a success, she must learn more of this species called the human race. Historical information is needed to gain knowledge of the human race's endurance during painful trials. She had learned, from previous subjects that historical documents are kept in museums and libraries all over the planet. And, while they were able to access the information, it did not prove beneficial to solving their biggest puzzle. She also must learn how the human race has survived when insurmountable obstacles were placed in its path, and she must have intelligence of their ability to interact with the species. Gaining this information has been a long, tedious, and most allusive venture. Several conundrums have been presented; one of which was how members of the species react with family members. They are willing to endure intolerable pain, even to the pain of death, to protect their families. They have been observed to be willing to do the same for fellow beings of their race whom they do not have an emotional tie with nor have ever seen before. Their proclivity to secure freedom from those who would oppress them, no matter how much more powerful, intelligent or militarily superior has continued to be a conundrum the

Bilkegine race has been unable to solve. It was thought that the only means by which this information and knowledge could be obtained was to become a member of the race and come to this knowledge first hand. Karna and many of her superiors believe that it will be done through careful manipulation of the right human subjects. Sean is the final test subject from whom they hope to gain their knowledge. The primary problem has been that while attempting to ascertain absolute understanding of the human psyche with finality, they continued to see variations in both reasoning and performance of their human subjects, especially in the males. Karna is convinced they have finally found the right human subject and that he will provide the key to that understanding. Under past leadership, concepts to accomplish this task were numerous. One means was surgical alteration of physical bodies to pass for human. This failed grossly due to their lack of knowledge of the human anatomy and lack of surgical prowess. Attempts were made to correct their lack of knowledge by abduction and dissection. Many volunteers came forth from the Bilkegine people to undergo the physical alterations, but most met a horrifying death. The direction then changed to cross breeding, hoping that genetic alteration and DNA grafting might produce a being both Human and Bilkegine. The new species would possess the human body, perfect in every way, but the Bilkegine mind and intelligence. Through additional abductions and manipulation of DNA this offspring would be able to freely gain access to places where data was stored and be able to develop emotional relationships with humans to gain insight to the interpersonal aspects of the race. Another goal of the same experiment would be the mating of this new species with that of a human to produce a virtual army of information gathers. These attempts failed miserably as well. Not only did the joining of the DNA's usually result in a dismal survival rate, but offspring who did survive became much stronger physically than any human or Bilkegine and their tendency to be extremely violent led to the total destruction of an advanced scouting vessel.

These failures and the years lost to that end have brought Karna to where she is today, now the Supreme Commander of this information quest and the Star Vessel Spiruthun. She and a few others have been modified to resemble a human on the outside while remaining Bilkegine everywhere else. There were others that were modified in the face alone and still others who were not physically modified for appearance but modified to allow them to produce the sounds necessary to speak the language of the humans. Karna being the most drastically modified Bilkegine and her willingness to alter her appearance and spend decades learning the rudimentary language skills needed to communicate with humans from many continents made her the right one to command this final expedition. If this mission fails, their entire race will eventually expire forever. Their only hope is learning how to defeat the human race emotionally so there would be no uprisings. This would allow them to use humans as slaves to build the infrastructure needed for the Bilkegine race to exist on this planet. If they were physically able to perform this work, they would have simply destroyed the entire human race decades ago and rebuilt the planet to suit them. But since they cannot exist on the planet in its current atmospheric condition they must rely on the human slaves to build the machinery to facilitate a friendly environment to the Bilkegine. Karna initiated long range communication with her superiors to update her progress.

"We are now preparing the male subject for phase one," Karna reports. "Steps have been taken to cause him great pain in an effort to provoke his immediate escape. Further steps will be taken to convince him that great harm, even death, is imminent to the female. These steps will produce the reactions we need to proceed. I am confident that success will be immediate. I will not fail." Transmission ended.

Karna returned to the Piiderk and crossed its great expanse to one of the hundreds of doorways and corridors. There were no landmarks just the brilliant light everywhere, and since every door and every hall looked just like the one before, knowing how the aliens found their way had been a mystery to every one of Sean's predecessors. It was as though they were following a scent trail like a Blood Hound. Maybe it was possible for them to see in a dimension or range of color that humans could not see. For whatever reason they knew exactly how to get where they were going amid the thousands of doors. She headed into the isolation chamber that Sean was encapsulated in and stood outside. It was nothing short of an old fashion torture chamber. The walls became translucent, and Sean could see her peering inside at him. Trying to remain in control and not show his fear, he grit his teeth as the pain returned to him. The more he held out, the more intense it became, until he broke down and screamed, "Ahhhh stop!" Sean had been broken numerous times. After every torture, he thought of how he would escape, but foremost in his thoughts were what they might be doing to Nancy.

"Has he demonstrated anything that will be beneficial to us?" Karna asked of his tormentor.

"Not yet, only his unusual thoughts which are more confusing than helpful." He responded. "An amazing and unexplainable event takes place within the human race. They actually care about other members of their race beyond how their actions serve the greater good. Individuality, freedom and helping the oppressed seemed to be the overriding motivation of this race. Even under extreme duress they are mentally linked to others of their race. This male is especially linked to the female we brought with him," he continued.

Karna and the tormentor watched in silence as the conditioning continued.

The pain stopped, and a period of peace came. Then a weightless feeling came over Sean as he began to lift off the floor. Unable to grasp the side of the cylindrical shaped cell he was imprisoned in, he went higher and higher. Looking up he saw sharp mechanical blades turning in every direction. I'll be cut into pieces, he thought. How will I get out of this? It was difficult for him to think rationally while in a situation where fear was his only emotion, but it was something that Sean had learned to live with his entire life. He stopped looking up and looked directly at the cold, black, shark like eyes of Karna. Remembering what she had told him, "You have a superior intelligence, a knowledge we must learn," he thought that his response, not his death, was what they were after, so he simply dropped his arms and continued to stare at Karna, as if to say, you will not get anything from me that I do not wish to give you.

Immediately, gravity returned to the chamber and Sean slammed to the floor, and the intense pain returned to him again. This time he did not brace himself for the pain. He simply tried to concentrate on staring at

Karna. Repeatedly the pain came and left, and with each came a different test. Sean realized that the threat of impending death was only an illusion since it changed from swirling knives, to fire, to bubbling acid. The pain began to lose its effect when Sean realized that the less he struggled the less it hurt. The test was over, or so he thought.

"It would appear we have failed in this test," the tormentor said.

"Not so," said Karna. "We have learned that humans care deeply for their own kind and will do anything to protect them. This male and female have demonstrated a weakness that will prove a useful advantage. The Bilkegine will use this weakness to perfect a means of overcoming their race.

Karna ordered the door opened and Sean stepped out.

"Is that all you've got?" he seethed.

"You are free to go back to your room now," she said. "Take the male back to his quarters."

Without question, two of the huge men standing nearby began to restrain Sean even though he was not putting up a fight. Walking behind them, Karna made plans to introduce other characters for Sean to adopt. She had to give Sean even more motivation to make his stand against insurmountable odds in order to learn the most before she had them all killed.

The door swished open and the two men shoved Sean into the room. He stopped and looked around. Much has changed since he was in the room last. The table with the food and bed were new, but Nancy was gone and that shifted his thinking immediately to her. Sean turned to the door and began banging on it. Within seconds the door opened and Karna was standing in the doorway.

"What do you want?" Sean asked hatefully.

"My role is to be your councilor. I wish to help you adapt to your new environment."

"Don't bother, lady. I won't be staying long. Where have you taken Nancy?"

"Nancy? Do you mean the female?"

"Yes, the female. She has a name, individuality unlike anyone else around here. It's something you wouldn't understand. Her name is Nancy! So, where is she?"

"Do not make worry for her," Karna offered.

"For the love of Pete, if you're going to speak the language—at least get it right, it's don't worry about her, you freak!"

"Why are you angry with me? I'm trying to help you fulfill your needs."

"Okay, black eyes, my need is to have Nancy here with me now!"

"Why do you yell at me when you know it might cause you to experience pain for doing so?"

"You or your people can't hurt me lady, and I use the term 'lady' loosely, very loosely."

"You have experienced the pain, and it has hurt you."

"That's not what I'm talking about, lady. What I mean to say is that I really don't care what you do to me! I want Nancy, now!"

"I will return shortly. Be ready for additional testing."

"Lady, when I get out of this place, I'm going to hurt you—real—bad. You don't understand the meaning of bad, do you lady? But it's coming and you're going to be sorry you ever saw me!"

Trying to work his way back toward the open door, Sean continued to yell at Karna. Knowing that she wanted to learn from him gave him an edge. He figured that she would stay and listen, if just for the opportunity to observe his nature. Moving in circles while he spoke, he said, "listen, freak, why don't you black eyed, green skinned, giants just let me and my lady friend off at the next block, and we'll forget all about this."

"I do not understand," she said. "Forget about what?"

"No! It's me who doesn't get it; you freaks just can't be insulted can you?"

"Is there something I can do for you?" she asked again.

"Yeah, you can do something for me. You can drop over dead and start to decay, cause you already stink like road kill!"

"Why won't you let me do something for you?"

"I know what it is now," Sean continued ranting. "You have no passion."

By now Sean had gone completely around her and had his back to the door. It was now or never, and he turned and bolted for the door. He glanced over his shoulder, and to his surprise saw no one following him. That is, there was no one running after him. There were people after him, but walking after him. This is the strangest thing, he thought. No one ever gets excited around here. No passion, no anger, no excitement. No one ran anywhere. A fire could break out in someone's shorts, and they would walk to the water cooler to put them out. He continued to run toward the column of light. That was the only place he had as a reference to the great hall. The door that he knew would open to him was not far from there. He would go there and see if it went anywhere before he would look for Nancy. Just as he made it to the light, three of Karna's big green goons grabbed for him. Running at full speed, it was hard to see them standing there since the light blinded him. It was like looking out of the window of a plane flying at thirty-five thousand feet and seeing nothing but white fluffy looking light. All of a sudden he ran smack into three eight-foot tall, green skinned, masked monsters, robots or something. They were stronger than an ape and ready and able to tear him limb from limb without so much as breaking a sweat. Ducking into this light will be a safe place to hide he thought, since Karna never does more than reach in and search with her arm to pull them out. He waited for a moment but when the feeling of peaceful warmth started to hit him, he knew he had better get out while he could. He didn't know what that thing was, but he also knew that if he stayed there be might never get out.

Looking around the best as he could, he headed for the hallway and door that opened for him and jumped through. It opened to another huge corridor that resembled the main terminal at LAX. It had everything an airport terminal had and then some. The main hallway was sixty feet wide with small forty foot square slips lining both sides, armed guards were everywhere, security booths, long boarding lines everywhere, different terminals heading in every direction and even the ubiquitous crowds. What it didn't have were windows and airliners themselves. No planes and no windows, if this wasn't an airport then what was it? And where was he, if not on foreign ground? At any rate it looked like a way out of where he was but not a place he wanted to be without Nancy. With that thought complete, he turned back through the doorway just in time to see five more of the green goons coming his way with Karna in tow.

"There he is. Take him now," she said in an almost monotone voice.

Sean turned and ducked under the empty grasp of two of them and under the legs of another. If it hadn't been for their height and slow speed he would surely have been caught. He jumped into the column of light again for a quick pick-me-up. Sean hadn't eaten anything since his bagel with cream cheese and coffee the morning of his abduction. This light was the only think that kept him moving. That and fear. Still not being able to see far ahead, he started for an area otherwise undiscovered. Not fifty feet away from the other side of the light he came to another room. The door opened when he came to it, and for the first time, he could see where he was.

The room was clear, significantly more dimly lit, and was the first room he had come to that had things in the room. He quickly looked around for something to jamb the door. Finding a container with small triangle shaped metal pieces, he picked up several and using a heavy square piece of material exactly like that of the wall and floor of his room, he pounded the triangle shaped pieces around the edge of the door. He had time to think. He didn't know how long it would be before they found him, or how long the door would hold when they did, so he would have to make the most of the time he had. He began to search the room. It was two hundred eighty feet, by one hundred feet and twenty feet tall. From where he was standing, it looked like the door he entered by was the only way in or out, so it could be defensible if he could find the right weapon, but there were a lot of containers along the wall that could be hiding other doorways. He started scanning open containers quickly looking for a weapon that he thought might be effective against the goliath like men he'd been struggling against. Picking up a heavy metal pipe-like rod briefly, and then dropping it for a sharp sword-like metal lance, he felt like he had a weapon worthy of defending his position. Now he had to look for another way out, if there was one. Running down a central hall amid the containers, he became aware that he was inside a huge warehouse. If this is a warehouse, he thought, where were the loading docks and where were the huge doors? Twenty feet ahead he saw a large opening in the hallway. Surely that must be them, he thought. He slowed to a walk, thinking there might be guards or workers around the doorway. Cautiously walking to the last stack of containers, with his back against them, he turned his head around the corner and nearly went faint at what he saw. He stepped from the containers and staggered to the center of the wide hallway and toward the front of the warehouse. His arms dropped to his side and he dropped the sword he had picked up as he was struck with awe and disbelief upon discovering to his amazement that he had in fact seen an airport but he had seen an airport from the air to the ground, not from the ground to the air. He was staring out a giant window into the black of space looking down at a tiny planet. The tiny blue planet was earth.

CHAPTER FIVE

The Sheriff got up to leave the office for home to tell his wife what was going on.

"Hey boys, I'm taking the rest of the day. You boys hold down the fort."

"Okay Sheriff. Everything alright?" the senior deputy asked.

"Oh yeah, I just thought while everything was slow, I'd catch up on my fishing."

Just then one of the junior deputies came running in all excited. "Hey Sheriff, did you know someone creamed your squad car?"

"Yes Justin, I'm aware of it." the Sheriff said. "I'm the top dog, I'm aware of everything that goes on here."

With that a couple of the deputies snickered.

"That's funny? How about pulling a few back to back all nighters?"

"Ah, no thanks Sheriff, we were laughing at the green hornet."

"Try to keep things quiet." the Sheriff ordered as he left.

He drove up to his mountain cabin. When he drove up, his wife was hanging the wash out. Because he never came home during the middle of the day, she knew something must be wrong. He drove up the drive, went inside and poured a cup of coffee and sat at the table and waited for her to come inside.

"What's wrong, Bruce?"

"Why would you say somethin like that, Maggie?"

"Well, in twenty years you've only come home three times during the day, twice when your babies were being born, and during the flood in '67. That's why."

"At ease, woman. I'll tell you. But, you'd better sit down."

"I'm listening." She said as she pulled out a chair at the kitchen table.

"I saw something this morning that this old mountain man can't explain, and I don't mind telling you it's got me plain scared."

"What was it, Bruce."

"I saw Sean Daniels and some woman disappear right in front of my eyes."

"What woman, and what do you mean…disappear?"

"I can't be for certain, but I think it was that gal, Nancy that rented Ben and Hilda's place." He said scratching his head.

"What about them disappearing, what did you mean by that?"

"What part of disappear don't you understand? The dis, or the, appear?" They just plain vanished!—in broad daylight, right in front of the hardware store, right before my eyes, in front of folks walking down the street, in front of God and everyone."

"Now, settle down Bruce. You're starting to scare me, too."

"I called in an expert and you're the only one who knows about it 'cept me."

"What about all the other people they vanished in front of?" She asked.

"You know, that's the weird thing. I asked them about it and nobody saw nothing."

"What about this expert? Won't he think you're crazy? I mean if you are the only one that saw anything, and all?"

"Nope, he's heard it all, or so he said. He's flying in with special equipment today."

"Today, from where?"

"New York. He was pretty excited when he heard about it. He'll be here in an hour or so. I came home to tell you not to expect me home for supper."

"You could have called like you always do."

"Well…I guess I needed to talk it out with someone I trusted."

"Ok, when do you think you'll be home?"

"I don't know, but I'll have dispatch keep you informed as our investigation continues. I told them I was gonna catch up on my fishin, so I'll call in a missing persons report like it came from someone else. Hopefully nobody will panic since everyone around here takes off once and awhile."

"Alright, Honey bear, but you be careful."

He got up and gave her a big mountain man bear hug and left for the airport. The mountains are pretty, especially in spring, but he didn't take notice because he was lost in thought. The winding roads make it impossible to get from one point to another in a hurry. Bruce used the time to make up a convincing story to call in to the station. Forty-five minutes later he pulled up to the airport, parked his car, and called into the station.

"Dispatch, this is the Sheriff."

"Go ahead, Sheriff."

"Anything going on that I need to know about?"

"Nothin' at all, I thought you were taking the day off?"

"Well, I was on my way out to Piney Ridge and got waved down about a missing person."

"We never got a call Sheriff, who flagged you down?"

"That's not important, just listen. Open a missing person file and make sure someone is manning the phone 24/7 until we find the fellow."

"Ok boss, who's come up missin?"

"Sean Daniels. He never opened the store this morning, and he's not at home. It seems the last person to see him this morning was Jane down at the Bagel Shop."

"Maybe he just took the day off and went fishin'," he said laughing.

"I don't think this is funny! The Sheriff yelled. "Cant' you ever take anything serious! Everything is a big joke with you isn't it! Maybe you should give up being a Sheriff's Deputy and become a stand-up comic."

"Sorry Sheriff. I like my job real fine. I'll shut-up."

"I was with him this morning at breakfast. He was on his way to the store."

"Oh, who should I say reported it, for the report?"

"Just put my name in."

"You got it, Sheriff."

"One more thing, I'll be working with an expert on abductions from New York. Patch everything you get through to me right away. Okay?"

"Is it a fed?" The deputy asked meekly. "I thought someone had to be missing more than twenty-four hours before they'd get involved."

"You don't have to see the fox to know your chicken coops been raided do you?" The Sheriff yelled back. "Just do what you're told and keep quiet,—out!"

The jet landed, and the Sheriff walked to greet it.

"Hello, Sheriff?" The man asked with his hand extended.

"Hey. I'm Sheriff Faulkner, folks round here just call me Bruce." he said taking the man's hand and squeezing firmly.

"Hi, Bruce, I'm James. Let's get things rolling shall we?"

They jumped into Bruce's squad car and headed down town. They didn't want to draw too much attention to themselves, so they kept a low profile as they took the readings with James' special equipment.

"Well, what do you think so far?" asked Bruce.

"Very interesting," James replied. "These radiation readings are pegged out."

"I'm sorry, James. I'm just a dumb mountain Sheriff. You're going to have to spell it out for me."

"What I mean is that the radiation levels are so high that the equipment that I brought with me cannot read it. The needle has moved all the way over and hit this little peg mark here, see it?"

"Oh yeah, and that's not good?"

"Well, not good in the sense that your friend has probably been abducted by aliens but good in the sense that we have undeniable proof that something has left a radiation trail, and that something has to be alien in nature."

"Why alien in nature?"

"We don't have anything that can produce that type of a radiation trail. Not a portable device that is. The only portable thing we have that could leave a trail this strong is a nuclear bomb, and clearly that has not happened. And we know it's a different radiation signature because while it does peg out our meter, which only checks radiation, there are no residual radioactive markers like burns, sickness, etc."

"How does an ordinary television show host come into this knowledge and or special equipment for that matter?"

"Contacts, my man, contacts."

"So, what's the next step? Bruce asked.

"We must notify our strategic command center that an alien abduction has occurred. And we must do that quickly." James said as he packed up his equipment.

"You're not really who you say you are. Are you?"

"Well, yes and no."

"Look! I'm the Sheriff of Morgan County, and it was my friend who was taken, and I'm running this investigation! Are you or are you not who you say you are?"

"That is on a need to know basis, Sheriff." James replied with a stern look.

"Hey! You're not in the big city here pal! You're out here in the middle of the mountains where men have been known to go and never return again. Out here they call me Bruce the Spruce! Do I need to show you why they call me that? I'll tell you this, I have a need to know and you're going to tell me, right now!"

"Settle down, big boy. Okay, No. I use the show to gather information and stories for the government project, Flash Back."

"Project, 'Flash Back'. Come on, are you trying to pull my chain now, big-city?"

"I wish I were, Bruce. Point is, I work for the National Security Agency and we have had a lot of activity the last five years, especially with abductions. We started the show in hopes of getting people to bring their stories to us. Knowing that most people don't buy into the whole UFO bit, we needed to make a way for those who do believe could bring us information that we needed. What we don't need is a panic. This abduction is the seventh this week, and it's only Monday morning. All the radiation readings have been the same. The only difference in this abduction, the one that scares us the most is this; last Friday a general was abducted from Washington, D.C., and this morning a Mr. Sean Michael

Daniels, previously, Lt. Sean Michael Daniels. The same man who was awarded three Purple Hearts, a Bronze Star with Clusters and promoted from Sergeant to First Lieutenant by a special Act of Congress, all during Vietnam for heroism during combat while under the command of this missing general."

"Our—Sean Daniels," Bruce asked in awe. "The same guy I had breakfast with this morning?"

"Yes your Sean Daniels."

"We never heard any of that. Why do you think he never told us anything?"

"It's our guess that Sean moved up here to get away from the stories. Face it. Our boys didn't exactly get a warm welcome home from our Nation after Vietnam."

"So, what's that got to do with this alien abduction and a general that came up missing?"

"The way we have it, they've been looking for someone who can help them."

"And they think the general is that man?"

"No, they needed the general to tell them who that man is."

"And Sean is that man? Com-on that's a stretch isn't it?"

"No, I'm afraid not, Bruce. We think Sean is that same man."

"No way, there's no way Sean's gonna help no space freak or any other freak for that matter."

"Oh, I'm sure he wouldn't want to."

"Listen here, Mr. Government man! Sean won't do anything he doesn't want to do. It's how he's built. I've known him since he moved up here."

"He didn't want to go to Vietnam, did he?"

"That was different and you know it. That was for his country, not to save his own skin. And if he won all those medals, he must have been a good fighter or he would have just layed down and given up."

"He survived to save his own life. That's the sad truth of the matter, Bruce."

"Well, I don't care what you say! I've known him for the past fifteen years. How long have you known him?"

"I hope you're right, Bruce."

"It's Sheriff Faulkner to you, sir."

"Now don't get your dander up, Sheriff, I want to help as much as you do. I'm your friend in this as much as I'm Sean's friend. I just know that it is human nature to try to preserve one's own life."

"Well, maybe in the big city, but down here I've seen a total stranger put his life in harm's way just to save someone. And, Mister, Sean is that type of man."

"Bruce, if he's half the man you are, I won't have anything to worry about."

By the time they had finished their tests several people walking down the street had stopped to see what the commotion was all about. Bruce noticed a crowd gathered and suggested that they carry on their conversation elsewhere. They got into the car and drove away.

"So, what's the next step? And, what's your real name?"

"Sorry I tried to deceive you, Sheriff. It's part of the job. My name is James. Agent, James Rose."

"And what's the next step?"

"For me, the next step is to get back to our command base in Colorado and start trying to track this thing somehow. Would you like to come along? We could use someone who knows Sean."

"Just try and stop me."

They Sheriff headed toward the mountains, away from the airport and ten minutes of silence passed before the National Security Agent said anything. "Hey, Bruce, aren't we heading the wrong direction?"

"I've got to pack a few things and let my wife know I'll be out of town a while."

"I'm sorry, how dumb of me."

"If you don't mind, I'm going to tell her you're an FBI agent about a missing person's report. I already told her about the vanishing, and she'll bug me about it, but I'll figure out something to tell her while I pack. I just don't want her to worry about it. It's not like a lie to my wife or nothin' like that. It's just that she worries a lot."

"I understand completely, and it won't be a lie, because I really am an FBI agent as well."

"Bruce looked at him strangely and said, "Boy you really get around don't you?"

They pulled up to the Sheriff's cabin and got out. James followed him inside, where his wife was waiting. "I was worried when I didn't hear anything, Bruce. I thought you were going to have dispatch call me."

"I'm sorry, Mags. I got busy and forgot. This is James; he's an FBI agent."

"Hi, Ma'am," he said politely.

"Mags, I've got to make a trip with Agent Rose. We've got to investigate this missing person case."

"Where are you going?"

"Where are we going, James?"

"Uh, we're going to be moving around following leads, Ma'am."

"But Bruce, you told me they vanished in front of you?"

"Well, Hon, I guess the lights were in my eyes or something, 'cause no one else saw anything like that."

He left the room to pack, and Maggie made polite conversation with Agent Rose.

"Would you like something to eat, Mr. Rose?"

"No, Ma'am. I ate on the plane on the way down."

"Some coffee then?" she asked.

"Yes, please. That would be nice."

"How long do you think you and Bruce will be gone?" she asked walking to the kitchen.

"To be honest, Ma'am, it's possible that we'll be gone a couple of weeks."

"Oh, my, you think it will take that long?"

Before James could answer, Bruce came back with his suitcase packed and sat it by the door. He had already changed into his civilian clothes and Stetson. "I've already made a call to Mikey. He'll be checking in on you every morning and night. If you need anything just tell him, okay Mags, anything?"

"Okay." she replied.

Bruce sat down beside James and Maggie poured him some coffee. James wrote down a cell phone number that he could be reached anywhere in the country, at any time of the day or night, and gave it to Maggie. He also gave her his secretary's name and phone number, in case she needed to leave a message for Bruce that wasn't an emergency.

"Now, Honey." Bruce said, "Don't worry about a thing. If this wasn't Sean who was missing, I would let the feds take it from here, but it is, and we go way back. It's just the right thing to do and the right time to do it."

"I know, Bruce. I'm not worried about a thing. You just go do what you have to do and get back."

They all got up and Bruce and James left. They stopped at the Sheriff's Station and had one of the deputies take them to the airport, where the jet was standing by to take them to Colorado. As far as they knew, Bruce was off to New York with the FBI on a missing person case. Once in flight, James asked, "Bruce, I've got to know one thing, but don't take this the wrong way. I'm not questioning your judgment or anything like that. It's just a containment issue."

"Shoot."

"Who is Mikey? And, how much does he know?"

"Is that all? Heck."

"Yeah, that's it."

"Mikey's my kid brother, I told him the same thing I told Maggie. That I'm going with the FBI to New York for a couple of weeks to investigate a missing person case, and asked him to look after Maggie for me. That's about it."

✳✳✳

Five men in masks rolled Nancy into an examination room. Under another brilliant light in the middle of the room they took sharp knives and moved toward her.

"No! Get away from me!" she screamed.

She could not move but was trying to squirm out of her restraints so hard that they were cutting into her arms and legs. Just as they got to the table, she let out a blood-curdling scream that filled the examination room. They picked up some shiny metal instruments and began to poke and prod her. She screamed as loud as she could, but it was as though they were completely deaf as they continued to examine her. Her restraints were beginning to restrict her circulation, and she was losing feeling in her legs and hands.

"Please, let me go!" she cried. "It hurts!"

The men had no reason to do any experiments. All their knowledge of the human anatomy had been done decades ago on previous journeys under other commands. Their goal was to illicit fear, so great a fear that she would do anything to make it stop. Karna had ordered this exercise solely as an unforgettable experience in fear for Nancy, with the hope that it would motivate Sean to divulge the limit he could take before he surrendered. Karna needed to learn how much fear and terror it would take to succeed. The decades before had proven to be so unsuccessful that unless Karna succeeded now, there would be no hope for her race. This was not an option for her. In order for the fear and terror to be real, there must be physical manifestations. So, Nancy was taken to the examination chamber, and there would be marks left on her body to match the mental torment she now endured. Karna knew that fear and terror was the key to victory. If she could illicit enough fear to Sean, he would surrender, become compliant and she would succeed. She only needed to find out what kind and how much fear and terror it would take to scare the bravest human subject into complete submission. Terror will defeat reason and without reason people will surrender.

In submission Nancy pleaded with her captors, "Please stop. Please, I beg you. I have done nothing to you. I have done nothing to deserve this."

It was obvious that the women of the human race, at least this woman, were weak. They would give up easily and perform whatever task easily. However, the women lacked the strength and knowledge in too many areas for the Bilkegine to merely wipe out all men from the planet and let the human women make the planet habitable for them. Additionally, they thought that once the men had been eradicated the women would no longer be compliant. They thought that they would rebel and might themselves take up arms against the Bilkegine race even though they would certainly fail. Yes, they thought the human race was a unique race unlike anything they had ever come across in all of their exploration. Never had they seen a race of beings that cared so much for, not only the well-being of other beings but for abstract concepts like freedom.

They placed a device over her head that removed all her hair. They took a long knife and made a long incision from the base of her skull around her ears and across her forehead. Pulling the incision slightly open, they poured a solution inside. The solution burned like salt. Clamps were then placed over her head and tightened so hard she thought her skull was going to crack. To this clamp wires were connected that resembled clear tubing with lights pulsing through them. Suddenly, she could hear a high frequency squelch that burned in her head like fingernails on a blackboard. Then without any warning, jolts of electric current shot through her head causing her whole body to convulse.

She lost consciousness and the procedures were halted until she was cognizant of the experience. They needed her to feel and remember every aspect of the torture in order to facilitate the anger in Sean to grow until he desired nothing more than escape. During his escape attempt their plan was to demonstrate how impossible it would be to overcome them with their superior weapons and intellect. The information they needed to extract from Sean was what his breaking point would be. If he was in fact the bravest and most battle worthy human on the planet, if they could apply that knowledge to the rest of the world they could finally obtain victory.

As Nancy slowly began to regain consciousness, she could hear her captors talking in an excited voice. It was the language the She had heard Karna speaking before, and she could only imagine what they were saying. She started to pull and strain at the restraints again but to no avail. All she managed to do was knock an instrument to the ground and make the Bilkegine butchers aware that she was awake.

When they saw her awake, they took the clamps off her head and began probing the holes left in her scalp from the clamps. They then cut her tunic open and made another incision from just below her sternum to just below her belly button. Like the other incisions, it was only deep enough to draw a lot of blood but with the chemical being added, it felt like they had cut her deep. She had taken all that she was physically and mentally able to take and began screaming repeatedly as loud as her lungs would allow. Then she began to cry and finally lost all control over her body as her arms and legs went limp, and she fainted again. Though Nancy was already in shock and completely unaware of her surroundings, by passing out again she had just saved herself anymore agony.

During the entire examination the team had been careful to keep what they had been doing to Nancy in her plain view. They put the burning fluid on all her incisions to give her the sensation that the wounds were much worse than they really were. They pulled the skin apart slightly to make the incisions bleed more so that when the blood clotted they would look much worse. The entire experience was designed to cause mental anguish and to present an illusion of physical abuse so horrifying that it would incite their male subject to fight. They knew from past experience that if they could incite anger the next emotional response would be fighting and if they could get him to fight, they could break him and make him submit. Their hope was that the bruises and cuts on Nancy's wrists and ankles would only add to the effects and would expedite their male subject's desire for escape so they could observe his ultimate defeat and ultimate surrender to their obvious, undefeatable supremacy.

The leader of the team that had tortured Nancy reported to Karna that the treatments she ordered were complete, and that the female subject was unconscious.

"Take her back to her chamber and wait for me there," Karna instructed.

They took Nancy to her room on the cart and waited outside for Karna. When she arrived and stepped into the room, they let Nancy up and led her into the room behind Karna. Nancy awakened and was very sore and groggy. She staggered into the room using the walls for support and looked around the room for Sean. "Where is Sean?"

"We do not know," Karna responded.

"What do you mean, you do not know? How is that possible?"

"He has run away from us." Karna responded calmly.

"He wouldn't leave me alone! He just wouldn't do that!"

"Nevertheless, he has, but we will find him and bring him back. There is nowhere he can go."

"Why are you doing this to us? What do you hope to learn from all of this?" Nancy said motioning with her hands on her body."

"Everything we need. Your resting phase is beginning, Rest."

Karna turned and left.

Nancy dropped to the floor and began weeping. "Dear God, please bring us out of this place and these cruel people. I don't remember the details God, but when I was a child, the teachers at the little church I attended taught me that You were at all places at all times, if that is true, then you know that we're here and why. God, I believe that you exist and on faith alone believe that somehow you can get me and Sean out of this mess. The teachers in Sunday school also taught me that all I had to do was to believe in you, that I could put myself in your hands and I would find peace in your presence. God, I need your peace more than anything in my life right now. Will you come? Will you bring your peace into my heart and let me rest?"

Sean regained his composure and now fear was his guiding light. Fear mixed with anger, responsibility and obligation would guide his steps. Okay, he thought, first I've got to get back to Nancy. She's probably been stuck in that room going crazy. He picked up his sword and headed for the door. Running at break-neck speed, he got to the door and began banging with his bare hands on the wedges he'd put in the door. All he achieved was cutting his hands. He found the block he used to hammer the metal pieces into the door and started to pound them out, but they wouldn't budge. Boy, when I do something right, I really do something right, he thought. Well, there's no getting out this door.

He looked around for another door. Running to the other end of the warehouse he found another door like the first. It opened. Walking through very slowly and cautiously, he started for the column of light. So far, this was his only landmark inside this place. He got to within ten feet when two of the eight foot tall beings stepped in front of him. Sean raised the sword-like shaft of metal he found in the warehouse in a defensive position. As they reached for him, in an attempt to subdue him, he started swinging his sword violently from left to right. He was able to hold them back until one of them began to circle around him. Sean scanned the room as far as he could see in the bright lights of the Piiderk level where he was and saw two more of the giants heading in his direction. He knew he couldn't hold all of them off if they got him surrounded so he stepped back a few paces and bolted three steps left, then spun around and took five quick steps right. It was a move he learned playing college football. It worked. He was clear of the goons and on his way to the room. Sean couldn't understand why no one ever pursued him when he ran. Maybe they can't run. He thought. Maybe it has something to do with how they're built. For whatever reason, he was glad they let him run away.

When he was clear of them he stopped running and tried to figure out which of the fifty or more doors on the far wall was his. They all looked identical in every way, then he remembered looking left when they first took him out of the room and saw in the distance a high counter against a wall. He tried to judge the distance from that point to a door and stepped up to it. As before, he was denied access.

So far the only good that had come from his excursion was the fact that he had found a weapon of sorts. It wasn't much but it was enough to slow the last gang of giants from simply rushing him. Then he recognized something. He saw a penny on the floor by the wall just outside one of the doors. Walking over to the penny he picked it up. He turned around to get out of the middle of the room and ran head long into the biggest of the giants he had seen. The big green, masked goon put Sean in a bear hug and started to pick him off the ground when all of a sudden he stopped and fell back. Sean was amazed and somewhat shocked that something that big went down that fast, but being impaled with a sword will do that to a thing of any size, he thought. He jumped up and scanned the room for more of the beasts. Then in a far distance, through the fog of brilliant light, he saw four more of them coming his way.

"Great!" he said out-loud. "What am I going to do now? Think, man think!" he said.

He ran back to the giant he had killed and grabbed one of his arms and dragged him toward the door. Man this thing is heavy. He thought. He made it to the door but it still would not open. He had to get the giant to his feet but no matter how hard he tried, there was just no way for him to lift him up. "Come on! I know that when these things walk up to a door

58

it opens, so what gives, maybe something in their clothes." He grabbed his sword-like metal shaft and cut away the jacket it was wearing. Seeing the others still heading toward him, Sean began to panic. He was waving the jacket widely in front of the door but it still didn't open. Oh, come on! What could it be man, think…think. It's got to be in his head. He thought. So, he turned and lifted his make-shift sword over his head and brought it down over the giant's neck with all his strength, severing the head from the body. He quickly lifted the head to the door and it opened.

He threw the head inside and reached out for the body, dragging it into the room.

"Close…close!" he yelled at the door.

Nancy looked over when she heard something hit the floor and screamed with she saw the huge bloody, stinking head pointing up at her.

"Shush!" Sean said. "It's me!"

Nancy watched in horror as Sean dragged the body inside the room and around the corner stuffing it into the corner of the little bathroom that had been provided for them.

"Go wait on the bed. I'll be there in a minute," Sean told Nancy briskly.

He grabbed up the head again and the towel from the bathroom and held the head up to open the door. Going out again, he looked around to make sure he was unseen. The giants who had been coming after him apparently left, so Sean started cleaning up the oily black blood and puss from the floor. He didn't want any evidence left behind that would cause Nancy and him more trouble. Holding up the head for the last time he re-entered the room and after tossing the head and towel into the toilet and washing his hands, he went over to the bed to console Nancy.

Taking one look at her, Sean asked excitedly, "What on earth did they do to you? Oh my dear God, are you alright, Honey?"

"Where have you been?" she said weeping. "I need you here, stay here, please."

"Oh, I'm so sorry Nancy; I was looking for a way out. I never thought they would do anything to you. I thought they only wanted something from me. Let's get you cleaned up."

Sean left her on the bed and went for a wet towel and clean tunic.

"What happened? When did they do this?" He asked as he began to wipe away the dried blood from her wounds.

"Shortly after they took you away, Karna took me to the light. At first it was wonderful. I don't know how long I was there, but I remember not wanting to leave. Karna had arranged to have these things brought in at my request." She said pointing to the food, bed, and clean clothing. "But, just as I was changing into a clean tunic and laying down, the same three giants that took you came in and took me. It was horrifying the way they approached me. They stood at the foot of the bed and just stood there and stared at me. Then one of them left and the other two climbed up on the bed and began crawling over to where I was sitting in that corner. They didn't say a word or anything. They just stared at me and I didn't know what they wanted. Anyway, they took me outside and strapped me down to some kind of cart like you see in a hospital. I thought they were going to kill me, but I was so scared the only thing I could do was scream. Then they took me to a room, shaved all my hair off and performed some kind of experiments on me. Thy poked me, and touched me all over then they cut me and put some kind of clamp on my head. Look." She removed a towel she had put over her head. "When I woke up I was outside the room, and they were taking the straps off of me. Sean? Can you get us out of here now? We need to leave before they come for us again."

"Honey, I'm sure going to try, but we're going to need to rest for a while. They don't know I'm here and there is no reason for them to think I would come back here. So I think we're safe for a while. Now that we have a way through any door, I think we've got a good chance of getting out of here."

"Don't you think they will come back for me to try to find you?"

"When were they here last?"

"It wasn't too long before you got here that they left."

"I'm sure we'll be alright for a while, just after they were done with me, before I escaped, the queen of contempt herself told me to rest for my upcoming test. Since they can't find me I think it will be a while anyway."

"I don't get her. She came in here all nice and polite asking me what I needed to be more comfortable. Then as soon as I got something, they took me away and did this to me. It's just like that big light out there. You feel great inside, but just when you think all your needs are met they wear off, leaving you more depressed and angry than before. What do they hope to achieve with this treatment?"

"I think they are baiting us. It must be part of the testing she is talking about. I've got a plan. When the old sleaze comes back to take you to the light, we'll be gone. Now that we can get into any of the doors around here they'll never be able to track us down. One of those doors has to lead us out of here." Sean didn't want to tell her where they really were yet.

The light began to dim as Karna said it would at the resting phase. Sean and Nancy laid down together on the bed. While Nancy slept heavily, Sean contemplated their next move. His plan seemed to be their only option, but he didn't want any more surprises, and he was just about fed up with being toyed with and tortured. It would be different if they had been torturing him for the information they seemed so intent on learning. At least he could understand that. Under the circumstances he would tell them whatever they wanted, and since he was the one that had this special knowledge of something, they wouldn't know if he was being truthful or not. But this…giving them something pleasant and then make them hurt routine was getting old fast. Sean fell asleep and for a while there was peace.

Nancy began to stir first. The light was still dim and she knew the resting phase was not over yet, but something woke her. She watched Sean sleep and thought for the first time that she might be falling for him. It was the first time that she had any rational thoughts or even considered the fact that he was a handsome guy. He certainly had strong character and a sense of responsibility. He had been her strength so far and continued to show a sincere caring for her. Just then her thoughts were interrupted again by a strange sound in the room. She looked back over her shoulder without moving her body but could not see anything. She returned to her warming thoughts of Sean. She had heard that it was common for victims of violent acts to fall in love with their rescuer, but Nancy dismissed this thought. She really believed that she was falling in love with him and believed that Sean felt the same way about her. She moved closer to Sean and snuggled up against him. Putting her arm over his strong, athletic shoulders, she wondered how Karna was able to throw him across the room so easily when Sean first attacked her. Sean opened his eyes to meet hers staring back at his. "Are you alright? He asked.

"At this moment in time I'm alright." she responded.

"Is it time to get up already?"

"No, something woke me up and I was just thinking, that's all, go back to sleep."

Just then she heard the sound again. This time Sean heard it too.

"What was that?" Sean whispered.

"Sh-h, listen," she said.

They both got really quiet and waited to hear it again. Sean lifted his head and looked behind them. Suddenly he saw movement at the end of the bed.

"There is something in the room with us." he whispered very quietly. "Don't move. I'm going to see what it is."

CHAPTER SIX

Karna was busy in the observation deck making preparations for Sean's adopted family and the subsequent experiments. The time was coming soon for Sean's next test. She must know how he will react when given more to be responsible over, especially when he has no history with or caring for them, but his escape was not in her plans. She needed to find him now. Unfortunately, in order to know how to fight your opponent you must know your opponent. This had been a distinct disadvantage for Karna, and now was proving to be more of a challenge than perceived. Sean had taken off and was in hiding someplace on the vessel of humongous proportions and without knowing how he thought, she didn't know where to begin her search. An organized search of the entire vessel was also out of the question, due to its size and number of accessible levels. The limited crewmembers available for the search could take forever if they only searched the obvious hiding places. She must try, knowing what she had already learned about him, to think like he would think.

"Take five Quod and search every accessible room beginning at the keel point of the Piiderk. And lock every room after it has been searched." She ordered.

"That will take a torod," the Piiderk Commander questioned. "We don't have that kind of time!"

Without verbal response Karna turned and shot him with a treshol, a sound-wave transmitting weapon so lethal it killed him instantly. She then looked at the goth, the male of their species, standing next to him and said, "You are now Piiderk Commander. Do you have any questions?"

"None, Commander!" he said with his head bowed.

Searching for one human male, even in the limited access area was not going to be a simple task. The newly appointed Piiderk Commander knew that, but also knew what failure would mean.

Karna went to the command center to call a general meeting. "Lt. Commander Brodem, call the officer staff to the briefing chamber immediately," said Karna.

Lt. Commander Brodem was the first to arrive at the briefing chamber. He was apprehensive about the meeting having already heard about the Piiderk Commander being killed. The Commander was very stern and did not tolerate anyone questioning her command in any way. Nor did she allow anyone, at any time, to fail in the execution of their duties. This offense was punishable by either death or being turned into a mindless drone, and her opinion was the only one that counted. The briefing chamber filled quickly. No one wanted to be the last one to appear in the briefing chamber, and no one definitely wanted to appear after the Commander.

Karna marched into the briefing chamber and everyone in the room snapped to attention and saluted her by stomping one foot twice and bowing their heads. "This meeting will be very brief." She began. "Our principle male subject has escaped from us and is eluding us somewhere on the vessel. We desired that he try to escape and fail but as we allowed in order to observe him. A team of Quod lead by the new Piiderk Commander, Captain Thoy, is searching the Piiderk level forward as we speak. However, much of the vessel is still available for the human to hide in. We require as many of your personnel available to search all unsecured areas of the vessel. Do not waste time searching area that will not open without implants. Do not fail me. I do not have to remind any of you what failure will mean."

Karna got up and before they could all rise and salute, she was out the door. "You have your orders," the Lt. Commander said, and they all left.

They needed to learn how to break a man's spirit; how to make a man give up on his individuality? More importantly, how to get him to give up on his love of freedom? Karna had learned from Sean's abduction a month earlier that he was the perfect human subject for the test she developed. Although there were other officers on board that couldn't see it, Sean, in her opinion, was the only human they had ever abducted that was capable of teaching them everything they had to learn before they could attack the planet, and her opinion was the only one that mattered. In his past, the experiences and fears he coped with not only resulted in his continued life and the life of his brothers-in-arms without capture, but resulted in his being decorated with three Purple Hearts, a Bronze Star and a Silver Star with Clusters by war's end, not to mention a Meritorious Field Promotion from Sergeant to Lieutenant by an Act of Congress. His tactical skills were unmatched. Many thought he was bound for military greatness after the war, but Sean was only in it for survival. What the government thought was tactical genius, he thought was running scared and fighting like a dying dog for his life.

An earlier abduction of an American general, whose war record suggested he would be the one human that Karna desired, proved to be nothing more than an old man who had out lived his usefulness, as far as military intelligence was concerned. The first thing Karna said when she saw this old man shaking in his boots was, "This is one of their top leaders? "Look he is so weak he is shaking and has soiled his clothes! This weak old human is what is so hard to defeat? Am I to understand we can't break a race of humans like him?"

"No, Commander," The head of their research team reported, "We took him for his knowledge alone, but have discovered that despite his weak body, his mind remains strong and resolved when it came to losing his freedom. We have seen it before in nearly every subject. Furthermore, we have discovered that while they will yield against extreme pain and suffering in their old age, when it comes to captivity they will not yield, even to the point of death."

"Then you have failed to learn anything new. What good is an old man, even to the humans?"

"That is not entirely true, Commander. While they may be weak of body, they posses experience and the respect of those younger and use that knowledge and authority to incite the younger humans to fight to the death to secure freedom at any cost. We have heard them say, "Without Freedom, you are dead already."

"Have you learned anything that we can use?" Karna asked impatiently.

"Yes. During the interrogation, this old general specifically remembered a man named Sean Daniels. In his anger he told us of this human's exploits and told us that there were many like him that would rather die than surrender as slaves." As he replied, he turned and asked an assistant for the file then continued. "The general recounted, "This young man was drafted into the army during the Vietnam War. It was a war where one side of a country was trying to force another side of its own country to live without freedom and individuality, two things that we as Americans take very seriously. We entered the war on the side of democracy to assist the weaker side in retaining their freedom. This young man entered the war as the lowest ranking member and was very quickly promoted to an officer. He had an uncanny ability to see a trap and avoid capture. Furthermore, he was consistently leading his troops around ambush and into victory. His military genius and strategic battle plans were decades ahead of his time. He developed plans of attack that generals and other great military planners had never ever considered possible, yet he made them look easy. Men began requesting to be assigned to his unit because of his success in battle and the low number of fatalities during battles. There was one mission in particular that won him one Purple Heart and a Silver Star. He was dropped into a HLZ in the Delta during one of the most active times of the war. It was a small reconnaissance team on a search and destroy mission. But, due to poor intelligence, the enemy had moved its major strike force forward to their position more than ten kilometers and instead of being a safe distance from the enemy, they ended up being dropped in the middle of a hell storm of bullets and mortar fire. Ten men went into the field and because Lieutenant Daniels was dedicated to bringing all his boys home, he decided to divide and conquer. He fell back into a swamp and spread his troops out about thirty yards apart. Having each man lay under the mud on their backs, with only their noses sticking out of the mud let the advancing army pass right over them. Thinking that they had tucked tail and run, the advancing army dropped their guards. When they could not find them they retreated and set camp right at the edge of the swamp not one hundred feet from where Lt. Daniels and his men were lying in the cold mud. He got up, and moving low and slow, went to each man and told him to work his way around the edge of the swamp to the far edge away from the camp. When he was sure each man was at the prearranged pick up point, he went back in under cover of night, armed with nothing more than a knife, and silently cut the throat of more than thirty men. Having taken the camp single handedly, he went back, got his troops and called in an air strike on the larger advancing army. Thanks to his bravery and dedication, more than a thousand soldiers were saved, and a major turn in the war resulted. When interviewed, he was asked where he found the bravery to take out the thirty men single handedly, and he replied, "It wasn't bravery, it was cowardice. I was afraid they would come and find me and kill me, so I went to kill them first. No one believed him. No one does something like that out of cowardice. He was just being modest."

He had remembered Sean from his Vietnam days as the bravest, smartest, strongest man he had ever seen. The only man he knew who would never give up, no matter what, and the man that this general wanted to be especially when it came to being under duress. So you see, Commander, we obtained much from this human."

✯✯✯

The National Security Agency jet landed in Colorado at the military airport at Cheyenne Mountain. James and Bruce were transported to the top secret military tracking base deep inside the mountain, where Operation 'Flash Back' had been set up to try and track any extraterrestrial spaceship movement. Since its initiation there had been one hundred seventy two abductions, thirty-three military, forty-nine government contract personnel, and the balance civilian. Many of the civilian abductions were prior military with only one, Sean, having the record that he had in combat and a mind for strategy. The military was very concerned since the aliens had him, and they did not.

"Bruce, let's get a security badge for you right off the get-go." James said.

"Whatever we need to get Sean back," Bruce replied with his arms held out to his side implying anything was acceptable.

"Now, you'll have to get sworn in, and remember that what you see here never leaves here."

"No problem. After all, who am I gonna tell?"

"Good attitude, Bruce. Corporal, this is Sheriff Faulkner. He'll be working with NSA on operation Flash Back."

"Yes Sir."

"I'll need to scan your right hand sir," the Corporal said. "We'll have to wait for a few moments for background clearance and verification of identity."

"Fine son, where should I put it," he said laughing while holding up his hand.

"Right here, Sir." he responded without so much as a smile.

"Is that it, young man?"

"Not quite sir. I'll also need a blood sample."

"A blood sample, well I…" the Sheriff started looking at James.

"Not to worry, Bruce, it's just a finger stick. It's standard procedure."

"Hold out your index finger please." the corporal asked.

"Heck, is that it? I've had tick bites that hurt worse than that."

Bruce watched as his palm and finger scan came up on a computer screen and a program highlighted groupings of areas that would verify the identity of Bruce. Then the computer prompted the operator to insert the small tube of blood into another machine.

"Boy, this stuff sure is complicated. I still can't program my VCR." Bruce said laughing. "How 'bout you James, are you up on all this stuff?"

"Afraid so, it kinda comes with the territory."

The computer sounded that it was complete and the printer spit out an identification card that had Bruce's specifics all there in black and white. It had a current picture, his thumb print, age, weight and blood type all on the card for the world to see.

"Is everything accurate, Sir?" the corporal asked.

"Uh, yeah, it looks ok to me."

"Very good, Sirs, welcome to Cheyenne Mountain."

"That will get you anywhere within the compound, but you will have to be with me or another NSA agent to get in or out. Understood?" James said.

"Got it, now let's get to work."

"Are you hungry or thirsty?" James asked.

"Just point me to the coffee pot, and let's get busy."

"It's this way."

✳✳✳

Karna returned to her personal quarters to ponder what was going on and try to figure out this male subject. She had to get inside his mind, and she had to get inside fast. Her life was also on the line and she was in no hurry to lose her life because of failure in her duty. Many had failed before her and her entire race would die if she failed. Decades were spent trying to procure this tiny planet. If their race had the ability to make the planet habitable themselves they wouldn't even need the humans, but they didn't so the point was moot, and time was running out. They only had fifty earth years left to have the planet ready for transformation and habitation of their race. After that, the humans were expendable.

Karna went to a desk and contacted the communication center. "Send the counselor," she said. She sat down on a small couch and waited. Moments later there was a knock on her door. "Come," she said.

The door opened and an old, thin Bilkegine lugoth, their female, entered. She was over six feet tall, had the typical Bilkegine appearance, greenish/gray skin with black spots resembling freckles, black eyes set very wide apart, gaunt facial features and short dark hair. Her forehead was extraordinarily long compared to human, and her nose, was almost non-existent, with just a thin ridge running the distance between her eyes to her mouth and three small holes no bigger than small peas in the shape of a v. The most pronounced feature of the Bilkegine, goth or lugoth was their mouths. It was three times the size of an average human mouth, had two rows of remarkably sharp teeth, and no lips at all. Tagging behind her was an uncharacteristically petite, young and pretty human girl with blond hair and blue eyes. Her cheerful voice and disposition were as uncommon in this place as her appearance, yet she acted like she was one of them.

"Hi, Karna." the young girl said happily.

"Well, hello." Karna replied, almost cheerful.

"Wow, I've never been up here before. It's really cool up here!"

"Yes, I suppose it is," Karna said not having any idea what the girl really meant. "How have you been? I am sorry but I have been so busy I haven't had much time to spend with you lately."

"I've been cool, you know, staying fly, busy in school, and hanging out."

"Yes, school work, is it going well with you. Are you staying busy as well?" Karna asked as though she was really interested in the girl.

Without answering her question and while looking around the room, the girl said, "You have to run this big place?"

"So, tell me, Nakita, how is your counseling going?"

"It's been okay, I guess."

Without looking at the older Bilkegine lugoth, who escorted the young girl, Karna said, "You may go now." Then looking at Nakita she said, "Nakita, how have you really been since we found you?"

"Well, I was really lost you know with the amnesia and everything, and was really bummed about my parents dying in the accident and all, but I've found a new family here and, it's been two years now and I really like it here now."

"I'm sorry we had to tell you about their death. But it was for your own good that you know all the truth about what happened." Karna said sounding sympathetic. "I'm really happy for you. I was so worried for you when we first found you alone and lost."

"Oh, you were the best Karna. You were like a mom to me, like always looking out for me and like that. You're the one who spent all that time with me the first year teaching me who I was. You told me about our people and about all the other people trying to destroy our way of life and trying to kill us. You were the one who showed me where our planet was before those people destroyed it, and how my parents were the first to discover a new one for our people. You told me that is why I look and talk differently than some of you, that because my family was away looking for a new planet to live on the evil people came and attacked our planet, and during the attack burned much of the cities, causing most to die. And that the only ones who lived are here in this city. And the reason they all talk differently and are a different color is because they were hurt in the wars. I know if it weren't for you I would think I was different. You are my best friend."

"Nakita, I've got a favor to ask."

"Okay, anything! You know I'd be glad to help you out Karna."

"I wouldn't ask unless it was really important."

"I know, but I'm happy to help you, whatever it is."

"There is a goth and lugoth who are staying with us that look like you do. I think they are trying to hurt our way of life. We don't know how they got here but we know they are telling people that we captured them, and that we are doing bad things to them, but none of these things are true."

"I know you wouldn't do anything like that. Why do they want to hurt us?"

"We don't know. Anyway, I would like you to join them and act like you are like them. Act like we took you and you are trying to get away from us so you can live with them. That way you can tell us what they are doing. Do you think you can do that for me?"

"It sounds scary. Will they hurt me?"

"No, Nakita. We will be watching you the whole time to make sure you are safe. If one of them tries to hurt you, we will just put them out of our city and forget about them."

"What would happen to them if they were put out of the city, Karna?"

"I am afraid they would die and I do not want that. Do you think you can help us fix them so we do not have to put them out?"

Yes, I think I can do that. In our class we are pretending all the time. In one of our classes we pretend to be another type of people called humans."

"That is what these people are calling themselves. They are bad people though. Can you pretend that you are scared and cry a lot? Can you pretend that you do not know a lot about us, and that you have been taken by us, but that you have been hiding on our vessel and make up a story about hiding someplace?"

"Yes, I think I can. I know a lot about this vessel and places where I could say I was hiding."

"Good—Nakita very good."

"I will be very good at this job, Karna. I will do a good job for our people against these bad people."

"I know you will, Nakita. I will tell you when it is time for you to go. For now you go back to your room. Do not go back to school. You must go and prepare for your new job for your people."

"Yes Karna. I will make you proud."

"Goodbye, Nakita."

Nakita and Karna left together. After Karna left Nakita in her room, she returned to the operations chamber to check on the status of locating Sean.

"Report," Karna ordered.

"Reports are coming in now from all over the vessel Commander but nothing new."

"How could he have gotten away from us?" asked Karna.

"I'm sure I don't know," the watch officer replied.

"No, I'm sure you don't!" Karna yelled.

The officer wanted to run and hide at this point. "Tell the Lieutenant Commander to meet me in the briefing chamber now!" Karna screamed.

"Yes Sir, at once Commander."

Karna stormed into the briefing chamber and waited for the Lt. Commander. Seconds later the Lt. Commander rushed in. "Yes, Commander, you wish my presence?"

"No, Lt. Commander, I'll tell you what I wish. I wish my principle male subject back in his quarters NOW! My resting phase is past due. When my resting phase is over, my principle subject better be in his quarters. Is that clear Lt. Commander?"

"Yes Commander, perfectly clear."

Without another word Karna left the briefing chamber for her quarters and went to sleep.

Lt. Commander Brodem called for all department commanders to report to the briefing chamber. Upon their arrival the meeting was very short and to the point.

"I just had another meeting with the Commander and where she implied that, unless the principle male subject was found by the end of her resting phase, the penalty would be more than I was willing to pay. She was speaking about death, mainly mine. While she is in her resting phase I am in complete command of this vessel and I am telling all of you that, unless the principle male subject is found by the end of her resting phase, death will result, and I mean yours. You have fourteen jitorians to find him from right now. I want every single Goth, Quod and Drone looking for him in every single chamber except locked chambers and officers' chambers. I don't mean every grot not working either, I mean every grot. I want him found NOW! I am going to find this human. This will not be the day I lose my life because of some useless human! Am I being clear enough?"

The search continued through the resting phase and Karna woke. Before checking in at the command center she decided to take the female subject to the cinbiote for fulfillment and keep appearances up as her councilor. Heading through the Piiderk on her way to the main subjects chamber she was hailed by a member of the search team looking for Sean.

"Commander, your presence is required on the command deck immediately."

"What is it?" She asked.

"I do not know, Commander, only that it was of extreme importance and that they tried to hail you, but all communication systems are down," he responded.

"Very well," she said walking out of the room.

CHAPTER SEVEN

Sean crouched down like a tiger stalking its prey. Each movement he made was calculated and extremely slow. As he moved toward the end of the bed Nancy moved closer to the wall. As if the abduction wasn't enough, there seemed to be a constant barrage of one horrifying experience after another, every one taking her closer to the mental breakdown that she had experienced as a child and that was hidden deep inside her soul. The yo-yo effect of persevering one emotional trauma after another was more than she could stand, and it was beginning to show.

"God, where are you?" she cried. "If there ever was a time that we need you it is now. Please give me some more peace and deliver us from these people, whoever they are."

Her prayers alone brought her some peace, but the emotional scars were not as healed as she had thought, and she was weak and ready to surrender.

The last thing we need now is more surprises. Sean thought. When is it going to be enough already?

Not knowing what to expect, Sean was mad at himself for not having the presence of mind to keep his new weapon closer to him in the bed. He lifted his legs into a crouching position preparing to spring off the bed and attack whatever it was. Just a couple of feet more and he could see it.

Then—swish! This snake like thing came out of nowhere right at him! He jumped back and yelled.

Nancy jumped and screamed. "What is it?"

Sean screamed, "I don't know!"

Then the little boy started to cry. A baby is crying? Sean thought. There is a baby in my room?

The child had been playing with a small length of rope about two feet long and was flinging it back and forth. When Sean had reached the end of the bed, the child decided to fling it up and down and when it flew up right into Sean's face it freaked him out. His nerves were already on edge with everything that he had been through and the things that he had done to the Quods. The kid in the room and the rope just put him over the edge.

How in the world did that child get in here? He thought.

"It's a baby boy!" Sean told Nancy in a somewhat strained and surprised tone. This was no strange, foreign little child. Sean thought. It doesn't have greenish/gray skin and black eyes. He's a normal looking little boy that looked like he could belong to almost any normal American family. His blond hair, along with the typical breakfast bowl haircut and light blue eyes made him look like John Doe America. He was wearing clothes that seemed a bit worn and faded, but other than that, he looked like every other kid Sean had ever seen. "He's a hefty little, fat cheeked, rope chewing carpet monkey," Sean proclaimed. "But what is he doing here?"

Nancy didn't know where here was but Sean did and that made him a much bigger enigma. And an even bigger conundrum was who put him there and why? Remembering how he got into the room himself, Sean sprang to his feet and across the floor to the bathroom. The head was still in the toilet and the humungous body was still in the corner by the sink. So once again, how did the kid get in here? He didn't just walk in here. Sean knew he couldn't get in earlier. Looking at the decapitated head in the toilet, he thought, there must be something in this freak's head that activates the doors when he gets close enough to them, something that I don't have. He thought. And, while the queen of mean looks more like us than them, she must have something as well.

There are just too many questions and not enough answers. New plan! Sean thought. I've got to either jar this door like the other, or I've got to leave now. But, now I've got this kid, but the kid is not my problem. If I jar the door, I'm drawing attention to the fact that I'm in here, and I can't stay here forever. But the kid is still not my problem. If I stay here the kid becomes my problem. And, if Nancy touches, sees, or talks to the kid, he becomes an even bigger problem. Ergo, the kid is my new problem. Okay, the kid is my problem. New Plan! Sean thinks, I've got to get rid of the body but I've got to keep the head somehow. Think, think!

He ran to the bed and pulled back the pad. He took his sword and started prying at the platform. "Yes." He whispered to himself as the platform began to lift. He was able to lift a section up high enough to put the body of the dead giant thing in it. It won't be pleasant to sleep on in a couple of days, but hopefully we will be gone by then. I can hide the sword under the pad but where to put the head. For now I'll cover it with a dirty tunic in the corner of the bathroom. That would buy me some time. Maybe by then I could cut it open and see if it was something inside that allows the doors to open.

By the time he got the body moved and everything cleaned up and put back together, the baby boy and Nancy had become good friends.

"Are you good mates now, Nancy?" Sean asked.

"Isn't he cute, Sean? Can we keep him?"

"It isn't a puppy, Nancy. Besides, don't we have enough problems of our own already?"

"He is not it!" Nancy complained. Anyway he's different than those other monsters. He's one of us? We have to protect him and get him back to his mother."

"Oh, ok. I guess we can look after him for a little while.

Sean crawled back into bed and Nancy brought the boy and crawled in with him. They were just lying down when they were shaken so violently they were nearly thrown off the bed. The entire vessel shuddered and the sounds of buckling metal and gale force winds could be heard through the doors.

"What in the name of everything holy was that!" screamed Nancy.

"I don't know!" Sean said trying to steady himself against a wall, "but

I don't like it." If Nancy knew where she was, he thought, she would be in a complete panic by now.

"You and Junior stay here, and I'll check it out."

✳ ✳ ✳

The Spiruthun was orbiting in the direct path of the oncoming meteoroid and collided so violently it split the meteoroid into hundreds of pieces. If the Spiruthun hadn't been in the frozen vacuum of space, it surely would have been demolished along with the meteoroid. While it did not sustain critical damage, it was however thrown spinning like a top out of its orbit toward the planet. Although the vessel was built to sustain direct hits from smaller meteoroids and other space debris, it was not designed for a meteoroid over one mile in diameter. The consequential rip through the hull of the ship caused an immediate decompression of deck twenty-four and the loss of everyone on board between decks twenty-three and twenty-five, from mid ship to the hull, and peeled back a section of the outer hull six hundred feet long.

As Karna was walking toward the command center as requested, the meteoroid hit the Spiruthun and the shock knocked her off her feet and rolled her around on the Piiderk floor. As soon as the shaking stopped enough to allow her to get back on her feet, she reported to the command center to find it full of smoke and in a general state of panic. Blue flashing strobes and alarms were everywhere and grots were frantically trying to gain control over the ship.

"Report!" yelled Karna.

"Emergency evacuations are under way on decks twenty-one through twenty-seven commander."

"Any breach?"

"Yes, Commander, there is a breach on deck twenty-four. All grot are lost."

"Were containment procedures initiated?"

"No, Commander, we didn't have the time. We didn't see it coming."

"Was there any damage to the central core?"

"No! But all communication and observation systems are down. We're sitting blind and…"

"Was there any significant damage to survival equipment or inner core disbursement?"

"I am waiting for the reports now, Commander Nuubiya."

"Report!" she screamed insistently. "Tell me now!"

"Commander, the communications are down, lateral stabilizers are not functioning and damage reports must be delivered by runners!"

"I want the answers now, report!"

"Here they come now, Commander. Inner core disbursement is not functioning at all. Survival equipment was lost on decks twenty-four and twenty-five and inner core is overheating and imminent disruption is moments away!"

"What about weapons and navigation?"

"They are both down as well, Commander. Maintenance drones are working on them as we speak."

"So what you are telling me is that we were blindsided by a meteoroid, and it has disabled my entire vessel?"

"Yes Commander."

"Why was evasive action not taken?"

"Uh…"

"Report, I want to know why this ship was not moved!"

"Commander, an Officer was not on command deck Sir."

"Why not?"

"All hands search, Commander."

"Search for my principle male subject?"

"Yes Commander."

"Using essential personnel?"

"Yes Sir, using all personnel, Commander."

"On whose orders?"

"By—your orders, Commander."

"By whose?"

"On your orders Commander, through Lieutenant Commander Brodem Sir."

"Call Lieutenant Commander Brodem to the War Chamber now!"

"To the uh—War Chamber?"

"Need I repeat myself?"

"No, Commander," he replied nervously.

Commander Karna left to the adjacent War Chamber and waited there. It was a chamber directly adjacent to the command chamber specifically designated to execute command decisions pertaining to battle and a room where challenges for command could be settled in private. The victor came out alone and assumed command of the vessel. Karna waited with her weapon drawn. There would be no battle and she would be the victor.

Expecting to be ambushed, Lt. Commander Brodem dove into the War Chamber screaming. His life lasted less than one second and the weapon used was the chot, the Commander's favorite personal weapon and the most powerful the Bilkegine people had at their disposal. It rendered the Lt. Commander's body into a puddle of green, bubbling, stinking ooze. War was over.

"Col. Rashintar, report to the briefing chamber." Karna said.

"Yes Sir, at once, Sir." He said leaving his area.

Colonel Rashintar walked briskly into the command center then into the briefing chamber although he was somewhat apprehensive. The last person to meet her there was turned into a mindless drone. "Yes, Sir." he said as he entered the chamber.

"Colonel Rashintar, you are hereby promoted to Lt. Commander."

"Thank you, Sir. I will not let you down, Sir," he said.

"I trust you will not," she said.

"Anything else?" he asked.

"I will go now to visit my principle female subject. If the principle male subject has not been found, and I trust he has not although I do not yet have that knowledge, I hope you will carry out that matter without haste."

Having gone to the bathroom and extracted the severed head from its hiding place, Sean held it up and opened the outer door of their prison chambers to go out and investigate the violent shaking. He stood with his back to the wall and as he had seen in so many cop movies on TV, he bobbed his head quickly around the corner of the doorway for a quick glance to see if the coast was clear just in time to see Karna coming his way. Great! Karna the cruel, just what I don't need right now. He thought. With shaking hands he quickly held the head up and closed the door, hoping beyond all hope that she hadn't seen him or the door closing. He hid the head and ran for the bed making the last ten feet airborne as he flew onto the bed and slid under the cover. There was no place to hide so he told Nancy to go along with whatever he made up. Karna was bound to try and discover how he came to be back in the room.

The door opened and Karna stepped into the room.

"Well, what a surprise," she said looking directly at Sean. "I wasn't expecting to see you here."

"I wouldn't be here if your crew wasn't so efficient, I'm sure," he replied.

"My crew?" Karna questioned in disbelief.

"Don't by coy with me, Karna. I now know more than you think I do but let's just keep it between you and me," he said glancing at Nancy.

"Yes, let's do that."

She walked slowly toward the bed, looking around the room slowly with her black eyes. "I see you have a new member with you. How did that come about?"

"We don't know. He just showed up," Nancy said joyfully. "I think he's cute."

"Amazing how things just…happen…to occur around here isn't it Karna?" Sean said with a smug look on his face.

Without responding to the remark Karna turned away from them and walked to the other side of the room. "So, how long ago were you detained, Sean?"

"Oh, just about an hour or so I guess." Sean said not wanting to show his hand and let her know everything he knew. "I think I was just about to get outside cause I thought I heard some big trucks running when your big, ugly, green goons caught up with me."

"Outside," Karna asked surprised.

"Yeah, I was going to find those trucks I heard and hide inside one of them and let them take me out of here?" He continued.

"You were going to leave your friend here alone?"

"Yes, but I was planning on bringing the Feds back with

reinforcements and get her back. You really don't think you can hold us here forever do you? People we know and love will be looking for us!"

"It is good that my guards captured you then, isn't it?"

"If I could have figured out how to open these stupid doors I could have gotten away sooner. I don't know who you people are but I will get away, and when I do you'll be sorry you ever met me. Mark my words; you'll be sorry you ever met Sean Daniels."

Karna started walking toward the door and Sean thought his lies must have been convincing. But then she stopped at the hall by the bathroom. Sean held his breath. She turned as though she was going to go inside but stopped just in the doorway. Sean was about to explode with fear that she would find the head when she turned back and said, "I'll send someone to clean this room. It stinks. Oh, and one more thing. I was the one who sent the small boy to you. We found him on the compound several months ago. Some uncaring mother probably abandoned him and I figured that…Nancy…would make a good caregiver to him. Is that all right with you, Nancy? Will you take good care of the child?"

She started to walk out again and stopped one more time. "Is there anything else you require?"

"Yes," Nancy said, "is there a place we could wash?" We have both been here many days and are beginning to, ah, well, we need showers."

"Yes, I agree. I will make arrangements," Karna said, and she left.

As soon as she left Sean let out a big sigh. "I thought we were going to be found out for sure. I don't know if she bought it or not, but I think she did. I know one thing for sure, that boy was not abandoned by his mother. More likely, Karna abducted him just like she abducted us."

"Why would they kidnap a mere boy?" Nancy asked.

"Who knows? Why have they done anything they've done?"

"Sean, we're going to need some things for the baby."

"Okay, when you see Karna again, ask her. It looks like he's been taken care of so far. Just tell her what you need, and she'll get them for you. In the mean time, you take care of the boy, and I'll take care of getting us out of here." Sean said confidently, adding, "Somehow," under his breath.

Sean went to the bathroom to get to work on the head. It was not going to be pleasant, but he had to cut it open to see if there was something inside that was causing the doors to open when these things got within a few feet of them. He took his sword into the bathroom. Placing the head onto the toilet facing him, he took the sword, lifted it over his head then stopped. "Hold on, this thing has a screen over its face." He whispered to himself. "What do you really look like you big freak?" Sean pinched at the material and tried to pull it away from the face of the giant but it would not move. He examined the entire head looking for an edge but discovered that it was growing from behind the monsters skin just in front of where his ears should have been. "I know this thing can hear, Karna was ordering them around, but where is its ears?" Sean examined the thing some more and decided to cut the web-like screen from the face. He picked up the sword and tried to push the tip into the screen but the head just twisted away from him. "Oh this is so nasty!" He said quietly while putting his left knee onto the face of the giant's head to keep it from moving. Once again he picked up the sword and pushed the tip into the material. It took a tremendous amount of pressure but finally began to rip. Sean found out that the material was not some kind of metal screen, but was in fact living tissue, very tough living tissue, but living nonetheless. "Anything that bleeds has to be living." He whispered. As he continued to tear away the screen-like growth Sean finally got a good look at what these things looked like. "Oh boy, you are one ugly freak." He said out-loud. Nancy could barely make it out over the sounds the child was making so she got up and started walking to the bathroom. She turned the corner into the hallway and just before stepping into the bathroom she stopped and said, "Sean, are you decent?"

"Uh—uh—no," he quickly said. "Don't come in."

The last thing he needed was for Nancy to see the giant's decapitated head sitting face up on a toilet without the mask covering it. Sean didn't think she had discovered that these beings were not human yet and he wanted to keep it that way as long as he could.

"I thought I heard you say something. She said. "What was it?"

"Oh that, I was just talking to myself that's all."

"Oh, o—k." she replied. "You're sure you're alright?"

"Yeah, I'm fine Nancy; you better stay with the child."

"Ok." She responded.

That was close, Sean thought. I'd better be quiet. Sean went back to work on his giant head. He had torn enough of the growth away to see the entire face now. "Ugly just isn't a strong enough word to describe you pal," Sean whispered. Not only was the face extremely disfigured, in comparison to a human face, but it had the weirdest color and smell. The face was very long, thin and gaunt. It had huge nodules all over it that oozed a very viscous, light green and purple puss that was so pungent it burned the nose. The eyes were double the size of normal human eyes but absolutely black. There was no contrast to distinguish one part of the eye from another. They were just two enormous black orbs sticking out of shallow sockets without eyelids of any kind. The nose was pretty much non-existent. There was an open space that was filled with mucous, but it resembled the cross section of a human nose one sees on an MRI. It was as if someone had come along and cut his nose off even with the rest of his face and skin grew over it. It was just open canals that oozed mucous. His mouth was as bad as his nose. It jutted out from his face at least four inches and he had no lips at all, the skin around his mouth just grew up to the gum line and ended, leaving two rows of huge, black and extremely sharp teeth exposed. Each tooth was serrated but didn't touch the teeth on either side. The inside of the mouth was also black and purple. Sean pretty much figured out what everything was except for three holes across the giant's forehead. The holes looked very deep but were dry. It was the only part of this beast's face that wasn't oozing something. The skin was the hardest for Sean to describe because of the color variations, it is why he had earlier thought of them as greenish, but in fact, they were more ashen colored with various size black spots. They not only smelled dead, but up close they looked it too. "Enough is enough." He whispered. "Let's just stop at that and say you are so ugly!" Sean decided he had seen more than he really wanted by that time and certainly more than he could ever forget in his lifetime. He also remembered that he didn't have much time before they would have visitors again. Sean turned the skull face down, picked up the sword, and brought it down over the back of the skull cracking it like a walnut. It split into two pieces, spraying a mist of blood and some kind of thick gray slime all over the walls and him. Laying down his sword he picked up the skull and continued prying it open. It oozed blue-gray slime all over the floor and smelled like road kill that had been rotting three days on a blistering Arizona highway. Even though Sean was trying to breath from his mouth, the strong sweet stench was getting into his nose and lungs, and that coupled with the act itself, had his gag reflex was working over-time. Sean barely made it to the sink as he emptied the contents of his stomach. This is nothing like sorting nuts and bolts. This isn't even close to my worst nightmare after Vietnam. He thought. Finally, with all the strength Sean could muster, the last crack echoed in the small bathroom and the skull flew into two separate pieces as flesh, slime and puss flew on the wall, floor and Sean. He threw up again.

Forcing himself to continue out of desperation, Sean laid down one half of the skull, closed his eyes, and then sank one hand into the brains. Squeezing the flesh through his fingers like a sieve, he fished around in the muck, slime and puss for something that didn't feel like it should belong there. Had there been anything on the doors at all that may have indicated some other means of automation, Sean would have avoided the whole dissection. "Nothing!" he whispered. "I hope I'm not going through this experience for nothing." He picked up the other side and repeated the entire loathsome exercise. "Nothing—How could there be nothing?" He said to himself. Something has to make those doors open. Come on man, think. There are no openings for keys, no type of imaging device or scanners that I can see. It has to be inside them somewhere. And since the door only opens when the body is vertical it must be in or on the head. It's got to be something like a magnet or maybe an electronic microchip like they put into dogs.

Sean had to try again. But he had a better idea. He took the skull and emptied it into the bowl and stirred it around like he was panning for gold, then repeated the same with the other half. With both skull halves empty he laid them down and washed the brain tissue. Slowly lifting them out, he examined the bottom of the water. Nothing! How can this be? He was getting upset. Think rationally. He thought to himself again. Forcing all the fluid and brains down the small drain, he began to clean up the mess. He went back to the skull pieces and washed them off in clean water. He began to peel the flesh from the outside of the skull halves. When he got to the eyes he thought that it may have something to do with their black eyes so he pulled one out and gently squeezed it in the palm of his hand until it popped. When it did his hand was filled with a thick, black tar like substance that smelled like vomit. The sight alone would have been enough to make Sean retch again but with the added aroma of vomit, that's exactly what he did. I've got to get this over with before it kills me. With nothing of value in the eyes themselves he finished stripping the flesh from the skulls and cleaned them again with fresh water. He picked up one half and began to examine it thoroughly then moved to the second. "Eureka!" He said somewhat loudly. Attached to the inside of the Frontal Lobe of the skull was a very small microchip. This has to be my ticket into every door on this ship. Being careful not to damage the chip, he took his sword and broke the bone around the chip leaving a piece one inch square. Then, taking up the sword again, he continued to break the remainder of the large skull into pieces that would fit down the small drain until there was no evidence of the skull left. He cleaned the bathroom until it was usable again and then himself. It will likely take years for me to get over this experience but to get off this ship, it was worth it.

He returned to the bed and saw Nancy sleeping with the boy. He took his sword and tucked it under the padding one the bed. He was exhausted and decided he had better catch a quick nap before anything else happened when he became aware of how bad he looked and smelled. The tunic he was given was covered top to bottom with blood, guts, puss and eye juice, not to mention the brain pieces. He laid the chip down, stripped off his tunic and tore it into pieces small enough to go down the drain. After destroying all the evidence, he washed up at the small sink the best he could and put on the fresh tunic Karna had provided for them. "Now for that nap, that is if I can ever sleep again after that." He said to himself. Just before he lay down, he reached his arms high over his head to relieve the stiffness in his neck and shoulders from being hunched over the sink so long. Unwittingly, he was still holding the chip in his hand and to his surprise, a secret storage door, hidden in the wall, popped open a couple of inches. This thing is going to come in very useful, he thought.

He went to the door and pushed it open a little further. It was dark inside and very dusty. It was obvious that it hadn't been used in a very long time. It was dank, dusty and filled with old containers holding all sorts of personal items that looked like things belonging to people who had been abducted from years before. What he had accidentally discovered was a virtual treasure trove of personal effects. It wasn't just clothing, it was things that could be used as weapons and tools of escape.

"This is just what I needed." Sean said as he stepped further into the room.

It was ten foot square and with the exception of about four feet in the middle, it was full of stacked containers each filled with all types of stuff. One box looked like the effects of a troop of Boy Scouts. Merit badges, pocketknives, rope, a magnifying glass, matches, a compass, etc... Another box had a purse with some keys, money, "Oh, here's an interesting item." he whispered to himself. "Mace" Sean knew he could spend hours in the room. He found an old flashlight but the batteries were dead.

"Hold everything! Matches, where did I see the matches?"

He went back to the second container he had opened and found the matches. He struck a match and looked around the room. The first thought to hit him once he saw the room with a little more light was, 'The Hiding Place'. A book he had read about a Jewish girl during Hitler's reign. They had a special room built in their home that was hidden behind a bookshelf. They would hide Jews that were trying to flee Germany. They could search this ship from fore to aft and never find us. Providing the boy was quiet. That is going to be a problem. The boy was going to be a problem and he knew it from the beginning. Maybe that is what Karna had in mind by putting him in here to begin with. The boy will have to go; it's as simple as that.

Sean left the room and pulled the door closed. Now, where can I hide this magic key? He looked around the room for a very special place to hide the chip. I know Karna will send a cleaning crew and we don't want them to find it. They will no doubt try to find the source of that awful smell and might possibly find a dead, not so jolly, green giant. There is no place in the room to hide it. The bathroom has no nooks or crannies, and the tunics they provided for us don't have any pockets. The bed had the pad but they would surely look there.

Thinking about them finding the dead giant reminded him to move his sword. He quickly retrieved it from under the pad and moved it to the secret closet and while he was thinking about it locked the door.

"Now for the body." he whispered.

He took the chip and opened the outside door. Looking around to make sure it was safe first he reentered the room and woke Nancy and had her move over. With more strength than he thought he had, Sean dragged the colossal giant out from under their bed and across the room. Pausing to open the outer door, he checked for seclusion then dragged it out of the room. Quickly and painfully he heaved the giant around a corner one hundred feet from his door and saw a hole in the floor near a wall. Looking around, Sean dropped to the floor and peered into the whole to see where it went. All he could see was light. So without questioning himself any longer, he pushed the body into the hole and ran back to the room with his chip in hand.

Who will they say did it? Not me, I can't get out of my room. He thought.

"Abracadabra!" he said as he got to his room and raised his hand holding the chip. The door slid open and he jumped through looking behind him as he did.

Okay, have I taken care of everything? The chip! Where can I hide the chip?

"I've got it!" he said talking to himself.

He went back to the hidden closet where he had remembered seeing a pocket knife. He found the Boy Scout container and took out the knife. It wasn't very sharp but it would do. He whittled down the edges of the bone very carefully until he had it just bigger than the chip itself, three eights of an inch square and one eighth thick. He returned the knife back in the closet and once again locked the door.

Although the thought of it grossed him out, he would carry the chip in the side of his mouth between his cheek and gums. It was better than the alternative cavities of his body and was at the right height for operating the doors. Still, the thought of having a pinch of skull between his cheek and gums didn't have the same allure that tobacco did.

Nancy was beginning to stir now and Sean was ready to lie down.

Too much time had passed since Karna left them alone, and she was on a mission. Her plans were taking shape and now that she had Sean where she needed him, and Nakita was ready to be plugged in, all she had to do was play her hand.

"Nancy, I'm tired and need to rest before the queen of cruel comes back. Can you take Tiny there and play with him on the other side of the room for a while?"

"Sure. Come on, Sweetie, let's go play and let Daddy go sleepy."

"Hey!" Sean protested. "Go easy on that Daddy stuff. I am not his Daddy!"

"Oh, stop. It's just baby talk. Don't be silly."

"You're the one talking silly, if you ask me."

Sean lay down and covered his ears and eyes with his arm and tried to sleep while Nancy started playing with the baby.

"Ok, little man, what should we call you?" she said. "How about— Sandy or does that sound too feminine? I know—we'll call you, Richard. That was my Daddy's name. He was a good man, and you're my little man."

She began to play and sing to Richard as Sean slept. She noticed the little rope he was chewing on was filthy and started to take it away from him.

"Oh no, dirty, dirty," she said. "Uky."

The child screamed in the same horrifying mechanical pitch she had heard Karna speak in, and she saw his eyes flash from bright blue to black.

CHAPTER EIGHT

"All hands red alert, red alert!" was the warning coming through the alarm system inside Cheyenne Mountain. James and Bruce had both been up for more than sixty hours and had been pouring coffee into their systems, trying to stay vertical. Bruce had been doing it for a couple of decades, but for James it was a relatively new venture, and his nerves were beginning to rattle like a baby toy. He could feel his entire insides shaking as if he were sitting on the edge of the bed in one of those cheesy motel rooms that have a massage-o-bed, but the control was on the fritz and wouldn't turn off.

They both ran down the hall to the central command center where a twenty-foot tall map of the world hung on one wall. Bruce looked over at James, who by now was a pasty color and said, "You alright James? You don't look so good."

"Yes, fine."

"What's all the commotion?" Bruce asked.

"We've got a contact!"

"Hot dang, we're goin' huntin' tonight!"

"Hold on big Spruce, this isn't a hunting party; it's a scouting party."

"Just the same, we're getting closer to that big game aren't we?"

"Yes we are."

They stepped up to a rail on the top balcony and watched all the commotion below. All the military men hustled as a red light flashed on the wall and a siren wailed. After the entire team had assembled, a short thirty seconds, the siren stopped and the red light stopped flashing and glowed constantly. A general walked into the theatre and everyone bolted to their feet, and one man near the door yelled "Attention on deck!"

"As you were," the general said, and they hurriedly went about their duties. He went to a desk in the middle of the room two levels up from the bottom level and sat down. Picking up a red phone, without dialing, he said, "Get me the President."

He waited for two minutes.

"Mr. President, Sir. We have confirmation of a hostile target, Sir."

There was a pause.

"Yes, Sir... No, Sir... We do not know, Sir... No, Sir. We cannot reach them with anything conventional, Sir... We will be in Washington in three days with more intelligence, Sir... Very well, Sir." At which time he hung up.

"Does he know it's four A.M. in D.C.?"

"Oh, I'm sure he knows exactly what time it is in D.C., Bruce."

"Boy, what I'd give to be a fly in that General's ear just then," said Bruce.

"Easy there, Bruce. It's thinking like that, that gets you a job like mine."

They watched the big board as things progressed. James explained as things lit up.

"You see those lights up there in the corner over the Atlantic Ocean? They are, or at least it was, a meteoroid. It either exploded due to the stress of Earth's gravitational pull, or it collided with something that wasn't supposed to be there. Or shall I say it collided with something that is not there according to every piece of detection equipment we have. We don't usually track meteoroids. That job normally falls to the civilians. But, we do constantly track space for incoming, fast moving objects. If we see a fast moving object we trace its origin, speed and trajectory to see where it is going to land and to identify its objective and potential threat to our nation. If there is no national threat, let's say like a meteoroid, we just ignore it. Unless of course it will strike a populated area, in which case we take the appropriate measures. Anyway, this fast moving object came up from the south here," he said pointing to the South Pole, "and the red alert warning woke everyone up. We began tracking it immediately. We were in the middle of computing its origin and trajectory and bam! Like I said, it either just came apart or ran smack dab into something that isn't out there. Now isn't that a coincidence? Anyway, I digress. The little lights, now hundreds of them, are being tracked. They represent either pieces of the meteoroid that blew apart and are useless to us, or pieces of what they hit, which will be very valuable to us. We are trying to track every one of those hundreds of pieces to the exact place they land, a task that will prove almost impossible. The military will spend millions of dollars and thousands of man-hours extracting everything from space rocks to ice, just for the chance that it did hit something and we're able to get a piece of it, it of course being the thing that isn't out there. If we're successful in obtaining a piece of something extraterrestrial and able to analyze it, it very well could mean the difference between our survival and our demise."

"Then what you are saying is that Roswell was real?"

"How did you get that from what I just told you?"

"Hey, I'm an old mountain man but I still know that two plus two equals four. In other words, you must have some previous experience to gamble that many man hours and tax dollars. You know what I'm saying?"

"That may be, and I'm not saying you're right, but the possibility does exist."

"Oh, it does, does it? Hey, I was born during the day, but it wasn't yesterday James." Bruce said with a big grin.

"Okay I guess, but since you already have inside information, so to speak, why do you think we're calling this Project Flash-Back? Hum?"

"So, there really are little green men out there?"

"Well," he said pulling Bruce aside and whispering, "I didn't say this, but, yes, we think they are green, well greenish. But we think the little part was some kind of experiment."

"What makes you think that of all things?"

"Simply put, because we examined them."

"And by examined you mean dissected them?"

"Ok look. You're not cleared for any of this information. But since you are here and already know what you know I'll give you this much. When they were examined, we found some human DNA but everything else was alien from their black eyes and weird head to their reproductive organs. Like I said, I didn't tell you anything and I've gone as far as I'm willing to go on this matter. Let's just concentrate on the job in front of us for now."

"If what you say is true, and I have no reason to doubt you, my buddy is in real trouble isn't he?"

"I'd say we're all in trouble if this is what is really happening right now."

"Boy, James, you really know how to freak a guy out!" Bruce said shaking all over.

"Let's just deal with what we know to be fact, and go on with our day. What do you say," James replied slapping Bruce on the shoulder, "ready for some breakfast?"

"Uh—no, you go ahead. I just need to ponder on this a while."

"Alright then, I'll see you later."

✼ ✼ ✼

At the same time the alarms sounded inside Cheyenne Mountain, two young college students working on their thesis in Hawaii were in the dome of the observatory watching an obscure meteoroid, just recently discovered, make its turn around the sun, when it apparently collided with something. The girls could not see anything but normal looking constellations, and certainly nothing close enough for the meteoroid to have run into. Nevertheless the meteoroid was now circumfusing in every direction. Confused and determined to find out more, they called their professor.

"Dr. Weiss, this is Cathy Crudens."

"Yes, Cathy, how can I help you?" The professor replied.

"I'm sorry to call so late, but Rachel and I ware in the lab and have been watching the new meteoroid M46H."

"Yes?"

"We, we were watching it come around the sun and it blew up!"

"What do you mean it blew up?"

"It just blew up! Well, it looked like it blew up, or, ah, more like it blew out or something like that." It looked like it ran into something, you know?"

"I'm sorry Cathy; I only know what you tell me."

"I'm sorry, Dr., we looked to see if there was anything to make the meteoroid splinter like it did but there wasn't anything there."

"I see," the Professor said patiently.

"Dr. Weiss, if the meteoroid did hit something, it would have to be something really big to make it blow up like it did, wouldn't it?"

"Yes, I suppose it would. However, if the meteoroid was large enough and was traveling at a high rate of speed, and the height, weight, and it's own mass were working against it and it had a high enough stress level due to the magnetic pull of the sun and perhaps our planet, it may have just simply flown apart

"Oh, I see what you are getting at," Cathy said, disappointed. "I thought we might have witnessed something spectacular."

"Perhaps, you may have." The professor said, consoling.

"Could you come and see?" She asked hesitantly, because of the late hour.

"I'll be right there."

"Thank you, Professor. Thank you very much!"

Since it was his day off, and he was used to staying up nights, the professor was both up, alert and still in his bath robe. He quickly pulled on some gray wrinkled Dockers that were laying over the arm of the recliner in the living room and picked out the least offensive dress shirt from the laundry basket. He was going to do laundry that day, but procrastinated, a habit common among night-shift workers in the field of astronomy. It seemed that sleeping through the day and working through the night alone gave them no reason to fuss with setting hard fast priorities, especially with mundane things like laundry. Not wanting to offend his two your impressionable students, he pulled a sweater over his lightly offensive shirt which not only covered the smell but covered the fact that he was not wearing a belt. He left his house to walk the just over a mile to the telescope.

He was a relatively handsome man and still in excellent shape for a man in his late fifties from walking to his lab and home at least twice a day. Nevertheless, he was in a lab staring through the peeping glass of a telescope most of his life, and that alone gave him little or no time with the opposite sex, besides those of his students. It may have been for that reason that he lost all hope of marriage and just gave up. At times he looked like Albert Einstein and acted like Goober from the Andy Griffith Show. At other times it was as though a fashion consultant dressed him, a stylist did his hair, a linguist taught him to speak all over again and a speech writer rewrote his speeches to keep them short and to the point. He would be tall, dark and handsome with enough charm to go around for all the ladies that would flock to him. In those times, the professor would have his brightest hour. But that was when he was the speaker at some symposium on Astrophysics or Astronomy. Most of the time the dear professor wasn't bright enough to light a five-watt bulb and couldn't charm a street bum to take a five-dollar bill.

He left his little bungalow by the beach in such a hurry he even forgot to change out of his slippers.

He didn't want his students to know, but he had already studied the meteoroid. He knew the estimated weight, mass and speed. He knew its trajectory. He knew where it had come from and where it was going. He also knew that there was no stress on it due to a gravitational pull either from the sun or any other celestial body because it wasn't going to enter the earth's atmosphere, and he knew without a shadow of doubt that there was nothing in its flight path with which to impact.

He got to the lab and entered the code to gain access. By the time he made it to the telescope, the two students were anxiously awaiting him.

"Good morning, girls," he said.

"Good morning?" They replied inquisitively.

He pointed to his watch and said, "It's almost four A.M., no?"

They both laughed and said, "Oh, yeah," and laughed again.

"Now, let's get started, shall we ladies?"

"Okay Dr. Weiss. What do you want us to do first?"

"First tell me everything again, only this time more calmly and with more detail than before."

"Okay," Cathy said. "I was on the rail, and Rachel was at the computer. We had trained the telescope to the site where the meteoroid would appear when it came around the sun and would appear in our horizon. Rachel had programmed the computer to record, digitize, enhance, and modify any abnormality observed."

"What did you observe when the meteoroid appeared on our horizon?"

"It was traveling toward our moon at just over sixteen thousand miles and suddenly burst into hundreds of smaller pieces."

"When this occurred, were there any flames, a burst of light or any indication that any significant release of energy had occurred?"

"Nothing that I could see through the telescope, she explained. It simply burst apart and smaller pieces went in every direction."

"Hum. Let me think for a moment," he said scratching his beard stubble.

Cathy and Rachel stood and watched him patiently. Dr. Weiss paced back and forth between the stairs that lead to the telescope gantry and the computer station where Rachel was standing. The two students looked at each other and then at the Professor. Minutes passed before anyone spoke.

"Ladies, I would like to try a few things. Would you be of assistance?"

"Sure, anything!" they replied together.

"Fine," he said as he began walking up the stairs leading to the gantry.

"What would you like me to do?" asked Cathy.

"Just do as I ask, when I ask, please."

"Should I do the same then?" Asked Rachel

"Yes, yes, that will do nicely." he replied distracted.

"Alright then, Cathy, open the iris to the precise location the meteoroid…blew up…as you said."

"It's already in the same location, professor. We didn't move anything."

"Good, very good, go ahead and open the iris."

Cathy went to Rachel and gave her the instructions to open the iris. Rachel input the commands and the steel iris began to slowly open. The cold night air filled the lab quickly reducing the temperature of the lab to sixty degrees. The professor was glad he had thrown a sweater over his dirty dress shirt.

"Good. Now Cathy, focus the telescope at the precise location that the meteoroid came apart."

Once again the orders were translated to Rachel and were carried out. The professor looked into the telescope for a very long time at the site where the students said the meteoroid blew up. He knew those constellations as well as he knew his way home. He had looked at those stars for more than thirty years and had taught them to his students for more than half of those years. He saw nothing out of the ordinary and certainly nothing that would explain why the meteoroid would simply disintegrate.

Seeing nothing in the telescope, he came down to the lab and went to the computer. The two students went to meet him.

"Well, Ladies, I cannot see anything that the meteoroid could have struck. Therefore, it must have simply shattered under immense stress. I'm sorry. I know you were hoping that you were involved in much more."

"Yes, we were," said Rachel

"I was hoping for something big for my paper," said Cathy.

"To bring your grade up I trust." Dr. Weiss said with a smile. "We had better lock up now, ladies."

"Goodnight, Professor," the two students said together.

"Yes goodnight."

The two students walked out and headed back to the dorms, but before the professor left, he went to the computer and copied everything that the girls had recorded onto a compact disk. Then he took it into a new lab that had just been completed by NASA. The new lab was designed to take digital telescopic data and digitally enhance it. It was also able to take recordings in all spectrums and modify them to enable them to be watched in full color visible to the human eyes, thereby allowing them to see in full color what they would not be able to see if, for instance, a recording was made in infrared only. The last thing it did was allow a photograph to be viewed as if it were in real time on earth. The best feature of the program was that it could combine any or all of the features at one time.

The professor took the disk into the lab and started to plug information his students had recorded into the program. The computer started to extrapolate the information and compile bits of data and export this information to a high definition plasma screen eight feet tall by twelve feet wide. When the program stopped running nearly four hours and some twenty cups of coffee later, it was ready to view.

CHAPTER NINE

The vessel was in a complete bustle with all crewmen busy preparing for the upcoming journey to the planet surface. They had regained control of their vessel and reestablished the orbit. Once the knowledge was theirs on how to overcome the human psyche, they would transfer to the surface and begin their siege. Although they had been making preparations for decades, the unexpected collision with the meteoroid damaged the ship severely. That would have to be repaired before anything else could proceed. Karna was still more than a little upset that the command center was left completely abandoned while they searched for Sean. The only good news that Karna had was that Sean had been found. The Bilkegine race worked and lived on a thirty-eight hour day, and they were working around the clock to make repairs to their vessel. Had the outer hull breach that occurred during the impact with the meteoroid reached the central core, the vessel would have imploded violently with everything being sucked into the vacuum of space in a fraction of a second. The inner nuclear core would have melt down instantly, resembling the super nova of a small sun. Observers on the planet would have thought they witnessed the birth of a new star in a distant solar system. It wasn't the possibility of these things that made Karna mad enough to kill her first in command, it was the fact that she represented her race's last chance for survival, and his lack of responsibility to save his own skin had almost put the lives of their entire race in jeopardy.

Karna called the Chief Operations Officer. "Chief Loetiffe, are the repairs complete?" she asked.

"They will be by the next resting phase sir," he replied.

"Are the surface ships ready to board landing parties, and the Chief of Arms checked in with you yet?"

"The ships are ready sir, but the Chief of Arms has not checked in with me or any of my officers, to my knowledge."

"Very well, Chief, let me know at once when the repairs are complete."

"Yes Sir."

Karna was in the command center and pushed a few buttons on a console. A voice came through, "Armory Duty Officer."

"This is Commander Karna. I want the Chief of Arms in the Briefing Chamber immediately!" she ordered.

"Yes, Sir!" he replied

The duty officer jumped up and walked briskly down a small hallway and into a small office and through another hallway into the Chief's office. Out of breath, he said, "the Com…"

"Now just hold it there!" the Chief said. "You just don't barge in on me and start shouting at me! You report to me with respect. I am your superior officer. I am the Chief of Arms for this vessel. Do you know what that means here?"

"Yes Sir."

"Don't you think that it is important to show some modicum of order on a military vessel?"

"Well, yes, Sir, I do."

"I have killed Jr. Officers for less serious infractions! Do you want to try again or would you like to join the ranks of the drones?"

Against his better judgment the Duty Officer stepped outside the Chief's door and knocked. Then opened the door and stepped in and began to speak. The Chief held up his hand, and the Duty Officer stopped talking.

"No. Stop. Go back to your desk. Start over from the beginning and do it right. Nothing can be so important that we dismiss protocol. When you do it the way a Bilkegine Officer should, you may continue."

"But, Sir, you don't understand, the Com…"

Once again the Chief held up his hand to stop him from speaking. "I said to stop and go back and do it the correct way!"

The Duty Officer left and thought on the way, I hope he is turned into a drone for this. Who does he think he is, the Commander? Minutes had passed since he received the message from the command center. Being only a few doors away certainly didn't leave any excuses for this tardiness.

The Duty Officer walked back to his desk as ordered, sat down, waited for a few seconds, then got up, walked briskly back to the small office, through the inside hallway, and stopped at the Chiefs door. He knocked.

"Enter," the Chief said.

"Chief Copehag, Sir," the Duty Officer reported. "The Commander has ordered your presence in the Briefing Chamber immediately, Sir!"

"Why, you fool, are you trying to get me killed? Why didn't you tell me?"

"I tried to, Sir, but you were trying to teach me military protocol, Sir."

The Chief left, running for the door as fast as possible. It was the first time that one of the Bilkegine elite officers had done more that walked briskly on the vessel. News of Karna's impatience had traveled around since the demise of her late Lt. Commander, and no one wanted to be the next to disappoint her.

"What took you so long, and why are you out of breath?" Karna asked as the Chief quickly popped into the Briefing Chamber.

"I was, ah, busy making preparations for the surface ships, Sir."

"You were?"

"Yes Sir!"

"Who were you making these preparations with?"

"I was going over my written plans, Sir."

"Have you spoken with the Chief of Operations about your plans?"

"Yes Sir. We are ready to go."

"Then we can disembark now?"

"We need only prepare our weapons, Sir."

"Then tell me, Chief, how do we defeat the humans? How do we overcome their proclivity for freedom and their ability to overcome insurmountable odds and superior weaponry?"

"Well, Sir, we haven't been briefed on that yet."

"But you just said we were ready to attack Chief. You just said that you had a written plan. You just said you had spoken to the Operations Chief, and that he was ready, and that we only needed to ready our weapons."

"Yes Sir."

"Chief, show me your plans, and I'll call the Operations Chief up for a meeting. We'll get this assault started so our race can prepare the planet for our survival. We have been waiting for so many phases it will be exciting to finally see everything begin. I will send a report at once that we are ready to begin. Good work, Chief."

As she reached for the communication panel the Chief said hesitantly, "Uh, Sir, I, uh, don't think the plan is fool-proof yet. I was looking it over and thought I saw a few flaws."

"Oh, you saw a few flaws?"

"Yes Sir."

"I'll tell you what you saw, Chief."

"Sir, I am not...?"

"You probably saw everyone else on this ship diligently working toward the good of the entire Bilkegine race except you. You probably saw yourself in a position of immense authority when we finally realize our dream of finding and acquiring a planet for our people to survive on. You probably saw the back side of your green eye lids. And let's see what else you saw."

Karna stopped and walked outside the Briefing room, leaving the Chief to wait inside in fear. She walked outside the chamber and down the hall through the Piiderk to the Armory. Walking inside, the Duty Officer, who had never seen the Commander in person before, nearly choked and jumped to his feet.

"Commander!" he said excitedly

"Lieutenant."

"Yes Sir!"

"How long have you been on duty?"

"I have been active thirty four jitorians, twelve tactars Sir!"

"In that time has the Chief left his office?"

"No, Sir."

"Has he had any outside communication with any other command center?"

"Not on a secure communication line, Sir."

"Has he been in communication with the Chief of Operations?"

"No Sir!"

"Have you been in his office during that time?"

"Yes Sir! I have been in his office nine times in the past four jitorians, Sir."

"What have you done for him in the last nine visits, Lieutenant?"

"I brought him food and drink four times, female companionship twice, reading material once and orders from you twice."

"Orders from me twice, I only ordered for him once. Explain."

"Yes Sir. He made me deliver the orders properly, Sir.

"Properly, what is a proper way to deliver an order from me?"

"The Chief said by following military protocol with respect and a modicum of order, Sir."

"And he knew the orders were from me?"

"No, Sir, he never let me complete the order the first time."

"How many times have you served under the Chief in the past duty cycle?"

"Me...I have...uh, seventy nine times, Sir." He replied very nervously.

"How many times did you serve with other officers?"

"That would be about one hundred twenty, Sir."

"Of your times serving other officers, how many times had you ever taken them female companions?"

"Not one time, Sir."

"How about bringing food?"

"Again, Commander, I've never..."

"What about reading material other than official documents or orders."

"I have not...uh, never, Commander Nuubiya, Sir."

"Of all the officers you have served under, who is the highest ranking officer?"

"Chief Copehag, Sir."

"Carry on Lieutenant."

Karna went back to the Briefing Chamber stopping briefly at the command center. She made a communication call to the Chief of Arms ready room. "Chief Cremo, will you report to the Briefing Chamber immediately?"

"Right away," he said.

She walked into the ready room.

"Chief Copehag, it would appear that your evaluation of the upcoming assault is not only decidedly devoid of thought and merit of any kind, but you have devoted no time or effort of any kind to this mission or placed any value on anything or anyone but yourself. The only effort shown is in self gratification."

At that time Chief Cremo walked into the room.

Karna continued. "Chief Cremo will take over command of Arms from this point forward. Your new mission in life will be to serve the needs of others as a drone."

With horror in his eyes, the Chief got up and quickly headed out the door. Before he could get out, two of the giant Quods were blocking the way and grabbed him. Kicking and screaming, they dragged him away.

"He will take his place among the drones where he belongs," Karna said. "There is no place for his kind in our new world."

"I believe I know fully what our mission is, Commander. Is there any update I need to be made aware of?" Chief Cremo asked.

"Not at this time," Karna said. "However, you must take the rest of Copehag's duty."

"Yes, Sir." he said and walked away.

Back in Sean and Nancy's prison room, the ordeal with the small boy was becoming a battle in itself. The cute little boy had become a monster. Once Nancy had taken his little toy away from him, his temper made him a living nightmare. He became ugly and distorted, and his cute little two-toothed smile became a snarled growl. Drooling and growling, he lunged at Nancy and clamped down on her arm twisting his teeth into the flesh of her arm. She screamed in torment beating at him. She finally kicked her way free of him, but he was on her again, this time at her thigh, biting and chewing unmercifully. Sean awakened as from his nightmare, bolted to his feet and flew across the room to see that the cute little boy had become a monster resembling the unofficial Roswell photos of aliens everyone was familiar with around the world. His head had become swollen, his skin was turning greenish-gray, his nose was shorter and wrinkled up like a growling dog, his mouth a mere slit with his sharp little teeth showing and his eyes doubled in size and were pitch black like Karna's and all the other beings on the ship. Sean took action immediately and began to beat and kick the demon to free Nancy. Finally, it turned its attention from Nancy and began chasing Sean around the room. Sean ran to his secret closet and when he got within three feet of the wall the door sprung open. As the ferocious little monster was chewing ravenously on Sean's foot and ankle, Sean reached inside, searched blindly for his sword and once he found it, picked it up and with one fatal swoop split the demented demon's head spilling his brains and other fluids all over the floor and himself. The obvious freak of nature was something that neither of them was prepared for. It was what Karna had knowledge of as the cross between human and Bilkegine.

"What was that thing?" Nancy screamed.

"It was one of them." Sean replied wishing he had reworded his response.

"One of them what, Sean, I don't understand!"

Nancy began to sob bitterly again. "Everything is so wrong here! Big green skinned people who don't talk right or not at all. People getting their heads cut off and food that doesn't taste like real food. Light that makes you feel like you're in heaven. Men attacking me and cutting my body up and cutting off my hair! Nothing is right here! When are we getting out of here?"

Sean had limped over to Nancy and sat down quietly next to her as she ranted about everything she had experienced. She was definitely in the middle of a full blown mental breakdown and there was nothing Sean could do to help.

"Soon, Nancy, real soon." was all he could say as he reached out to cradle Nancy in his arms in an attempt to comfort her in his own way.

Karna walked with the two Quods who were escorting the kicking, screaming former Chief of Arms, to a chamber across the Piiderk. The chamber was used to transform intelligent members of their race who had become either useless in their current positions or a threat to the sitting power into mindless, unthinking drones used to carry out tasks like cleaning and repairs that would prove fatal to essential personnel. They were expendable. The procedure was extremely painful, as evidenced by the torturous screams heard from behind the chamber doors. It took several tactars to complete. While it required no invasive procedures, it nevertheless caused blood loss from the trauma. Many who witnessed the procedure reported that they would rather be killed than go through it. They reported that blood and other vital body fluids would run from the nose, eyes, ears and mouth during the process, leaving them a mindless walking zombie, willing to follow any command without regard to their own welfare. Karna didn't need more drones on the vessel. Her only motivation in doing this was to make an example of this poor excuse for a Bilkegine officer. She had already killed one officer for failure to execute his orders with proper thought. Now she would kill this officer's ability to think and act on his own behalf. This would send a message to the rest of the crew that she would stop at nothing to get the results she was after. If there were any doubts that she was in command of this vessel, they would end with this action. When the screaming started and blood and other fluids began to flow from his black eyes, Karna turned and walked out the door.

Thinking the time was right for Nakita to be introduced to her primary male subject, Karna went to give them the opportunity of escape but under closer observation this time. She knew they could not gain access to locked chambers. At least she thought they had no access to locked chambers. Once they were out, she would have Nakita run into them accidentally, thereby making it look like the girl was running away from her as well, and would be trusted by the humans. She thought her plan was genius. Walking to Nakita's chamber she formulated her final plans.

The door opened. "Nakita, are you ready for the mission we talked about earlier?"

"Yes, I am. I will be proud to help our people," Nakita responded.

"The time has come for you to do just that. I will take you to the cinbiote. I have heard the humans call it the great light. When you are there do not go inside. They will not stay long, for they know of its hypnotic effect. When they come out of the cinbiote, you will run into them and act as though you are frightened. You have had enough practice to pretend from there on your own."

"I believe I know what to do. What is the final goal?" Nakita asked.

"Just go along with whatever he wants to do. I only desire to observe his actions to learn how he thinks under pressure, so I can gain the knowledge our people need to defeat our enemy who has long made our race suffer." She lied.

"How have they made us suffer, Karna?"

"They have attacked us without reason for brenaides. Only this morning they attacked us. Did you not feel the shock from the attack?"

"Yes, I did. Is that what it was?"

"Yes, and they nearly killed all of us."

"Why do they want to destroy us, Karna?"

"Because, we are different then they are, Nakita, nothing more."

"I am ready to go now."

"Remember, tell them nothing that he does not ask. And remember, you can only access areas of the vessel that do not require an implant."

"I've forgotten which area those are, Karna."

"Be aware. When you approach a door that requires the implant to open, you will feel a light buzzing feeling in your head. Stop before you get there. That will be a door that requires an implant. Pretend that you have never been in that chamber, and forget what is in that chamber."

"Okay, I've got it."

"Leave now and wait by the cinbiote."

Karna left and went up twelve levels to the Piiderk. She went to the holding chamber where Sean and Nancy were and went inside. As soon as Sean saw her come inside, he jumped out of bed and ran to greet her.

"What do you mean sending this monster in here with us?" he yelled at her, pointing to the dead kid.

"I don't understand what you mean," she said acting puzzled.

"Don't play dumb with me! This is one of yours!"

"I am sure I don't know what you mean."

"That thing attacked Nancy and nearly ate her arm and leg off! And look at my foot!" he yelled again, holding his leg out for her to see.

"I'm sorry that you were injured. I will have our medical staff look at it immediately."

"I can hardly walk on it, and Nancy is in really bad shape!"

Karna thought for a minute. This really was a problem she didn't need just then. She needed him to be able to move around quickly in order for him to escape, and she knew he wouldn't leave without the woman.

"Again, I am very sorry it happened, but I assure you I had no idea that the child was not just a boy. We found him on the compound just outside. I was assumed his mother abandoned him, and I just thought that he w…"

"Don't waste your breath lady," Sean interrupted, "I'm not buying a word of it anyway."

"I have no reason to lie to you."

"And another thing, how about getting us that shower you promised and some real food. And get this stinking thing out of here! Oh, and how about something real to eat. We haven't had anything real to eat or drink since we got here days ago!"

"It will be done." Karna said, disappointed that her plans would have to wait for some time. She turned and left.

Sean thought for a minute he had really messed up when he pointed out the dead kid. He was sure that Karna was going to ask how he came to split the kid's skull. Maybe she did wonder, but just didn't ask, maybe not. The only thing to do now was to wait and find out. A few minutes later, the door opened and several people came to the room. Without speaking a word, three men came over and began to dress their wounds. The bites and rips in Nancy's arm and leg were closed with some kind of laser, and then dressed. Then a wand of some kind was waved over them and she began to feel better right away. They then turned their attention to Sean's ankle. Two drones came in and took out the body of the child monster and cleaned up the mess. Another went to the wall on the opposite side of the room from the bathroom and began to scan the wall with some electronic device. When he had placed it in the right position, a panel opened and was removed revealing another short hallway leading to another door. He stepped into the hallway and when he approached the door it opened and he went inside. A few seconds later he returned to the room, gathered up the other two drones and left. They were all in and out within a few minutes.

Sean was just getting up to investigate the new hallway when the door opened again, and three lugoth entered the room with a cart. They had hot food and cold drink on the cart. Sean and Nancy went right for the food. It had been so many days since Sean had anything at all to eat or since Nancy had anything but some fake tasting grapes and some water, their stomachs ached. Sean grabbed a piece of warm meat and put it into his mouth. It was hot, sweet and tasted like pork chops. It was good. He didn't recognize the texture, color or shape, but it tasted good and went down easy so he devoured it. The beverage they sent was likewise different from anything he had before. It was very cold and bubbly. Very carbonated, somewhat grainy and had a bitter aftertaste. If he would have had to guess, he would swear he was drinking an old beer. Never having acquired a taste for beer, he put it down and tried the blue drink that resembled the fluid you put in your car to wash your windshield, bug juice. He gave it a try and thought it was rather good. It tasted like a mix of really sweet grape juice and lemon lime soda that had gone flat. The meal wasn't Mickey D's, but it was hot and it was real. Nancy's pallet was more refined than Sean's, but then he was used to eating day old pizza left in the box and fruit he had to shave before eating. She found the meat too confusing to eat but found the vegetable edible. They were prepared similar to steamed vegetables in a fine restaurant, and while they had a different shape, color and texture than anything she had ever eaten in her life, still they were hot and palatable. Somehow in all the excitement of their food, they had forgotten about their wounds. Or, it would have been the medical treatment and medication. Sean thought about the medications they received and was reminded of morphine he was given after being shot in Vietnam. They both stuffed themselves and headed for the room that was opened up for them.

Sean stepped into the hallway hesitantly. With extreme caution he stuck his head around the corner and peered inside another small room. The room had clear walls on all sides, the ceiling was ten foot tall and it had what looked like a shower head six feet in diameter hanging a few inches off the ceiling in the center of the room. Sean slowly stepped inside and seconds later, it began to rain. He jumped back into the hallway and the rain stopped and a gentle warm breeze began to blow from the ceiling of the hallway. Wow, Sean thought. I've never even imagined anything like this before. When I get home I'm going to patent this thing and sell it exclusively in my hardware store.

"Hey Nancy, it's another bathroom!" he said excitedly, "Except it's a shower!"

Nancy came running into the new hallway where Sean was standing looking inside.

"I don't see any handles. How does it work?"

"Just like the bathroom I guess." Sean explained. "It somehow senses you inside and turns on."

"Ladies First," he said as he stepped aside.

"Uh, there are a few problems," she said.

"What's that?"

"There's no door, the walls are transparent, there isn't any towels, and…"

"And," Sean questioned in a puzzled voice.

"And, we're not married."

"Oh, how dumb am I. I'm sorry, I wasn't thinking…I was just…you know, I better just shut up before I dig myself into a hole I can't get out of."

"It's ok. I'm just not comfortable with…

"Say no more, I understand. Why don't I just go lay down until you're finished and dressed." Sean said with a sheepish smile.

"Thank you, Sean."

Sean left for the bed, and Nancy stepped out of her tunic and into the room. It was the greatest experience of her life next to the cinbiote. The hot water lasted forever. It was the perfect temperature, like it was warmed inside the earth and brought up through a hot spring, pumped into the shower and dropped like rain. It was soft. She looked around for soap and shampoo, and just when she was about to get disappointed, her body started to lather. This is amazing, she thought. About fifteen minutes into her shower, the water started to clear and her body was rinsed off. "This is great, an automatic shower just like the car wash but at home. Sean is going to love this." She whispered.

"Ok, your turn!" she said as she was putting on a clean tunic.

There was no answer from the room.

"Sean, it's your turn!" she repeated coming out of the air dryer.

Sean was not in the room. "Where has he gone?"

CHAPTER TEN

Now that the professor had his evidence confirmed, he could call the government and tell them what he saw, or more specifically, what he did not see.

"Yes, Ma'am, may I speak to the Department of the Interior." The professor asked.

"Whom do you wish to speak with?" A secretary requested.

"I'm not sure. What I mean to say is that I don't have a name specifically."

"I'm sorry, Sir, but I have to have a name before I can transfer a call."

"Can you transfer me to Washington Information?"

"Yes Sir. Please hold."

The professor was on hold for twenty minutes when someone said, "Information, how may I help you?"

"Yes, I wish to speak to someone from the Department of the Interior. I am Dr. Oscar Weiss, PhD. From the University of Hawaii, Astronomy and have discovered an anomaly that could pose a threat to our nation. I do not have a name and have difficulty getting through to them without one. Can you help me?"

"One minute, please."

Once again the professor was on hold for more than thirty minutes. It was good that the professor was a patient man. It came with his profession. Finally a man came to the phone and in a very monotone voice, introduced himself as being not from the Department of the Interior, but from the National Security Agency.

"Hello, Sir. My name is Agent James Rose, from NSA."

"Yes, I've been on hold for some time now and I have..."

"I'm sorry, Sir. I was passed to you but was not given your name only that you had important information that may be connected to a case I'm working on."

"Oh yes, my apology, my name is Dr. Oscar Weiss, PhD., from the University of Hawaii, Astronomy Department."

"Thank you, Professor, please go on."

"Thank you. As I was saying, I called to speak to someone in the Department of the Interior."

"What was the issue you wished to discuss with them?"

"As I said before, I am an astronomer. A student had recently brought to my attention a meteoroid she was tracking. She reported to me that it had collided with something, or simply divided due to stress and is now spreading out in different directions. Some of the pieces are going to speed out into space, some will burn up in our atmosphere, but some will become meteorites and crash into the planet."

"Yes, Professor, I am aware of the meteoroid."

"Oh! You are aware of this meteoroid?"

"Yes, we are. How or why does this concern you, and why do you think it may be a threat to our nation?"

"Uh, oh, yes. Acting on a theory that I had regarding the breaking up of the meteoroid, it was my contention that the meteoroid could not have in fact broken up due to stress. Nor could it collide with something since there, simply put, couldn't be anything for it to collide with. Therefore I took the data that was collected and did some analysis of it and arrived at a rather shocking conclusion that, I dare say, I fear to expatiate over the phone."

"I see, Doctor, nor I. Are you able to travel?"

"Yes, I can travel. To where would I be traveling?"

"Colorado."

"When may I come? The information I must disseminate is of the utmost importance."

"Can you be ready to leave in a four hours?"

"I'm confident the airport doesn't have a flight out until at least one o'clock this afternoon. I do travel quite a bit for speaking engagements and the first available flight is usually early afternoon. But…"

"I will have our jet pick you up in Hawaii at your convenience, Professor."

"Very well, I will go to the airport in a couple of hours and wait there. Where will the jet be?"

"Go to the military gate. I will arrange to have a car waiting for you there."

"One more question, Agent Rose."

"Yes Sir?"

"Where am I going?"

"I'm afraid I cannot tell you that until you are airborne."

"I understand. I'll see you then."

The professor hung up and proceeded home to pack for his trip. He had never in his career been involved in anything so cloak and dagger before, nor had he seen anything so puzzling. He knew he was involved in something that would change his life forever.

"Hey, Bruce, I've got to take another trip." James said.

"Need some company?"

"Sure, why not. Not much you can do here right now anyway."

"Where are we going?"

"Ever been to Hawaii?"

"Hawaii? Nope, but the wife's been naggin' me for years to take her there."

"We've got to go pick up some help. He's got some new info for our scouting party."

"Sounds good to me, got anything to do with that fireworks show we saw earlier?"

"Yeah, it sure does, and then some I suspect."

They left the mountain and got in a jeep to go to the military airport and the jet. It was fueled and waiting by the time they arrived. It only took three hours and fifty-three minutes to get from Colorado Springs, Colorado to Hawaii and pick up the Dr. He wasn't what either Bruce or

James was expecting to see when he walked up to the gate, carrying his fifty year old suit case, thirty-nine year old umbrella, and World War II rain coat complete with insignia. He wasn't in the war; he just got a good deal at the Army Surplus store. He looked more like a homeless street person without the ubiquitous shopping cart than a big university professor with credentials as long as the jet, but he had what they needed, and that was all that counted. The door to the jet opened and James went out to greet the doctor. They met each other about half way and stopped to shake hands.

"Hello, Dr. Weiss. I'm Agent James Rose. We spoke on the phone."

"Yes, Oscar Weiss," he said holding out his hand.

"Please." James said directing him to the jet.

They walked to the jet together, and James motioned for the professor to board first. Once they had both boarded, the door was shut and they prepared to take off. As they were seated they got more acquainted.

"Dr. Weiss, this is Sheriff Bruce Faulkner."

"Hello Doc." Bruce said

"Bruce, the doctor is an astronomer at the University here in Hawaii. He's been observing a meteoroid that has, shall we say, something to do with our case. We'll discuss it in detail when we get back on base."

"Why the secrecy, Agent Rose? Isn't the plane a safe location to speak?" the professor asked.

"We would like to think so, since it's ours, but we have to take fuel and have maintenance and the like in un-secure locations at times and are not always in control of the security, so we don't take unnecessary chances."

"I see. How long is the flight?"

"It will be just under four hours, why not just sit back and relax."

"Would you like some coffee, Doc? I'm heading that way." Bruce offered raising his coffee cup in the air.

"Yes, please, Sheriff. I could use some stimulation."

"Stimulation, ha, that's a good one, Doc."

"James, can I get you a jolt?"

"No! My liver can't take any more of your coffee for another seventy-two hours, maybe more. It's strong enough to peel paint."

The flight time was faster on the return trip due to a tail wind, and the three of them stopped at the security station to procure a security badge for the professor.

"I will need a brief before we have our first session Professor, we'll need to make sure we have everything the General will need to report to Washington. Charts, files and reports will have to be typed and duplicated for the briefing before we can start, and there is very little time."

"I believe I brought most of what you will need Agent Rose, so all you need do is get them reproduced."

"Let's get started right away. I'll get the 'IT' department right on it." James said reaching for the case Dr. Weiss was carrying. "At the end of the hall is a bathroom. Just to the right is a small room with a bed and nightstand. I'm sorry for the accommodations. This isn't meant to be a five star hotel. Just follow the yellow tape along the floor. When you leave your room, you'll follow the red tape to a briefing room. It's the large room with a table about forty feet long and a large viewing screen at one end. Please go unpack and freshen up now and meet us there as soon as possible. We'll start the briefing as soon as you are ready. Is there anything you need?"

"What are the computer capabilities in the briefing room?"

"What do you need them to be?"

"It would be easier for me to write them down, Agent Rose. I don't mean to insult your intelligence, but the computer must meet critical specifications, or the disk I have will be useless, and the computer will not be able to be programmed."

"No apologies necessary, doctor. There are no egos here. Whatever is required to ensure the security of our nation is all we are interested in. Just give me the list and it will be done."

The professor wrote down the specifications for the computer and gave them to James. He looked them over briefly and put them in his pocket.

"I'll have our 'IT' boys get right on this, and they'll have what you need by the time of our brief. Let's say one hour from now. Is that sufficient?"

"That will be more than sufficient, Agent Rose. Thank you."

✷✷✷

Nakita went to the cinbiote to wait for the humans to appear. She knew that Karna was on her way to their room and would not be there long. Planning her accidental meeting, Nakita slipped into the cinbiote for a quick pick-me-up. She liked the effects it had on her. She was not always allowed inside the cinbiote. She couldn't remember her childhood but from the time she could remember, she was scolded for entering the cinbiote. She thought it was because it reminded her of her past, but those memories were long gone now. She can't remember what the big deal could have been anyway. What could have been so horrible about her past to be yelled at for remembering it? She thought. Was I bad or something, how bad could I have been? I couldn't have been more than five years old, since I'm only twelve now. "Come on." she said out loud. "Let's get started already!"

Nakita was the only natural 'English' speaking person on the vessel besides the human abductees that were being used by the Bilkegine. Without her knowledge, Nakita had been used as a teacher since her abduction. The Bilkegine kept her because they needed to learn the language and customs of the humans. They needed someone who was young enough to not remember her past easily, but old enough to have a complete understanding of the language. She was not the only child taken when the Spiruthun arrived to relieve the previous vessel. There were children taken from all parts of the world. Karna had learned all the languages from the children and tried to foster relationships with all of them in order to use them to their up-most potential, but her relationship with Nakita was different. While she wouldn't have been able to explain it, there was a special relationship between the two.

Nakita had learned the Bilkegine language in her education on board. It was her least favorite subject because of the unnatural humming and clicking noises she had to make hidden behind each word. That coupled with the fact that there were more than three hundred symbols to their written language, and one word could have up to twenty-five meanings depending on those difficult hums and clicks or grunts used with it, made it very difficult and boring.

As she stood in the warming, fulfilling rays of the cinbiote, a peace came over her but, due to her complete brain washing, she no longer had the memories from her childhood, nor did she have the peace of being a carefree child in a happy place where love abounds. She only knew the joy of serving, and the honor of sacrifice. The irony of this race's creed was that the more insight and knowledge they had of the human race, the more they came to act and believe in the thought of individual service and freedoms. The thought of individual survival was one thought that was running rampant around the vessel lately, especially with Karna in command.

Karna stepped into the chamber where Sean and Nancy were being held. She walked in just as Nancy had come out of the shower looking for Sean.

"Karna!" she said, shocked.

"I require you both to accompany me to the cinbiote," she said.

"The cinbiote, what's a cinbiote?" Nancy asked.

"The great light as you call it," replied Karna.

"Oh, that. Uh, we're not ready yet." Nancy offered.

"No matter, we must go now. Where is the male?"

"Sean?" Nancy asked trying to stall.

"Is there another male? Yes, Sean!"

"Uh, he is in the shower," she lied. "I will tell him," she said as she turned and began walking to the shower.

"I will tell him myself." Karna said sternly as she pushed past Nancy.

Nancy jumped in front of Karna to stop her from learning that Sean was not there. "You can't go in there!" she cried out.

"Why not," Karna asked puzzled, "is he not cleaning himself?"

"Apparently, you don't know much about males," Nancy began. "You go in there and he'll never do anything you want again."

"Why not, it does not make any sense to me?"

"Who knows? Men are private that way. They don't like for women to see them naked, unless it's their idea first."

"That is ridiculous. The time is come. We must go now!"

"It might be ridiculous to you, but if you go in there, I'm telling you, the only way he will go anywhere again is if you are dragging him."

"Stupid males," Karna said storming away. "When do you think he will be ready?"

"I would say in thirty minutes. Give or take."

"You tell him that he will have half of that!"

"I'll tell him."

Karna stormed out of the room and briskly headed across the Piiderk toward the cinbiote.

Nancy watched the door close and turned nervously back toward the shower. Mumbling under her breath, "Sean, where on earth did you go?"

The secret door cracked open and Sean poked his head out. Nancy jumped and screamed. "It's okay Nancy, it's me. Is the coast clear?"

"Yes the coast is clear. I didn't know where you went."

"What did black eyes want?"

"She came to get us for something. Oh, yeah, she wanted to take us to the light for something. I had to tell her you were in the shower, and she tried to walk in there to get you! Then I had to stop her and bluff her from going in there. She must have really wanted you badly for her to back down."

"Yeah, I heard part of the conversation. She wants me badly alright, but God only knows what for."

"Why did you hide from her in the first place?"

"I heard the shower blower come on and mistook it for the outer door. I thought it was someone coming in and didn't want to get caught with this door opened so I jumped inside and pushed it closed behind me."

"What's in there anyway?"

"It's an old storage closet and from the looks of it, it's been forgotten about for some time. It's full of all sorts of junk, but I think I'll be able to use some of it for our escape. I'm going through it little by little for things we can use."

"Is there anything really good in there?"

"Not yet. Listen, we better get ready for the creepy queen to come back. Let me grab a quick shower."

Karna reached the cinbiote and found Nikita still basking in the light.

She reached inside and pulled her out roughly. "Ouch! That hurt!" Nakita cried.

"Stop whining!" Karna demanded.

"Why did you do that?" Nakita protested.

"Because instead of waiting for the male and female to join with them like I commanded, I find you here playing in the cinbiote."

"I wasn't playing; I was fulfilling myself for the long mission."

"No, you were not. I saw you enter when I went into the prison chamber. You forget my black vision has no problem seeing through the fog of brilliant light like yours does. Don't forget what you see and what I can see are two different things."

"I'm sorry, Karna. I got caught up in the light. I didn't realize how much time had passed."

"No you didn't! Your kind...I mean those of your age, never realize how long they are in."

"Why do you never enter the cinbiote, Karna?"

"I do not require fulfillment any longer."

"You do not require to be fulfilled?"

"I do not find enjoyment in it any longer. Let's leave it at that."

"Yes Sir."

"Now, back to our current mission, I will now go and bring the male and female. I will leave them at the cinbiote. I will tell them that I must leave for a brief time and not to get out without my help. It is then I expect you to join with them and do whatever the male tells you to do and nothing else. From this time forward do not try and contact me, no matter what. Do you understand, under no circumstances?"

Sean was just coming out of the shower blow dryer and throwing on his clean tunic when Karna came through the door. "It's about time you are finished," she said.

Sean came back with, "You ever hear of knocking you rude, obnoxious, pig?"

"Come with me, it is time for you to go to the cinb...the light."

"Oh, no thanks," said Sean. "We ate a big supper just a bit ago, and I don't have to tell you, we're still stuffed," he said tapping his stomach.

"You don't understand," Karna continued. "It's not only for food. It is for our protection against germs which you may be carrying that we have not been vaccinated against."

"That was quick thinking," Sean said under his breath.

They left with Karna leading the way as usual. Upon reaching the cinbiote Karna motioned for them to enter and said, "I will leave you here while I attend to an urgent matter. Do not leave until I come for you. You must stay in the light a designated time for the required effect. Do you understand?"

"Yeah, yeah," Sean said.

Sean and Nancy stepped into the light, and Karna turned and walked away. Moving far enough away that she knew they couldn't' see her through the fog of light; she stopped to watch what they would do. Just as she hoped, they walked out the other side and there was Nakita waiting, acting as though she had been running and was out of breath.

"Oh! Who are you?" Nakita asked startled.

"I'm Sean. Who are you?"

"Nakita, hurry we've got to get out of here. They will be back for us!"

"How did you get here sweetie?" Nancy asked.

"Come on!" Nakita said starting to run.

She started to run toward the doorway that Sean had already examined and found to be too busy to be a good hiding place.

"No, not in there," he said. "I've got a better idea."

He took Nakita with one hand and Nancy with the other and started to run toward the warehouse he had been to before. Knowing that Nancy didn't know where they were, and not knowing Nakita's story yet, he didn't want them to see the big window, so he kept them close to the door as they entered the warehouse. Because of the obstacles between the cinbiote and the warehouse, and because they had changed directions, Karna had no idea where they had gone. Thinking they had gone into the transportation chamber, she called for the Chief of Security to call his team to have them watched and report all of their actions to her in order to learn what she needed.

"Okay, Nakita, this is Nancy. How long have you been here?"

"A very long time," she replied with a lie.

"How did you escape your compartment?"

"They brought me to the cinbiote, and when they put me inside, I crawled out the other side and ran away. Then I saw you coming and thought that you could help me."

"What's a cinbiote?" Sean asked. It wasn't a term he had heard.

"The cinbiote, it's where we just left, the bright light."

"Ah, how do you know what they call it?"

"I…uh…" she began explaining trying to stall for time to think.

"Never mind, where are they keeping you?" Sean asked.

"In one of those rooms," Nakita replied pointing to the wall.

"How did you know the door that you were going into would open?"

"I've been gone for a few days, and when no one is around I go around and try to get inside different doors."

Wait a minute! Sean thought. She said she had just escaped from the light and saw us coming.

"Have you had anything to eat or drink since you escaped?"

"No, I keep sneaking back to the cinbiote. It seems to give me the energy to keep going."

"How can you make yourself come out of there?" Nancy asked.

Yeah, good question Nancy. Sean thought again.

"It's not easy. There is something about that place that makes you feel so good. It's hard I admit but somehow I just find the courage to leave."

"Let's just hide out here while I think of a plan for our escape. Somehow we've got to get to the trucks I heard outside. Maybe we can grab one and drive out of here." Sean said just to give them hope and to throw Nakita off, just in case she was another one of Karna's spies.

Sean sat quietly and thought of where they were and the impossible task ahead. He really thought that there was no hope of escape, and that his only real objective should be to destroy the ship and everyone on it. If not to protect the planet, just to get even with that black-eyed snake Karna. The girls talked as girls will do. Nancy talked about everything they had done to here and her horrifying experience with the boy. Nakita told Nancy about school. The odd thing about Nakita's stories, though, was that they seemed shallow. Sean thought they lacked the everyday detail that girls instinctively put into every sentence they speak. There weren't any boys in her stories, no shopping trips to the malls, no clothes, bad hair days, no negative teachers or anything else he had overheard a hundred times while waiting at the local bus stop while walking to work. The friends that traded at his hardware store would tell him stories of a typical night at home, where their teenage daughters would tie up the phone from the time they got home from school until past bedtime, and he was not hearing anything remotely close to detail like that. Something sure is different about her. He thought. He remembered being at the local pizza joint and listening to all the girls gossiping and giggling over boys, so he thought it was normal behavior for every teenage girl to at least mention a boy, or clothes or shopping in at least one story. At least Sean had never, not heard other girls, about her age, talking about boys and the like. The other thing that Sean thought was wrong about her was her clothes. She wasn't dressed right. The current dress for girls her age was retro sixties, an age he would like to forget ever existed. Nevertheless, it was popular again, but no headband, no hip hugger bellbottom jeans, no peasant blouse, no beads, nothing. She was wearing clothes that looked like they came out of the old Salvation Army or Goodwill dumpster from the nineties. Something was different about this girl, and Sean was on his guard, especially after the incident with the boy. He got up and walked toward the door.

"Where are you going?" asked Nancy.

"Just going to take a peek around, I'll be right back."

He walked outside and looked for the tell tale signs of the resting phase. Everything got a lot quieter, and the lights were lower during the resting phase. Not yet. He went back inside.

"Any news," Nancy inquired.

"Not yet. I'm gonna have a look around. You two stay here."

Remembering what Karna had instructed Nakita to do, she thought up more lies to talk about.

Sean started to take a closer look at what was in the containers. He found a large bar and started forcing open some of the containers. He couldn't read the strange markings on the containers, so he went for the largest one first. When he opened it he found what looked like a huge weapon. This didn't look good at all. He looked around the huge warehouse for other boxes with the same size and markings and found hundreds of them. He opened another container and found little packages of something. He pulled on open with his teeth, wishing he had pockets to carry one of the pocket-knives he had found, and discovered what he thought was some kind of food. He hesitantly took a small bite. "Oh! That's terrible!" He said as he spat it out and wanted to lick the side of the crate just to get the taste off his tongue. "What was that? I don't think I want to know." He whispered. Throwing it down he went to another box.

"I'll take what's in box number three, Bob." He said quietly.

He forced it open and some packing material fell around his feet. Standing in the middle of the container was a rack holding objects that resembled hand guns. They were long and black and had a curvy body. The curvy part was about an inch think and two inches wide and was tapered from two inches at the top and about five inches at the opposite end. On the bottom of the wider side was a potato shaped bulge. He picked up one and began to examine it closer. It wasn't heavy even though it looked like solid cast iron. The small end had an opening one quarter of an inch round. The ball shape underneath was warm to the touch. Sean palmed the ball and a short burst of heat came out the other end expanding as it left, growing in a circular motion like a heat wave. Within a split second it reached a stack of containers several high and burst them apart almost silently. "Oh Yes!" he said excitedly. "This is perfect. It's lightweight, easy to conceal and a blast of fun, he perfect terrorist weapon. I'll take two," he said. "Can I get them gift wrapped?" Examining even closer he discovered a small oval depression on the side of the ball end. He needed to fully understand how they worked and what they fired. He pressed on the depression and the breech opened on the underside of the curved barrel. There was no chamber to put a conventional round as he knew it. Then he saw it. "Oh, how clever, there is a clip." The weapon was like the old over and under, with a pistol on the top and shotgun on the bottom. It loaded the chambers individually and fired them individually, but with one trigger. Each round was no bigger than the diameter of a pencil lead and was one inch long. The magazine only weighed a few ounces, and the entire weapon loaded was no more than a pound in weight. This is phenomenal, he thought. "I've got to try this baby out again!" He whispered.

He pointed the weapon at a stack of crates at the other side of the warehouse. Then once again palming the ball on the underside he squeezed. Whoosh, the weapon sent out the energy wave again but because the target was so far away this time, it had dissipated too much to cause any damage. Well that's disappointing. Pointing again at the same target, Sean squeezed the ball and depressed the oval depression at the same time. An almost silent zing sound came from the weapon this time followed by a huge bang. The energy wave preceded two of the small pins as they left the chamber and then exploded on contact with the force of eight ounces of plastic explosives sending splinters of whatever those containers were made of flying through the warehouse.

"Oh, Yes!" Sean yelled. "Meet my new best friend!"

"What was that?" Nancy screamed.

"Oh, it's okay Nancy, it's only me. I found something, something wonderful. Everything is fine, go on back to your conversation."

Sean reached into the box and searched through the packing in the bottom for more ammunition. He found several of the ball shapes and pulled them out. Grabbing another of the weapons he tucked them under his tunic and headed back to the girls. "Okay, ladies, time to head back."

"Where are we going?" Nakita asked.

"Back to our room, Sean replied."

"Your room," Nakita questioned surprised.

"Yes, our room." Sean replied "Should we be going someplace else?"

"I thought you were trying to escape?"

"Where did you get an idea like that?" Sean asked frowning.

"From Ka…, well I just thought you would be, like me."

Sean glared at her for an instant. My doubts in her may have some merit after all. He thought.

They arrived back at the room they were being held in and Sean went ahead. "You girls wait here, and I'll see if the door is open."

Sean knew it would be closed, but not wanting to show his hand yet, and knowing the fog would conceal his ability to open the locked doors, it would give him a chance to get inside, stash his weapons in his hidden closet and get back without Nakita knowing anything.

He ran to the door, went inside, hid his loot and went to get the girls.

"It's locked." He said as he walked up to them. "We'll just have to wait around for someone to open it for us."

"Is that a good thing to do Sean?" Nancy asked.

"I don't have a better idea."

They didn't have to wait long before two of the big Quods came and grabbed Nancy and Sean by the arms and dragged them toward the room leaving Nakita standing in the Püderk. Sean looked back to see Nakita just standing there surprised and confused at what to do. Suddenly Karna was there and grabbed Nakita. "There you are you little brat," she said. "We've been looking all over for you. You may as well join your new friends."

Just as Sean and Nancy were thrown into the room, Karna dragged Nakita into the room and threw her onto the floor. "I see the three of you have met. I expected you to try and escape, but am relieved to see that you have returned to your room."

"Then why did you have the goons throw us in here?" Sean asked angrily.

"They don't think much, they just react. They saw you were out without an escort and they reacted. It's what they do."

"The next time they react, I'm going to react myself. I'm getting tired of being pushed around!" Sean yelled.

"I do not think you are any match for their strength."

"Don't patronize me you black eyed, black hearted queen of cruelty. You would be surprised at what my strengths are."

"We will see tomorrow." She replied leaving the room.

Nancy crawled over to Sean and whispered, "Why do you try to make her mad like that? Don't you know that will only make things worse?"

"I don't know, I guess it's because I know who she really is."

"Who is she, really?"

Nakita was straining to hear, but Sean was not ready to trust her yet. Especially after just watching her stand there when they had been grabbed. The normal response to the giants showing up would be to run like hell was chasing you but she just stood and look confused.

"Let's just say that no one here is who they seem to be except you and me."

The lights dimmed signaling the resting phase, so Sean and Nancy went to the bed. Nakita lay on the floor near the door and they all went to sleep.

CHAPTER ELEVEN

Inside Cheyenne Mountain the top-secret military compound, the brief was about to begin. The professor had met with Agent Rose to prepare for the brief, and everything was in order. The 'IT' department reconfigured all the computers needed for the briefing as Dr. Weiss had instructed in record time as usual. They had also provided printed material including hard copies of every screen he would use during his PowerPoint presentation. Those in attendance would be the highest-ranking brass from each of the armed forces, the Chief of Staff, the Secretary of the Defense, General Whiting, Head of Cheyenne Mountain and the Vice-President of the United States. Never before in the history of the United States had such a prestigious team of statesmen been in one room inside Cheyenne Mountain.

Everyone was in attendance, and it was time to begin.

"Gentlemen," said the Vice-President, "Let's begin, Agent Rose?"

Agent Rose went to the front of the room and everyone got quiet and settled down.

"Gentlemen, let me present Dr. Oscar Weiss. Dr. Weiss is Dean of Astronomy at the University of Hawaii at Honolulu. He has been director since 1998 and before that he was the director for NASA's Hubble project in its infancy. He has been chair on symposiums across the world and has been published in every journal read by a variety of scientists in many fields of expertise, including astronomers. He is the foremost authority on astronomy and a renowned speaker on imagery. He also holds doctorate degrees in Astrophysics, Language, and Theoretical Mathematics and Probability. He is here by invitation from the White House to explain in further detail, that which we only just learned of through him. Some of you might not even know why you are here, yet, but since Dr. Weiss made this discovery, we felt it only prudent that he should explain what we will be looking at. I have also been told that new data will be forthcoming as well. Before we continue, we have closed this meeting of all incoming or outgoing communication because of the risk to national security. Please give Dr. Weiss your complete and uninterrupted attention. Dr. Weiss?" Agent Rose said motioning for him to begin. "You have the floor."

The room grew exceptionally quiet in anticipation to what they would all hear. The doors had been locked and were being guarded by armed Marines, and all communication except the direct line to the White House was disabled. Only essential personnel holding a security clearance of 'Final Secret' or above were allowed in the briefing room with the exception of Bruce Faulkner and the Professor, and soundproofing and an electromagnetic sound barrier were in place to ensure absolute secrecy.

Dr. Weiss stood up and began to walk slowly to the front of the room. He was wearing the suit and tie he normally wore while speaking in front of his peers, and presented himself with authority and confidence. As he reached the center of the room, he calmly organized his material on the podium in front of him and began his prepared speech. "Gentlemen," he said, looking around the room as he made eye contact with everyone present, "what you are about to see and hear is critically important, and need I say, of upmost secrecy. Early this morning, two of my graduate students were working on their thesis in the lab and were following a meteoroid that you are aware of called M46H. You are further aware that the meteoroid fell apart, and that some of the pieces are on a collision course with earth. As we speak this facility is tracking what is left of that meteoroid. As I'm sure you are aware, NASA has developed an advanced program dubbed DART, which stands for Digital, Analyzing and Re-imaging Technology. We have been one of the few universities fortunate enough to have been endowed with this system, and having already studied the meteoroid in question, I knew that with its size, speed and mass, the integrity of the meteoroid was not in question. Therefore, when my students came to me with their story of it exploding, I knew that there must have been something out there that intercepted the meteoroid and caused it to disintegrate. I knew there was no celestial body in its orbit to have collided with and being a man of science, I could only have drawn one conclusion, something must have moved into its orbit. I immediately went to the telescope and vectored in on the coordinates of the collision but found nothing. Of course our strongest telescopes can barely see the moons of Mars on a clear night so to expect to see something that could cause a meteoroid one hundred meters by two hundred fifty meters to split into a hundred pieces was no surprise. However, in an attempt to explore every conceivable avenue, I took the recorded data: photographic, infrared, and gamma, entered the data into DART, programmed the potential filters needed to reflect possible light emissions from the collision with the meteoroid, potential solar radiation, energetic charged protons and electrons produced by cosmic ray showers and solar emissions—captive in the Val Allen region and solar winds, and allowed the computer to extrapolate the data. I also calculated and filtered out the possibility for cosmic dust or energetic particles that come to earth from space that would be present. These have been identified above the atmosphere as elementary particles mainly the nuclei of hydrogen and helium atoms. Ultraviolet and x-ray observations of the sun have revealed the emissions of these radiations inline spectra unlike the continuous visible portion of the solar spectrum. When the analysis was complete gentlemen, this is what was revealed. And, I assure you, DART can only show you what is really there. It cannot speculate. This image is certainly not a trick with smoke and mirrors. This gentlemen, is pure science, not science fiction. If it were not, I would not be here."

The room went dark, dark and cold as Halloween in Haiti. The computer started to run the file and the ten by twelve foot screen started its five minute show that would change what every man in the room thought about the eternal question, are we alone in the universe? The show, if it had a title would be called, "The New Beginning," or perhaps, "The Beginning of the End," It began by showing the sun in the right of the screen and the pin lights of other stars to the left of the screen. The rest of the screen was black. It would have been a brilliant beginning to an otherwise normal sci-fi movie just for the fact of its original true magnificent color and magnitude. Then the star of the movie appeared. The meteoroid itself came from behind the sun and moved toward the center of the screen, streaming silently, gracefully flowing as on ice through the frozen timelessness of space in a never ending quest for nothing. Suddenly and unexpectedly, there was an astronomical collision. A brilliant light was emitted and the meteoroid was destroyed. Its quest was ended in a millisecond, with its remains falling down like tears into the earth's ravenous grasp. Shakespeare couldn't have written a better tragedy, and now this one was over. Then the final curtain call came. The thing all the king's horses and all the kings' men were here to witness. The cause of the meteoroids demise was there right in front of them all the time, but no one saw it until that moment. Prior to the meteoroid making contact, whatever it was, had been projecting the normal constellations it was blocking in order to camouflage its identity and location. When the meteoroid struck it, the star pattern it was projecting went black leaving a black hole spinning in space for seconds before shifting momentarily to a cuneiform shaped symbol then black again. It was only for a few brief seconds. Not enough to be seen by the naked eye or by a telescope.

The movie ended and the screen went blank. The lights came on and the room sat quietly in shock and amazement by what they had just witnessed. Many hoped what they saw was just an old man's over active imagination, but the facts spoke for themselves.

"Dr. Weiss." Agent Rose said again quietly, motioning him to the front of the room again.

"Gentlemen, again I must reiterate that what you have seen is hard data that has been digitally recorded using the most recent, technically advanced systems available to us today. I'm sure that the only reason we stumbled on this before the military is that you weren't interested in meteoroids that aren't a threat to our planet and this one was more than sixteen thousand miles from earth in a flight path that, in all likelihood, would not bring it back around in our lifetimes. The cuneiform shaped symbol you saw near the end puzzled me, as it no doubt did you. I knew

I had seen it before but couldn't remember where. Then it hit me. The earliest form of writing, circa 3000 B.C., consisted of outline pictures drawn on lumps of damp clay. Each picture represented a word whose meaning was identified with, or close to, the object pictured. The curves of these original pictograms were, in the course of time, replaced by straight lines and the signs came to be drawn ninety degrees counterclockwise relative to their original position; by 2500 B.C. there were few signs whose original remained recognizable. By impressing the edge of a reed of triangular cross section, straight lines were made without the blurred edges which drawing produced; this technique gave the characteristic wedge shape designated cuneiform. After 300 B.C. cuneiform was written only for astrological purposes, the last datable example coming from 75 A.D. The cuneiform symbol you saw briefly displayed when the meteor struck the unidentifiable object in space was the symbol for earth. It creates many more questions on the topic of early Mesopotamian writing, but that is another topic for discussion at a different time and place."

Instantly there was a murmur between all the members in the room. Assistants who had been standing against the wall of the briefing room were summoned and orders were whispered to them as they hurried off.

"Gentlemen," Agent Rose said. "Gentlemen, Dr. Weiss has more."

The room came to a hush again and the Dr. continued.

"I fear the worst news is yet to be spoken. I have confirmed my findings five times using three different methods, and am one hundred percent sure of my findings. I am furthermore confident that the military has methods that I am not aware of. However, I am at your disposal should you feel it necessary to explore other avenues of research in an effort to gain more knowledge of this subject.

There is without question an alien vessel in a geo-synchronous orbit around earth. It is not however orbiting earth at what we would expect to be the normal thirty-six thousand kilometers, but I estimate the orbit to be somewhere closer to forty-eight thousand two hundred kilometers. We know that our satellites, when placed in a geo-synchronous orbit at a mere thirty-six thousand kilometers cover eighty-five percent of the globe which includes ninety-five percent of the population. How much more are they possible of observing? I also have taken measurements that show the vessel to be nearly nine-hundred kilometers, about one-fourth the size of our moon. That makes the earth roughly twenty times greater in size than that of the alien vessel. In size alone, not in mass, it is no small wonder, given this fact, that the meteoroid was destroyed when it collided with a ship of that size. Secondly, a ship is hollow and no doubt can accommodate a vast amount of man and machine. Our space station, pale in comparison, hosts six state-of-the-art laboratories and is capable of sustaining a team of twelve for six months without support. I have gone back through my charts and compared infrared images of this sector since I have been Dean at the University. Luckily the computer regularly compares infrared images and tags those images that show frequency deviancies outside a preset upper and lower control limit for future scrutiny. Unfortunately, the time had not been allotted to review those old files, a task usually given to graduate students needing some extra credit. However, I studied the files and discovered that a shift in the Infrared and gamma frequencies did occur in that sector on May 12, 1998 and remained the same since. Gentlemen, it is my contention that the vessel that caused the meteoroid to destruct is the cause for the shift in the infrared and gamma frequency and has been in that orbit for just over six years. I believe it came into our orbit very slowly to keep from drawing any attention and concealed itself by projecting the celestial bodies that it was masking.

I apologize for my circumlocution but felt it necessary in order to educate you fully to the severity of the situation."

Before the professor could take his seat the room was in complete uproar. Everyone was shouting back and forth at each other with possible solutions and questions that had no answers. Arguing over the correct way to attack the problem seemed to be the only topic in the room at that moment, until finally the Vice-President stood up and shouted over everyone in the room. "Can we please have a modicum of order?"

The room quieted down instantly. "Dr. Weiss," he continued, "since you seem to be the only one on the planet to have seen this thing, can you give us the coordinates?"

"Yes, sir, I have all the data you will need on this disk," he said, holding up a CD.

"Get that disk to the War Room!" The Vice-President ordered to a page standing nearby. "Dr. Weiss, will you stay as our guest and assist us with whatever means you are able during this time of crisis?"

"It would be my honor, Sir."

"Where are your quarters, Doctor?"

"There by the toilet. Mr. Vice-President."

"By the toilet, what idiot put you by the toilet?" he asked, "Rose?"

"Yes sir." He said jumping to his feet.

"See to it that he is moved to the Executive Suites immediately."

"Yes, Sir, right away, Mr. Vice-President."

"Thank you, Dr. Weiss. Your insight and effort has been most valuable. I will see that the President hears about this."

"Not necessary, Sir, I assure you."

"Nevertheless," he said as he held out his hand.

They shook hands and the Vice-President turned the leave. By this time all the generals and Chief of Staff had left. The Secretary of Defense left with the Vice-President and the room was empty, with the exception of Dr. Weiss, Agent Rose, and the Sheriff. The three stood silently for a couple of minutes gathering their thoughts before Bruce broke the silence with a question.

"Who's up for a cup of joe?"

"You go ahead," said Agent Rose

Bruce left and Agent Rose started to help the professor gather his notes.

"Hey Professor, look, I'm sorry about that room. I only meant it to be temporary. I didn't even know if you were going to stay overnight."

"Don't worry about it, Agent Rose."

"Please, call me James."

"Okay, James, Don't worry about it. I only thought it would be one night anyway, and if you saw my apartment you would think that room by the toilet was a five star hotel."

"If that's the case, just wait until you see your new room. You'll think you're a high roller in Vegas."

✳✳✳

Back on the Spiruthun a meeting was beginning. In the bowels of the vessel near the radium core, a central core nearly one hundred and forty feet in diameter that ran through the entire ship, stood three Bilkegine men. The green pulsating flow from the core was barely enough light for them to see each other. One feature of the earth that was going to be difficult for their race was the lack of enough light. On their dying planet, which had two Suns, they had grown so accustomed to an abundance of light that everywhere else seemed dark by comparison. By the light of our earth's sun, even though it was more than twice the size of just one of theirs, it would seem more like twilight then broad daylight. It would be a fact they would have to get used to. Now, in the belly of this huge Goliath of a ship, these three men stood in light so dimly lit, to them it were as though they were standing in pitch black. As their faces gleamed by this flickering green light, they were plotting. Unlike any of their kind before them, they were defying their ancestors and putting themselves and another race before the needs of the Shem and the needs of the Bilkegine race. Like Communism on Earth, their race had developed a government hierarchy and structure that lead people to be ruled by fear. They were afraid to speak against the leaders; for fear that they would be either executed without so much as a trial, or turned into a mindless, unthinking, unchallenging drone, capable of following orders and nothing more. It had the same faults as communism. It had two classes of beings—the all-powerful ruling alliance known as the Shem, and the rest of the population consisting of several other alliances. In addition to the normal Bilkegine though, the ruling alliance also had created two creatures through DNA manipulation and cloning they called Quod. They were designed to be extremely large, strong and loyal servants and were considered expendable. The Quod were further divided into two distinct groups. Some were built for security and were able to make a few decisions on their own, while the others were designed specifically for war. The Warrior Quods were much more developed physically but lacked the ability to think at all, and also lacked the ability to feel pain. The weaker Bilkegine people were the backbone of their race. They had nothing: starvation when they should have had plenty, division when they should have had unity and classes when they should have had a classless society. The saying; power corrupts, and absolute power corrupts absolutely was as prevalent with the Bilkegine people as with any other race anywhere. Now these three men found themselves in the middle of a war. It wasn't a revolt against the government of the Bilkegine, nor a civil war between two powers among the Bilkegine. It was a war between what is right and what is wrong. What is wrong is taking a world away from one race, making that race your slaves, ordering them to modify their world to fit your needs and then destroying them. That was wrong and these three men and others like them knew right from wrong. It wasn't a matter of their rights. No one has the right to do something like that. It wasn't that they wanted to die or that they wanted their families to die. They just thought that they wouldn't want it to happen to them. It was too far away from the way they were taught from birth; they didn't have any other good reason. They couldn't think about it as a matter of principle because they didn't have any principles. They were taught that the greater good always outweighed individual good. Because the Bilkegine were superior to any other species they had ever made contact with, they had every duty to ensure their survival. Even at the expense of the Bilkegine themselves.

"We've been here for more than six coratrons and we've all seen it, the preparations for our initial engagement is almost complete." said Gebel, the leader of a weaker alliance called the Tahar.

"What will you have us do Gebel?" said Zawn. "If we're caught, that will be the end of everything we've worked so hard to do. Why do you think it's taken us six years to get this far? Our efforts to slow down the process have been very effective!"

"I know Zawn but listen; we must do more if we are to stop the engagement! I overheard Supreme Commander Karna, at the beginning of the resting phase order Lieutenant Commander Rashintar to be ready to engage in battle as soon as her principle male subject gives her what she needs."

"Who is her principle male subject now, Gebel?" asked the third man present.

"I don't know yet. I'm trying to find out. As soon as I do, I'll make contact."

"You're going to get us all killed!" yelled Zawn.

"Are you not prepared to give your life for this cause, Zawn?" asked Gebel harshly.

"Of course I am! And every man with us, but what will it gain us if it happened today?"

"It won't, trust me."

"Trust you, all you ever say anymore is trust me, Gebel!"

"Calm down, Zawn. Gebel is right; we must make contact with Karna's subject if we are to find out what she needs. All we know is that her plan involves finding a way to control the humans. We must do everything in our power to get to whatever it is she thinks will bring her victory. If we do not, well…then it will be for nothing, and I do not want to die for nothing."

"We're not going to die for nothing, Strothe. None of us are. You and Zawn have served me well these six coratrons, and we will be victorious. The efforts to slow down the advance have brought us more than time, and without raising any suspicions. We must proceed with our plan to thwart Karna's plan of planetary domination of earth and return home."

"What if there is no 'home' to go to?" asked Zawn. "Then we will find another in planet and make it our home, but we will not be taking this one even if it means destroying the Spiruthun and everyone aboard."

"You're right, Gebel. It's just that me and many others are afraid of Karna, and the fear for our families at home is very strong. We don't want them to experience any hardship. We don't want to get caught." said Zawn.

"We won't get caught if we stay alert and follow our plan like always, Zawn. When Gebel and I joined the Spiruthun, the resistance was already underway, and we didn't even know it. We just thought that it was normal breakdowns, and so did everyone else, including Karna. Don't worry about it."

"Listen, both of you. The time may come when it might be impossible to hide the fact that there is a resistance faction on board the Spiruthun. If that time comes, just remember to play dumb, and remember that we are more than five thousand strong. Also try and think about the fact that there are also more than twelve million Bilkegine on this vessel. Trying to find us is going to be virtually impossible."

"Yes, you are right." Zawn said.

"Now, I will make it my top priority to find Karna's male subject and make contact. Zawn, find a way through security in the transport terminal and disable the life support systems in the entire sector. As always, make it look like a routing or sub-system failure in the venting or radiation input chamber. We all know we require that additional radiation to survive. Since this planets' solar radiation output is much less than ours, we've had to add the additional radiation from our central core, so find a way to cut that off without raising suspicions."

"What about causing a small meltdown in the sub-route along one of the horizontal pathways from the central core to the transportation terminal? By building up the temperature someplace and letting the radiation take over, it would look like a natural occurrence caused by excessive radiation build up and put that entire section out of operation for more than ten phases."

"Sounds good to me, check it out with your team. Strothe, you and your team will have a bigger task. We had managed to corrupt the Chief of Arms, but Karna discovered his changed habits and had him converted. The new Chief will not be corrupted, especially after having heard Karna give the order for his conversion. You must find another means of gaining access to the armory and damaging the ammunition stores that have been set aside for the first mission. It is imperative that they look and feel normal but do not work well. It would be great if they did not work at all or came back on the one that fired them, but do whatever you can do. Do either of you have any questions?"

"No," They both answered.

"Good, then let's go do this thing. And be careful. I will get word to you as to time and place of our next meeting."

Zawn and Strothe left the area very slowly in different directions. As though walking through a warehouse blindfolded, they had their arms held out in front of them to help feel for doorways and containers that might be blocking their paths. Gebel sat down where he had been standing and waited fifteen minutes to give them a safe head start before he got up to follow them out. Since he worked in a different field altogether, on a different level of the ship and was a different rank and class, he didn't want them to be seen with him. It would have raised too many questions. Just as he was getting up to leave, he heard a ring behind him. It was the sound a small, lightweight tool would make if it fell from a table and struck a concrete floor. It rang out and echoed in the vastness of the empty room with nothing to absorb the sound wave. He froze in his steps. Someone was there with him in the room, and it was not one of his fellow resistance fighters. The time had come for him to make a decision he knew he would have to make when he decided to fight against his own race. He knew that someone had been in the room when the three of them went in to have their meeting, and that whoever it was had heard everything that was said. The question now burning in his head was, had the person been told of the meeting beforehand and been instructed where to go and hide, or was it just an accident?

CHAPTER TWELVE

The resting phase was over, and Sean was sitting up and thinking about where he was, what he was going to do about it and Nancy. Everything in his life seemed to be a battle. Fear seemed to be his constant companion. Even in times of seeming normalcy he was haunted by fear in his dreams. I know one thing, he thought, I'm not giving an inch. They can kill me, Nancy and everyone else on this ship but they're not getting me to give them anything they can use against earth. Just then he was startled by the swishing of the door as it opened and three of the drones came in carrying trays of food. He waited expecting to see Karna, but she wasn't there.

"Wake up," he said gently touching Nancy's shoulder. "Breakfast is up."

"Huh?' she said groggily.

"Breakfast," Sean repeated pointing to the table.

"Oh, I'm not hungry. I just want to get clean and go home." she said as she got out of bed and shuffled off toward the shower.

"Yeah, me too...me too," he whispered to himself.

He looked over and saw Nikita devouring the food. She was acting like she hadn't eaten in a very long time.

"Hey, slow down there, kid. You'll get a belly ache!"

"Oh, it's so good."

"Haven't they feed you since they brought you here?"

"No, I don't get this kind of food, I get hysynk."

"Hysynk?" Sounds bad, what is it?"

"I don't know," she said while munching down some kind of meat.

"It sounds like garbage."

"Garbage?"

"Yeah, you know trash, refuse—garbage."

She ignored him and continued eating. He reached over and picked up some of the meat she was eating and examined it closer. He smelled it then quickly turned up his nose and threw it down.

"Pew, that stinks! How can you eat that?"

"It's good!"

"So what grade were you in when you were taken?" he asked nonchalantly.

"What grade?"

"Yeah, grade, you know a marked level of achievement."

"I was almost finished." she said not knowing the right answer. It had been almost seven years since her abduction and too many sessions of brainwashing for her to remember. She really was convinced that she was Bilkegine. As far as she was concerned, she hadn't been taken by anyone. The sad truth was that everything she knew from her past was completely foreign to her.

"So what was your favorite subject?" Sean continued.

Still not knowing how to answer, she got mad.

"Why are you asking me all these questions? I'm trying to eat, and I'm trying to get away from these mean people and all you can do is ask stupid questions. Why don't you try and be cool, Old Man!"

"Fine, you want me to leave you alone, you got it! I'll just put you outside that door and leave you where I found you and you can be alone again. While you're at it, stop eating my food!" he said as he grabbed the food from her and took a huge bite. Resisting the urge to spit it out, he stared at her and chewed it slowly and swallowed hard.

Nancy came out of the shower room looking refreshed and wearing a clean tunic. "What's going on?" she asked.

"Oh, nothing, your new girlfriend here is just a little touchy is all."

"What happened?"

"All I did was asked her a couple of friendly questions about her school and she came unglued; told me to take a hike."

"Maybe she's just not a morning person, Sean."

"Forget it; I'm taking a shower before the queen of mean comes back."

Knowing that Sean was talking about Karna made Nikita even madder at him. Karna is always nice to me except when I screw up, Nikita thought. He only says that because he is trying to destroy us and wants to make me mad at Karna, too. I just have to remember what she told me. Play along and give him something to fight for. I must get information from him." I'm messing up already! I have to make him want to keep me with him.

"Nancy, is Sean mad at me?"

"It sounds like that to me."

"Well, he was asking all these questions and I was…"

"What questions?"

"Well, he asked what grade I was in, and what my favorite subject was."

"What's wrong with that?"

"I don't know the answers."

"How can you not know the answers to what grade you are in?"

"I don't remember what grade I am in. I remember what school is, and what grade means, but I don't have any personal memories of it." She lied.

"Nikita, how long have you been here, wherever 'here' is?"

"You don't know where you are?"

"Of course not, I was abducted and woke up in this room."

"But Karna told me that…I mean Karna told me to stay with you, because you obviously knew your way around when she threw me in here with you."

"We've only been here for a few days, Nikita. I don't know what Karna has told you but it isn't true."

"Then how did you know where to go and hide before when we were running?"

"I didn't know anything, and neither did Sean. We were just running away from them. We ran this direction because they were that direction. It was that simple."

"Oh, me too I guess."

"How long have you been here, really?"

"I don't know."

"You seemed very hungry before, and I heard you say you normally got to eat, what was it, Hysynk?"

"Yes, Hysynk, it is synthetic food, not like this."

"Nikita, do you want our help?"

"Yes, I do. I want you to keep me with you and take me everywhere you go."

"I'm afraid we're not in control of either who is with us or where we go, but if and when that time comes, do you want our help?"

"Yes, I want you and Sean to help me."

"Then you have to trust us. It's obvious you've been here quite a while. Sean thinks it's a compound of some type, maybe underground. Can you tell me how long?"

"A little longer than you, I think."

Nancy thought for a few seconds then said, "Did they cut your hair?"

Nakita thought carefully for a brief moment. What kind of question is that? Is it a trick question? Can any danger come from answering this question? When she had thought through it carefully, she answered, "Yes, it was longer."

"Well, then." Nancy said. "That was easy wasn't it?"

It was a test. Nikita thought again. I can do this, if I concentrate and don't lose my temper. "Yes, that was easy." She answered.

"Let's try another. Are those the clothes you remember buying for yourself?"

"Yes, I bought these."

"Where did you buy them, from a catalog or a store?"

"A catalog," Nikita answered quickly, thinking she was doing very well.

"Was it Montgomery Ward's?"

"Yes, it was. How did you know?"

"Just a lucky guess, I've bought clothes from them too. You sit tight, I should check on Sean."

Nancy got up to talk to Sean and communicate her suspicion about

Nikita. There is something about a woman's ability to sniff out a lie, especially about wardrobe, and Nancy suspected Nikita's story about her shopping trip stunk like yesterday's fish. Before she made it to the shower room to spill the beans, as it were, she heard the familiar swish of the door opening and turned quickly to find Karna standing in the room.

"I'll get Sean," Nancy said as she quickened the pace. "It won't take but a second."

"That won't be necessary, I'll wait." said Karna.

Sean was oblivious to the fact that Karna was now standing in their room, when he came around the corner from the hall already in mid-thought and sentence started.

"Hey, Nancy, what do you bet that the head sneeze herself comes rolling in here this... Oh, speak of the devil."

"Yes, I have decided to let you go. Before I can do that I will give you a detailed tour of our compound including our, truck bay, as you called it yesterday."

"Why the change, two days ago you were threatening to chop me up and you nearly cut Nancy stem to stern."

"You shall see. By the way, in case you were contemplating an escape attempt you will be heavily guarded by three of my Quods. I believe you have become intimate with them over the past three days."

"Why escape if you are going to let us go. Weren't those your own words?" "Let us go?"

"Yes, they were, and I always do what I say I will do...always. As to your question, I desire that you have a thorough knowledge of our compound so you can know what you have been up against, and so you can realize that at any moment I could have killed you."

"How thoughtful of you, thinking of me the way you do, and me not remembering our anniversary or anything."

Sean's wit, sarcasm and insults had no impact on Karna but he couldn't keep himself from venting.

"We will leave now." Karna said in a commanding voice.

"No! We will leave when I am dressed in the clothes I came here in, when my belly is full and not before. If you think I'm going to walk home like this, you have another think coming."

"Sean! She said she's letting us walk out!" Nancy whispered.

"No, she didn't Nancy! She said she was letting us go. It's a big difference."

Sean stood there staring at Karna and waiting for an answer. At length she finally agreed.

"Fine, bring his clothes." Karna ordered to the Quod waiting to escort them.

"Let's not forget about Nancy!" Sean added.

"The woman's as well," ordered Karna.

Karna turned to leave. As she was walking out the door, and in her consistent monotone voice, she said, "I will return for you briefly."

"One more thing," Sean yelled out.

"What is it?"

"Take this with you." he said, pushing Nikita by the back of the neck through the open door and into Karna's arms. "She's not mine!"

The door shut, and Sean, took the towel he was holding and threw it against the wall.

"What's wrong Sean? She said they are letting us go. We're going home!"

"We're not going home, Honey." Sean spoke quietly.

"Sure we are, didn't you hear her? She said…"

"She said she was going to let us go."

"Yeah, let us go…send us home, same, same."

"No Honey, send us home would be something. But, 'let us go,' considering where we are, isn't anything. It certainly isn't anything to jump up and down over."

"You know where we are? Sean that's great! Maybe that's why she is letting us go."

"She will never let us go alive. If she is letting us go, it's either because she no longer needs me or she can't stand me and will put up with worse to get rid of me. Either way we lose."

"Sean, I don't get it."

"The test she had been harping on since we've been here. We're going to move it up and do it now."

"Maybe she'll let us go after the test then? Why aren't you excited?"

"I doubt, it but if we can finally execute my escape plan, and if it happens the way I believe it will happen, then at least we'll have a fighting chance. And if so, then I will be stoked."

"Stoked this, pumped that, why can't guys use real words?"

"All I know is that we will be given our old clothes back."

"Big deal, if we don't get to go home."

"Yes, it will be a big deal. When it happens, I'm betting they will be able to see it with the naked eye."

"They who… See what?" she asked puzzled.

"See what will happen to this place when we're done with it."

Nancy started to turn away frustrated when she remembered what she was going to tell Sean before Karna showed up.

"Oh yeah, before Karna came in here I was heading in to tell you something I learned about Nikita."

"What?"

"I was a little suspicious of her."

"You're not the only one, Sweetie. What clued you in?"

"I was asking her why she was so upset about you asking such simple questions, and she said it was because she didn't have the answers. So, I asked her a couple of my own."

"What did you ask her?"

"My first question was how long she had been here, and I said, wherever here is. She looked at me really puzzled and asked me if I really didn't know where I was. I told her where you thought we were. She said she didn't know how long she had been here. I asked her if she really wanted our help. She told me yes, that she wanted us to take her everywhere we went and that she wanted to do everything we did. I told her that we weren't the ones who determined where we went and what we did, but when we were if she wanted our help she would have to trust us. Then I asked her if she wanted our help again. She said yes. I asked her how long she was here again and she told me about the same, maybe a little longer than us. So, I asked her if they had cut her hair since they had taken her, and she said yes, but only after waiting quite a while to answer."

"I don't get the hair question. How would that determine how long she's been here? They haven't cut my hair either." Sean asked puzzled.

"Because when we were talking before in the warehouse, I asked her if she always wore her hair short, and she said no, she just got it cut."

"You think she slipped before or that she really had short hair before?"

"No, don't you see? It isn't a fresh cut but she said they cut it. It was an inconsistency."

"What else did you ask her?"

"Then I asked her about her clothes. I asked her specifically if she remembered going shopping for the clothes she was wearing, and she said yes."

"I guess that was a problem, too, right?"

"You bet it's a problem. The style now is retro sixties, not retro late eighties. At least a girl her age wouldn't be caught dead in them no matter how square she was."

"Anything else?"

"Yeah, the biggest tip off. I asked her if she shopped the Montgomery Ward catalog or went to the mall for her shopping. And…"

"Let me guess, Monkey Wards."

"Yep!"

"We've got to face the facts about this girl, Nancy. Something just doesn't add up. Either she is one very skillfully made imposter, or she is who she claims but has been stripped of her own identity. Either way she could have meant trouble for us and I didn't think we can trust her."

"That's why you threw her out? What if she does really need our help Sean?"

"I've been thinking about it since she happened to find us. It was just all too convenient. It was like the kid showing up in our room with his chew toy. Everything looks cute, little boy on the outside but inside there is a Pitt Bull Tasmanian devil mix ready to have parts of you for lunch."

"What should we do?"

"As soon as we get some food and our clothes, we'll take our grand tour. It will be no doubt our last meal so pack it in. Then we'll load down my backpack, your purse and our pockets with some of the things I found in the closet and while we're on the nickel tour we'll slip away. It's either what that cold-hearted waste of space wants or our only hope, and I can't figure out which."

Minutes turned into hours, and there was no sign of any clothes. He didn't know what was going on, but sitting in a room waiting to die when he had a way out seemed like lunacy. Just when he was about to take Nancy by the hand and leave, the door swished open and a dozen drones backed by the goon squad came into the room. They had the clothes that Sean and Nancy were wearing the morning of their abduction along with fresh towels and tunics. Much of the food that was brought in earlier was not edible in Nancy's opinion but Sean had told her to "pack it in", so pack it in is what she did. The drones that brought the clothes also cleaned the room as though they were making arrangements for another guest to check in later that afternoon. As soon as they left Sean didn't waste any time in making his own preparations. He first checked all the clothing to make sure it wasn't bugged. He didn't know if it was from watching too many spy movies as a kid, or if he was really a conspiracy theorist at heart, but whatever the cause, he checked all the clothing, the purse and his back pack meticulously. He knew he was running out of time and Karna the cruel would soon be there to retrieve them, so he told Nancy to stand guard, as it were, and scream if the door started to open. He hoped the screaming would stall whoever it was long enough for him to jump out and close the door behind him. He went to the wall and it opened. He was most of all grateful for the microchip that one of the green giants so graciously donated to the cause. He quickly went into the closet and this time was ripping through the containers looking for items that might come in useful. He didn't know if he would ever see the room again and had to take the chance that he would not, so he took everything he had found useful and stuffed it into the backpack. He stuck the pocketknife he found into his pocket along with a magnifying glass, and a sewing kit. He found another box that was filled with survival gear. From the looks of it the previous owner was an accomplished survivalist. He didn't have time to go through it all so he just dumped the entire box into the backpack and moved on to another box. He was just about to open another, when Nancy screamed. Holy sweat! He thought as he jumped through the door, slamming it behind him, and slipped quickly into the shower room.

"What's going on?" He said rushing out of the shower with his bag in tow.

"Oh it's nothing. The door startled me when it opened that's all."

Karna stood and looked the room over with her usual prudish stance then looked over at Sean. "I see you are dressed and ready to leave."

"Yeah, I've had all of you I can stand. Why don't you show me your precious compound so we can get out of here, already?"

He walked over to Nancy and took her arm. Handing her purse to her, he said. "Here, Honey, you don't want to forget your purse."

They left for their tour, a tour that Karna hoped would give her what she so desperately needed and one Sean thought would let him, "Be All He Could Be," just like the recruitment posters promised him so many years ago.

CHAPTER THIRTEEN

Twelve hours had passed and the information was coming in slower than they wanted. They now knew the alien ship was out there. They couldn't see it from where they were, but had seen the short clip that Dr. Weiss prepared for them.

Information was needed much quicker than they were getting it, and no one was happy, especially the big brass in Washington. The professor had joined the team and was working around the clock, thanks to the good sheriff's coffee. They were working on a plan to take military controlled spy satellites and turn them around to peer into space in hopes of obtaining some live imagery of the ship. It wasn't going to be an easy task because they were not designed to look outward and the satellites programs had to be changed in order to turn them about. Bruce, when not making coffee, was helping Agent Rose track reports coming in from around the United States and the United Kingdom of similar abductions that had taken place earlier that week. An outline was beginning to take shape pertaining to who was taken and why, except for Sean. Although he had a brilliant military career while on active duty during Vietnam, He hadn't done anything since then. He wasn't a scientist, government agent, never ran for any political office, wasn't a career military officer or even head chef at Trader Vics. He was just Sean, and it was Bruce's job to help James figure out why they had taken him. There were other indications coming in that lead them to believe his role was important. One report in particular seemed more interesting than others. Among the abductees taken the month before Sean, one in particular shared a common experience. He and Sean were both in Vietnam. They were at one time in the same unit, and Sean saved his life. Although he was an emotional wreck, he was able to ask over and over again about Sean. Somehow they found out about his record, his acts of bravery and service during the Vietnam War, and they thought he could help them somehow.

"Do we have control of the satellites yet, Doctor." asked General Stephens, the base commander.

"We're just about there. A couple more commands and we'll be able to turn them around and get a good look at what's out there."

"I can't emphasis how timely everything is now."

"Yes, I know commander. These things were never designed to look out and we must re-program the computer to tell the thrusters how to fire in order to facilitate the maneuver."

"Please inform me as soon as we can turn her about and get a look at that thing out there. I need some hard intelligence on this thing and fast."

The briefing room had been scheduled for a meeting between Bruce and a well-known psychologist. His goal would be to try and determine what significant role Sean was playing in the drama. Drawing from Bruce's more than twenty year friendship with Sean, he hoped to develop a profile that would give the authorities a better picture of who Sean was and how, if any, he would be able to help them from where he was.

"It's just up ahead, Dr. Ross." Agent Rose said pointing.

"Will the Sheriff be there?"

"I told him to meet us there at 0600."

"You sure begin early around here."

"The early bird and all of that, you know."

"I suppose so. Can you tell me what this is all about?"

"All I can say is that it's a matter of National Security that we know as much about his guy as we can. We need to get inside his head, and that's why we called you in."

"Fine, this Sheriff I am meeting with, is he the one that knows this man the best?"

"If anyone knows him, he does. They have been close friends for more than twenty years. I understand they see each other nearly every day."

"I see."

"How long will it take for you to get a good picture of our man, doctor?"

"As soon as the interview is over, I'd say no more than a few hours to get all the data I need and then perhaps another hour to draft my profile."

"Can you be more specific? Time is of the essence on this matter."

"Can you give me three hours total? I could do it faster but the profile might not be as specific as you need it."

"No, that's good. Okay it's here," Agent Rose said, pointing at a doorway and motioning the doctor to go ahead of him.

They walked into the briefing room and found Bruce there waiting with his usual cup of coffee in hand. He was sitting in the far darkened corner of the room quietly, almost prayerfully, and the two men went unnoticed at first because of his deep concentration. Finally he heard the noise of the door close and jumped slightly, startled to see them coming toward him. He stood up and went to greet them. Agent Rose introduced the men and left the room so the doctor could begin his interview right away.

"Shall we begin, Sheriff?"

"The sooner the better I guess. I've never talked to a shrink before. Uh, no insult intended."

"Nor I a Sheriff, and none taken."

"So, let me understand, doc. You're gonna get inside our man's head by getting into mine? That about sum it up?"

"Yes, precisely, shall we begin?"

"Okay then, shoot."

"What I need you to do is expound on any question that I ask. I need you to offer any insight that you may think of along the way. It will be easier, since you are in criminal justice and know what makes people think the way they do."

"You mean, what makes them tick so to speak?"

"Precisely."

"Okay, let's do this thing."

"Describe as completely as you can, what's his name," he asked looking at his notes, "Sean Daniels."

"Sure, Sean is a quiet, down to earth guy who owns a hardware store in a very small mountain community in North Carolina. He moved there around 1974 I guess. I think it was just after he got back from Vietnam."

"Would you say he was mad about having to serve in the war? My file reports that he was drafted."

"Mad? No. To be honest, he never spoke much about it. Until I got here and found out more about what was going on, I didn't know that much about his life before he moved into town. Fact is I've never seen Sean really mad about anything. He's always been kinda easy going if you know what I mean."

"Did you find it odd that he didn't talk about his past?"

"No I guess not. Where I come from folks like to keep themselves to themselves. If folks don't offer any information you don't ask, that simple."

"Was there ever a time when you tried to look up any information on him?"

"Never had a cause, without a cause, that'd just be nosy. If he wanted to tell me about his past, I figured he would."

"Tell me about Sean as a person. What makes him mad?"

"Well, like I said. He doesn't get mad often. But as I recall there was one instance that stands out now that I think about it. He hates to see women treated badly and will always stand up for them no matter what the odds are against his success. He is the same way for kids. One time some drunk ran a red light and nearly took out a bunch of kids walking home from school. Now Sean ain't a preacher or nothing and has been known to have a drink from time to time, but he doesn't think people should be toasted by three in the afternoon either. He especially doesn't think they should be driving when they've been out lightin' one up. He was so mad, he chased down this car on foot, and the driver got so worried seeing someone chasing him, he stopped looking where he was going and drove smack dab into a creek. Sean dragged his sorry behind out of the car through the window and nearly beat the stuffing out of him by the time I got there. The sad part was that the drunk was so tanked, he

152

didn't feel a thing. Anyway, I guess he figured since me or my deputies weren't there to arrest him, he would."

"Tell me about his job."

"Friendly, down-home hardware business, what's to tell? He's just like all the other shop owners. He opens by nine and closes by five, pays his bills and keeps a nice, clean and very meticulously organized parts bin."

"So one might say he was neat and clean all the time?"

"Well one might, but they'd be lying through their teeth." Bruce said with a chuckle. "Unless of course you're talking about the store, in that case yes, I might go as far as saying, now how does that go, excessive compulsive would describe him there."

"What about his personal life?"

"Let me see. He works hard and once in a great while he goes out for a brew with the guys. He takes in a game or two at the lanes in the winter and plays softball for the Baptist church in the summer."

"Let's go back to his cleanliness. How about his home? Is it meticulously organized and clean as well?"

"Heck no, when it comes to home, the boy can't spell meticulous. It's clean I guess, but I wouldn't eat off the floor, if that's what you mean. And you don't want to go anywhere near his frig."

"I see. Does Sean have any bad habits?"

"Hum, bad habits. I guess it depends on who you ask really. Not as far as I'm concerned, but if you were to ask the reverend down at the church he might say he has a bad habit of playing poker with the boys once a month."

Bruce had never heard questions put like this before. There didn't seem to be any rhyme or reason to them at all. He was used to interrogating a prisoner or suspect in a crime by asking more direct questions like, where were you on this night and this time, or how did you get that blood on your bumper, questions that had real answers. These questions seemed more like something a priest would be expected to answer if he was being considered to be pope. Bruce thought it all depended on who you asked to what answer you were going to get in reply. He told his deputies one time; if you ask a car thief, who was seen taking a car off of the street in broad daylight if he was the one that took the car you can expect him to lie. He knows he's on his way to jail. Do you expect him to say yes, I took the car, lock me away for five years? Yes, Bruce thought this line of questioning was stupid and was wondering what in the world how clean a guy keeps his home had to do with being taken by aliens. Bruce was deep in thought and the doctor had lost his attention.

"I'm going to ask a couple of hypothetical questions now. Do you understand what I mean by that Sheriff? Sheriff, are you still with me?"

"Oh, I'm sorry doc. I didn't sleep much last night."

"No problem. I'll repeat the statement," the psychologist said smugly. "I'm going to ask a couple of hypothetical questions. Do you understand what I mean by that?"

"Sure I do!" Bruce replied somewhat annoyed with the doctor's smugness and implication that Bruce was a dumb hick. "I didn't fall off the turnip truck yesterday!"

"I'm sorry. I did not mean to insult your intelligence. I simply wanted to ensure that the question was clearly understood." Dr. Ross said quietly, while still sounding condescending at the same time. Bruce just shrugged at him and nodded to suggest he continue. "Let's say that Sean was walking home from work one evening minding his own business, and on the way home decided to stop at the bank to make his nightly deposit, now, let's say that someone came up to him and demanded his money. Is Sean the kind of guy to just hand the money over or put up a fight?"

"Is the guy armed?"

"Why do you ask?"

"It's important, doc. You just gonna hand over your pocket money 'cause I tell you to?"

"Yes, the mugger is armed with a knife."

"No, he wouldn't give him the money."

"Why not?"

"'Cause I'm sure that Sean would think he could take a guy with a knife."

"Okay then, let's give the mugger a gun. Will he give up the money then?"

"Is it just the two of them on the street?"

"Why do you ask that?"

"Cause I'm sure that Sean would be thinking about innocent by-standers getting shot if he tried to take the gun away from him and it went off by accident. You know, Doc, if you're gonna come up with these make believe stories, they've got to have some bit of reality to them or they don't make sense."

Without pausing to comment on what Bruce said, the doctor simply continued. "Let's say, no, no other people."

"No question then. Sean wouldn't give it up."

"Why not?"

"Same as before, cause Sean could probably take the guy out and keep his money. Besides, I think Sean would rather die trying then just lie down and give up."

"Let's say there are other people on the street, and they might get hurt. What would you say Sean would do then?"

"I think he would give up the money, and in the process of handing it over or shortly after, get his money back. I still don't see him just lying down and taking it once the threat of innocent by-standers getting hurt is past."

"Let's put him in one more situation. Let's say that Sean is in the middle of a hostage situation where there are multiple hostages and a lot of potential for people getting hurt or killed innocently, and he is the only one who can stop them from getting hurt. Would he give up himself to save their lives?"

"Boy, where do you come up with these lose, lose situations? Let me get this straight. If he gives up his life the others are assured their safety?"

"That's right."

"Sean would give up his own life for the lives of the others, hoping for a shot at saving his own later."

"What if there are no guarantees that any lives would be saved?"

"Easy, Sean would take whatever chances he would have to take, but only after talking it over and doing what the majority of the people decided to do."

"Even if it meant the majority decided to hope for life and do nothing."

"Yep."

The doctor continued asking Bruce more hypothetical questions for another hour before he finally stopped talking and thumbed through Sean's file. After reviewing it for about ten minutes he closed the file, made a few more notes and wrapped up his interview.

"I think that's it, Sheriff. I think I can put something together based on what you have told me and what I have already learned from his file. Thanks for your candor."

"Just help me save my friend, that's all I ask."

Bruce left Dr. Ross in the briefing room going over Sean's file and making notes for his profile, and went to the war room where all the action was. It was the only place where anything was happening at every hour of the day or night. The small pieces of the meteor that started this whole thing in the War Room were long gone. The pieces that were going off into space were no longer traceable and the ones that were heading to earth either burned up entering the atmosphere or crashed someplace on the planet without fan-fare. The one and only concern on everyone's mind now was this alien ship, and Bruce could not believe that he was a part of the whole nightmare. His only wish at this time would be to have his bride on one arm and his friend by his side. James came into the room and saw Bruce looking over the big board.

"See anything interesting?"

"Nope, just wished this whole thing was over, I guess."

"Yeah buddy, me too."

"Back there in the briefing room you were startled."

"Oh, that. Yeah I was pondering. Sometimes I concentrate so hard I forget where I am and what I'm doing."

"What were you thinking about, as if I have to ask?"

"This crazy business we're all caught up in. It makes me wonder about a lot more things. You know?"

"What kind of things?"

"Roswell, Devil's Triangle, Stonehenge you know: all the great mysteries that none of us has ever been able to explain. If we're out here able to put huge telescopes and satellites in space and all of that, how come we can't figure out the Devil's Triangle or Stonehenge? If we're on such a low level mentally, where does that put them?" He said pointing to a red light on the big board.

"Those are good questions, Bruce. I wish I had the answers for you. Maybe when we're through with all of this we will all have more answers?"

"Maybe, if we're still around. Or maybe we won't care about them anymore now that we've seen what someone else from someplace else is capable of doing. Kinda makes us look like the pre-schooler in the crowd of college kids doesn't it?"

"I guess it does at that."

The two swinging doors at the top of the gallery swung open and two young enlisted men ran in announcing that the satellites had finally come online and they had control. The room erupted in cheers for a brief moment but was short lived when the reason why became evident in everyone's mind. At least they would have the intelligence they so desperately needed to gain some insight of this alien ship parked on their front doorstep. Everyone was sure that they had a long way to go, but the first of many long and sleepless nights was behind them and the first of many victories hopefully won as the satellites came online and the first pictures lit up the big screen.

CHAPTER FOURTEEN

Sean took his backpack and Nancy's arm and walked out the door behind Karna. The food they were carrying along with the weapons, ammo and other supplies from the hidden closet were much bulkier and heavier than the pack had originally been. Sean was holding his breath hoping that it went unnoticed. The original contents of his pack included some papers he was to return to his accountant for taxes, a couple of parts catalogs he had been perusing in his leisure time and a new ball glove he was breaking in for softball season. When he had filled the pack with the new items he simply dumped the old stuff into one of the boxes. He figured everything was replaceable and especially wasn't fond of the tax papers. They headed through the Piiderk toward the cinbiote, and all the time Sean was straining his eyes trying to see through the bright light for some details of movement around other areas of the vessel. He could only see a short distance, but did see several groups of ten or so men walking in formation into a room next to theirs. That's one room I will leave off my list to investigate, he thought. They reached the center of the Piiderk when Karna stopped and reached into the light of the cinbiote. Sean was wondering who she was taking out this time and why she never just walked into the light to get them out. His mind was running wild with questions there were no real answers too when Nakita appeared from inside the light, firmly held by Karna.

"Your time is finished, wait here." Karna demanded.

"Please," Karna motioned, "before we can continue, I must insist that we decontaminate you."

"I would like to decontaminate her alright!" Sean whispered to Nancy.

"It will only take a few moments and we will be able to continue our tour. I'm very excited to show you our compound."

Oh, yeah, you really look excited, Sean thought to himself.

They stepped into the light and immediately started to fall into the trance like state that felt so good before. For whatever reason, Nancy seemed to be more affected than Sean. She easily surrendered to the power that the cinbiote had over her, while Sean resisted it. This time, Karna stayed true to her word. Just as the light was beginning to take hold of Sean, she reached in and pulled them free from the light.

"I believe that if you didn't pull us out of this thing, we would stay in there forever," Nancy said.

"Yes, you would. You would stay in there until you died."

"Can we get this show on the road, Highness?" Sean asked sarcastically.

"Follow me and do exactly what I tell you. To do any less may result in your immediate death."

They left the Piiderk with Karna in the lead, and Sean noticed that the girl, Nakita, was following them. He considered that she might, in fact, be a victim of these aliens and did, in fact, need his help. However, knowing that he had a weakness for women in distress, regardless of their age, he cautioned himself against making a bad decision. He was resolved to destroy the ship and everyone on it, including Nancy and himself unless he could figure out a way off and destroy it at the same time. Either way he had to figure out a way of destroying the ship.

They began their tour of the vessel on the Piiderk. Karna took them to the command center. She pointed out every aspect of their control of the ship from that one position but failed to point out that they were, in fact, in the middle of the frozen expanse of space thousands of miles from earth. Sean had always imagined what the control panels would look like on an alien ship but realized upon seeing the real deal, that his imagination was mostly driven by whatever science fiction movies he had seen throughout his life. The reality of it was that the controls were nothing like

159

the movies. Everything in the room seemed black to him. There was a high elevated seat in the middle of a long thin room that was no doubt where the captain of the ship sat while in command. There was a counter like table that was angled against the wall at about sixty degrees and was forty feet wide. In front of the table were more than twenty angled chairs that resembled un-padded recliners in the opened position. The floor was the same hard, granite like substance, the walls were black and shiny but had a rough texture, and the wall behind the counter looked like polished brass. Sean thought it was weird that everywhere else on the ship was so bright he could barely see through it but in this room, it was absolutely dark except for an extremely bright spot light immediately over every chair in the room. Sean couldn't figure out whether Karna knew that he had discovered the weapons cash in the massive warehouse or not, but was gambling that she did not. He looked around cautiously to see if this would be the place to stage his war when the time came. He remembered his military training and experience as it came back to him instantly. He assessed the entrances and exits, number of staff in the general location and decided that it might be a defensible position when he knew more about the ship and its functions. Even though there was still much more intelligence to gather, Sean briefly considered making his stand right then and there. No, he thought, now is not the time, I've got to be patient and wait until I know more.

Just before they left the room, as Sean was standing in the doorway, the table began to light up like a Christmas tree. The once black table had thousands of large square lights blinking on and off at different pulses and with each pulse a series of high pitched clicks. And most important of all, he saw the polished brass wall clear to a transparent view of the earth as seen from space just like he had seen on the NASA channel. In the corner of his eye he caught the staff coming into the room through a door he had not seen, then hearing noise behind him another big group coming from another seemingly invisible door. Each one wore a dark hooded robe like garment except for the last five figures who were dressed more like Karna. They were very much larger than the other workers and more importantly, he noticed they were heavily armed. God only knows how many other doors come in or out of here that I didn't see," Sean thought.

It's a good thing I didn't try to make my stand just then.

Even though the figures he had seen coming through the door had their heads covered, Sean did notice that they looked nothing like the other beings he had already seen. Karna was the only being so far that even came close to resembling a human. Then he realized that everyone else he had come in contact with since he'd been there had their face covered with some kind of mask or screen. He turned around taking the first step out of the room and ran directly into Karna who had realized that Sean wasn't following them and came back to see what he was up too.

"Hey, watch where you're going!" Sean yelled into her face.

"I did not want you to lose yourself. I want you to stay near me for your safety." She replied calmly.

"Oh I bet you're really concerned for my well being. Just like you were when you were torturing me, and just like you were so concerned for Nancy when you ordered her cut up like you did. I'm touched, really." Sean said as he pushed by her.

They proceeded around the Piiderk and stopped at several locations that were mostly private quarters for the officers and operations equipment and personnel. Nancy began to slow down then came to a complete stop. She began looking around and asked, "Sean, where is everyone. We haven't seen anyone other than Karna. Someone has to be working at these places don't they?"

"You're right, Nancy, it is possible that they were told to stay out of sight while we were around. God only knows what evil Karna has planned for us but I'm betting it isn't what she has been telling us."

They were walking toward an area that began to look familiar to Sean. Through the haze of light he realized they were coming up to the warehouse that he had discovered earlier and began to fear that his fight might come earlier than he wanted. He figured as soon as Karna saw the damage inside and the busted crates, she would suspect that Sean was responsible. The second Karna nearly walked into the door when it failed to open caught her off guard. Fear instantly gripped Sean. This is it. He thought. Surely she will go around to the other door and discover the damage I caused and the missing weapons. To his surprise she shrugged it off as a malfunction and turned to explain that it was merely a warehouse. Sean figured that she wouldn't just dismiss it but would report it to some kind of maintenance crew that would address the problem. If that happened, it would certainly be revealed that someone had gained access and found the weapons. Not knowing about the other abductees, he assumed that she would summarize that someone to be him since he had been missing and the warehouse had an unsecured entry. Sean was thinking hard of a way to get information from her about the warehouse, without sounding too interested in it, and before they had gone too far. He thought it might cast her suspicion away from him and onto someone else.

"Is that the only way into the warehouse?" he asked. "I'd kind of like to see it. Since my business is hardware, you never know where a good idea for storage will come from."

"There is nothing of importance in there," Karna replied, "just stacks of stores and supplies needed for support. But to answer your question, yes, there are two other entrances. One is on the other side of the Piiderk, and the other is through the loading bay that opens to the outside. If you really want to see it badly enough we can go there before we continue."

"No, that's alright, I don't want you to have to go out of your way. If you seen one warehouse I guess you seen them all."

Continuing their tour, they went around the perimeter of the Piiderk until they came to a hole in the floor beside a wall. Sean remembered shoving a rather large corpse down a shaft identical to this one on the other side of the Piiderk. I wondered what that hole was for, he thought. Karna walked up to the hole and stood for a brief moment. As if by magic an elevator like pod appeared. It resembled an old type telephone booth except it was round and there was no door on it.

"This is our vertical conveyance system." Karna declared.

"That's funny," Sean whispered to Nancy, "looks like an elevator to me. But hey, what do I know?"

"We will take this to the lowest level of our facility and work our way back to the Piiderk and your rooms. Then I will arrange for your release."

"Sure you will." Sean mumbled.

"It is only capable of carrying two at a time so the girl and I will go first and wait for you at the lowest level. You need not worry," she continued,

"It will not stop at any other level before reaching the bottom, so you won't get lost."

Karna and Nakita stepped into the elevator and it began to descend. Sean leaned over to watch as it proceeded to the bottom but he lost sight of it within a few feet due to the brightness of the light below. While Sean and Nancy waited for their ride, Sean took the opportunity to outline his thoughts to Nancy.

"Okay, here is what I'm planning. At some point in our tour, after I think I have seen enough and know my way around, I will give you a signal. Be prepared to run."

"What will the signal be?"

"I'll tell Karna that I'm feeling weak and need to visit the light thing and when she gets near enough, I will try to push her inside. Whatever you do, don't let go of my hand."

"What about the girl?"

"You would have to ask about her. If she keeps up she can stay with us, but the moment she drops back, I'll assume that she prefers the company of Karna and her goons over us and leave her. Are we clear?"

"Okay, whatever you think."

The elevator appeared and came to a stop and they stepped inside. Sean could not see how the thing worked since it was void of any buttons or switches to operate, but without so much as a hum, it began its slow descent. Sean could see much better as they passed the decks below. With every level they went down, the light seemed to get dimmer until it reached the final level. They stepped off and Karna motioned for them to follow her. The lowest level suited Sean especially well. It was like midnight on the Delta under a full moon, dark and secure, but with just enough light to move around quickly without running into anything. It was clear to see that Karna was having difficulty seeing clearly because she dropped her almighty posture for one of caution. She was walking as she would walk through a kid's room barefoot in the middle of the night, cautiously avoiding any hazardous obstacles that might be lying around. She walked not more than twenty feet from the elevator until a glittering green light could be seen in the distance and stopped. "This is our central core. It is the life of the vessel and what generates our power. You would refer to it as a cold fusion reactor, but we call it our digherg rapitor. The containment field is necessary to concentrate the elements within and separate sub-atomic particles at a molecular level. The resulting gas becomes denser as the particles are extracted and a chain reaction occurs resulting in immense amounts of energy and radiation. The bigger the central core, the more gasses converted, resulting in faster process and more energy output."

"Why is it green?" asked Nancy

"The color of the gas in its natural state when concentrated in one area is seen as this color."

"How thick is the containment you spoke of?" Sean asked expecting a dead black stare from Karna.

"I do not know."

"Yeah—right!" Sean mumbled.

"Is that it then, are we finished?" asked Nancy.

"No, there is much more for you to learn."

"I just want to go home and take a long hot bath."

"In time, in due time," Karna said.

Sean was looking further than the core the whole time Karna was describing it and its function. He was more interested in what was beyond. It was clear that Karna had problems seeing in the darkness, and Sean was feeling better than he had since he arrived on the ship. This is the place. He thought. This is the place to begin. I can always go on reconnaissance missions during their sleep phase and now that I can open these doors, ride the lift and have an advantage of the darkness, I think I'm ready to hold my ground.

"So, what else is down here?" He asked.

"Nothing, it is in an area that must be kept dark due to the core exposure. If light permeates the core while the process is in its beginning phase of separation, the fusion stops and must start over. It would take days to get the reactor core back to full energy output."

Why would she tell me that unless she knew I was about to die, or figured I was not a threat to her. Sean thought. He knew it was now or never.

"Karna, I am really feeling sick and very tired, can we go to the light?"

Karna looked at Sean somewhat suspiciously when Nancy spoke up and said, "Me too."

"Very well, we can end your tour now if you desire and return to your rooms, or we can stop at the light, as you say, on our way back after the tour."

"Now would be fine by me," Nancy said, "the sooner the better."

Karna turned and headed back to the lift without saying another word. As she stepped onto the lift and moved toward the back she motioned for the girl to get in with her. When the lift was about two feet off the floor, Sean reached in, grabbed Nakita by the wrist and pulled her out of the moving lift, yelling, "She can ride up with us, she's small." Karna reached out to catch her but was caught off guard and had to go up alone.

"What's going on Sean?" Nancy asked surprised.

"Change in plans! Listen," he said grabbing Nakita by both arms and turning her to face him, "Do you want our help or not? It's now or never!"

"Yes." She said meekly.

Sean took each of them by the arm and said, "Okay ladies, follow me."

The elevator stopped at the Piiderk level and Karna sent it back to the bottom knowing that they lacked the implant needed to call for the lift. She waited for five minutes but when the lift returned again empty she realized that Sean was about to give her what she had been waiting for. She had taken them to the central core to demonstrate their intellectual superiority and advanced technology, but she never considered that Sean would have chosen that time and place to try and escape. He was playing the game but it wasn't the game of hunter and hunted she had hoped to play. She was trapped in her own trap. With them escaping to the lowest level, she could not hunt them, she could not observe their movements and she had lost control of the game altogether. The realization that she could not learn from that which she was unable to observe drove her insanely angry. Now for the first time in her life she was experiencing something new, something no one of her kind had ever experienced before. She felt rage, complete unadulterated rage in all its glory.

Karna stormed through the Piiderk and ordered the Chief of Arms to her war room. Because of her short temper and harsh judgments in the past, no one desired to enter the war room with Karna alone. With no other choice, he reported as ordered.

"Chief Cremo, my principle subject has decidedly chosen to escape but has chosen the rapitor level in which to do so. Dispatch a team of Quods to that level immediately to flush him out. It shouldn't be too difficult. He has two earth women with him whom he will worry about. However, listen very closely. Instruct the Quods implicitly not to kill him. They can do what they want with the females, but he must be taken alive and brought back to me. They should assist them in leaving that deck for any other then allow him to escape again. As you know, he lacks the implants required to gain access to secure locations and, unfortunately the vertical transporter as well. He has also taken the human girl, Nakita. He thinks she is one of us and will not trust her. I believe he thinks he has some bargaining tool by her capture. She is no longer of any use to us. See to it immediately!"

"Yes, Commander!" he replied.

On his way out the Chief of Arms was thinking that he was certain to be the next drone assigned to the Spiruthun permanently. He asked himself, "How am I supposed to find three alien escapees in a place so dark I can't see what's directly in front of me? How am I to capture them when the lack of radiation on that level will drain the Quods and me in a matter of tactars? It is an impossible task."

CHAPTER FIFTEEN

The Bilkegine race had learned in their infancy that they must control individual thought in order to control the masses and avoid civil unrest. Although they were one race, there were fearsome wars between different sects, and each of them took their positions on government very serious. Not unlike the Human race, the Bilkegine had, among their high ranking and most powerful associations, who had won those wars in their past. From those days until now, they had maintained a strict order of strong government that promoted unity and oneness in thinking rather than individual thinking. Furthermore, when periods of unrest did occur, the ranking powers would simply squelch the rebellions and convert the revolutionist into unthinking drones as a means to eradicate the problem citizens without capital murder, a punishment that was banned from use with the exception of Officers commanding military vessels. In those instances the commanders were the judge, jury and executioners. Karna was one of the commanders who relished the opportunity to use lethal punishment as a means of dictating unquestioning obedience among her crewmen.

There were however thousands of underground Bilkegines who did not believe in the old system of government rule, and although quiet about their convictions, they were willing to die if need be to build a new association to defy the old order. Gebel, one of the resistance fighters on board the Spiruthun, was one of the highest ranking officers of the Tahar, the alliance or association fighting the sitting power of the Bilkegines. Along with sixty other ranking officers who had managed to be assigned to the Spiruthun, his orders were simple: stop Karna and the current sitting government from their attempts to overtake the planet Earth or any other planet by force. His Tahar brethren knew that their planet could not sustain life as the Bilkegine knew it for very many more years. However, they believed that a peaceful and more diplomatic approach was the answer to their problems not force. While it was true that not many other species could live within the same hostile environment needed to sustain the Bilkegine, there were some planets that had acceptable conditions already, and the uninhabited space that would accommodate them. It was through these channels that the Tahar were seeking to rebuild their world.

Caution was the standing order from the resistance alliance. If one of the Tahar members were caught, he had orders to take his own life before any interrogation could occur. Should any ranking officer of the alliance be arrested and forced to reveal information through mind conversion, his attempts to place a new government would be thwarted and years of organization wasted. Additionally, they also had provisions in their standing orders to take the life of a fellow Tahar members should they fail to take their own life before interrogation occurred.

The gradual and incremental means of usurping power from the ruling association meant that many sacrifices would have to be made and serving under Karna was one of those sacrifices. Gabel knew that his mission to disrupt, and if need be remove, any possibility to take earth by military means was the highest priority of his alliance. He furthermore knew that without victory in his mission, his association had no chance to seize power over the Bilkegine people.

The nearly fatal crash with the meteoroid was, in Gebel's opinion, more than mere chance. He believed that a higher power was at play in determining the direction that his people were going. Now more than any other time in the past, it was possible to capitalize on the errors made by command and create sabotage with exacting precision and blame it on the meteoroid strike, thereby removing any possible glare from suspecting eyes and allow them to carry out their mission successfully.

At their last meeting Gabel heard a suspicious sound that led him to believe that someone other than a member of his association had over-heard their plans of sabotage and would no doubt report what had been heard. Gabel could not allow that to happen this close to success. He waited just outside the doorway to the elevators for hours waiting for that person to come out and reveal himself. Standing in the dark, without the presence of the supplemental radiation made him feel tired and somewhat sick. He knew that whoever was hiding within the dighergant rapitor chamber would be in a much weaker state than he was and hoped that whoever it was would break down and head for the light before him. He was beginning to lose all hope of catching the spy, when he heard the elevator descending with Karna and her human subjects in tow. However, not knowing who was coming or why he had no choice but to surrender his chance of ambush and escape to the darkness of the rapitor level.

As he turned his attention away from the central core and his potential spy he heard another sound very close. He froze. Now at a crossroad of doubt and indecision he didn't know whether to flee from the elevator and potential trouble explaining why he was there or stay and subdue the potential spy. Seconds seemed to drag through time as he attempted to make his decision. Then finally a body appeared in the doorway and his decision was made for him. He struck without thinking and a battle ensued. His opponent was equally matched in strength but due to his lengthy stay in the dighergant rapitor chamber, he had significantly less stamina.

Hand to hand combat was a lesson well learned by all the Tahar soldiers, and Gebel was no exception to the rule. The depth and subsequent damage of each blow began to take its toll on his opponent until finally he slumped to the floor dead. Seconds remained until the elevator would be in full view of the area they had battled in, and he knew that he must leave immediately. Quickly grabbing his fallen opponent by the arms, Gebel dragged his limp, lifeless corpse into the recesses of the dark abyss and waited. Although he had been in the darkened room for hours, and was completely wasted with fatigue, he was forced to stand alone against uncertain forces. It would have been such a relief if the next person he would see was a concerned comrade but when he recognized Karna through the darkness of the room he nearly collapsed in fear. At first all he could think about was his failure to complete his mission if he was discovered. Then he wondered why the Supreme Commander of the Spiruthun would ever lower herself to come to the rapitor level of the vessel. He was even more confused when she arrived with a young earth girl and stood waiting by the lift. Who would she be waiting for? He wondered. And, why would she come down here herself? He concluded that it must be her prized male subject since her total concentration had been nothing but him since she became aware of his existence more than a week ago. His strength and stamina began to drift out of his conscience thought as he waited to see if his assumptions were correct. In the silence, while he was waiting to see what was going to happen next, he heard faint voices in his own tongue.

"Listen carefully, Nakita," Karna spoke quietly, "whatever happens today you make sure and stay with the male and do as he instructs you to do. He will try to escape before he is locked up again in his room. Stay with him and when we have learned from him all there is to know, we will catch him and you can report everything back to me. Do you understand clearly?"

"Yes, Karna, but what if he does something dangerous. What if he really does escape? Should I contact you and let you know?"

"No!" Karna said in a very stern voice that made Nakita shrink back away from her. "You will do nothing but what the human male tells you."

"I will Karna. I will do as you say."

"Be still now, don't say a word, they are coming."

As soon as Sean and Nancy appeared in the lift Gebel realized a new sense of courage and strength. He now knew that Karna was putting her plan into effect by demonstrating to the earthling how powerful and seemingly invincible the Bilkegine people were. Somehow he would have to make contact with him, but when?

He listened intently as Karna explained the operation of their central core and answer questions. With his renewed courage and strength he felt that he might take the opportunity to try and overpower Karna and take command of the star vessel Spiruthun himself. Because of the great numbers of his Tahar personnel on board, he believed that he not only had the manpower to execute such a plan but thought that with the number of officers in his command and the element of surprise on his side, that they would be successful. His plan was simple. Leap out from the cover of darkness, attack and kill Karna and seize power over the ship. He knew it wouldn't be that easy to overpower Karna, especially in his weakened state, but it might be the only chance he would get with her alone without her Quods to protect her. It's now or never, he thought. Just as he was preparing to attack, Karna stepped onto the lift with Nakita. Suddenly the human male grabbed Nakita from the lift and it began to ascend leaving the three earthlings alone. Stunned at first, he then realized that a golden opportunity had just presented itself to him. He waited for another moment and stepped into the dim light of the room making his presence known.

Sean immediately reached for his pack to draw the weapon inside when Gebel raised his arms toward Sean with his palms facing up indicating he had no weapon nor intended any harm. Having recognized Nakita and overhearing Karna's plan for her, he said in his native tongue, "Nakita, is that you?"

Surprised to see another Bilkegine she stopped dead in her tracks and answered slowly, "Yes it is me. Do I know you?"

Before he could reply, Sean asked, "What is going on here, Nakita?"

She did not answer him. Nakita looked back and forth between Gebel, who was walking toward her with open arms and Sean who was looking at both of them with a puzzled look on his face. "Nakita," he demanded, "Who or what are you talking too?"

"I am Bilkegine and like you too... I don't know." She replied scared and confused.

"You know him? Can you understand him? What is he saying?" Sean said finally obtaining the weapon and pointing it at both Nakita and the stranger.

"Yes, uh no, I mean...yes, let me find out."

She began speaking in their tongue, but without the familiar clicks and digital sounding murmur that Nancy had heard before when listening to

Karna speak to the Quods. Nancy looked at Nakita in shock and amazement believing her to be a normal teenage girl, and now discovering that she spoke their language. While it sounded differently, the newcomer apparently understood everything she said. "What is going on here, Sean?"

"I'm not sure. Let's just hold out a minute longer."

Again Gebel spoke to her—"Nakita child, what are you doing here?"

Not knowing how to answer or what to do Nakita finally replied; "I am attempting to escape!" More confused than ever, she decided to play along as Karna had instructed.

"Nakita," Sean yelled, "I need to know what is going on here right now!"

The newcomer began to speak again, "I am on your side," he said in Bilkegine. "Do not be alarmed."

"What do you mean you are on our side?" Nakita asked in response. "Whose side are you on?"

Knowing Nakita was playing out Karna's hand, Gebel had to come up with an answer quickly to put her at rest. He couldn't allow his cover as a loyal Bilkegine Officer to be compromised. "Listen carefully child, I know Karna's plan and I too am a part of her deception. Play along or we will both be in trouble."

Nakita nodded her understanding and began to explain what was happening to Sean. "He said he is on your side don't be alarmed."

"Our side, what does he mean on our side. How does he know there are even sides to be on here?"

"He knows about your capture and wants to help you."

As Nakita was translating what Gebel said, he interrupted. "We must leave now. There will be Quods sent for you. They are very large and strong. You will not have a chance against them. We must leave!"

Again she relayed the information to Sean, and they all agreed to follow him into the darkness. Sean was not sure he trusted Nakita and now he was expected to trust one of the aliens he had just met in the dark yet hasn't seen clearly yet. It could be a trap, he thought.

"Where is he taking us?" Sean asked.

Nakita translated and waited for a reply. "To a safe place," she reported.

"Good," Said Nancy. "It will be nice to be in a safe place for a while."

"Tell him we need to stop and talk about our plans."

"Why Sean," Nancy asked. "He said he is taking us to safety. Why not trust him?"

"Come on Nancy, you can't be serious after everything we've been through. We haven't even seen this guy yet and you want to trust him? Based on what?"

Nakita translated Sean's demand and waited for Gebel's response. He stopped walking, turned around and spoke quickly. Nakita relayed what he said, "He said in a few minutes we will all be out of danger, and that we can stop and talk more then, but for now we must avoid the Quods who will surely come looking for us."

"But how do we know you can be trusted?" Sean asked looking directly at Gebel and listening to Nakita's translation.

"I am too weak to stop here. I understand your distrust but if we do not proceed, we will all be killed."

Sean agreed by signaling for Gebel to continue and they proceeded through the dark one short cautious step at a time.

Due to the vastness of the space around them, they heard very loud sounds coming from behind them. They not only heard numerous loud crashes, but a series of grunts and growls. At one point it sounded like a pack of hungry lions on the prowl for small game. Nancy became so scared that she ran in front of Sean and grasp his arm very tightly. The sounds were growing closer by the minute yet Sean thought they were moving at a snail's pace. "We've got to get moving faster!" he whispered loudly. "Nakita, tell him to get a move on or we're all dead!"

Nakita spoke to Gebel and he stopped short and turned abruptly nearly running into Sean and Nancy. He looked at Sean but spoke to Nakita and told her where they needed to go. He explained that he could not see more than an arm's reach in front of him and gave her directions to their destination. Nakita translated the directions to Sean and he quickly grabbed Nancy's arm with one hand and Gebel's in the other. "Stay close, Nakita!" he said as he took off running. By the sounds behind them Sean believed the Quod were getting closer by the second and asked, "If you can't see down here, how are they gaining on us."

Gebel replied through Nakita. "They are following your scent. You have a very distinct odor."

"I have an odor? Have you smelled those things lately? You've got to be kidding me!"

Just then they turned the last corner and reached the place where Sean was directed to go. It was a dead end.

CHAPTER SIXTEEN

Nearly two weeks had passed since Sean's abduction and the military command center had just obtained control of the satellites. The satellites they had virtually stolen were under the control of NASA and were used for weather prediction and observation to facilitate launches of many kinds. Many on the team wondered why the military didn't simply go to NASA and take control of the satellites there, but the powers in command of the alien project dubbed "Flash Back" knew the answer to that question all too well. Since the unsuccessful attempt to cover up the Roswell incident, the government has been hounded by alien enthusiasts and proactive anti-government groups to release information. They did not want a repeat of those mistakes. In order to have the NASA team that was already working with the satellites turn them around, hundreds of people would have to be brought in on the project. The government knew from past experiences that keeping a matter "Top Secret" was difficult with a group of twenty, let alone trying to do so with hundreds. In their opinion it just couldn't be done. The security around the base, in the work environments and in the homes of workers on the project would have had to be so tight it would have required months of planning and preparations just to screen all the potential workers needed to facilitate the return of the satellites and their maneuvers. No, this would have to be a black ops mission, and they would have to hack into the system and literally steal the satellites. Plausible deniability was the government's standard operating procedure and it would be easier to deny if only a dozen men had access to the mission.

The staff responsible for acquiring the satellites was made up of specially trained Air Force officers, a team of five MIT graduates who specialized in computer technology, and several Air Force enlisted men who had experience working with the satellites directly. The entire team was coordinated by the military and working closely with Dr. Oscar Weiss, PhD, whose job was to ensure the safety of the satellites and to create a new flight plan avoiding problem areas in space.

The two enlisted men had just burst through the doors of the Operations Command Center and announced that they had succeeded in acquiring the satellites.

"Finally," responded Major General Stephens, Base Commander of Cheyenne Mountain Air Force Base, "we can finally get a good look at that thing out there!"

Professor Weiss walked into the room following the two enlisted men and announced that a flight plan had been transmitted and received by the satellites and would be in position to get the first images of the alien craft in fourteen hours.

"Fourteen hours?" asked General Stephens.

"Yes, sir," replied the professor. "The two satellites we borrowed, so to speak, were being used by NASA to observe weather conditions on both coasts to ensure a safe launch of the shuttle that is due to initiate in twelve hours. When we interrupted the satellites orders and ordered them to this location," he said pointing to a spot on the big board with a laser pen, "they began to panic and we had a small technological tug of war in order to get them close enough to get the detailed images we need. They must travel around the world on a very complicated flight plan in order to establish the geo-synchronous orbit needed and that flight will take fourteen hours to complete."

"What about security? NASA is going to want those birds back. What security measures have been taken to ensure that NASA can't just take them back for one thing or worse, see what we will be seeing?"

"That will not be possible, General," said Dr. Weiss. "When we took control over the crafts we reprogrammed the access codes. They will be able to track the craft and determine its flight plan but will not be able to access any of the data banks or send and receive conflicting orders."

"Won't they undoubtedly assume that they have been pirated and attempt to hack their way back in to retrieve them, Doctor?"

"Of course," Dr. Weiss replied. "However, because of my knowledge of the NASA systems, from working with the Hubble Space Telescope, and the expertise of writing code by the MIT boys, they will fail. Your MIT officers are all genius. They have used a brilliant encryption code to program into the transponders. The NASA team will not be able to access anything. I am very confident, Commander."

"Very good, Doctor. Let me know the instant we are able to get an image, no matter how far out or blurred it may be."

"Yes, Commander Stephens. I will do so personally. However, for now may I request some time to get some sleep? It's been a couple of days since I've been able to sleep more than a few minutes at a time and I am extremely exhausted."

"By all means Dr. Weiss, and thank you for all your expertise and assistance."

Bruce was in a meeting with Agent Rose and Dr. Ross going over the profile that was created on Sean. As the Sheriff read the profile he was becoming agitated at what he was reading. He stopped reading the report about half way through and tossed it down on the table and rubbed his eyes. It was clear that he was sleep deprived and edgy before the meeting began, but due to the severe and potentially dangerous situation at hand, they wanted to get the profile into the general's hands as soon as possible. The Vice-President and Chief of Staff had already returned to Washington but the heads of the other military branches and the Secretary of Defense were still there and needed the report on Sean as soon as it was available.

"Was I in the same room with you when you were taking down the information on Sean?" Bruce asked angrily while looking at Dr. Ross.

"I believe the profile represents Sean very accurately, given what I had to work with," Dr. Ross replied in defense of his work.

"This isn't the same man I know at all, Doctor!"

"What don't you agree with so far? You haven't even read the entire profile."

"The whole thing, I haven't read anything that remotely sounds like Sean to me! What's this business about him being anti-government, anti-authority? Did you just make that up on your way here?"

"Let's just all calm down, Bruce," said Agent Rose.

"I am calm! Listen, you guys asked me here to help you get to know Sean, and I have been here doing whatever was needed to help. But I'm tired, hungry and pretty ticked off at this whole ordeal! Now, I'm 'posed to just sit back here and read this; this fictitious profile and agree with someone who I don't even know tell me everything about someone I've known for more than twenty years?"

"At least finish the profile before you cast dispersions on my work and reputation, Sheriff," Dr. Ross said emphatically.

"No, you listen up pal. I'm done with you. I'm done with this fairytale story you've written, and I'm going home! You guys do what you want, but you ain't no closer to understanding Sean than you are in understanding how he was taken in the first place!"

With that, Bruce stood up abruptly and stormed out of the room, leaving Agent Rose and the psychiatrist sitting there staring at each other.

"I'll go talk to him, Dr. Ross."

"Someone better get a grip on that rather large, man, and his temper before he becomes a problem."

Agent Rose left the room and went looking for Bruce. He caught up with him in his room throwing his clothes from his locker into his small suitcase, mumbling under his breath. This huge angry man was not a man the Agent wanted to have to deal with, but given the circumstances, had little choice in the matter. He hesitantly stepped into the doorway of the sheriff's room and leaned against the door in an unaggressive manner.

"What do, you want?" Bruce asked annoyed.

"So, you're packing it in then?"

"Boy, you're sharp as a tack," he said sarcastically.

"Hey, don't vent on me, man. I'm just trying to get to the bottom of this whole thing same as you! The doctor is one of the best in his field and you sat there and accused him of making everything up. For Christ's sake, he's the one who trained half of the FBI on profiling."

"Well, let's just say I call 'em like I see 'em. He couldn't have heard a thing I said during the interview. It was like I was talking to a wall or something. If all I'm doing is sitting around wasting my time, there are a lot better places to do it than here!"

"What if I were to tell you that the Base has been shut down, and no one is allowed to come or go right now?"

"You just watch me leave. What are they gonna do, shoot me?"

"Yes. If they have to, I'm sure they will."

Bruce stopped throwing his clothes and stared at James. After a few moments he seemed to calm down and said, "I guess I'm just tired and need a break. I miss my wife, my town is probably in the middle of a county wide bar fight, and I'm very ticked off with all these people who think they know everything, because they got a few initials after their names."

"Why don't' you take a few hours and rest. Give your people back home a call and think about it. If after that, you still want to go home. I'll personally check you out and get you on the jet."

"Yeah?" he said. "Sounds alright, I guess, but I'm done with that shrink!"

"I'll turn in the report but let the brass know that you strongly disagree with the conclusions that the doctor came up with."

"Oh, alright, but if I stay I want a more active role in decisions made where Sean is concerned. Nobody here knows him better than I do, and that's it! Can you live with that?"

"The decision isn't mine Bruce, but I'm sure that General Stephens can't argue with your logic. I'll let you know."

On his way out, Agent Rose stopped and turned back toward Bruce and whistled softly to get his attention, "Hey Bruce, one more thing."

"Yeah, what is it?"

"The satellite snatch was a success. We'll be able to see something in about fourteen hours according to Dr. Weiss. Just thought you might like to know. Here catch." He said, and tossed his private cell phone to him. "You'll have to go outside to get a signal, and I've never seen that phone before."

"Thanks, James."

CHAPTER SEVENTEEN

Gebel had directed them as they ran through the darkness of the Rapitor Level. He had a clear picture of the layout in his head and since Sean, Nancy and Nakita could all see clearly, their escape went easier than Gebel thought it would. They reached the point that Gebel had directed them to but nothing was there. It was a dead end and Sean was angry, thinking he had been trapped. He turned around and began to yell, "What is this, did you bring us here to die?"

By this time, Nakita had gone into automatic translation mode, and immediately began to translate if anyone said anything. Gebel understood what Sean was thinking and instructed them to look for a panel in the wall near the corner. Sean and Nancy split up and Sean searched the wall for any indication of a panel. He didn't have to search long when a panel popped open as he approached it. "Over here," he yelled.

"How did you open the panel?" asked Gabel

"I didn't. It just opened by itself," Sean replied.

"You must have an implant. It's the only way to unlock the doors." Gebel responded puzzled.

Watching Nakita closely for any telltale signs of shock, Sean said, "Yes, I have an implant."

"I don't understand. How could you have been implanted in such a short time, and why?" Nakita was just as interested in Sean's answer as Gebel had been when asking the question.

"I will tell you later. Let's just get out of here!"

Nakita was a good translator, but Sean was uncomfortable sharing what he knew with everything having to go through her for interpretation. There were just too many inconsistencies in her story to add up to her being here a short time and now that he knew she could speak the language, he knew she had lied to them.

As they all passed behind the hidden panel and into a small dimly lit room, Sean pulled Nakita aside to warn her not to betray him.

"Listen sweetie, I don't know what your game is, but if you betray me you will be the first to die. If you are in fact human as you claim, you must have been here for some time to be able to speak their language. So just watch yourself, because you can bet your life that I'll be watching you!"

Once the door was closed, Gebel groped the walls for a light panel. He pulled a tool out of his pocket and inserted it into the control. The light in the room increased and as everyone got a clear view of Gebel, he pulled a communicator from his pocket and called for help.

"Strothe, this is Gebel. Are you there?"

"Gebel, where are you? We've been looking all over for you."

"I am still on the Rapitor level and have the Commander's principal subjects with me now."

"Do you require assistance?"

"Yes, bring me a dighergant treatment immediately, but beware of Quods on this level. I heard them chasing us and we barely escaped. I'm sure they are hunting the human subjects but if you are seen, they will no doubt take you, or kill you. We are hiding inside the maintenance passage that holds the symhyphonic transmitter."

"I'll be there in a few minutes. Hold fast, and I will bring help."

"Also find Rotusea and have her come with you. I require her assistance in communicating with the humans."

While Gebel was talking to someone through his communicator, Sean was finishing his warning to Nakita not to betray them. "Are you clear on this Nakita, I swear if we come to any harm, I will kill you first."

"I will promise. I just want to stay with you and Nancy."

During the entire ordeal of being chased by the Quods, Nancy was so scared that she had no real idea what was happening around her. She was focused on staying close to Sean and when they finally reached a place where she thought she was safe, she sat down against a wall and began to stare at Gebel. At first, Sean didn't realize what she was doing. He merely thought she was tired and scared from running and needed to rest. He was too concerned that he was being betrayed by either Nakita or Gebel or both. Sean turned his attention away from Nakita and back to Gebel. Now able to clearly see him for the first time, Sean was taken back with his appearance. Sean had only seen the Quod and Karna up close and personal and now he was seeing what the Bilkegine people really looked like. Gebel was about the same height as Sean, but was extremely thin. His face was long and gaunt just like the Quod, but many of his facial features were exaggerated. His eyes were jet black just like all the other aliens he had seen, but they were twice normal size, at least normal as Sean had ever known. Remembering his college science classes, he remembered that most animals that lived in extreme darkness had larger eyes to capture more light, but this was the exact opposite. Their large eyes allowed them to see in the bright light, but lacking the ability for their eyes to adjust to darkness, they were nearly blind in low light conditions. His cheek bones were very prominent and sat high on his face, nearly circling his eyes. And his forehead, although exceptionally long had an extruding bony structure just above the brow line. His jaw bone protruded outward making it stand away from his face about two inches and his lips were very thin, almost non-existent. The only feature not over-sized in Sean's opinion was his nose, which was so small it seemed to barely stand out at all. As Sean was staring, Gebel realized that Sean had not yet seen a Bilkegine in their natural state. He spoke quietly to Sean, "Yes my friend, this is what my kind really look like. Except of course the Quod, who I trust you have already seen." Sean turned to Nakita and listed to the translation.

"Sorry, I didn't mean to stare at you. It's just that everything is so...so different." He replied thinking of a way to say what he was thinking.

Sean immediately turned to Nancy and was concerned with how she had handled seeing an alien up close and personal. When he saw her sitting in the same manner as before when she had gone into shock, Sean ran over to her quickly and knelt down directly in front of her. "Nancy," he whispered, "are you alright?"

Sean reached out and gently wiped the tears away from her soft cheeks then leaned into her and gave her a gentle peck on the forehead. "Everything will be okay. I promise." He said, thinking that he didn't like to lie to her but at the same time he wanted to protect her from the truth that they were all likely to die. Nancy reached out and took Sean by the hands and pulled them close to her heart.

Seconds later a loud crash was heard just outside the door of the maintenance passage. It was the Quods searching for Sean and Nancy. They had picked up their scent and, like the infamous bloodhounds, had tracked them through the darkness of the Rapitor.

"Will they find us in here, Sean?" asked Nancy.

"I don't think so. Remember what Karna said about them being big and strong, but also dumb and loyal?"

"Yeah, but what…"

"They followed us by smell but are no doubt confused about where we could have vanished because we were touching every wall out there looking for this passage, remember? Listen. They are out there banging into everything trying to find us. If they knew exactly where we were they would have been inside by now."

"It won't be long now," said Gebel. "They will lose all their strength to the darkness and will soon die searching for you."

"I don't understand. How could they die from being in the darkness? And if that's the case, why aren't you already dead, or are you different from them?"

"No, we are the same with one exception. They are so big and strong and exert so much energy that they will grow weak before me since I have been mostly still the whole time I have been down here."

"That answers the why but not the how. How can being in the dark kill you?"

"I understand your confusion. It is not the darkness that kills us it is the lack of radiation. Our people need a lot of radiation to live. The light you see is full of radioactive particles. It is what gives us our strength but also what sustains our lives."

"Oh great, isn't that just peachy. If I understand you then, Nancy and me along with the girl here will die from radiation poisoning?"

"No, you have been protected. The light in the chamber where you have been kept is shielded from the radiation outside. Also, have you not been taken to the cinbiote? It is the large brilliantly lit column in the center of the Piiderk level."

"Yes, we have spent considerable time in that thing. Karna told us it was to decontaminate us, to protect them from us."

"No, that was a lie. It is a healing chamber designed to keep the human subjects from dying to quickly. It cures radiation poisoning."

The pounding stopped, and Gebel knew that the Quods had either given up or had died. All they could do was wait for the Tahar comrades to rescue them. Suddenly the door of the passage began buckling under the violent pounding of a Quod. One Quod had found them and was pounding the door so hard it was crumpling like a piece of tin. Each blow seemed harder and more penetrative as the Quod attempted to extricate them from their hiding place.

Sean had learned that the Quod had several traits that made them a fearsome enemy. They had the strength of ten power lifters, the tenacity of a fox hound, the nose of a blood hound, and the intelligence of an ape. Normally a low intelligence would be a negative trait for a warrior, but in their case it gave them purpose. They followed orders without question, even to the death. Sean and Gebel both knew that this Quod would not give up until he was dead, and they were both hoping that it would run out of life before the door collapsed. As suddenly as the pounding began it stopped and just when they thought they were safe, the door burst open.

They all jumped back inside the passage as far as they could expecting a mammoth ashen arm to reach in and destroy them, but were relieved to see that it was in fact another member of the Tahar that had come to their aid.

"Are you alright, Gebel?" asked the Tahar soldier.

"Yes, but did you bring the treatment?"

"Here it is," he said passing a clear tube to Gebel. "Take it quickly. We must leave now!"

Gebel took the vial that contained a treatment consisting of a potent cocktail of dighergant particles and let out a big sigh. It was as if he was an addict and had just received his fix for the morning. As soon as the dighergant sped into his bloodstream, Gebel sat back for a moment and let it course through his system. Sean was half expecting Gebel to get up and say something like, "Boy, I really needed that," when he jumped to his feet and took control over their escape. One at a time everyone stepped out of the small hiding place and as each one entered the corridor outside they were instantly assaulted by the odor of the dead Quods lying dead on the floor just outside the door. Sean and Nancy were the last to leave and Sean, having already experienced the sight and smell of a dead Quod up close and personal, instructed Nancy to breathe through her mouth and keep her eyes closed until he instructed her otherwise. She stepped behind Sean and wrapped her arms around his waist so he could guide her out.

"Your assistance is most appreciated, Droge," Gebel said as he patted him on the shoulder. "Did you bring Rotusea with you? I need her to translate for me," he whispered.

"Yes sir. She is waiting in your private chamber."

Nakita who was still translating was puzzled when another Bilkegine officer appeared to help Gebel. She also was suspicious when he leaned into the other officer and spoke so quietly. "Who is Rotusea?" She asked. But instead of getting an answer, Gebel simply looked over his shoulder at her and said, "Good. Then let's get out of here." He motioned for the others to follow.

"Where is he taking us, Nakita," asked Sean.

"To his private room," she replied.

"How do we know we can trust him?"

"You don't."

Sean took Nancy by the hand and followed Gebel and Droge out of the room letting Nakita follow them. When they got to an elevator, Gebel and Droge got on first.

Gebel looked back at them and said, "We will go and make sure it is safe for you to come up. When the conveyance passes a level that appears to have a yellow light, get off and allow the conveyance to continue up empty. It will be monitored on the floors above to ensure that you are not on board. If we find Quod on the level we will not send the conveyance back down. If that happens, go back to the passage we hid in and you will be safe there. When it is safe for you to continue, I'll send someone after you."

He waited and watched Nakita to ensure that she would translate the message correctly and to see if Sean seemed to understand. When Sean motioned for him to continue, he turned and proceeded to the falkoe level.

"Do you think it will be safe with them, Sean?" asked Nancy.

"I think so, but if it isn't, I do have a back-up plan." Sean said then turned toward Nakita.

"Nakita, I need to know that I can trust you. Can you tell me why I should?"

Nakita thought about his question for a brief moment before answering. "I can't tell you why but please don't leave me behind."

"Kid, if you cannot give me a good reason to keep you, I'm through with you. I have some issues with you, some truths that I have discovered that show you to be a liar."

"Please, give me another chance!" She cried out. "What do you want to know, I'll tell you."

"You can start out by telling me how long you've been here and how you came to speak their language."

"I am speaking the truth. I don't know what you're talking about. I was told that my parents abandoned me here and these people took me in. I know I am different, like you but I don't know how. I have been taught the language in school."

"What is your relationship to Karna? And remember, before you answer I already know about some things so if you lie to me I'll know about it and we'll leave you here."

Nakita was not sure how much to divulge nor did she know exactly what Sean knew about her or how he came to know it. She also was very confused about who exactly was on whose side now that there were many more people involved. Gebel had told her that he was in on Karna's plan, but said nothing about anyone else being in on it. Furthermore, she was now aware that at least three other Bilkegine were involved somehow. Finally she answered, "Karna is my councilor. She instructs me in their ways and teaches me many things. She also comforts me when I am feeling sad. She is my friend."

"We'll see." Sean replied hesitantly. "I'm sure that those two who just left will know the truth about you, and if you've been lying to us, God help you."

The elevator came back down and Sean assumed that the coast must have been clear for them to go up. The three of them stepped into the elevator and, due to the cramped condition they all stood facing one another with their bodies pressed together. Sean reached his arms out and embraced Nakita and Nancy pulling them in closer to him so they wouldn't be hurt passing through the small openings in each floor. As the elevator began to climb, a Quod came out of the darkness and attempted to pull them off the lift. Nancy screamed when she felt it brush against her ankle nearly pulling her off the elevator. They came up to a level that was emitting a yellow light just as Gebel predicted. They stepped off and two Tahar men waiting for them grabbed them by the arm and hurried them down a long narrow hall and into a room. Gebel's quarters were very simple by earth's standards, and lacked anything that would suggest that he had any interest other than his job on the ship. The lights were bright inside the room but were still quite a bit darker than the other levels. Gebel brought a small female over to them. Gebel spoke something to her, and before Nakita could translate, she began explaining what was going on.

One of the Bilkegine men that accompanied them to the room walked over to Gebel and whispered something. They both turned to face Nakita for a moment then continued with their conversation. When they were finished, the two men who led them there walked over to Nakita and escorted her out into the hallway.

"Hey, she said in their language, "What are you doing? He needs me to translate. I'm to stay with the male subject on Karna's orders."

Neither of them responded to her pleading to stay. They took her down the hallway and into another room. "Sit." One of them instructed her. When she complied, they returned to the door and stood as if guarding her.

Back in Gebel's quarters, the Bilkegine woman began to speak to Sean.

"Hello. They call me Rotusea. I am a member of the Tahar, an association of Bilkegine people who are fighting against our ruling parties and against the domination of your planet."

"Our planet?" asked Nancy, confused by what she had just heard.

"Yes Honey, our planet. You have to have known something was terribly wrong here, but I've been trying to protect you from the truth of where we really are."

"Sure I did, I'm not an idiot. I thought we were taken and drugged by terrorists. And, based on what they did to me, I thought they were performing some illegal DNA manipulation or even cloning. But after seeing that man," she said pointing to Gebel, "and the others that just left, I'm more confused and angry than I am anything else. Tell me what is really going on here."

The truth of the matter was that she wasn't thinking clearly at all since they were abducted. Nancy had been on the verge of an emotional breakdown several times, and at the very least was in a state of shock and denial. Sean recognized some of the symptoms from his experience working with Vietnam vets who had breakdowns after long and intense battles. He was going to have to give her this news gently. He had to choose his words with extreme caution or she would certainly go over the edge.

"Nancy, this isn't going to be easy to comprehend. Believe me, I've been struggling with it myself, so I know. But, before I tell you I need you to understand that I am here with you and will do everything in my power to keep you from harm. I know I haven't been able to protect you at all times since we've been here but I promise to from now on."

"What is it, Sean? Just tell me!"

"You were partly right. We have been abducted, but by an alien race not terrorists. I didn't want you to know because of your past experience as a child, but there is no way to hide it now."

Nancy looked at Sean for a second in confusion then glanced over at Gebel and Rotusea, who were standing nearby, then back to Sean. Her eyes were fixed and wide open as the reality of what Sean had said sank in. Then, as Sean predicted, her eyes rolled back in her head and she passed out. Sean reached out and grabbed her to break her fall, then picked her up and carried her to a thin mat on the floor and laid her down gently. He gently brushed the side of her face and tried to revive her. "Nancy," Sean said calmly, "Nancy. Come on honey, snap out of it."

Within a few moments, Nancy started to stir. She opened her eyes long enough to see Sean sitting beside her and feel his warm touch on her hand and face. Then she closed her eyes and fell asleep.

"Will she be alright?" Rotusea asked.

"I believe she is in shock," Sean replied. "Can I get a blanket or something to cover her up with?"

"Here," she said handing Sean a thin piece of material similar to that of their uniforms. "Will this do?"

"Yes, thanks, how about something to raise her feet a little?"

Rotusea scanned the room quickly and retrieved a small box from a table and handed it to Sean. Gebel told Sean that they had Tahar officers that were familiar with human anatomy and asked if they were needed.

"No, that might make things worse. She'll be fine in a couple of hours. She just needs to rest."

Rotusea walked over to Sean as he stood up and turned around. "May we continue now? It is very important."

"By the way, where did they take Nakita?" Sean asked.

"She is not what you think she is," Rotusea said. "The young human woman has been with the Bilkegine for the past six years and has been mentally confused to believe that she is one of us. Until her memory has been returned to her, she is a danger to you. We have known of her existence for several years but have not been successful in reaching her until today. Gebel just learned that she is working close to Karna as a spy. She was instructed just an hour ago to stay with you and play along with whatever you did and was ordered to report everything back to Karna upon your re-capture."

"So, you're saying my escape was planned...allowed?"

"Yes, we believe that to be the case, but also believe that Karna did not expect you to choose the rapitor level to make your attempt and that has given you a distinct advantage."

"Okay, so what's next?"

"There is a vessel wide search going on for you right now. The Commander believes that you are stuck on the rapitor level since you are unable to operate the vertical conveyance. We must use this time to educate you on what is happening and how you can assist us in defeating the Shem, the ruling party association."

189

"But if Karna thinks we are on the rapitor level than why is there a vessel wide search going on, and if she does realize later that we are not on that level, won't there be more trouble for us both?"

"First of all you must know that the human girl, Nakita was implanted with a chip that allows her to not only use the vertical conveyance, but open doors to low security areas as well. If you are found on the upper levels, which we will not allow to happen, Karna would simply believe that Nakita was helping you as she was ordered to do. Also, the darkness of the rapitor level is your advantage. It lacks the light that carries dighergant particles that keep us healthy and strong. Everyone that she sends to look for you on that level will either fail or die from the lack of the dighergant."

"I don't understand, what is this dighergant you're talking about? Is that the stuff Gebel took a while ago that brought back his strength?

"Yes, you are correct. The dighergant is—I believe the word you use is—radiation. It is crucial for us to survive and deadly for you. Therefore, in its absence you have a distinct advantage."

"I understand that part. Gebel explained it to me before, but if you have this stuff that can cure you why won't they just take a supply with them while they search for us there?"

"It is not readily available like that. The Tahar have developed the synthetic dighergant to give us an advantage of strength in areas of low production of natural dighergant and as an emergency supply of energy in the event that we were forced to completely destroy the dighergant core. It also has not been perfected and we suffer physically with every use."

"Alright then, can you tell me why I am here?"

Gebel took over the conversation and Rotusea translated.

"We believe that Karna has been looking for a human subject that has demonstrated a superior knowledge of warfare and cunning in battle, and has proven to be fearless as well. Since we have been here over the past six years, we have abducted thousands of your species in that quest. The search has become more frantic since Karna has learned that our planet is deteriorating more quickly than anyone had predicted."

"Boy is she wrong about me! Where did she get her information, and how did she find me?"

"We have several crewmen on board our vessel who have gone through extensive physical modification, and could possibly fool any human of their true identity. They have done so at considerable cost to their own bodies. The procedure has not yet been perfected and many volunteers have died due to complications. Those chosen to receive modifications, like Rotusea, have been placed on the surface of your planet in order to gain information needed to defeat you during battle for your planet. Their missions were to find essential humans and force them to cooperate by holding their families hostage on our vessel. Many of your species surrendered to these threats and gave Karna the information she needed."

"But you don't look human to me, at least not up close," he said looking at Rotusea. "How could you pass for human enough to capture these people?

"First let me say that I had no part in those missions. I volunteered for another reason entirely. I went through the conversion in order to speak peace with your people once we had overthrown our leading party associations. But to answer your question, they used the cover of darkness to travel in secure areas and abduct them."

"How did you overcome our planet's lack of radiation?"

"They could not. Even if they had our treatment of dighergant, they could not sustain life long enough to stay on the surface for long periods of time. Many died on the surface and had to be retrieved similar to how you were brought here. Each one of them had a tracking implant that we were able to follow in the event of their demise."

"Oh, that's great! You're saying I've got something inside of me that helps them find me whenever they want to?"

"Yes, that is correct. We can remove it if you like."

"I'm almost afraid to ask, but where is it?"

"It is implanted inside your skull, just behind your ear."

"Does Nancy have one as well?"

"It is not certain. We believe she was touching you when you were transported by our crystalline star chamber onto one of our smaller shuttle vessels."

"So, if you can take this thing out of my head, will it hurt?"

"Yes, we can remove it but it is possible that you might expire if we tried. It would be much easier and just as beneficial if we simply disabled it."

"Fine, let's do that."

"It will take some time to obtain the equipment. We will do it as soon as we can."

"Okay, now, how can I get off this vessel and back home?"

"We have not been able to plan for that yet, but we are working on the problem. If you simply disappear, Karna will grow suspicious and our presence and purpose will be discovered."

"So if I'm getting this, you can't help me escape?"

"No not until we have complete control over this vessel and Karna is eliminated."

"I'm all over that! How can I help you defeat Karna?"

"Be yourself, but never, ever give up. She is looking for a way to break the spirit of your species. If she succeeds in taking away your desire for freedom and convinces you that any resistance is useless, then she will have what she needs to take over your planet and force your species into slavery."

"Slavery, to what end?"

"I'm sorry I do not understand your question."

"Why does she need slaves? Why use us at all?"

"Like Rotusea said earlier, we lack the ability to operate on your planet safely. Therefore, we need your species to ready the planet for our occupation."

"So let me get this straight. She wants us to change our planet's atmosphere to accommodate your species at the peril of mine—to somehow raise the radiation level so that every living thing on my planet dies? What if she fails?"

"That too is bad news for your kind. She has orders to destroy the planet and everything on it."

"For what—punishment for not playing fairly?"

Rotusea explained the plans of the Shem Alliance and how they reasoned. She explained how driven Karna was and how irrational she had become since her deadline was moved up. "She is ready and waiting to learn the key to human domination and when she gets that information, she already has hundreds of thousands of warrior Quod ready to attack the surface. They will not be concerned with what they look like either. They have developed specialized equipment that will protect each warrior for up to forty-eight of your earth hours. They will win if it comes to that."

"If she is determined to attack the planet, with my knowledge or without it, what can you do to stop her?"

"We will die to protect your species and your planet. Our goal is to obtain a peaceful agreement with neighboring planets to allow us to cohabitate with them. Before we fail at that task, we will destroy this vessel and sentence our entire species to final eradication."

"Hold on. Did you just say neighboring planets would agree to a peaceful co-existence? You are telling me there are more than your race and mine out there?"

"Yes." Rotusea replied, turning to look at Gebel as if amazed at Sean's lack of knowledge.

"Where—where are they? I mean—what planet are they on?"

"They are located in the Limeethrian Quadrant. I believe your people call it the Epsilon Eridani. It is ten point five light-years from your sun."

Sean stood staring strangely at both Gebel and Rotusea for a couple of moments. It was a mix of bewilderment and disbelief. Finally snapping out of his awe inspired daze, Sean continued. "We didn't know. I'll deal with that knowledge some other time. Meanwhile, let's get busy stopping Karna. And just to let you know, I'm prepared to sacrifice my life to keep her from winning also."

The door opened unexpectedly causing everyone to jump. Without warning, three Quods entered the room in a very aggressive manner toward Sean. As if the other Bilkegine present or Nancy did not exist, they reached for Sean. Gebel, who had been standing silently while watching the meeting take place between Sean and Rotusea ran to the wall closest to the door and removed a weapon from a hidden panel. He pointed the weapon at the Quods, fired, and a short bright light, that resembled lightning, shot from the end of the weapon. The Quods immediately dropped to the floor flopping violently and screaming a horrific yelp, as yellow foam and blood bubbled out of their mouths. Before Sean's eyes, the bodies began to decompose and bubble until all that was left was a seven foot long pile of bubbling ooze. The sight and smell was enough to make anyone, no matter how strong of a stomach they had, retch. The smell actually burned Sean's eyes and nasal passages.

"I guess they are not restricting their search to the dark level any longer," Sean said. "In fact, I guess they're looking everywhere."

Gebel looked into Rotusea's eyes and spoke a few words then looked at Sean while he waited for her to translate.

"It has begun," she said. "Our time is upon us."

CHAPTER EIGHTEEN

Bruce walked to the security booth just inside the main gate of the mountain. He had come to help Sean but was regretting it more and more each day. Not only did he feel completely out of place among the geeks and military personnel, but he missed his wife and his mountain. While he probably would never have admitted it, he missed the bar fights, clan wars and his lazy deputies as well.

The security guard at the gate motioned for him to stop, but not really paying attention, Bruce just flipped up his badge and kept walking. That was not how security worked on the mountain though.

"Hey, pal! I said halt!" the MP yelled as he jumped to his feet and stepped in front of Bruce.

"Hey, no need to get your shorts in a knot, Buddy!" Bruce said as he stopped and raised his hands.

"Move back behind the gate!" The MP said loudly and firm.

Bruce was in no mood to put up with some military hotshot who thought he was bad. He turned around and put his arms down. "Fine—what do you want—a mother may I?"

"What I want is for you to follow procedures and sign out. Another thing I want is for you to surrender your cell phone!" he yelled again, reaching for the phone Bruce was carrying.

Bruce pulled back the hand holding the phone and held it out of reach from the much shorter and much thinner MP. "Okay, Hotshot! I'll sign out but you don't touch me or the phone. Get it?"

As Bruce signed the logbook and threw the pen down, he noticed the MP unlatching his holster. Oh boy, he thought, some little schoolboy, punk kid with a gun. He turned around and faced the MP who now had his hand on his nine-millimeter colt automatic.

"I'm all a-shudder, Boy. What? You gonna shoot me to get my phone?"

"You cannot make calls from this base without a secure line, Sheriff. It's my job and my butt if you do, and I'm not going to let that happen," he warned, pointing at Bruce with his finger.

Bruce was getting hotter by the second. He was not in any mood to put up with some scrawny little teenage kid, with or without a gun, no matter what his orders were.

"I tell you what, Kid, why don't you just pretend that you never saw me, huh? I think we'd get along much better if you did. I'm in no mood to put up with some little boy who wants to play war. And if you don't put that finger away, I'm gonna break it off and feed it to you!"

Bruce started walking toward the outside gate when he heard the gun slip from the leather holster. He stopped inches from the door and, without turning around, said, "Go ahead and shoot! Shoot me!"

"If I have to, I will, but you're not leaving with that phone!"

"No! I'll tell you, you put that thing away, or I'll personally come over there and beat you with it! You got me kid? Bruce yelled, thinking it would intimidate the young private. As he reached for the door and heard a shot ring out and strike the door over his head.

Now he was really mad. He turned around and marched right for the kid, who by now was shaking like a leaf. The MP had never fired his gun at a living person before, and the adrenalin was coursing through his veins with every massive beat of his heart.

"Fine, you want the phone, take it! He said, holding it out for the MP. As soon as the kid reached for the phone, the Sheriff grabbed him with one arm and stripped the gun away while choking him with his other arm. He pressed him up against the wall and started to squeeze. Bruce was not in danger of losing his head completely. He took the kid's gun and held it up to his temple. "You want to play war with me, you got it. How does it feel having a gun to your brain? Does it feel real enough for you?"

The MP was turning blue and was about to pass out when Agent Rose came running down the corridor.

"Let him go, Bruce! What's the matter with you?"

"The dang fool kid almost shot me!"

"For what?" he asked as he tried to pull Bruce's arm down to release the guard.

The guard was choking and grasping for air as he fell to the floor. Color started coming back in his face, and he was holding his throat. As he sat on the floor trying to regain his composure, he gave Bruce a look that translated, anger and revenge at the same time.

"I wasn't gonna hurt the kid, James!"

"Man, you have gone off the edge! Get a grip, will you?"

"How would you feel? Look, I don't like it when people shoot at me, especially over making a phone call!" He yelled as he wiped sweat from his brow. "Unless you want to shoot me in the back now, I'm calling my wife."

"Go ahead, but make it quick!"

Bruce walked out the door and slammed it behind him as James helped the MP back onto his feet. He was still shaking and shocked at almost being strangled and shot by the giant.

"Private! Do you have any idea who you were just shooting at? Are you authorized to use deadly force to keep anyone—any single person inside this facility?"

"Yes Sir uh, I mean no Sir. I'm not sure, Sir. I was just trying to follow my orders, Sir." It was just some old Sheriff—one that wasn't following orders."

"No, Private! You weren't—just—doing anything. You were shooting at perhaps the only man on the planet who has vital knowledge pertinent to our current crisis. From now on, you'd better think before you act, and you better keep that gun in its holster, unless you want it fed to you. Am I clear on that, Private?"

"Sir, yes Sir!"

"Get out of here then!" Agent Rose commanded.

"But I can't leave…"

"Private, you are inches form a court marshal. You are dismissed, and I had better not hear, or see, a single word about this entire experience, or you'll be digging latrines in Alaska! You got me?"

"Yes, Sir," he replied. Then he performed an about-face and walked briskly down the corridor.

Agent Rose was not accustomed to taking orders from a private, any more than Bruce was, but thought that given his experience as Sheriff for so many years, he could have handled the situation better. James was going to have to make up something about the security station and get someone new assigned. "This kind of thing was the reason I got out of the military when I did and joined the NSA." James whispered to himself. "Sometimes the military just don't think before they act, they're always so black and white in an all gray world." James thought it wouldn't be appropriate to put: "I was just following my orders, no matter how stupid they are," on the MP's tombstone, but also thought if they would it might stimulate some thinking on behalf of the rest of the military. He remembered hearing someone say; "military intelligence was a contradiction in terms" and the more he dealt with them the more he thought just that. With them it was always, shoot first and then count the bodies, without the asking questions later part. He thought. If they asked questions at all that might mean someone was thinking and he didn't think that happened anymore. And, if he hadn't shown up when he did to stop Bruce from choking the kid to death it would have proved his theory right.

James picked up the phone at the guard shack and dialed the Officer of the Day.

"Captain, this is Agent James Rose from the NSA. I have relieved your guard at security checkpoint alpha. He was not feeling well, so I told him to report to his quarters. Can you assign a replacement right away?"

"Yes Sir. Right away, Sir" the Captain replied.

James waited for the new guard at the checkpoint and gave him further orders upon his arrival.

"Private Reynolds reporting as ordered, Sir, the Private said as he took his post.

"Very well private, you are to check for proper identification on anyone entering this compound. You understand that any attempt to gain access to this base by force can be dealt with lethal force, but only as a last resort. You are not, and I repeat not, to detain, harass or otherwise disturb anyone trying to leave. You may request that they sign out but you'd better do so politely. Do you have any questions?"

"Sir, am I to understand that you are superseding my previous orders?"

"What orders are you referring to, Private?"

"It is my understanding that the base is on high alert, condition red."

"That is correct, Private, and?"

"There are specific protocols to follow when we are under condition red, Sir."

"Specifically Private, I don't have all day."

"Under condition red, no personnel are allowed to exit, make unsecured phone calls, or interfere with a guard in the execution of his duties, Sir."

"Is this coming directly from the Officer of the Day?"

"Yes Sir."

"Let me explain the chain of command to you, Private. At the top of the food chain is the President of the United States, the Commander and Chief, then the Vice-President, then me, then the Officer of the Day, then anyone who outranks you. You are at the bottom, Private. Understand so far?"

"Yes Sir."

"So you understand no one but a higher ranking authority can supersede my orders, right?"

"Yes Sir."

"Know this Private, and pass it along to anyone who relieves you; I represent the President, the Commander and Chief during this operation. No one, and I repeat for clarity, no one present at this facility right now has a higher authority than I do, and here is my proof." Agent Rose said as he showed his identification and orders signed by the President.

"Yes Sir!" the Private replied, snapping to attention.

"At ease Private, you are here to keep unauthorized personnel from obtaining entry to this facility and logging personnel in or out who have authority to leave under condition red, yellow, orange or green and nothing more. Understood?"

"Sir Yes Sir!"

"Now, just to make sure your replacements understand, I will speak to the Officer of the Day and have those orders posted."

"Yes Sir."

"One more thing Private, have you seen the Sheriff that has been here the past two weeks?"

"Yes, Sir I have. He's the big guy, right?"

"That's him alright. Leave him alone. All you need to do with him is ask him to log in and out, politely. That's it. Understand?"

"Yes Sir, crystal clear, Sir."

"Good, carry on, Private Reynolds."

Bruce made his call back home to check in with his wife Maggie. She was still worrying about him, but she always had, so everything was fine. His brother Mikey was still living at the house and taking care of business, and Bruce got an update about the town while he was talking to her. Everything seemed to be back to normal in town—at least as normal as things could ever be again now that his knowledge of the world had been turned upside down.

Just as Agent Rose was about to leave, the door opened and Bruce stepped inside. He looked much better and his face wasn't beet red any longer. He walked slowly up to the guard shack and presented his identification and authorization papers. Without a word he picked up the pen and signed the register.

"Thank you, Sir." The Private said.

Bruce looked directly at James and asked, "We cool?"

"Yeah, we're cool. Do you feel better now?"

"I'm Ok, and for what it's worth, I'm sorry I lost my head back there."

"Can I have my phone back?" James asked, holding his hand out.

"Sure."

Inside the Command Center everything was buzzing. The satellites had made their turns and had now stopped several thousand miles from the alien craft. All the MIT techs were punching keyboards and setting the satellites for a close up view of the space ship. Dr. Weiss was standing in the center of the room staring at the big screen. He along with everyone else had been anticipating this moment for the past two days. The first image transmitted from the alpha satellite came up on the screen, and while it came into focus, every eye in the room was glued to the screen. The room grew exceptionally quiet as the image became crystal clear.

The morning sun was just beginning to crest when the edges of the craft became clear. There was just enough light hitting the surface of the craft to distinguish it from the blackness of space around it. Everyone was struck with awe as the details of the ship came into focus and a simultaneous "whoa" filled the air. The vessel was much larger than the professor had estimated, and the millions of lights glowing on the surface gave its proportion. It had a spherical shape over-all, and as the satellite zoomed in for a close-up view, it became obvious that there were several hundred levels within. Near the top of the spherical craft the damage caused by the meteor could be seen. Sections of the vessel were missing completely, while other areas were pulled away from the side extending out into space. A white gaseous fog surrounded the ship and some type of gas was escaping from the center of the top. On one hand it was the most amazing thing anyone had ever seen. On the other hand, it scared everyone to the core of their being.

Dr. Weiss was studying the lights that were being projected on the side facing the earth. He recognized several constellations and realized that his assumptions were true about the ship projecting the celestial bodies it would have otherwise blocked as a means of camouflage.

Moments later, someone in the room announced that the second satellite was coming online. An image showed up on a second screen directly beside the big screen. All eyes shifted to the new image which was showing the back side of the craft. It was completely different from the side facing earth. Instead of being black and projecting small lights it had the color of polished copper. It was extremely bright and nearly every opening had light pouring out. Everyone watched the screens with jaws slightly open in amazement when the General spoke.

"We are recording all of this aren't we, Doctor?"

"Yes, absolutely," he replied.

"Can we zoom in any closer?"

"One minute, General," the professor said as he moved to the control panel one of the MIT officers was sitting at. "Mr. Danforge, if we try to get a closer view, will you be able to extrapolate the data sufficient enough to get a clear image?"

Dr. Weiss and Captain Danforge entered a few commands and changed the program codes enough to produce the closer view that the General wanted. Minutes later the image went fuzzy and zoomed in. When it became clear, the image that filled the big screen was that of three distinct levels of the spacecraft. Windows became very clear and shadows could be seen behind the intense light inside.

"Good job. Now, do the same thing to the beta satellite." General Stephens commanded. "I want to get a good look into this thing if I can."

Just as before, a minute or two passed and a new close-up view came up on the smaller board. Everyone in the room was studying both images.

After viewing both sides of the craft for more than ten minutes, and recording a close up image of the entire surface from both vantage points, General Stephens looked down from his elevated position into the gallery below and said, "Lieutenant Goldwell, can you get a fix on the position of those two satellites and track their movements?"

"Yes Sir. No problem. I'm tracking their orbit as we speak."

"Show me on the beta screen." He ordered.

The graphic came up on the screen showing the globe and two pictograms indicating the alpha and beta satellites, and a white line indicating where they had been and where they were currently. Since they were in geo-synchronous orbits, the line did not indicate any further movement.

"That's real good, boys." The General remarked. "Now, I know we didn't know this thing was out there before, but now that we've got a good look up her skirt, can you get a fix on it electronically? Can you track this thing?"

"No, Sir," replied one of the technicians working just below the General. "It just doesn't show up on anything we have. We've tried everything except trying to bounce a laser off of it."

"Would that give me what I need to know?"

"It would if we measured the bounce of the laser against its hull," interrupted Dr. Weiss. "Do you have that capability here, General?"

"Dr. Weiss, I'm afraid that is on a 'need to know' basis and since you need to know, the answer is yes. Make it happen."

Three Air-Force technicians got up and left the room. Dr. Weiss, believing them to be leading the way, left behind them. As he was walking out, the General called his name.

"Dr. Weiss, I need this one a lot faster than before. How long before I can get a fix on this thing so I can blow it out of the sky?"

"We will do it as fast as humanly possible, General Stephens. You have my word on it."

"I want every inch of this thing recorded at maximum close-up gentlemen. We've been standing down here with our pants down around our ankles and I want to turn that around. Let's get a jump on that thing and take it out! We're burning daylight, let's get moving!"

True to his word, Dr. Weiss and the technicians configured the tracking laser to fire at the position directly between the two satellites in a best guess chance of hitting the surface. All they need accomplish was hitting the target anywhere. If they could do that, it would show up on the images in the command center as a bright sparkle and they would be able to adjust their aim based on the location of that ping. They knew they had no equipment capable of tracking the ship if it changed course, but it was all they had at that time. Dr. Weiss walked as briskly as he could back to the command center and gave the word to General Stephens that they were ready to fire the laser.

"Fire at will Dr. Weiss," General Stephens ordered.

Dr. Weiss walked over to another terminal and executed the command to fire three short bursts into space. As quickly as he could look up at the screen, he saw three distinct pings of light strike the spacecraft.

"Got you," General Stephens said under his breath. "Okay, get a fix on those three pings and…"

Before the General could finish his sentence he saw a bright flash come from inside the spacecraft as bright as the sun. Both screens showed nothing but white light from top to bottom, and then went black. Everyone in the room began to murmur as they attempted to discern what happened.

"What just happened?" General Stephens demanded.

No one said a word; they were all trying to figure out what had just happened to their equipment. Dr. Weiss ran over to the console that communicated with the satellites in an effort to solve the problem and realized that the satellites were no longer transmitting.

"Someone tell me what just happened!" the General ordered.

Dr. Weiss was the first to respond. "It appears that they have somehow disabled the satellites General."

"How—how could they have done that from so far away? Did they hack into them and shut them down or what?

"Unknown General." Dr. Weiss replied. "Perhaps the ship sent out an electromagnetic pulse. That would certainly have this effect on a satellite."

Both screens switched back to its normal tracking software and displayed tiny white dots indicating all the space debris that was regularly tracked. Suddenly the big screen began to blink red around the edges, an alarm sounded inside the command center, and a small red dot appeared on the image.

"Tracking!" yelled one of the technicians. "It's heading straight for the alpha satellite, General."

Before any evasive action could be taken the icon representing the alpha satellite disappeared from the image. Inside the control room chaos broke out as everyone was running between one panel and another. Everyone was attempting to discover what had happened to the alpha satellite when the same thing happened to the beta satellite.

"Everyone settle down." General Stephens ordered. "You've all had training for this contingency. Just follow protocol and we'll get to the bottom of this."

General Stephens walked over to his desk on the highest platform in the command center, picked up a red phone next to his chair and spoke in a controlled voice. "Get me the President," he said calmly. "Mr. President, Sir, they've just showed us their hand."

CHAPTER NINETEEN

The Spiruthun was at high alert. The ships sensors detected the three laser pings that had hit its surface and put the ship on alert. Karna was in the War Chamber when the alert sounded and immediately called the central command station. The newly appointed Lieutenant Commander had the watch and was not going to be blind-sided by anything. He didn't want the same fate his predecessor had experienced, and he had posted additional personnel to keep from being surprised by another meteoroid. They had no reason to suspect the humans even knew of their existence, and none of their observations had revealed any spacecraft capable of intersecting them without them being able to detect a launch. However, when the surface sensors picked up the three laser pings, they weren't going to take any chances and the Lieutenant Commander ordered continuous searches by their long-range scanners.

"Lt. Commander Rashintar, report!" called Karna from the War Chamber.

"On your screen, Commander," he replied. "Our surface scanners picked up three distinct pulses originating from the earth's surface. I immediately ordered continuous long-range scanning of the immediate area and discovered two earth spacecrafts. They were confirmed to be unmanned probes of some kind, similar to the type set in geo-synchronous orbits around the planet. However, these were not only much further into space, but directed toward our vessel. It has become evident that someone on earth is aware of our presence."

Karna observed the two satellites on her screen and knew they were of human origin. She ordered probes to be launched to investigate them closer.

"Probe launched, Commander," Rashintar reported, "data coming in now."

She watched as the probe sent back measurements and close up imagery of the craft. She could see no indication that it was a threat to her, but nonetheless did not like having something or someone observing her ship.

"Destroy the vessels," she ordered.

"Destroy Commander? Will that not give our position away?"

"It would appear that our position has already been compromised. Do I have to remind you that questioning my orders is punishable by death, Lieutenant Rashintar?

"No, Commander. Target has been acquired, firing!"

The weapons fired were high output particle separators. The principle behind the weapon was simple. The head generated by the device struck the target with highly accelerated dighergant particles. The concentrated radioactive beam was traveling at such a high speed that upon contact, it tore through the target as if it were made of paper. The effect was not unlike solar radioactive rays being focused through a magnifying glass, but was carried to within a hundred feet of the target by a nuclear powered, self targeting rocket resembling a torpedo.

"Objects destroyed, Commander."

"It would indeed appear that the humans know of our presence. Ready all combat troops and launch reconnaissance cruisers at once!" she ordered.

The cruisers were sent out to patrol the sector where the craft had been destroyed, and their on-board sensors picked up a vapor trail indicating the craft's flight path. They had orders to follow the vapor trail to verify its origin. Based on their course, they surmised that the crafts originated from two distinct geo-synchronous orbits; one on the east coast of the United States and the other from the west coast.

"Incoming transmission, Commander," reported Rashintar.

"Both crafts destroyed. We followed their vapor trails and discovered they were launched from two different geo-synchronous orbits above the United States."

"Continue to patrol over the United States if they did in fact originate there, it is possible that they will attempt another launch. Continue on high alert and report anything launched from the planet's surface." Karna ordered.

Lieutenant Commander Rashintar walked to the War Chamber where Karna was sitting and reported. "Everything is secure, Commander."

"No it is not. Lieutenant Commander Rashintar! If everything were secure we would have known that instant those vessels entered our area and would have been able to conceal our location before we were identified and before those probes sent back information about us!"

***

Sean was getting a brief of his own in Gebel's quarters. He was told about the ruling alliance and their goal of securing a planet. Gebel told him as much about the Tahar as he thought Sean needed to know and what the weaknesses were in the Bilkegine. Finally Sean was beginning to believe that he wasn't alone on his quest to destroy the ship.

"How many Tahar are on this ship?" Sean asked.

"We have over one hundred thousand on board that sympathize with you and will assist you in halting the occupation and annihilation of your planet."

"That sounds like a formidable army, why haven't you organized an attack strategy and taken over the ship?"

"The primary reason is the lack of adequate weapons. We have managed to obtain a few weapons like this," Gebel said, raising the weapon he had used to kill the Quod. "We are ever vigilant in our search for weapons but can only take weapons that would not be missed. Most of them were taken from those belonging to Quod that have died for one reason or another. But we do not have enough to overpower all the Quod and seize the vessel."

Sean smiled then reached into his backpack and presented the weapon and ammunition he had stolen from the warehouse. "Would something like this or bigger help you take control? I happen to know where you can get your hands on hundreds, perhaps thousands."

Gebel reached out and took the weapon from Sean. Rotusea stepped closer and examined the weapon with him. "Where did you find this? I have never seen anything like this before," Rotusea asked, "and you say there are many more?"

"Yes, I found this one in a warehouse on the bright level near the middle of the ship. I believe Karna referred to it as the Pii…"

"The Piiderk Level," Rotusea said completing his sentence.

Gebel interrupted Rotusea and said, "No, you must have found them somewhere else. The only thing on that deck would be stores and supplies used for this mission."

"I know what I know," Sean replied. "I found this one and many more when I was out doing reconnaissance a few days ago."

"I'm confused," Gebel said somewhat puzzled. "You were given the freedom to roam the ship without an escort?"

"Not exactly, I left our room during the time you refer to your resting phase. I was looking for a way to escape and discovered the warehouse. I blocked the main entrance by jamming some metal into the edge of the door, but there is another way inside."

"How did you leave your room? Was Nakita inside with you?" Rotusea asked.

"No Gebel, do you remember me telling you I had an implant and you were perplexed why they would have given me an implant?"

"Yes, now that you bring it up."

"Well, they didn't give it to me, I uh, took it."

"From where?" Rotusea asked, looking at Gebel.

Having reached a higher level of trust for Gebel, Sean opened his mouth and pulled out the microchip. "I, uh, took it out of one of the giant's head."

With a look of shock and disbelief, Gebel looked at the chip closely and repeated his question. "Where did you get this?"

"I cut it out of one of those big green goons," Sean replied. "No offense."

"But how—how did you overpower the Quod and take his implant?"

"It just kind of happened. I had escaped Karna and was hiding in the warehouse. Then I decided to go back to my quarters and ran into him. While in the warehouse, I also found a large piece of metal that was extremely sharp and shaped like a sword, and when the Quod grabbed me from behind, I ran the metal through his guts and he dropped dead right behind me. Since the doors simply opened when your people walked up to them, I dragged the dead Quod next to the door but nothing happened, so I deduced that it must have been in his head but I couldn't pick him up so I decapitated him and raised his head and the door opened. Believe me when I say that it was the hardest thing I've ever had to do in my life, but I used the sword to crack his head open and sifted through his brain. I finally noticed that chip attached to the front of his skull and cut it away."

Gebel was somewhat amazed that Sean could have killed the Quod, cut open the skull and remove his implant and it changed his perception of the human subject.

"What about nourishment?" Gebel asked.

"Karna was taking us to some bright light in the center of the big room."

"Yes, the cinbiote. You must not go back in there. It is your only hope of survival."

"Karna told us it was for your good—that it killed bacteria that could kill you."

"Karna has no truth in her soul. She will tell you anything that she thinks will keep you confused. Let me explain how the cinbiote works. The light of the cinbiote seems brighter only because it is filtered through several million scrubbers that have a microscopic reflective surface that reflects and magnifies the intensity. We use a process similar to your pair annihilation. It's a process in which a particle and antiparticle unite, annihilate each other, and produce one or more photons. The process is used to recover spent radiation particles that we need to sustain life. The radioactive particles recovered are circulated everywhere on the Spiruthun at different levels, and are generated by a reactor much like that of your sun but without the heat. The cinbiote is nothing more than our waste stream of spent radioactive sub-particles that we are depositing into space. By accident it was discovered that the cinbiote could remove foreign bacteria and viruses that can kill us."

"I don't understand, after we were put into the cinbiote the first time, wouldn't that have removed anything harmful to you? And if so, why would Karna continue to take us there?"

"There was a man here, another subject like you, who escaped. We searched the entire vessel for weeks and could not find him. One day a maintenance drone had bypassed the cinbiote discharge in order to clean the filters and discovered the dead body of the man inside."

"But I thought it helped us regain our strength?"

"No, you see the cinbiote does not provide anything beneficial to humans except the absence of radiation all around. While it can help your species by curing radiation sickness, there is no other positive benefit, but the eventual outcome far out weights the benefit of the cure. It is not known how it works exactly, but many believe that the scrubbers themselves, being so small, actually go inside your body with every breath and pick up the radiation in your blood through the as they enter and exit your body through your lungs."

"Then why does it feel so good—so satisfying and fulfilling?"

"We believe the cinbiote light and heat to be a 99.7 percent match to that of your sun. However, in the concentrated beam, void of any contact, air, movement or smell—your species rely solely on their sense of sight. Again we can only theorize, but we believe that when you lose your other senses your brain begins to release chemicals that cause a feeling that triggers another chemical release and so on, until your brain is in a chain reaction of its own. When that point occurs we believe you can only live a few minutes more. When this occurs, the brain has reached a critical state which causes a non-stop flow of endorphins that stimulate the sense of euphoria. Another chemical release causes the release of old memories locked away for years. Between the memories and the endorphins flowing freely inside your brain, it becomes somewhat addictive. Eventually you would die from an overdose of your own chemicals."

"So why did Karna take us there more than once if it only takes one time to kill off the bad bacteria or viruses."

"Only the special humans they desire to keep alive more than a few days are taken there to protect them from all the radiation in the air. Also, you enjoy the euphoric high from being in the cinbiote that it becomes addictive after just a few visits. Thus the more times you go the more times you want to go and the longer you stay each time. Before too long you eagerly await the visit to the cinbiote and become a slave to us in order to get to spend time there. But, because of the ill effects of the cinbiote, and because you are more important to her than any other human subject has been before, you are never allowed to be inside the cinbiote for more than a few minutes."

"That makes some sense, I guess, but if we don't go to the cinbiote how will we be healed from the radiation exposure outside the cinbiote?"

"That's all I need to hear. I'll not be a slave to anything, or anyone!" Sean said emphatically. "But if I don't go to the cinbiote to be cured of the radiation out here, how long will I live?"

"You need not worry about that. We have another way of treating radiation poisoning. We will take you all there for a treatment very soon."

Sean was amazed with the technology but was more concerned with the destruction of the ship and escaping than remaining on the ship even if they had a cure for radiation poisoning. "Okay, Gebel, back to the business at hand." I believe we were talking about weapons and the start of a military coup."

"Yes, indeed we were." Gebel said nodding. "Tell me exactly where this warehouse is located where you found the weapons."

"Okay, on the Piiderk level there is the cinbiote we were just talking about. Do you know where I was being held?" Sean asked.

"No, I do not."

"This is going to be harder to explain than I thought. I can't give you any bearings or landmarks. All I know is that I left my room, ran to the light, the cinbiote, then turned to my left and ran about one hundred yards. The only thing I can tell you for certain is that the warehouse has an enormous doorway to the outside about sixty feet tall and one hundred feet wide. Oh, and one more thing, it is on the same side as the command center." Sean instructed.

Gebel turned to Rotusea and declared, "He must be talking about the forward storage chamber."

Rotusea nodded in agreement and replied, "He can lead a small team there during the resting phase. We can send enough Tahar to carry enough weapons to stage an attack on the Command Chamber and seize control of the vessel." She said excitedly.

Gebel thought for a moment silently. He stepped just outside the door where two Tahar soldiers were standing guard. "Gather up as many men as possible and go to the forward storage chamber just after the resting phase begins. We have learned that there are several storage containers full of weapons inside. Take as many as you can carry and hide them on the rapitor level where we normally meet. Make as many trips as you can during the resting phase to ensure that we have at least one for every team. When you think you have retrieved enough weapons and ammunition to cease control of the ship, purge the remaining contents of the chamber into space."

One of the two Tahar men looked at Gebel very seriously and said, "You understand what you are ordering?"

"Yes I do. Since the only other controls to the chamber are inside the Command Chamber, the loading door must be opened from the inside. Ask for a volunteer and make sure they understand what they are volunteering for."

Gebel walked back inside his chamber and ordered Rotusea to take the humans to a hiding place deep in the bowels of the ship away from the radiation where they would be safe. "Rotusea, you must remain with them. Go to the maintenance passage under the planetary transport unit and wait for word from me. Tell the humans as much as you can about our people, our weaknesses and this vessel. Don't forget to take several dighergant treatments along, I don't know how long you will have to stay."

Rotusea turned to explain what was going to happen and asked if he had any additional questions before they left.

"Yeah, Gebel," he said turning to face him. "If I'm going to take an active role in this coup, I'll need more than one person who can speak my language. Of those on board, how many have been—what you said—modified to allow them to speak our language?"

"The Tahar have about two hundred who can speak your language, but there are many more. Some of them were modified by the Bilkegine Empire as liaisons between our people and earth's once occupation of the planet commenced. However, some speak your English, while others speak Russian, German, French, Spanish and many other languages. There is at least one hundred Bilkegine modified for every language on earth."

"Good," Sean said nodding. "Can you arrange for me to lead a team of Tahar soldiers that all speak English, so we don't lose any time waiting for someone to translate. I'm going to want to have a big part of this coup. And more than anything in the world, I want Karna for myself."

Rotusea translated and Gebel nodded to confirm and said, "I understand and agree but right now we need to get you and Nancy to safety while we prepare for our attack." Turning back to Rotusea he waited for her to translate then gave her more instructions.

Rotusea took two other Tahar members with her to escort Sean and Nancy to the hiding place. As they left the long corridor just outside Gebel's chamber, Sean stopped Rotusea by grabbing her arm and asked about Nakita.

"What about the girl, Nakita," Sean asked.

"Gebel ordered us to leave her behind." She replied.

"Why?" asked Nancy, looking at Sean.

"He did not say," Rotusea answered, "He just told us to leave her behind, and I have learned that he knows what is best for our people."

Gebel called for an immediate meeting of his highest-ranking officers to plan their mutiny and the possible destruction of the vessel Spiruthun.

CHAPTER TWENTY

Before Sean and Nancy left, Gebel told them one more thing to remember. Through his translator Rotusea, he said, "When you are traveling through the brightest levels of the vessel and are not able to see clearly because of the bright light, it is because your eyes are accustomed to much more dimly lit environment. We on the other hand are used to the brilliant light of our planet's two suns. I tell you this to point out that when you are not able to see more than twenty feet, we have no problem seeing clearly over several hundred feet. Please keep this in mind when you have to travel through an open area. Oh and one last tip—never run. It will only draw attention to you and that we cannot afford."

Gebel stayed behind in his quarters and planned for their next mission, while Rotusea and the other two Tahar soldiers lead Sean and Nancy through the ship. Since they were on the falkoe deck at level thirteen and had to pass through more than forty other decks to reach their goal, Rotusea led them away from heavily traveled areas of the vessel and avoided the elevators completely. The vessel had no stairs, so each level had to be negotiated by a series of ladders more than forty feet in length. The only problem they had was Nancy's fear of heights and the fact that she was more afraid of the heights than she was of being captured again.

"Come on Nancy! I'm right below you and will not let you fall."

"Sean I am moving as fast as I can! These rungs are too far apart for my short legs!"

Rotusea kept calling for them to hurry. They had gone only three levels and from the bustle of everything on each level it would appear that the search for Sean and Nancy had been increased.

Half way down a ladder between levels sixteen and seventeen all the lights suddenly grew very dim then went dark completely. Nancy started to panic and cry as Sean was urging her to keep moving. He could see that while she was physically fit for the climb her mental condition was worsening under all the stress she had endured over the past weeks. Now weeping and shaky, Nancy was becoming dangerous to them all. If one of the Quod heard her crying, they could be easily located and because they were on the ladder it was becoming possible that they could be trapped between levels. The ladders were primarily used by maintenance drones and Quod, so the rungs were more than two feet apart.

"I'm sorry we must use these maintenance ladders, but it's the safest way to travel since they are inside the maintenance corridors." Rotusea said, pleading Nancy to hurry.

"Why are these stupid rungs so far apart anyway? They're nearly three feet apart." She asked.

"Because, they are primarily used by the maintenance drones and Quod, and they are both very tall. They are bred as special workers and warriors. Not only are they the largest, strongest and most loyal members of the Bilkegine working class, but they are considered expendable and therefore used in the most dangerous areas of the vessel."

With each step Nancy took she had to literally hang from one rung with both arms and search for the next rung with her feet. The progress was slow going at best because of her fear of heights, and short legs, but now that the lights were out, progress nearly stopped altogether.

"Nancy, if you fall back too far, we will have to go on without you." Rotusea said. She not only lacked the authority to make a decision like that, but had no desire to do so either. She thought that it might encourage her to speed things up if she was pressed and tried to use the fear of being caught by the Quod as a motivator.

"No, we will not, Nancy! Don't listen to her. Just listen to my voice, and we can get off these ladders and find another way down."

"We cannot," interrupted Rotusea. "We will not be able to see anything."

Sean wasn't worried because, while it looked pitch black to the Bilkegines, there was actually some light coming from somewhere. It was very dim, like the light from a half moon, but his eyes were growing accustomed to it and he knew Nancy's were too. "Listen, Rotusea, you know the way with your eyes closed, and I can see enough to look for landmarks as you describe the way to me! So let's get moving!"

Rotusea agreed, and Nancy took the last few steps before she was safely on firm ground again.

"What caused the lights to go out?" Sean asked.

"When the Spiruthun was struck by the meteoroid, it damaged our dighergant generators evacuation chamber. Attempts have been made to correct the problem, but it would appear that the chamber was not repaired in time to cause the chain reaction to fail. It is a mishap that will work to our benefit now that everyone but you and Nancy cannot see and will begin to weaken until it is repaired."

"Doesn't that mean you three as well, Rotusea?"

"Yes, but we have an ample supply of dighergant treatments with us."

"I find it hard to believe that something as simple as a meteoroid strike can disable your ship and kill everyone aboard," Sean said. "If it was that easy, why didn't the Tahar think of it years ago to stop this aggression?"

"It has only temporarily disabled the Spiruthun. There are backup systems that will initiate in less than three phases. We have until then to reach our destination."

"How long is a phase?"

"It is about one and a half of your earth hours and also our day depending on the context used and the inflections of our voice. We better get moving before someone discovers us in this maintenance corridor."

While they searched through the dark for passageways and had to work around the locked doors due to the power failure, an overwhelming fear started to grip Sean. He could not understand why, now of all times, the fear was gripping him so hard. After everything he had already been through, and now in the company of a significant ally, he thought he should be feeling more relieved instead of more afraid. Suddenly the reason became evident as they all turned a corner and ran into the biggest obstacle he could have imagined.

✳ ✳ ✳

As everyone in the war room watched as the two satellites were destroyed, they stood in absolute silence. It was nothing they were prepared for. Even with the knowledge of Roswell more than fifty years behind them they couldn't understand how an alien spacecraft could have been sitting in an orbit around the earth without them knowing anything about it until now. The professor was the first to break the silence.

"Gentlemen, I believe we have seen our enemy."

Shaken from the image by the professor's words, General Stephens started snapping orders. "Captain Bowe, I want those images printed, duplicated and ready for a brief of the heads of state by 0100 hours!"

"Yes Sir! I'm on it!" he replied.

"Dr. Weiss, you and your MIT boys put your heads together and get me another plan for reconnaissance."

"Come on boys," said the professor, "let's get busy and find a way around that thing!"

Agent Rose and Bruce had been standing on the balcony overlooking the war room. They had nothing they could do at the moment so they stood and watched in silence. General Stephens shouted more orders to different stations in the war room and turned to give James a knowing look. James nodded and motioned Bruce to follow him out.

"Where're we going?" asked Bruce

"We're going to D.C."

"Do you need me any longer, 'cause I feel 'bout as useful as teats on a bore hog."

"More than ever before, my friend, more than you could ever imagine."

They packed quickly and headed for the gate. Within just a few minutes they were on their way to the airport and the jet. With all that had happened in the last week, everyone's beliefs were being challenged. The events that were unfolding were challenging what they all believed to be the truth; that they were the only intelligent beings in the universe. Everyone's belief, except for a very select few, already knew better. And they were not even able to comprehend all the challenges they were facing.

"Can you tell me where we're going specifically and why you need me, James?"

"Sure, we're going to the White House to speak face to face with the President. You are the only one who I can think of that knows what our chances will be up there if your friend is still alive."

"How is that?"

"Because you know him better than anyone else alive, and in spite of what Dr. Ross wrote in his report, you know that Sean may very well be our only hope."

The jet landed in D.C., and James and Bruce were picked up and driven to the White House by an FBI agent. It was now 0200 hours in Washington and for the first time since the Cuban missile crisis, the President was awakened for a matter of national security. Another first was also about to occur—the Heads of State for nearly every major power on the planet would be at the briefing.

"Bruce, there is something that I need to tell you before our brief with the President."

"Shoot."

"I'm not sure how to tell you this, but given the circumstances, I'm going to just come out with everything at once. It'll be hard to grasp, but I need you to keep an open mind."

"Then get on with it already!" Bruce said nervously.

"Ok. Here goes. In 1942 we were visited by aliens. It wasn't anything like you have heard. There wasn't a crash where alien bodies and a spaceship were recovered either."

"What? No little green men?"

"No, that part is true. They were little and their skin did have a green hue to it. The part that wasn't true was how we came to possess the spacecraft. Didn't it ever surprise you how fast our country came to have knowledge of an atom bomb, computer technology and advanced flying craft of our own so quickly? Did you ever give it any thought at all how in a short twenty years we went from single prop aircraft to a ship capable of leaving our planet to explore space and land on the moon? Well, it was because of them."

"You're talking about the 'them' we just saw on the big screen?"

"Yes, we believe they are the very same."

"What have we seen so far that would confirm that?"

"As the images were coming in from the satellites, they were being simultaneously enhanced and encrypted so they could be sent to Washington. One of those images had several small dark specs just to the side of the spacecraft. When that image was enhanced and enlarged it was discovered that they were smaller, individual craft just like the craft we recovered from before. Records were pulled and examined against the new images and it was confirmed. They are identical in shape, size and color."

"Wait a minute. You just said there was no crash where bodies were recovered."

"That's right we didn't recover the craft from a crash. Let me explain."

"Please, you've got my curiosity up now."

"We were visited by spacecraft from another world, but it wasn't an observation or exploration mission that the aliens were on. It was a siege. The entire planet was under attack by the aliens, but since practically the whole world was in the middle of World War II, and there was a sense of political unrest between the nations, President Roosevelt met with Signals Intelligence corps better known as the SIGINT, and other cryptologists to try to find and decode their communications. This group was of course the pre-cursor of the NSA which was not officially formed until November 4, 1952. Also present were high ranking officers from every branch of our military and a few civilians who had expertise in areas like physics, electronics and explosives. This meeting took place in a cave in Arkansas and the sole purpose was to discuss ways to defend the US against these aliens. Our own historical experts all agree that the whole thing could have ended much differently if it hadn't been for one mountain man like you. The man's name was Adelais Dubois. He was a Frenchman who immigrated to the United States in 1911 and settled in the Blue Ridge Mountains. He was one of many citizens who were abducted prior to the attack but was, like Sean, a man with history. He fought bravely during World War I and was awarded many metals for bravery under fire. After the war, he returned to the solace of the mountains to try to escape from his nightmares. The one thing that he had that made him different than other abductees was a propensity for freedom. Shortly after he was taken, he escaped on board the alien craft and hid out. The aliens eventually gave up looking for him and continued with their mission to destroy earth and everyone on it, if that was their goal. But, Adelais Dubois decided to fight, and fight he did. He singlehandedly seized a weapon and took out the alien craft that launched the attack. Whatever he did set off a chain reaction of some kind inside the spacecraft and within an hour it was destroyed. The craft's orbit began to decay and the earth's gravitation pulled it into our atmosphere. It eventually crashed in the desert of Arizona just thirty five miles from Flagstaff, where it was obliterated. People today know the site as 'Meteor Crater', but now you know the real story. The smaller attack crafts that survived eventually ran out of fuel and either drifted into space or burned up upon re-entry to earth. All but one, that is, somehow, old Adelais Dubois managed to stow away on one of their smaller crafts just before it launched from the mother ship. The two aliens who were piloting the craft were, according to Adelais, friendly. He insisted that he would have surely died if it hadn't been for their help. Before they died, though, they were helpful in giving us some technology that we built upon. Adelais would never divulge what he had seen or what he did to the ship to destroy it. All he would say was, "I was there, you weren't, and I never want to think about it again." He went back home to the mountains, and he was never seen or heard from again. Of course we have the spacecraft but it has proven to be more of a puzzle than we have been able to decipher."

"So how could all of that be kept secret for all these years without someone at least making a death bed confession about their involvement?"

"Some did, but because of the government cover-ups and the ridicule that the story tellers received when they did come forward, no one believed them. Several were committed to mental institutions for telling their stories. Now, after we borrowed their technology, they have returned. The biggest problem being we never learned how to use or build the weapons that the ships were carrying. The Atomic Bomb was the first technology to come out of what we were able to learn."

"You remember that part at the beginning of this story where you told me it would be hard to swallow?" Bruce said. "You're right, it is hard to swallow."

"You are about to be taken to a place that has been kept a secret for all these years. It isn't on a secret military base like you read in the tabloids either. It was originally studied on an abandoned Air Force base in Arizona then moved into a storage facility in New Mexico where it stayed until April 8, 1976. From there it was moved to its final resting place right here in the middle of Washington in the sub-basement of the Smithsonian National Air and Space Museum, and that is where our briefing will be today."

"And, explain it again. I'm important how?"

"You are the best friend of Sean Daniels—our modern day Adelais Dubois."

"You didn't say how your Adelais destroyed the ship, or how you came to know the story so well."

"He would say he got off with God's help."

"That answers half my question." Bruce said waving his hand toward him as if to say, 'come on with the rest'.

"Let's just say—I haven't been completely forthcoming about one little detail."

"Come on James, you gonna make me beat it out of you?"

"Okay, calm down. I've already seen you angry and I think once is enough for anyone." James smiled. "When I said that no one ever saw or heard from him again, that didn't include one particularly special person, my grandfather."

"I should have known you had government spook in your bloodline. You're just too good at it. And, you told me how Adelais explained his escape. What do you think really happened?"

"What I think—I would say that he either got really lucky, or he paid close attention to every detail of how things worked and used them to his advantage."

"Ah ha, and you think Sean can do all that too."

"Bruce—I pray that he can because in my opinion, he is our only hope."

The FBI van they were traveling in pulled up to the Smithsonian Air and Space museum and stopped. Bruce and James got out and went into the building that was now closed and guarded by several men. As they reached the door they pulled out their identification badges and were allowed inside.

They walked through the enormous empty corridor to a glass elevator located in the middle of the main exhibit hall. Bruce reached out and pushed the call button. Up was the only option indicated and Bruce looked at James and said, "I thought you said it was underneath the Smithsonian."

"Just wait, you'll see." James said with a smile.

The elevator hummed as it arrived and the door swished open. The two men stepped inside and waited for the door to close. James took out a special key and inserted it into a slot on the face of the control panel and tapped a button at the top of the panel marked with the letter 'A'. The elevator began to ascend as Bruce stepped up to the glass and looked down on the exhibits below. "Nice view," he stated.

It continued up past the ceiling of the main exhibit hall then stopped. The door slid open and James stepped out into the huge expanse of a rooftop atrium filled with an overwhelming variety of plant life. Bruce stopped just outside the elevator and stood looking out into the jungle of greenery. "What's all of this?" Bruce asked with his arms stretched out in front of him.

James laughed. "It's a greenhouse, what did you think?"

Bruce waved him off and began to follow him. James reached the center of the room and turned down a narrow path nearly overgrown with large leaves. Bruce pushed them aside as he followed closely behind. They came to a small clearing in front of a set of steel doors. Once again, James produced a special magnetic key card. He waved it over the center of the doors and they sprang open revealing another elevator much smaller than the first. James stepped inside first and moved aside allowing Bruce to fit in beside him. Bruce was amazed at how tight the security was without having to be guarded. "Boy you really know how to make something secure don't you?"

"It's harder than you think when you have to hide something in plain sight. If there were guards all around, it would make people suspicious and they would want to know what was inside."

"That makes sense."

"Let me tell you something before we go any further my friend. I can count the number of people who know about this entrance on one hand. I don't have to tell you—once you go past this point, there is no going back. Your life will never be the same again."

"Believe me James, my life has already been turned on its ear. My whole concept of life has been changed to the point that I'm not sure what is real anymore. You're not telling me nothin."

"I'm talking about security, Bruce. From now on you will have people watching you. They'll know what you do on a daily basis, where you go on vacation and who you talk to. I guess what I'm saying is that if you ever had a secret, you won't anymore. You sure you want to continue?"

"I've got nothing to hide, James. And if it makes the difference between my seeing my best friend again live, I'd do anything. Let's go!"

James hit a series of numbers on the control panel and a panel popped open on the side of the elevator wall. James placed his right hand on the panel and a blue light came on and scanned his palm. The light went out and James closed the door and leaned into the panel and said, "Agent James Albert Rose, 4873495701." The elevator began to descend rapidly then came to an abrupt stop. The doors slid open and James said, "We're here."

Bruce stepped out of the elevator and noticed a sign below a black icon that read 'B12'. "Does everyone that comes here have to go through that whole rig-a-ma-role?"

"Yes and no. If the few that know about the elevator entrance come then the answer is, yes. But for those who use the secret underground tram that links this place to the White House and other strategic buildings in Washington, then no. They have their own set of security protocols to go through. Believe me, those are a lot tougher to get through."

"So tell me, where exactly are we now?"

"We are now one hundred and twenty feet below the basement level of the Smithsonian. The elevator we used from the rooftop and the underground tram are the only ways in. This building was built for this purpose and the whole Smithsonian Air and Space Museum is a cover. The floors above us are air tight, lead lined and waterproof, and the first level below the museum basement level is covered with twenty feet of reinforced concrete. Most of the floors above are used to store extremely secret and sensitive materials, and have also served as maximum security prisons to hold political prisoners and spies that managed to breech security in some very special government agencies that most people don't even know exists, including most Presidents. This lowest level has been used by a few of our Presidents at one time or another, and both Kennedy and Nixon used it for strategic planning during times of war. They met here because of the tight security needed and the fact that it was the only place that could be guaranteed to be bug free."

"Why were they fearful of bugs?" Who would bug them?"

"You have to remember that the CIA and a few other agencies that I won't mention were very independent agencies, especially back then, and both Kennedy and Nixon were planning political assassinations, both foreign and domestic."

"Who were they planning on killing?"

"If I told you that, I'd have to kill you," James said laughing. "Just think about it a minute and you can come up with a few names they might have wanted to get rid of."

"Ah—yeah," Bruce mumbled rubbing his chin."

James started walking down a long hallway directly across from the elevator and Bruce followed close by until they stood outside a double door marked, 'Flash Back'.

"It's time," James said patting Bruce on the shoulder. "Just give them what you have, and be completely candid, and remember, you are the expert here where Sean is concerned."

"Alright, let's go."

CHAPTER TWENTY-ONE

With the power failure still a problem for the Bilkegine, Sean thought the trip to the hiding place that Gebel had told him about would be a breeze. Except for Nancy's fear of heights, it had been. However, just as they turned a corner a few levels down from Gebel's quarters, they ran into Quods. This time it wasn't just a couple, it was hundreds of them. Sean turned white with fear and nearly passed out at the sight of so many Quod warriors. Another thing that made them more opposing was the fact that they were armed. Rotusea took the lead and started to go right into the room with all the Quod, before Sean grabbed her arm and pulled her back.

"Are you crazy? There is no way I'm going in that room! There has to be another way." Sean screamed in a whisper.

"Do not worry, these Quods are warriors. Their mission is to take your planet by force, and they probably do not even know of your existence."

"They'll certainly know if we go through that room! Besides, Nancy is more afraid of them than I am. She'll freak out!"

"No Sean. Listen to me. For these Quod to react to you or us in any way would require that they think beyond what they have been ordered to do. They are not capable of individual thought beyond how to execute a specific order and they can only comprehend and remember one simple order at a time. Warrior Quods are programmed for one thing and one thing only—search and destroy."

"That's exactly what I am afraid of Rotusea. They will see us without having to search for us and they will execute us in the process of executing their last order."

"That is not how they think. A warrior Quod thinks in terms of fighting against armies not an individual man. Even on the planet surface while executing their direct orders to search and destroy, they are searching for groups of men, armies, not the individual. If you were to walk up to a warrior Quod alone, he would most likely just ignore you. I've seen it happen before. You have to trust me on this."

"I'm sorry—but that level of trust doesn't come that easy for me Rotusea. Besides, how can you tell the difference between a warrior Quod and the other big ugly Quod that have been guarding Karna since we arrived? They all look the same to me."

"No, they are not the same. Sure they were all cloned from the same breeding stock, but there is a distinct difference."

Rotusea stepped into the doorway to get a closer look at the crowd of Quod in the room. She scanned each group looking for a security Quod so she could point out the differences. "Look," she said pointing into the room. "Do you see the large transparent panel covering the Zurostian Chamber?"

"The Zuro, uh, sti, uh, what? I'm not sure."

"There," she pointed again, "the clear chamber with the blue haze inside, it is our Zurostian Chamber. What words would you use, uh, mind altering chamber?"

"You mean the octagon shaped box against the wall with the blue clouds inside?"

"Yes, that is it. Do you see the Quod standing near the controls? Look closely, he is a security Quod. See how he stands and the way his shoulders extend beyond his chest?"

"Yeah, I see that, kinda hunchback?"

"Now look at one of the armed warrior Quods. You see how much straighter his spine is and how his shoulders are in line with his neck? That is one way to tell them apart."

"That's it? I have to examine their posture and try to determine if their shoulders are rounded in front of them? That may not be that easy if there are a lot of them in a room."

"It is not the only way. The easiest way is to examine their faces. The security Quods have large nodules on their face but the warrior Quod have scale like skin on their whole bodies. Look at their arms up close and you can see it easily."

"It sounds extremely dangerous to me. It sounds like I would have to be within ten feet to see the difference and that's just a little too close for comfort."

"Well there is another way you can tell if there is a security Quod close enough to find you. They are trained by smell. When you were first brought here, you were stripped and given those tunics. Your clothes were given to the Quod in order to learn your smell. They can find anyone once they are trained for that person up to about seventy distinct odors. So, if you see a Quod looking around quickly, he has smelled you and is trying to determine where your scent is coming from."

"You mean to tell me that those humungous maniacs are like Bloodhounds?"

"I do not know what a—Bloodhound is."

"They are a species of canine with an extraordinary sense of smell, giving them an exceptional ability to track a person with their nose, once they have been given something with their scent on it."

"Then, yes, in that instance they are like your Bloodhound. So let's go."

"Hold on! We already know there's a security Quod in there. You just pointed him out to me. Are you crazy?"

"Sean, you must trust me. He will not be able to pick up your scent with the other warrior Quods so close to him. The warrior Quod odor is very distinct and overwhelming. With so many around him, it will cover up your scent."

"Okay, if you say so, I guess I'll trust you. But just in case, I want to be prepared," he said as he pulled the weapon out of his backpack.

"No!" Rotusea said quickly as she covered the weapon with her hands. "If just one of them sees that weapon, they might consider us a threat and fight us."

"Just a minute ago you said they would only attack an armed group?"

"Yes that is correct, and if you are armed, we become an armed group not just an individual."

"Oh, yeah, I see your point. Alright then, let's go," Sean replied, as he put the weapon away. "But let me explain this to Nancy and give her a moment to prepare mentally."

Sean went to where Nancy was leaning against the wall and explained what to expect when she rounded the corner. "Don't worry, I won't let go of your hand. Just stay behind me as close as you can and look down at the floor, we'll slowly walk right through them."

Rotusea took the lead and began to walk into the room. Sean and Nancy were immediately behind her, followed by the other two Tahar soldiers who were escorting them. As they walked by the Quod it was difficult not to unintentionally brush up against them because there were so many in the room. Sean's heart was beating three times the normal rate and he was sure that Nancy would be near collapse. They walked along one wall toward a door opposite where they had entered. They had made it past the Quod and only had about thirty yards to go before they were out of sight. It was difficult for Sean and Nancy to resist the overwhelming urge to run the remaining distance but they managed partly out of fear of drawing attention to themselves and because Rotusea was directly in front of them. They finally reached the doorway and even though the immediate danger was behind them, Sean could still feel the adrenalin rushing through his veins. Sean knew from his experience in Vietnam that intentionally ignoring the fight or flight response to a stressful situation always left him shaky and weak, so the biological effects he was feeling were no surprise. As Rotusea stepped through the door she ran into three security Quods. She instantaneously turned and yelled, "Hide!" but could not move fast enough to avoid being shoved to the floor as they reached for Sean.

Hide where, Sean thought as he grabbed Nancy and ran into the middle of the warrior Quods still milling around the room. They stopped and turned around to see if the three security Quods had successfully followed them, but it was exceedingly difficult for Sean to see over the heads of the warrior Quods, and was only able to catch an occasional glimpse through the crowd. He led Nancy across the room then turned and worked his way around the outside of the warrior Quods until he finally reached the door where Rotusea and the Tahar soldiers were waiting.

"Come on, let's get out of here." Sean said as he led Nancy through the door and onto another enormous expanse.

"Where to now, Rotusea?" Sean asked impatiently.

"Proceed another forty yards until you come to a corridor on your left. Stay close to the wall and make sure there are no Quods. There will be an access panel not more than twenty feet down that hallway on the right side near the floor."

It was getting darker and more difficult for Sean to see with each progressive level they passed, too dark for him to make out the access panel. I'm sure that I've gone at least twenty feet by now, he thought. He was walking down the right side of the corridor with his hands against the wall so he wouldn't miss it but feeling like he had traveled the distance that Rotusea instructed, he didn't know what to do.

"Rotusea, I don't see the access panel, and I know we've gone at least twenty feet. What should we do now?"

"I know another way but it would mean going down two more maintenance passageways on the ladders."

"No way," Nancy said firmly. "Sean, I am not getting on another ladder, especially when it's so dark. There has to be another way."

Rotusea was telling Nancy that it was the access panel or the maintenance passageways, one or the other when one of the Tahar escorts began talking to Rotusea. They argued for a couple of minutes before Rotusea explained.

"Wigdrake has offered another solution but I do not think it a very safe alternative. His idea involves us traveling right through the middle of two levels."

"That's fine with me," Nancy said. "Let's go already."

"What's your reservation with the plan, Rotusea?" Sean asked.

"We would have to maneuver them in total darkness and I do not believe it is possible. Besides that, you must remember that the Quod do not need sight to find you in the dark. They would be able to walk right up to you and take you without us seeing them come."

"I think it's worth the risk. Not only will we be able to avoid the ladders but we will make much better time getting where we're going." Sean commented.

"You have a valid point, but I have been charged with your safety and what would Gebel say if you were recaptured?"

"I don't know what he would say but this I do know. I am in charge of me and I am looking out for Nancy. I've done pretty well on my own this far and you have to admit you weren't much help back there when the three security Quods nearly caught me. If it hadn't been for my quick reflexes and fast thinking, they would have too. I guess you have to make the final call since I don't know where we're ultimately going, but I say we go for it."

"Very well, Sean." Rotusea relented. "You take the lead since you can see better than me, and we will all form a chain by grasping hands so no one gets left behind. We must walk briskly to get through quickly and avoid running into any Quod that might catch your scent."

Rotusea gave Sean the directions needed to successfully maneuver through the two levels, and instructed him on the landmarks that would ensure he was on the right course.

They made it through the first level without any problems and Sean thought that the second would be easier since there were less obstacles to avoid, but halfway across the lights began to come back on and they realized that the room they were in on that level had twelve security Quods inside with them. Sean knew if they were going to make it they would have to run blindly through them before the lights were back to one hundred percent. What he didn't know was that the Quods had picked up his scent the moment they stepped onto the level and had began walking toward the smell. As the lights got a little brighter, Sean was aware that the Quods had him surrounded and were moving slowly in. Rotusea and the Tahar had fallen behind and could not see clearly enough to know the danger Sean and Nancy were facing. Sean shoved Nancy to the floor while simultaneously removing his weapon. "I will not be taken again!" Sean yelled as loud as he could. He opened fire at the Quod directly in front of him and began to circle as he was firing. With each shot fired, Quod were literally blowing up. Blood, green slime and body parts were flying all over the room. Upon hearing the first shot ring out, Rotusea and the two Tahar men opened fire with their much smaller weapon but it had little effect to stave off the onslaught of Quod moving on Sean and Nancy. Each time Sean pulled the trigger two exploding rounds left the chamber and found a target. Within a few seconds the lights were at full brightness and Rotusea and the Tahar men could see the carnage Sean had caused. Still in a stage of panic, with the adrenalin pumping like he had never felt before, Sean continued circling and firing. The weapon began to heat up and a few seconds later, seized. Sean continued to pull the trigger but all he heard was a slight hum. Then, finally calming down a little bit, he realized that he had not only annihilated every last Quod in the room on that level and successfully created a path to the exit, but had inadvertently killed one of the Tahar escorts. He helped Nancy get to her feet and ran to where the dead soldier lay. Rotusea and the other Tahar soldier were knelt beside him looking somber.

Nancy covered her mouth with her hand and began to cry softly while Sean knelt down beside Rotusea. "I'm so sorry, Rotusea. I just lost my head. I didn't even think about you being in the line of fire. Oh, God, what have I done?" Sean said grieving over the loss of the Tahar man who had been looking out for them.

"What is done is done," Rotusea told the other soldier in her own language, as she looked up from her fallen comrade toward the other soldier. "He has died for his cause. Many more will fall before this task is fulfilled."

He nodded and reached down and took the secret communicator from the fallen soldier and passed it to Rotusea. They stood up and looked down at Sean who was still holding his face in his hands.

"Sean, he has died protecting you and fighting for your kind. His death will mean nothing if you do not survive. We must go on now."

Sean looked up at them both confused and amazed at how they reacted to their fallen brother in arms. He knew they were different, but indifference was something he did not expect. "How can you just leave him here? Don't you feel sympathetic for his death?

"Yes, we do. But what would you have us do? We all have sworn an oath to the death to make your planet and people safe. He has fulfilled his oath. We must go now or his death will be wasted."

Sean felt horrible for having taken a life by friendly fire. He knew it was not going to be as easy for him to get over as it seemed to be for the Tahar. He slowly got up and put his arms around Nancy and stood quiet while she finished a prayer for the fallen soldier.

Once again Rotusea called for Sean to hurry so Sean gently turned Nancy away from the dead Bilkegine man and lead her toward Rotusea. As before Sean lead the Tahar through the dimly lit room and into the corridor as he was instructed earlier. He could now see clearly where Rotusea wanted them to go and was waiting for her and the soldier to catch up. Just as he turned to see where they were, he caught sight of more Quod coming in the far distance.

"Let's go!" Sean said impatiently. "There are more Quod coming!" Rotusea and Wigdrake caught up, but before Sean took a step, Rotusea stopped him and explained that they wouldn't be able to get away.

"What's the hold up, Rotusea?"

"It will not work as we planned now. The Quod have found your scent and will only follow you until you are found." She explained.

"So what do we do, stop here and fight?"

"No, more will keep coming until you are either caught or run out of ammunition."

Sean knew she was right; that they were sure to track them until they were eventually caught. "Think man, think!" Sean said to himself. How can we get out of this mess? He thought. Then in dawned on him, the clothes… "We need to put them off our trail, just like the Bloodhounds." He said quickly. "Here, take this," he ordered as he took off his shirt.

Nancy followed suit removed her tee-shirt and handed it to Wigdrake.

"Take these," Sean instructed. "Go up several levels and then split up the clothes before you go a different direction. We will hide out on this level somewhere until the Quod pass us by and follow you. Hopefully they will pick up the scent and assume that we merely stopped here to rest and went on. If they are as dumb as a box of hammers like you said, perhaps they will just ignore us and go on."

"Not good enough," Rotusea interrupted. "The smell of your bodies will be stronger than the scent of your clothes. They will stay here and search until you are discovered."

Sean thought about it a second as he looked around the room for a fresh idea. "Oh, no they won't! I've got an idea. It won't be pleasant, but it will be better than the alternative. We will hide under those bodies." He said pointing to the mass of blood, puss and body parts lying around on the floor.

"Sean, no, there's no way I can lay under one of those things!" Nancy said in disgust. "No!" She repeated shaking her head. "It's not going to happen."

"Nancy, we don't have time to argue about it. It's either this or..."

"Or you are taken and Karna will enact her revenge." Rotusea said, completing Sean's sentence.

"Tell him to leave now and do as I instructed." Sean ordered.

Nancy walked up to face Sean. "Sean, please, isn't there some other way?" She pleaded.

"I'm afraid not, honey. Look, they are big enough to conceal us and they stink so badly that their smell will more than cover up ours. I know it's nasty and beyond your worst nightmare, but it's our only hope and they are getting closer." He said softly. "Come on, I don't want to lose you. It will be okay, I promise."

"No, it won't be okay, but I know you're only thinking of our survival, so, okay."

They all walked briskly toward the pile of bodies and Rotusea lifted up one of the bodies as Sean helped Nancy get underneath. "Close your eyes and think about something else." He instructed. "And, breathe through your mouth so you won't get sick."

As soon as Nancy was tucked securely under one of the dead Quod, Rotusea lifted another one about ten feet away and Sean climbed under. He was trying to imagine he was buried under the warm sand on a beach he once visited but as soon as some of the still warm blood and puss ran down his bare side he lost his imagination. Rotusea told them she would stay close by and retrieve them once the coast was clear.

No more than a few seconds after the Quod that Sean had seen in the distance appeared in the room where they were hiding, Nancy heard their grunts and growls as they entered the room and tried to hold her breath. The pressure of the humungous alien bodies was immense and she found it hard to breath when she finally tried to take another breathe. The Quod circled the mass of bodies as they tried to figure out what had happened. Then, as if an alarm sounded, they caught the smell of the clothes the Tahar soldier had taken with him and left the room following their trail. Rotusea waited for a couple more minutes before she went back to recover Sean and Nancy from their bloody graves. Nancy was the first to be freed and as she slid out from under the body she was crying and trembling from the stress of her ordeal. Sean came out gasping for breath as if he had been trying to hold his breath the entire time. He immediately went to Nancy's side and helped her to her feet and embraced her. They were both covered from head to foot with the blood, slime and some oily substance that made them almost retch. They stood in each other's arms for quite some time before Rotusea, who was standing silently beside them, began to speak.

"We had better get moving," she said quietly. It was not in her nature to be caring, at least not in the way that she saw in Sean and Nancy, but she was learning that the Human race had many good traits that she thought the Bilkegine people could benefit from.

Sean took Nancy's hand and Rotusea led them to their destination. At the very least, the solitude of the dark, cold maintenance passage would give them a break from all the running, but it would also give Sean more time to plan their escape, and Nancy time to recuperate from the ordeal. They all knew that it wouldn't be over for quite a while, but for the time being, they found some degree of comfort in each other's arms.

CHAPTER TWENTY-TWO

Gebel called a meeting of his Tahar soldiers. The time had come to begin the battle against Karna and the Shem, the ruling alliance of their planet. It was clear to all the Tahar leaders that a conventional battle against the Shem would be futile. Without the Quod on the side of the Tahar, the losses would be so great that one battle would decide the outcome of the Bilkegine, and that outcome would mean the annihilation of the human race.

Fifty Tahar officers had gathered in a maintenance corridor that was ran by drones. The corridor provided a safe place for them to meet because it was a treatment facility for the Bilkegine waste stream and was filled with chemical clouds hazardous enough to strip paint from a hundred feet away. The drones who were assigned to the treatment facility only had a life expectancy of several months because of their exposure to the chemicals, but were considered expendable due to some previous violation of offense they had done against a higher ranking officer. The site was a safe place to meet for that very reason, but it was also a health hazard for the Tahar. Gebel knew that the exposure would have long term effects on their health, but they all knew the risks when they signed up.

Gebel walked into the meeting room holding a cloth over his face in an effort to protect his lungs from the caustic cocktail of chemicals used to break down the waste. He began his meeting with the statement of resolve that they all swore to before leaving their planet.

"Tahar brothers, I have come to inform you that our final stand against the Shem, and Karna, has begun! When we left our planet we all knew that it would be a one-way mission. We sacrificially came across the cold vacuum of space to this tiny, blue planet with one goal in mind. That goal, my brothers was to stop the Shem at all costs! We all came here, leaving our families behind, with the knowledge that we may all die for the freedom to make a new life for them and all Bilkegine."

The Tahar soldiers cheered at the sound of freedom. The wars that had been fought in the shadows for three generations were not about simply taking power away from the Shem; it was about having the power to make change. The desired changes were so revolutionary to the Bilkegine thinking that many among the Tahar thought them unachievable, but worthy enough to fight for and to even die attempting: Freedom to live one's own life, to have individual thought and purpose and to rule no one by laws that weren't for everyone; including the Shem ruling alliance.

"We came united with conviction of heart that one race of beings cannot live on the backs of a weaker race, that the honor of the Bilkegine race is more important than life at any cost, that peaceful co-existence with other species is possible and should be the only avenue that the Bilkegine people pursue. Some of us have died, and others will follow in their footsteps, but the Tahar will not be defeated! Thousands of years before the Shem, our people lived in harmony with each other and with our planet and neighboring planets, but in only a few generations under the Shem, the Bilkegine people have become a race of takers. We will be no more!"

Again the crowd of Tahar officers cheered their leader. They had all sworn to fight to the death, if need be, to defeat the Shem and return the power of decision back to individuals who had a voice in all matters. Now the time had come for them to act.

"We will bring the fight to them. We will come out of the shadows and let the Shem leadership, including Karna, know that we are among them in numbers! No more will we hide in the darkness and sabotage missions silently. We will stand proud and strong against the tyranny that the Shem represents in the name of survival and let them know that, without our honor, life is not worth living! Join with me now to defeat the poison that has infected so many of the Bilkegine race! Join with me to stamp out the Quod and other slaves of the Shem belief! We are now the minority among the mighty but we all know in our hearts that good will overcome evil, that right will overcome wrong, and that tyranny has a name, and it is the Shem!"

For the last time, the Tahar soldiers cheered their leader. Gebel wasn't just a good motivator or speaker, he was a good leader, a tried and true disciple of peace through war, and they knew that he would be the first in battle to prove his loyalty and devotion to the cause that he was willing to die for and willing to lead others into death for.

During the cheers, Gebel nodded, and several top officers of the Tahar who had been standing in the front row came forward and faced the soldiers present. One by one, Gebel recognized the officers, introduced them to the soldiers and let each of them speak to the ones who would serve under them. Each of them had a specific mission and section of the Spiruthun they would be responsible for taking control of or destroying. They all made a brief speech that demonstrated to the soldiers how dedicated they were to the cause and ultimate goal for the Bilkegine. Gebel returned to the front of the soldiers and gave them their final orders.

"Fellow Tahar, take heed. This battle will be the most important we have ever fought. This battle will determine the outcome of the entire Bilkegine race and it will set us all apart as martyrs for the cause, if we should perish in our attempts. Pay close attention as you take your positions and strike against the Shem. The Quod, as many of you know, are a formidable enemy who does not have any conscience, regret or moral integrity. They were created by the Shem for one thing, and one thing only, to follow orders without thinking. None of them will feel pain as you and I may feel it. They will not go down easily, and since we are grossly out-numbered, by more than a hundred to one, we must fight smart. We must strike and strike hard, then retreat to strike again. We must be tenacious in successfully meeting our objectives and not waiver. As hard as it may seem, we must not attempt a rescue if one of our brothers is captured. We have all sworn to uphold our strict code of silence and to take our own lives before endangering the lives of our

Tahar brothers. Although it may be extremely difficult, we must also be willing to take the life of our brother if they lack the fortitude to take their own life if captured. Tahar brothers, I salute your courage and willingness to sacrifice your own lives for those of the human species."

Gebel stepped back a few paces and struck the Tahar salute, usually reserved for soldiers honoring their leaders, by kneeling on one knee and lowering his head. It was a gesture showing their loyalty and willingness to give their life sacrificially for their leader. The other Tahar officers then followed Gebel's example and held their salute until every soldier was able to recognize the salute and return the gesture.

"One last thing before I turn you over to your officers. There is a human man and woman on board the Spiruthun that are essential to the success of Karna's plan. He is in our care at present and is being instructed in ways that he can help our cause. He is believed to be the Earth's most intelligent, and bravest warrior and he has demonstrated his willingness and ability to defeat our enemies by single-handedly killing a Quod with nothing more than a piece of metal fashioned into a primitive weapon. Furthermore, he has discovered a new weapon that we were unaware of and given us the location so we might take possession. This weapon is unlike any that we have seen and is capable of delivering a massive blow to the Shem, so take comfort knowing that we will be equally armed against our foe."

At that time Gebel turned and faced the Tahar officers and saluted them. He then turned the soldiers over to the officers for their assignments and left the room. One at a time, the officers addressed the soldiers under them and divided them into groups of specialized attack teams. Each officer then appointed the team leaders, and when the teams had assembled, gave each of them a specific mission.

Gebel had already formed his teams in advance of the meeting and had assigned each man his individual mission. His team's first assignment was to retrieve the new weapons from their hiding place, and distribute them among the other teams. Their second assignment was to assassinate essential officers in Karna's alliance, saving Karna for himself.

CHAPTER TWENTY-THREE

The lowest level of the Smithsonian held decades of records that archived different Blue Book projects of the United States government, along with other artifacts of alien origin. When James and Bruce had gotten off the elevator, they stepped into a long, dark and musty smelling corridor several hundred feet long by ten feet wide. The lighting that had been installed during the construction was never intended to meet the needs of the modern day use of the facility and consisted of a single bulbed fixture every twenty feet. The old archway construction of the doorways was brick over concrete with many of the doors removed and bricked closed. As they walked in unison down the hallway the echo of each footstep could be heard seconds after they stopped. By all appearances, they were the only ones on the level. Nothing but the echo of their steps and voices could be heard, as Bruce questioned James.

"So, what else is stored down here beside all these files?" Bruce asked.

"If we have any time after the meeting, I'll give you the nickel tour of the place. Remember that you are now in a place unknown to all but a handful of people, and what you see here must never be discussed, not even with Maggie."

"Yes, I understand that, but you can't expect me not to be curious."

"No, I suppose not, but let's wait until after the briefing. I need you to be thinking about Sean and what you will say to those in attendance."

They stopped at a steel door that looked like it had been made by an old blacksmith. It had very thick panels that were welded and riveted together with thick, wide bands of iron. The door actually matched the brick archway design, until James opened a small panel made from the same materials as the door revealing an electric key pad and scanner. Like before, James entered a series of nine numbers, then placed his entire palm onto the scanner and waited for the blue light to pass down over his palm and back to the top. A beep sounded, and James then entered a second set of nine numbers before the door made a buzzing sound indicating that the door could be pushed open. When they stepped inside the next room, Bruce was amazed at what he saw. Not only was the room as brightly lit as a ball park, but there were at least fifty scientists in white lab coats running around a very sophisticated laboratory.

James led Bruce through the middle of the room, seemingly unnoticed by everyone working around them. As they walked through, Bruce was scanning the room in every direction looking at what everyone was working on, and the things he saw looked like something out of a science fiction movie. One particular item drew his attention. Behind a transparent wall, he saw a scaled down version of a flying machine that resembled the ubiquitous flying saucer. It even had a thick white fog surrounding it. What amazed him the most was the fact that it seemed to be flying itself. He looked to see a man standing inside and expected to see a remote control, but all he was doing was scanning the craft with a handheld electronic device of some kind. Everywhere he looked he saw something that he not only had never seen before, but didn't even know existed. Most of them were defying what physical laws he remembered from high-school science class.

It wasn't long before they came to another old hallway with several glass doors lining it. Painted on each door was a sign indicating the purpose for the room or a name indicating which project the room was dedicated. James walked immediately to the door marked "Flash Back", and let Bruce inside. This room, unlike the other, was filled from top to bottom with file drawers and every inch of the rooms walls were covered with this file system. It resembled the stacks in a major university library except instead of books there were file cabinets. The room was thirty feet tall and had three balconies around the edge of the room allowing files to be easily accessed. On one end of the room sat a large conference table made of heavy walnut, with forty high back leather chairs around it. Bruce thought it odd that the room was void of any modern equipment. There were no televisions, computers, security cameras or monitors, or recording devices, and upon closer examination, not even electrical outlets. It was as if they had stepped back in time a hundred years and were waiting for the members of a symposium to gather for a debate. He couldn't help but chuckle after having been in the most technologically advanced room he had ever seen or thought even existed.

"Something funny Bruce?" James said as he turned.

"Oh, it's nothing. I was just thinking…"

"Yeah, probably the same thing I thought the first time I was brought here. Where is the high tech stuff?"

"Yeah," Bruce smiled. "Somethin' like that, this where we're gonna have the briefing?"

"Yes, but we're a day early. We have to prepare for the meeting first."

"I thought I was just going to talk about Sean?"

"You are, but many of the top scientists working on different projects that are related will be presenting possible solutions to our problem as well."

"What do we have to get ready?"

"Documents—I have had a team of people working on these old files for months trying to gather information that will help us paint a picture for the Heads of State that we will be addressing."

"I'm confused. I thought you only found out about the spacecraft a few days ago with the rest of us."

"Yeah, that's right."

"Then why would you already have people working on it?"

"Simple, we didn't have specific knowledge of the spacecraft, but we did know that people were being abducted. We just didn't know how, when, why and where until the ship was located."

"So you knew it all along?" Bruce asked with a puzzled look on his face.

"Yes."

"But I don't get it. Why didn't the rest of the world know anything about it? Why keep these things a secret all these years? I thought the government was only hiding stuff like who killed Kennedy and whether the moon landing was real or staged."

James turned back and laughed when Bruce mentioned Kennedy and the moon landings but before he said anything else he walked over to one of the filing cabinets and pulled out a file. The jacket read, 'Prometheus'. He handed the file to Bruce, and as he was scanning through the pages, James began to answer his question.

"You will find within that document, detailed stories by credible witnesses of alien activity on our planet dating back as far as the early nineteen hundreds. At the time the earliest stories were documented, the country was going through a rough war that was tearing the world apart. Many of our countries' leaders were convinced that the United States was being attacked by another country. They believed that the alien activity was in fact an attempt to achieve military supremacy over the United States. In an attempt to ascertain the true meaning of those occurrences, they developed a team of researchers to investigate the unusual reports. The project was dubbed, Prometheus."

"Why Prometheus?"

"Prometheus was one of the Greek gods, and was the wisest Titan. His name means 'forethought' and he was known as the protector and benefactor of men."

"So, what you are telling me is that everything in this file and all of those files actually happened the way they are recorded?" And if used properly will help us protect man?" Bruce asked pointing to the files all around the room.

"Well—part of it is true. Yes, as near as we have been able to tell, everything happened just like they are recorded. But—they aren't all in these cabinets, on paper documents." He replied as he turned and walked to the other side of the room and opened a file drawer. He reached inside the cabinet and pulled all the file folders to the front, reached inside and activated a switch. He then pushed the files back to their original position, closed the drawer, and stepped back to the center of the room. James looked up and then back to Bruce, then back to the ceiling. As Bruce stood up and peered into the darkness of the ceiling more than thirty feet away, he heard a slight humming sound. A lighted column more than fifteen feet in diameter began to descend from the middle of the ceiling.

"What is it?" Bruce asked.

"Wait, you'll see."

When it finally stopped, it was table high and had a flat glass surface surrounding a stack of highly complex, computers. The entire table surface had touch sensitive glass keyboards and eight working stations each with their own monitors. James reached under the class table and pulled out and unfolded a seat then sat down and began to type. Suddenly the monitor began to display a streaming list of names, dates, places and times. "As you can see, nearly everything we believed to be of some importance has been archived on this computer. This file contains the names, places, dates and times of most of the abductions since they were first recorded. We even ran cross checks to see if there were any patterns, you know, like whether or not the descendants of an abductee was ever taken. Stuff like that."

Bruce was amazed as he watched the screen flow with names in alphabetical order. Then he noticed something peculiar, "Hold on, go back!"

"What is it?"

"Just go back a little bit." Bruce said. "There! You've got Sean Daniels name right there. How did his name get there so quickly?"

James stopped the automatic scrolling of the names and double clicked on Sean's name. The monitor displayed another page with a complete dossier on Sean that covered his life's history from the time he was born to present, including his current abduction.

"Hey, James, what does this mean?" He asked, pointing out the dates beside Sean's name.

James looked into Bruce's eyes for a couple of seconds before he answered. "Those are the dates that Sean has been abducted before."

"What? How is that possible?"

"We've been tracking Sean for years now, Bruce. Ever since he disappeared in front of his entire fire-team during a reconnaissance mission in Vietnam, then re-appeared two weeks later with the story that he blacked out."

"Did the story check out?"

"Not entirely. The rest of his entire squad was killed a week later while on another mission. All we had to go on was the report in his file. But, Sean was the only one in his team to survive the massacre and didn't remember a thing. When he first showed back up at camp, his commander suspected him of working with the enemy, but later, during other battles, Sean proved to be almost indestructible. Anyway, as I was saying before, years went by and other, more recent, reports came in to the group, and as the information continued to stream in, the investigators continued to examine it. These rooms are full of that evidence."

"And that's what those scientists are working on out there?"

"No, but they are working on more recent evidence. You remember I told you that our government leaders thought it was other countries at work?" Bruce nodded. "Well, they finally realized the truth."

"What truth is that, James?

"That we're not alone in the universe. That's the reason we pour so much money into space exploration and special defense weapons like the 'Star Wars' project just to name one."

"So what did they do with all the information that was studied?"

"As far as actions taken, they pulled the greatest minds together and started working out the why, when and how of the whole thing. Then they got their first break in 1930, August 27th to be exact. Strange lights were seen over our nation's capital and planes were sent to investigate. Something went wrong and two American fighter Mustangs were destroyed."

"Why keep it a secret though, why not let people know about it?"

"Bruce, you're not looking at the big picture. Can't you imagine the ramifications of people knowing that there are alien beings trying to seize our planet and kill, or take our citizens for God only knows why? There would be mass rioting everywhere. Our economy would crash worse than it did in the thirties, and our culture would digress to a time of small tribes warring against each other for food and other necessities. Really, would you put this kind of information in the hands of people who only care about themselves?"

"No, I guess not, now that you make your point." Bruce said solemnly.

"Enough of this for now, why don't we get busy putting this briefing together. We've got a lot of work ahead of us."

"What's the first step?"

"We will begin by sifting through all the documents that our team has put together for us relating to our current project and look for a common thread that you think Sean would be able to capitalize on. Recent abductees that came forward, as a direct result of the television program, like you did, should help. While they can't remember a lot of detail, they did have some recollection. That's why your knowledge of Sean is so critical to our planning. We must predict what he will try, knowing what little we know, and assist him if possible."

"But isn't that just it, we don't know what we're up against."

"Maybe not in the physical realm, but we know they've been here before, and who they've taken, and what they did to them, to a limited extent. If we can draw a picture of what they need from us, perhaps we can predict how they intend to use Sean. It's not much, but it's all we have to work with."

Bruce sat down at the huge table and began reading the file marked 'Prometheus', while James retrieved other files from the computer his team had assembled. If they had any hope of all of getting out of their situation, it would be someplace in the files. James printed off some of the files and left to retrieve them. Bringing back a carafe of coffee and a handful of documents, he sat next to Bruce. "Here are the files marked Priority One. They show the most potential for shedding some light on our problem."

CHAPTER TWENTY-FOUR

Karna was in the command center overlooking the operation of the ship when the power failure struck. She along with every other Bilkegine on the vessel was blind as a bat, even though there was a small amount of light coming into each room. To make matters even worse, the power failure caused every other support system on the Spiruthun to shut down except for life support, which was on a different redundant system. That meant that the orbit they were stationed in would begin to decay and the Spiruthun was in danger of drifting. That alone wouldn't be so bad if they weren't so close to the Earth and the possibility of being pulled into its atmosphere. If the Bilkegine could not restore full power to their ship within one hour, and it was pulled into the atmosphere, they lacked the ability to reach escape velocity and return to space. If they didn't return to full power within two hours it wouldn't matter because they would all be too weak to even work on the problem. Karna could not allow that to happen, not only for her sake and the sake of her crew, but for the sake of the entire race that had put all their trust and faith into this one small planet. If her ship crashed into the planet it would destroy all life. It would create tidal waves a thousand feet high, raise the sea level by so many hundreds of feet that the only dry land in America would be the mountains and high plains at altitudes greater than nine thousand feet and would most likely reach the deep lower mantle layer of the Earth causing volcanic eruptions proportionally larger than its formation. It would also send molten rock, glass and gasses so far into space that it would engulf the moon. If any organism did happen to survive, the nuclear winter that followed from the complete lack of solar radiation hitting the surface— would turn the planet into a solid mass of rock and ice. There was too much at stake to let any time elapse that was not spent on repairs to her ship and subsequent power. The redundant systems on board were designed to re-power the vessel in space over a greater amount of time not in an emergency situation. Since the meteoroid destroyed the mid-section of decks twenty-four and twenty-five, it also damaged the emissions conduit and caused the interruption of the fusion of their dighergant material, and subsequent failure in the chain reaction needed to produce constant energy.

Because the Bilkegine's planet had two suns at nearly opposite sides of their planet, it never got completely dark. The days were, of course much longer and they had their resting phase during those times when the twin stars were blocked by their moon. The normal rotation of their planet, moon and smallest sun, made each day forty hours long, with eight hours of diminished light they referred to as their resting phase. They had become so accustomed to these conditions that their eyes no longer dilated, explaining why they were nearly blind under dark conditions. Unfortunately, due to the power failure and long start-up time of their back-up reactor, the Spiruthun was experiencing the same conditions as their planets night and the Bilkegine could barely see anything. The lack of light was also causing another problem. It was slowing the repairs to the ship to a crawl, and no flashlight smaller than one powered by a nuclear fusion could produce enough light to solve the problem. Repairs would be slow and dangerous. A point of fact was that their twin suns were the ultimate reason the Bilkegine had even come to Earth in the first place. Several years before the Bilkegine's first visit, their planet was struck by a small meteorite. While it wasn't big enough to cause the immediate destruction of the planet, it was large enough to shift the planets axis. After years of catastrophic changes on the planet, they realized that the planet was being pulled apart by the gravitational pull of the two suns and they would be forced to find another planet to call home.

Another problem even more dangerous than that of total darkness was the lack of the dighergant crystals, or what earth called radiation, being generated and circulated into the ship. Like the need for brilliant light to see, the two suns on their planet put out enormous amounts of radiation. Since the Bilkegine atmosphere was also much thinner and had less magnetic energy released at its poles, it allowed more gamma radiation to strike the planet. The Bilkegine body was built to require the additional radiation to survive. When they could not get the radiation naturally, as on their ship thousands of light years from home, they generated it by means of the dighergant fusion and literally pumped it into the air they breathed. Unlike the condition experienced on earth when humans have a decreased amount of sunlight due to cold winter conditions, instead of merely getting a little depressed or getting cabin fever, the Bilkegine would die. What the cinbiote did to cure the human via the sub-atomic dighergant crystals removing the radiation that would cause radiation sickness and death, the air inside the Spiruthun, without the radiation, would cause the Bilkegine to get sick and eventually die. The maximum time period an average Bilkegine body could tolerate being without the dighergant crystals was six hours, but like humans with radiation sickness, they would be too sick to do anything long before they actually died from the illness. The Quod would die much quicker due to their extraordinary size and strength. The more energy they used, the more they needed, and the quicker they became sick and died without it. Without exception, every Bilkegine was in for a period of intense pain and sickness if they could not get the redundant systems up within a few minutes. Although Karna wanted more than anything for her crew to find the human subjects and bring them back to her, she had no recourse but to order every crewmember to stay at his or her assigned task until the vessel was in full operation again. She had problems beyond her wildest imagination and she was getting madder by the second, knowing that it was the incompetence of her now dead second in command that had ultimately caused all of the trouble she was having. If she could have resurrected him from the oily bubbling spot on the War Chamber floor to kill him again more slowly, she would have. However, since she could not, she would no doubt take out her anger on the next Bilkegine to make a mistake no matter how insignificant.

As Karna walked into and out of the control chamber in the dark, she grew more impatient and started screaming her orders and demands to everyone.

"I want power to my vessel now!" she screamed to the crew inside the operations room.

"Yes, Commander, we are working on it now." The ranking officer in the room replied.

She walked outside the chamber to try and see if the light was any brighter there since it had space observation portals on the outside bulkhead that would allow some ambient light from space come in. It was not any brighter, but even if it had been, it wouldn't have been bright enough to distinguish. She decided to stand in the Piiderk and wait for power to be returned to her.

As she was standing there, a crewmember crashed into her, knocking her to the floor. Not knowing who he had knocked down, the crewman went inside without helping or stopping to explain. That was not unusual for the Bilkegine people, and especially something that wouldn't happen from a Bilkegine person belonging to the Shem alliance. The person who had knocked her down was a message runner. Due to the power failure in the communication systems as well, all messages from engineering had to be relayed in person. The messenger stumbled into the room in the darkness and was calling for the commander when she stepped up behind him and pressed her body up against his and asked, "Are you the one who just knocked down the crewman in the Piiderk?"

Not knowing who he was addressing, he replied, "That's not important! I have important business with…"

"No you do not! The only thing you have is a death sentence!" She yelled, as she ran a bladed weapon into him. She twisted the blade then listened carefully for the thump of him hitting the floor as she removed the weapon. "Perhaps the next messenger will not be so hasty!" she yelled. "Where is my power?" She yelled again.

If she had taken the time, or had the patience to hear why the messenger was there, she would have learned that a battle with many casualties was underway on several decks. She would have learned that in the darkness of the power failure a group of Tahar, lead by the Earthling Sean was running through level after level destroying everyone and anything that moved. She would also have learned that the humans can in fact see very well in the darkness once their eyes had become accustomed to the lower light conditions. Then she would have heard that Sean was coming. He was coming after her!

✳✳✳

The briefing inside the Smithsonian was ready to begin. Bruce had spent the last twenty-two hours reading old reports and drinking coffee. He had learned more about Sean than he believed Sean knew about himself. He found it especially interesting to find out that he had, according to the NSA records, been abducted on six different occasions over the previous twenty years. He especially thought it beneficial to learn that during Sean's tour in Vietnam, he had been accredited with the destruction of an entire advanced VC scouting party. According to the report it had been done single-handedly. He also found out how decorated Sean was for his efforts during the war. There wasn't a lot of information that Bruce read that he had known before. He now had a deeper understanding of why the government felt they could not reveal the information they had. He knew that the only thing it would accomplish would be mass panic and riots everywhere. The thing that concerned Bruce was that he knew how many of the mountain men acted when it came to survival, and also realized that the murder rate alone would be astronomical from people trying to hoard supplies for themselves. Above all though, Bruce was glad that he had the opportunity to learn first-hand about his friend Sean and his mysterious history.

When Sean came to the mountains of North Carolina, Bruce was one of the first to welcome him with open arms. It would be years before the other locals would do as much, since people keep themselves to themselves in the mountain. But during the time when Sean moved into the mountains, the nation was having problems all over with Vietnam veterans coming home. It wasn't necessarily a problem for the average citizen; it was a problem for the vets themselves because they were not given the soldiers welcome home like they should have. They were not treated with dignity and respect for doing what their country ordered them to do. Not all, but many were shunned from their own communities and didn't fit in anywhere. Besides that, Bruce didn't think it was right to pry into a man's past if he didn't offer the information. Except of course the man guilty of committing a crime, in which case he had no rights as far as Bruce was concerned. As he sat reading Sean's dossier with twenty-twenty hind sight, Bruce wished he had pushed a little harder to get to know Sean better and that he would have known then, what he had just learned. Not that it would have made a difference whether or not he would have accepted Sean and welcomed him into the community, but to have known that Sean's past was riddled with lost memories, horrifying visions and nightmares, and that Sean was treated in the mental ward of the Veteran's Hospital before he moved. He would have known that Sean was a shy and reclusive person because he was always afraid. Bruce also now knew that the psychologist, who had written the profile on Sean, did know Sean better than he did after all.

The last nugget of knowledge Bruce learned from the report was that during his treatment for Traumatic Stress Disorder after the war, Sean was subjected to multiple hypnosis sessions where the horror of the abductions were brought to light. Without his knowledge, Sean gave the government investigators a vivid picture of the terror he was feeling every time he closed his eyes.

Now in a few minutes, pumped up with fear and caffeine, Bruce would have to tell a group of very powerful government heads a story that would rock their world, and he was going to have to tell them that his friend was their only hope. Then, as if that weren't enough, he was going to have to suggest that because of Sean's mental instability under stressful situations, he may not be reliable and that trying to destroy the ship might be their only other option.

CHAPTER TWENTY-FIVE

On the way to the maintenance passage Sean realized that the power failure was a blessing in disguise. He noticed that the Tahar fighters were growing increasingly fatigued just from walking without the light and subsequent radiation. When they avoided the security Quod by hiding under the dead Quod bodies he had killed, he also realized that in the darkness, he could strike any position onboard without the fear of reprisal. By now he thought that the remaining Tahar soldiers would have obtained the weapons cache he told them about and on their way to stage a battle in some essential area. He stopped running and called over the Tahar woman.

"Rotusea, I have a plan," he began. "You take Nancy to the passageway and leave me with one of your Tahar soldiers as a guide, and I will use this opportune moment to initiate an attack against Karna."

"Are you crazy?" she asked. "You wouldn't stand a chance against her!"

"I think I would stand a better chance because of the power failure and the reduced strength and endurance of the Quod. I believe the time for me to strike is now!"

"I can't argue with you. Gebel has given me orders to take you to the passageway for your own safety, but he did say for me to take my orders from you as well."

"It's settled then. You get someone to lead the way and we will leave you for the Piiderk and try to take out your leader."

"She is not my leader, Gebel is." She argued.

"You know what I mean."

"Either way, it's not a good plan. She will kill you on sight because of all the trouble you have caused her. I have not seen it myself but reports indicate that she has lost control of her faculties. She is responding to errors in anger which is more human than Bilkegine. Gebel and other high ranking Tahar leaders believe it is due to her constant contact with humans."

"Good, I can use that against her then. If she is acting more human then her anger will cloud her judgment and make her more vulnerable."

"How will you attack then?"

"I plan on taking the fight to her head on."

"You will take on Karna in her own command center?"

"I'll take on that evil hearted monster anywhere I have to! You just give me someone to lead the way."

Rotusea thought for a moment then said, "It will be me then. You stand a better chance if I lead you, since we can speak."

"Good. Then have one of your Tahar men take Nancy and we'll be on our way."

Rotusea called one of the Tahar leaders on the special communicator the Tahar had developed and requested he send two soldiers to guard Nancy and told him where they could be found. She then attempted to contact Gebel to inform him of Sean's plan but could not get through. While they waited for the soldier to arrive, Sean walked over to where Nancy had sat down against a wall to rest and knelt down beside her.

"Nancy, I have to tell you something very important and I want your word that you will do what I ask." He said softly.

"What is it, Sean?"

"Before I tell you I need you to know something else." He turned to look into her eyes. "I have been a pretty shy and reclusive guy the past twenty years and have pretty much stayed to myself. But, since our ordeal, I have grown very fond of you and care about you very much. I'm dreadfully sorry that you ever got involved with all of this. I also think that it's my fault. If you hadn't been so kind hearted and caring yourself, you wouldn't be here today. So, I'm sorry."

"No, Sean. I don't see you that way at all. If anything you have been my valiant knight in shining armor. If you hadn't been there to hold me and comfort me through all of this I wouldn't have survived this long. And, for the record, I too have grown to love you over the past few weeks." She paused and squeezed his hands. "But telling me this now is scaring me. What do you have planned that would make you want to tell me this?"

"I have to leave you for a short time. Rotusea and I are going to find Karna and I plan on killing her before we make our escape."

Nancy was already shaking her head no to what she was hearing and tears began to slowly run down her face.

"No, Sean. Please. Stay with me until it's safe and let Gebel and the other Tahar fight her. Then we can escape with their help."

"I'm sorry, Nancy, but it won't work that way. We need to take advantage of the darkness and her weakened condition while we can."

"Why does it have to be you? Why can't they do it?" she said looking at Rotusea and the two Tahar soldiers that had just arrived.

"Because they can't see any better than Karna and they too are weakened by the lack of radiation. It just has to be this way if we're to survive and escape."

Sean began to rise and Nancy tried pulling him back down. "Please, Nancy. Don't make this any harder on me then it has to be. Let me go so I can save us both."

Nancy loosened her grip on Sean and her hands slid out of his as he continued to stand up. Tears were now streaming down her face and as Sean turned to leave, she called him back.

"Sean!" She yelled as she got to her feet. "Promise me that you will come back. Promise me that everything will be alright and that we can go home together!"

"I do, Nancy. I do. Pray for us." He said as he started to walk backward away from her.

Nancy stood for a brief moment watching Sean walk away then abruptly ran to catch up with him. As the tears continued to flow down her cheek, she reached out and hugged him, gave him a long soft kiss then backed off and told him to be careful.

Rotusea had given her orders to the two Tahar soldiers that had come to relieve her and was outlining Sean's plan as he reached them. Sean couldn't understand them but thought she was telling them what to do if they didn't survive. He stood and watched silently as the two Tahar soldiers lead her down the dark corridor and into the blackness of the ship.

"Ok, let's rock and roll!" Sean declared.

Karna was in the command center waiting for the report that all the repairs were completed. The Spiruthun was drifting aimlessly and was beginning to shift on its axis. It would only be a few more hours before they lost the ability to power the ship and return to their orbit. For the first time since the meteoroid struck them they were visible to Earth's defenses. She was screaming orders to the crewmembers and it would only have taken one misplaced word or reply to set her off on another killing spree. Karna was in fact the most deadly and impatient commander the Bilkegine had ever had, and she didn't try to hide the fact.

✳✳✳

The staff inside Cheyenne Mountain was busier than ever before tracking the ship. Their telemetry showed exactly where in space the ship was and they had a lock on it. They believed the ship's orbit was decaying and would either drift off into space or enter the Earth's atmosphere in just under seventy-two hours. The general ordered a special team to work on different plans to defend against the alien craft. As they followed the ship's movement, the MIT team and the professor finally came up with a feasible plan of defense. The hard part was going to be convincing the military that their plan had some merit. Their plan would require the entire strength of the U.S. and other countries working together, and that would not be an easy task, since many of the other countries had no idea the craft was there. Dr. Weiss presented his team's plan to the general and waited. General Stephens discussed the plan with the other military leaders present then called the White House for approval and implementation.

"Get me the President," he said into the red phone beside him. The

President came on the line, and General Stephens outlined what the team had come up with as a line of defense against the aliens.

"Yes Sir. Here is the plan we have. An outline has been sent to you to follow via encrypted fax. You should have everything that I have in front of me now." He waited for the President to respond then continued. "The plan is straight forward. We know that they have weapons capable of destroying any ship we send too close, as evidenced by the destruction of our two satellites earlier. However, new data suggests that their ship is experiencing a power loss of some kind. The craft has already moved some two thousand miles toward earth and is still drifting."

"General Stephens, what data do you have to indicate the craft has lost power? I don't see that data here." The President asked.

Dr. Weiss, standing nearby heard the question and retrieved the data. He handed it to the general as he pointed to the data in question.

"I have it here, Mr. President. Earlier reconnaissance, we were able to obtain before the satellites were destroyed, showed the ship to be venting some kind of gas into space through a port on the top of the craft. Recent images obtained from a new satellite staged further away from the craft now indicate that the venting has stopped. At the time, I believed that it was possible that they stopped it intentionally, it's something that isn't required all the time, but at the time the craft stopped venting, it immediately began to drift. The telemetry verified this and ever since then the craft continued to drift."

"General Stephens, I know time is of the essence right now but this plan needs to be reviewed by strategic command, the Air Force, NASA, and our military to see if it has any merit. I have already given the order for a total recall of our military personnel and a meeting is already underway to come up with another plan. I'll get back to you as soon as I can."

"Can we go private, Mr. President." General Stephens requested quietly as he picked up the receiver and held it to his ear.

He heard a click on the other end of the phone and the Presidents voice, "What is it John?"

"Mr. President, We're on fourth down with two seconds on the clock right now. I don't think we have time for a feasibility study before we start doing something. We're already at defcon three, Sir, and I am getting ready to move it up to level two."

"I'm well aware of that John, but I'm not ready to put the lives of every man, woman and child on this planet in the hands of an old college professor and some MIT kids. This has to be done right the first time, because between you and me, there probably won't be a second chance."

"I didn't mean to suggest that we initiate, Mr. President, I just think it would be prudent to at least be working on something while greater minds come up with another plan just in case things escalate."

"Okay, John. Go ahead and get your plan started, but I want to know that you understand—you don't have authority to act until you have my go ahead."

"Yes Sir. I understand completely."

The President took the plan back into the war room inside the bunker he had been moved to and sat down at the table. Everyone stopped talking when he entered the room and watched quietly as he took his seat.

"Gentlemen, I just got off the phone with General Stephens. His team has come up with a plan that should be thrown into the ring. I've reviewed the high points and given him authority to start the ball rolling but he's waiting for the go ahead before he initiates anything. I need to know what, if anything, you've come up with as well. I'm not telling you anything you don't already know, but we don't have much time and whatever we do we had better do quickly. Mr. Robertson will give you what Stephens has come up with. Go ahead," he said nodding to the Secretary of Defense.

"I won't be the only one here that thinks this plan is full of holes, but like the President said, we have to look at every possible angle and do it quickly. The plan consists of utilizing the Hubble Space Telescope to get a close up of the craft to try and locate an area that might be vulnerable to attack. Then, utilizing our new Solar Pulse Laser satellite, we strike hard. We know that craft is pretty tough because it's still there after being hit almost head on by a meteoroid but the laser is intended to weaken the craft more, not take it out completely. The second phase of the plan calls for us to modify four shuttles with as many nuclear missiles as they can carry and launch them at the craft using laser guidance provided by the International Space Station. With the coordinated effort of the other super powers we can put enough nukes in space to obliterate the space craft. The only drawback I see in this plan is that we would have to demonstrate the awesome destructive power of our new "SPL" Satellite. The positive part of this plan is that we already have a lot of what we need in place. We already have the "SPL" Satellite in orbit, and it's been tested. The ISS is manned and has laser capabilities so it won't take long for them to adapt it for this type of use. And, we already have four shuttles in a state of operational readiness. We can short cut the launch of the shuttles and sent them out back to back if we ignore safety protocols and use both launch pads. And, of course, we already have an arsenal of laser guided nuclear missiles, despite what everyone believes. Now for the negative aspects of the plan, we do not have any kind of launching mechanism designed to fire missiles from a Space Shuttle. We would have to launch the Shuttles with the missiles already armed, and pray that we don't have another incident like Challenger. And, we would have to reveal that we, one, have more nuclear missiles than we have been reporting over the last five decades, and two, we're going to have to show our hold card and use the "SPL". That's it, any questions?"

The very second he stopped talking, the room instantly filled with questions and loud objections. Everyone in the room except the Secretary of Defense and the President were trying to talk louder than the person next to them so they could be heard. The President stood up and yelled to be heard over the chaos that had irrupted in the room.

"Quiet! Let's have a modicum of order here!"

As quickly as the yelling and chaos started, it stopped and every eye was on the President. "One at a time, gentlemen, I know you all have valid points to make, but we don't have the luxury of wasting time here. General Watkins, if you would?"

General Watkins stood up and began to voice his concerns with the plan. "As far as the Air Force is concerned, I think we should consider using the S51F with the new ram air jet engines. They can be launched off the belly of a 747 and be in space before NASA could get just one Shuttle on the launch pad. It would be a whole lot easier to modify it to carry nukes and they wouldn't have to be armed until they were ready to launch. I like the idea of using the Hubble Space Telescope to get the intell on the craft and I like the idea of using the ISS to laser the site, but that's it. We have two S51F's operationally ready and they too have already been proven. And it would mean we wouldn't have to try and modify the Shuttles to carry then launch missiles from their cargo bays. God only knows what would happen if you tried. I'm in favor of using the S51F's. It's the way to go in my opinion."

As General Watson began to sit down, three other military leaders stood up and began to put their bid in for the task at hand. Once again, the President nodded at one individual and the other two took their seats quietly. Fleet Admiral William DeLeahy began to explain what part the Navy could play in the mission. "As I see it gentlemen, the Navy is not the option to use for this mission, at least in a leadership role. However, we too have capabilities that will be needed if your plan fails. We will have our recovery teams on standby in the event that something goes wrong. As for which plan to attempt, I can see merit it both plans. Now I'm not here to step on anyone's toes but knowing what I do about the S51F's abilities, and limitations, I can't see them taking out a craft of that size. While it may be true that the ISS can laser the site for you I believe the SPL must first be used to weaken the obviously formidable defenses that spacecraft must have. I also think it would be prudent to at least try to modify the Shuttles to carry and deploy nuclear missiles if the S51F's can't get the job done.

"You're right, General Watkins, we don't know what would happen if we tried to launch missiles from the cargo bays of the Shuttles, but if your plan were to fail, what other options would we have? Lie down and surrender? What I believe to be the case here is simple. The Air Force should be the one taking the lead on this attack. They are the only branch of our military that has the expertise and abilities to reach space; well, them and NASA. What I would like to know is what part NASA can play? If anyone would know, Dr. Weiss would. He practically lived there for thirty years before he retired to take his teaching position. If anyone knows space, it's him. I think he should stay in the loop and at least have some input here. That's all I have to say, gentlemen."

President Fleming stood up and addressed the room again. "Gentlemen, the DOD has had a long and prestigious history. We also know that not every plan that's been conceived behind these walls have been good ones. We have had our share of disasters. And, while it may not be a matter of public record, we have also conceived military plans that bordered on genius. With extremely favorable outcomes, I might add. However, now is not the time to let petty egos and competition get in the way of coming together and making a plan that will not fail. Sure, we don't have the intelligence we would like to have. And we don't have any weapons that can even compare to the technologically advanced weapons the aliens have already demonstrated. But what we do have, no matter what the cost in dollars, secrets or pride, we need to use against these aggressors. It's not just our livelihood, our economy, or democratic way of governing or even our national security at risk here; it is our lives and the lives of every human on the planet. I guess the reason I'm saying this is that I believe we should not only show our enemies and allies what we are capable of technologically speaking, we should use them and invite the other governments to aid and assist in any way they can. I believe that Dr. Weiss was on the right path when he said it would take the cooperation of the entire world to defeat them and that is what we are going to do. See to it, gentlemen, and whether you're a believer or not, I think we should all say a prayer while we're at it."

As the President turned to leave, everyone stood up. They waited until he had left then took their seats, and the Secretary of Defense, Mr. Dakota Robertson, began to address them.

"The President is on his way to speak to the Ambassadors of the world as we speak. We estimate that we only have seventy-two hours before action must take place of some kind. If that craft regains control of their ship and becomes hostile, we won't have a prayer. We know they are aggressive because they took out those two satellites, but on the other hand, it very well could have been a defensive action as well. No one knows, but we're certainly not ready to sit back and find out either. Let's get a plan together, see what help, if any, our allies or enemies can be and be prepared to initiate at a moment's notice. One more thing, when we are meeting with our enemies leave your personal opinions at home, especially if we are meeting face to face. The last thing we need right now is some hot-head causing a war down here when the real battle will be up there." He instructed as he pointed to the ceiling. "Let's get busy, operation "Laser Tag" is our only priority."

Hours had passed since the meeting of the top military brass and the intelligence briefing was about to begin in another area of the Smithsonian bunker. While the military top brass was not present, they each had assigned ranking officers to assist by attending the meeting. The Secretary of Defense was the only one in attendance that had current information pertinent to a military offensive against the spacecraft. As he walked briskly into the room, everyone stood, and the ranking officers snapped to attention.

"As you were," he said, taking a seat at the conference table. "Go ahead, Agent Rose."

Agent Rose stood up and walked to the center of the room so everyone could both see and hear him easily. "Good evening ladies and gentlemen, my name is James Rose. I am an agent with the NSA and have been assigned to act as liaison between your governments and the United States, and disseminator of the intelligence we currently have on the alien spacecraft that is orbiting our planet. Let me assure you all that we are all here with for a single purpose: to share information and ascertain if the intelligence we have been able to obtain about the alien craft is beneficial to our ultimate cause. Our teams have been working tirelessly to sift through decades of data in order to divulge any hidden information that could prove essential to our mission. In a gesture of good will, let me begin by saying that we have been testing—how should I say—alien technology and other artifacts that we were able to recover over the past few decades in hopes of finding something that we can use against our alien aggressor. There has, no doubt, been alien activity all around the world and if you have experienced anything like the US, as I'm sure you have, you know how important it is that we work together on the defense of our planet and our individual nations. Furthermore, you all need to know that the United States is holding nothing back to this end. We all know that there have been times when our governments have not seen eye to eye. To that end, we all have kept things from one another and those secrets have caused division, suspicions, distrust and, I dare say, hatred for one another. I am here today to put an end to that in the name of humanity as a whole. The things you will learn today may shock you, disturb you and possibly anger you, but some of that goes both ways and at this place and at this time we cannot allow anything to interfere with mutual cooperation toward the destruction of the alien spacecraft that is a threat to our cultures, our governments and the lives of our citizens. We are not here to formulate a plan of attack; that task has been delegated to the expert military departments of our countries. What we are here to do is to gather information and postulate ideas that we can present as credible intelligence useful in the planning phase of our mission. In addition to having alien technology, that we will delve into later, we have first hand reports about a person who has been abducted numerous times and reported detailed data, of inestimable worth, while under hypnosis. Furthermore, the person to whom I refer is currently on board that spacecraft and his name is Sean Daniels."

Up to this time, those in attendance had listened quietly for the most part. There were a few grumbles when the facts were released about the alien technology and the mention of giving up secrets and mutual cooperation, but when James said Sean was currently onboard the spacecraft, it caught most of them by surprise and the surprise was obvious by their responses. Agent Rose continued. "Ladies and gentlemen, let me introduce Sherriff Bruce Faulkner, he has pertinent information about Mr. Sean Daniels. Sherriff Faulkner."

"Hi folks my name is Bruce. I'm a little outside my comfort zone here, but Sean Daniels is my best friend and I've been asked here to search through data and give you my best gut feeling on what he'll do out there. You have each been given a comprehensive profile on him that was prepared by our team here as well as a profile done by the FBI's top psychologist." He waited for a couple of moments for everyone to fine the report and review it. "Sean and I go back more than twenty years. And like James, I mean, Agent Rose told you, Sean has been abducted before. Six times to be exact. As you can see there in your profile, Sean was first abducted while he was on a reconnaissance mission in Vietnam. He was the highest ranking NCO, uh, that's non-commissioned officer, in his squad and that made him the fire-team leader. He was leading his team through the jungle and as they stepped into a rice patty in the middle of a large clearing, the enemy began firing on their position. They all scattered except Sean and the men on his fire-team were screaming for him to get behind some cover but it was like he couldn't even hear them. They reported afterward that he was frozen for a few seconds then a bright light came out of nowhere and he just vanished in front of them. Sean didn't return to his unit for nearly two weeks. It was during his debriefing that his commanding officer suspected he was acting as a spy for the enemy and ordered Sean to have a comprehensive psychological evaluation. The doctor that performed the analysis used drugs and hypnosis during his evaluation and discovered that something very peculiar did happen to Sean but his findings weren't conclusive enough to be certain about anything. He reported what Sean had told him and they left it at that. At least everyone thought so. In reality, there was someone interested in the mere fact that he had disappeared in front of his men and that someone knew what had happened because he had seen it before and was in charge of an operation called "Blue Book". Sean was followed and observed for over two decades by either the colonel or someone else and interviewed under hypnosis each time. Sean was never aware of the abductions, the government involvement, the interviews or the hypnosis." Agent Rose stood up in the back of the room indicating to Bruce that his time was just about up. "I guess I'm here to tell you what I know about Sean and what I think he can do for all of us. I've seen Sean in action many times when an injustice has been done. It ain't a pretty thing. I know that if he's threatened, he will fight back, if he's trapped, he will find a way out, and if someone else's life is threatened, especially a woman, if a way exists, he will find a way to defeat them. He is resourceful, he will not give up, and he has shown a remarkable knack for persevering against tremendous odds. That's what I know. What the psychologist thinks is written in that file, and one thing he wrote that I absolutely agree with is this, and I quote: "He has a propensity to violence when he feels threatened." Folks, my time is just about over, but I want you to know that Sean is probably seeing everything that could set him off. He has been captured, his life has probably been threatened, and a human woman from our town was taken with him and he will no doubt protect her with his life. Now I don't even know if my friend is still alive, but mark my words, if he is, they'll have hell to pay, uh, pardon my French. I guess that's all I have to say."

Bruce started to sit back down when Mr. Robertson, the Secretary of Defense asked him a question. Bruce quickly stood back up and answered him.

"Sherriff Faulkner, what do you think your friend can do for us, specifically, and how would we know if he was able to help us out?"

"Specifically Sir, I can't say, but like I said before, I know Sean better than pretty much everyone, and I know that he won't just sit around and do nothin'. I also know that if he is able to do somethin' we will know when he does it. I'm sure that he would give us some kind of signal if for no other reason than to draw attention to the craft in case we didn't know it was out there."

"One more thing, Sherriff, you said there was another person taken at the same time. Have we verified that? How did you come to that conclusion?"

"I saw it with my own two eyes, Sir."

"So, what you're telling us is that there are at least two humans onboard that alien craft and probably more, and if we don't see some kind of signal that would demonstrate that he was successful in thwarting their mission, whatever it is, than they are going to be killed when we blow the craft out of space?"

"Yes, Sir, but I think I'm saying more than that. I think that we should use the plan that Dr. Weiss came up with, or some other plan as a last resort."

With no other questions posed, Bruce took his seat and James addressed the group again.

"If I might add one more thought. We have been monitoring Sean for years as a matter of national security, and if anyone has the potential to stop these aliens at whatever they are planning, Sean does. What we must agree on is if the alien ship isn't posing an immediate threat, we must not initiate a preemptive strike against them and allow Sean more time to act."

The room filled with murmurs and Mr. Robertson voiced his own opinion quickly. "To what end, Agent Rose? Are you suggesting that our governments just sit on our hands and do nothing until it's too late?"

"Yes and no Sir. Sure, it's imperative that we plan for the inevitable, but we must only act if the alien craft initiates an aggressive action toward us. The point I'm trying to make is that, while the mere presence of an alien spacecraft does present a potential threat to our national security and the security of the rest of the world, they have done nothing to indicate that they are aggressive in nature. And as such, we should stay any aggressive action of our own."

"Let me point out to everyone here that your purpose is to gather intelligence, ascertain its usefulness, and make your recommendations to your leaders. The decision to initiate or not is not yours to make."

"Yes, you are absolutely correct it is not our decision, nevertheless, the fact that we have a decorated and experienced soldier in the enemy camp, as it were, is definitely to our advantage, and we should recommend that a preemptive attack should at the very least be avoided unless irrefutable evidence tells us otherwise. I'm just saying, with the intelligence and physical evidence we now have, it would be prudent to give Sean as much time as we can."

"Point taken Agent Rose, may we continue?"

James continued with the briefing and over the next seven hours, demonstrated how technologically advanced the aliens were, and suggested what they were capable of doing if in fact their plans were something other than observation and experimentation. The world leaders watched in amazement as they learned of everything the United States had uncovered about the alien race and many presented their own intelligence after much trepidation.

CHAPTER TWENTY-SIX

Gebel took his strike team of sixty Tahar men to the warehouse that Sean told him about and found the weapons just as he had said. The weapons were new to Gebel and the other officers, and they could easily see that they were more primitive than their usual weapons. The weapons were designed to destroy everything with which they came into contact, where their normal weapons utilized a more surgical approach and only destroyed the flesh of the targets. It was obvious to Gebel that the new weapons had been designed to not only demonstrate the Bilkegine superiority while the battle was taking place, but to also destroy more than one target with each precise deployment.

The Tahar soldiers each received a weapon and several hundred rounds and staged themselves inside the warehouse for an attack. Gebel took his officers aside and gave each of them their specific assignments and the overall battle plans.

"Listen, because there is only one working door in or out of this warehouse, we must stage our battle from here if we are to have our backs covered. Every precaution must be made to ensure that everyone is in position before the first wave. Before we engage the Quod, we must first disable the Star Docking Bay Entrance. If we attack and have to retreat to regroup, they will discover where we are and simply open the Bay entrance from the command center and suck us all into space. If we override the operation control panel at the site, no one will be able to override them from outside the warehouse. It's possible that it may be blamed on the meteoroid collision since so much has gone wrong since then. Our primary target will be in one of three key areas of the Piiderk so we must hit all three simultaneously. Listen very carefully. If we are to succeed in our ultimate purpose we must not destroy any essential operations system because doing so would not only mean an end to the ship, but the planet as well. If this ship ever lost complete control, it would no doubt eventually end up in the earth's atmosphere. I will give each of you your specific target areas individually. In the meantime, get with your men and become familiar with the new weapons. Are there any questions?" He waited for a few seconds for an officer to ask a question or object. When he was assured they all understood and had no further questions or comments, he continued. "Captain Theoinis, you take your team and stage them outside the main engineering level. Your assignment will be to gain access and secure that location and be prepared to regain control of the Spiruthun once the controls from the main control center have been transferred to you. Once you have command, disengage the primary communication controls so the bridge cannot override your commands. You must also lock out any other satellite control stations. Is everything clear?"

Captain Theoinis nodded and began to leave, but Gebel stopped him.

"One more minute, Captain, do not begin your attack until the seventeenth phase. At the precise moment the phase begins, attack with extreme prejudice but remember to exercise caution so no vital system is damaged with those primitive weapons. Go!"

Gebel warned the remaining officers that the power could be returned to full strength at any time, and that the Quod would certainly be up to fighting strength within half a phase. He ordered his officers to distribute the dighergant injections and use them immediately.

"Captain Briges, you and Lieutenant Ziils take two teams to the Quod barracks and isolate them. They will be there resting and trying to conserve their energy until the power is returned. Send your two best engineering men to bypass the dighergant ducts so no new dighergant crystals enter the barracks. That will keep them weak and unable to fight even if the power is returned to full. Make that your first priority, then quickly block or destroy any and all means of them traveling between decks. If they are able to move around the Spiruthun, then we will be doomed, and the earth will fall as well. Your orders are to isolate, control and if detected, kill whatever moves and determine if it was Quod later. As a precaution against friendly fire, every Tahar soldier will be wearing their Tahar crest for everyone to see. This will provide for two things. Avoid shooting one of our own, and just as importantly, proclaim that we are Tahar so there will be no going back to the way things have been. Some innocent Bilkegine will die during this battle but we have all sworn to embrace the same future to protect Earth and its inhabitants."

As before, they acknowledged their orders, rallied their teams and left quickly and quietly. The cover of darkness made everything more difficult, but it gave them the element of surprise and allowed them to leave the warehouse without being detected.

Gebel had just three officers left at the warehouse. He wanted to utilize them the best he could until the remaining army of Tahar soldiers could be deployed safely from where they were when the ship lost power. He knew that some of them would already be in a strategic position to command surrender of that work area once they were armed, so he ordered two groups of ten men to continually distribute the new weapons and ammunition to those waiting Tahar officers and soldiers. Then, knowing the only other station that was both under Quod command and of vital importance, he decided to send all but ten Tahar soldiers to the Space Port and Transportation hanger.

"Major Rusos, you take Captain Rigeila and all but ten soldiers to transportation. Besides the command center, the Space Port is the most important area to seize. Not only is it the most important because there are thousands upon thousands of warrior Quods waiting to deploy there, but because we will need surface shuttles or the z-bolt transporter to safely deliver our human captives home again, and as you know, they are both in that area. I have selected you and Captain Rigeila for this specific mission because you are both well seasoned warriors and will be facing overwhelming odds. I will not deceive you. You will most likely lose all your men attempting to secure that position until reinforcements arrive. But it will be up to you and you alone to ensure that every battle fighter, troop shuttle and surface destroyer is destroyed before they can be launched. You must leave no ship large enough for them to battle the planet with. I know that alone will not secure the safety of the planet, but it will at least stop the Quod from attacking the planet. Prepare your soldiers well before you engage and lastly—may the spirit of the Tahar be with each of you."

Gebel saluted each of them and asked if they had any questions. Captain Rigeila turned and walked toward his men leaving Major Rusos behind with Gebel.

"Is there something else, Major Rusos?" Gebel asked.

"Yes Sir, Commander, I desire to speak a word of encouragement to you as you have us during this difficult mission."

"Yes Major?"

"I know it is not the Bilkegine way, but since observing many of the humans on board the Spiruthun, I wish to say that you have been and will always be a good leader and I am fortunate to die with you here."

"I understand. I too am fortunate to die for the cause along with those who have served me so willingly."

"Where is it you intend to battle?"

"I will take these ten brave soldiers and attempt to seize control of the command center and kill Commander Karna. She will no doubt have several security Quods at her side, and since we cannot destroy the control center before we are able to transfer control to engineering, we must draw them out first and then stage our attack. Until Karna is dead, we will never command the Spiruthun. It is our only hope."

"I understand, Commander Gebel, embrace your death in honor."

"I will major. I have no other choice."

As Major Rusos left with his men, Gebel called for the last soldiers to join him. He explained his strategy for seizing control over the ship and ensured that each of them had a working knowledge of the weapon.

Gebel knew that it was not going to be an easy battle but believed in what he was doing so much that he was willing to give up everything to win. When he volunteered to command the Tahar on the mission, he did not expect to ever see his family again. He told his helpmate that he would die in battle protecting the humans and, as was customary to the

Bilkegine, he passed his authority for his family to his oldest brother. He told her that the Shem were a power seeking alliance and told them that he wasn't only giving his life up for the humans, he was surrendering his life to ensure a better and more peaceful life for his family and the family of all the Tahar and other alliances that disagreed with the Shem. He also explained that the Shem would fall if their plans to dominate Earth and enslave the humans failed and said it was his responsibility to do everything he could to make that happen.

Karna was his supreme commander on the Spiruthun but was a despicable tyrant and high council of the enemy alliance. Gebel had watched as power and control of the ship and the mission was handed over to her, and he knew that very day that open, public war between the Tahar and the Shem would begin and end onboard her ship. He also knew that while she was very intelligent, she was nevertheless weak in other ways. She was extremely intolerant and violently impatient when it came to crewmembers taking her orders, and it would be her demise. Furthermore, he not only had a grudge against the Shem, Karna's own alliance, but also had a personal grudge against Karna's family. His father had been killed by Karna's uncle and everyone in the Nuubiya clan was as evil as he had been. While Karna had no idea of his relationship, or clan association when she approved his application to volunteer for the mission, he secretly hoped that he would be the one responsible for her death. He wanted to enact vengeance for his clan and reciprocity for his father.

Everything was coming down to the ultimate battle that could be over within one phase, and Gebel knew that the next few hours would decide the fate of his people.

Gebel took his team out of the warehouse and started through the Piiderk toward the command center and Karna. He was moving slowly around the perimeter of the room in single file when he heard the new weapons' devastating report. Trying to determine where the sound came from, he squinted as much as possible to try and see through the darkness. Suddenly he was blinded by the brilliant flash resulting from another explosion as it struck the command center. Who could that be? He thought. Why were his men not at their post, and why were they attacking his position? Gebel rallied his men and struck out for the command center. Just as he was moving into striking distance, another flash erupted a few hundred feet in front of him. In the glow of the fire and explosion he could see several Quods lying dead. As he looked behind him to see who was firing, he was amazed to see Sean and Rotusea running toward him.

The battle started on the Quod barracks in much the same manner as it had on the Piiderk. Each position was engaged with a divided team firing the new weapon blindly into hundreds of Quod as they were ordered. Because the Tahar had barricaded both exits into the barracks, the only means of escape for the weakened or injured Quod were the ladders that were stationed at all corners. However, having destroyed the ladders with the first well placed blasts, the Quod were trapped in a hell-storm of explosions and subsequent fire. The already putrid smell of the concentration of Quod in one space was worsened by their shredded bodies and burning flesh. With each explosion, more pieces of Quod anatomy was flying through the air and sticking to every surface. It appeared to the Captain in charge of the attack that they were winning. The Quod, having been in an advanced weakened state were easy pickings for the Tahar with their explosive weapons. Never in the Tahar history had a battle been so one sided against the Quod.

The battle against the transportation hanger was not as successful as the barracks was. Because of the concentration of armed warrior Quod, and due to the artificial dighergant generator on board the attack ships, the Tahar met a formidable enemy who could fire back. Even in a slightly weakened state, it was clear to see that the warrior Quod were not going to lose. Two hundred Tahar soldiers against an army of thousands of warrior Quods was decidedly a mistake to undertake. The first volley of explosions destroyed twenty-two shuttles, but also cost the Tahar over a thirty soldiers due to blast back. The Major was defeated and decided to fall back to regroup. It was the best course of action in his opinion, but as he was retreating he became cut off from his escape route and realized that he was not going to make it out alive. Taking his last soldiers, he struck against the largest troop transport shuttle in the hanger. The vessel he attacked was capable of carrying six thousand Quod to the surface fully armed. Major Rusos knew it wasn't going to be 'all' the ships destroyed as he was ordered, but it was the main attack vessel, and without it, the Quod would only be one hundred strong with each of the smaller shuttles reaching earth at a time. He ran into the battle, and facing fifty Quod with the same weapons he was using, prepared to fire on the weakest section of the transport. Just as he about to pull the trigger, an explosion ripped through the deck he was standing on and threw him into the air. Landing hard and completely wasted of all his strength, the Major pointed the weapon at the transport and fired.

Before all the positions could be taken, the lights suddenly returned and with it full power to the vessel. The immediate surge of energy, from the power coming online, shoved Gebel and Sean back against the far wall of the Piiderk. The battle was over, and the only thing left for them to do was run and hide. If they could not defeat Karna now, it would have to be later or not at all. Sean, Rotusea and Gebel took off toward the ladders and the lower levels to hide inside the maintenance passageways. The Quod barracks were destroyed and burning along with ninety percent of the Quod on that level. Unfortunately, thousands of Quod survived on other levels of the ship. While engineering was successfully taken, the Tahar did not have adequate time to isolate the command center from operating the ship. The battle was lost but the war would continue. Gebel called for all his Tahar officers to retreat and reorganize. Then in a moment of acumen, Gebel made contact with them again and ordered them to cut off the upper and lower decks from the Piiderk, which was located in the middle of the ship. He calculated that if all his Tahar soldiers and officers were on the four mid-ship levels directly above and below the Piiderk, they had a fighting chance against the Quod and certain defeat. All over the vessel, Tahar soldiers abandoned their posts and made their way to the mid-ship decks. When the last surviving alliance members passed through the connecting corridors, simultaneous explosions ripped through the ship, closing off all but five levels.

Karna came storming out of the command center upon return of power to assess the damage to her ship. Just as she was scanning the Piiderk, she saw three figures running for the far corner and recognized one of her attackers as Sean. She also realized for the first time that there were mutineers on her ship. She immediately sent for all the security Quod as well as her Chief of Arms. When the chief reported, she pulled out her favorite weapon, the chot, and pointed it the chief's head. Pausing for a moment to see his response, she said, "You have failed to carry out your duties; how dare you allow traitors to board my ship!"

The chief knew that anything he said would be perceived as an excuse and would likely result in his death so he remained silent.

"Do you not have any excuse for your failure?"

Again, he remained silent.

"Answer me!" she screamed.

Realizing he had no choice but to reply, he said, "Commander Nuubiya, when you appointed me Chief of Arms, I swore to defend you and the alliance to the death. If it is you who would take my life, I understand, but how then will I continue to serve when I am dead?"

Fuming with anger but knowing the chief was right; she pointed the weapon at the nearest drone and fired. Without looking at the chief again, she turned away and began walking calmly back to the command center. She stopped in the doorway, turned briefly and yelled, "Get the human! I will kill him personally!"

The chief froze until she was out of sight, wiped the sweat from his brow, and ran as fast as he could away from the command center and toward his security chamber.

CHAPTER TWENTY-SEVEN

The Chief of Arms took little time in forming an attack team consisting of several armory personnel and the Quod that managed to survive the Tahar attack on the barracks. He called for reinforcements from other decks and discovered right then what the last explosions were about. He instructed the Quods to find and destroy the treasonous Tahar alliance members and capture the human. He knew his task would be more difficult without the aid of more Quod, but he would either produce the human subject and the Tahar alliance members onboard, or he would suffer death for his failure. He concluded that he would be held responsible for the Tahar traitor's success in cutting off the mid-ship levels, but also thought that the return of the human male and news of all the traitor's deaths might be his salvation. The security force he assembled was armed and ready to search every available level enthusiastically; his only hope was in the Tahar being within reach. The Chief of Arms went to the main security chamber and locked down the ladder passageways using a high frequency force-field that he alone could deactivate. He alone could open and close the force-fields remotely, allowing only himself and his security team access between the remaining levels. He knew that other access passageways existed for maintenance between levels, but they were in complete darkness to the Quod and every other Bilkegine. He thought that Sean would not know the way around the vessel alone and concluded that the passageways could not be used.

He was sure he had trapped the Tahar on whatever level they were on and could systematically annihilate each one as they were found.

Sean and Rotusea stayed with Gebel when they fled the Piiderk. As they reached the ladder exits several quod were coming up and they had to retreat. Luckily for them, Karna, who had recognized Sean, had left the Piiderk for the command center and did not see them retreat back into the Piiderk. Sean was now leading the two Tahar members and decided the safest place for them now would be his old quarters. They quickly ducked into the chamber and the door closed behind them. Out of breath and completely exhausted from their time without light or dighergant, Gebel and Rotusea collapsed on the floor just inside the door. Sean took a quick break and decided that he would investigate the storage closet he had found earlier. He went to the wall and as the door opened Gebel asked Rotusea, "What is that?"

Rotusea translated as usual as Sean explained what he had found.

"It's a storage closet used to store the personal effects from humans who have been taken over the past years from the looks of it," Sean replied. "Come look for yourself."

Although they were both fatigued, Gebel and Rotusea rose and walked slowly into the closet. Sean pulled down a container he hadn't looked through and opened it. Gebel read the markings on the container and gave Rotusea a knowing glance. The marking read, "Goyruine voqutili bezy-yal kleg—statl 2, hiprai 38, p-tactar 18, Befil 45312."

Sean noticed Gebel's response at the container, and as he pulled items from it, he asked, "What do the markings say?"

"Specifically it would translate, possessions taken of skull walker family."

"Let me rephrase my question then, what do the markings mean?"

"Specifically," she said glancing briefly at Gebel, "it would mean personal effects of human family taken from quadrant 2, section 38, partial minute 18, Befil 45312, which is the third month of our sixteen month annual calendar, in the year 45312." Rotusea answered. "You would say in your month of December, 1987."

"Where is quadrant 2, section 38, partial minute 18?"

"Specifically it would be North America, State of Missouri, and City of Saint James.

"Saint James, Missouri, 1987," Sean mumbled as he rummaged through the container, "is this the latest date you see in here?"

Rotusea moved into the closet a little deeper and began to read the containers. She noticed one container that was from a more recent time and pulled it down.

"Most are from an earlier time. Every-one except…this one," she said pulling another container down. "This is marked, North America primary male subject, Corathron 45571. This would be close to your February, 2004."

Sean put the open container aside and took the new box Rotusea had pulled down. He opened it and began to sort through the contents. Then, almost in a daze, he dropped the contents into the box and stared at Gebel as if hypnotized.

"What is it?" Gebel said looking at Rotusea. She asked Sean but did not get an immediate response. "Sean, what is it?"

"These are some of my things," he mumbled softly, "things I thought I had lost early this year. Here are the keys to my apartment and store!" He spoke louder with underlying anger in his voice. "How can this be possible?"

"You must have been here before." Rotusea responded as if merely stating an obvious fact.

"How…how could I have been on this God forsaken ship and not remembered it? How could I have forgotten the Quod?" For that matter, how could I have forgotten anything like this? It's impossible!"

"The cinbiote, it will remove all current memories of your encounter up to a week."

Gebel grasped Rotusea by the arm and asked what was going on. After she answered him, he stepped up to Sean and said, "It would appear you have been here before. There can be no other explanation."

Sean began to ask another question when they heard the outer door open. He quickly grabbed the door to the closet and closed it. Sean's imagination was running wild when fear enveloped him again. Great! He thought. Coming back here was the stupidest thing I could have done. Now we're stuck in this closet.

Several Quod came into the room and were sniffing around. Sean could hear them outside the door. He heard them throwing things around the room and one of them stopped just outside the panel in the wall that lead to the closet and begin to sniff loudly. As the Quod stepped closer to the panel, the door came unlocked and Sean quickly grabbed it and urgently braced his legs against the wall and leaned against the door to keep it closed. Suddenly a Quod began to strike the wall with his weapon.

✳ ✳ ✳

The generals and Chief of Staff were making final plans for the launch of the new S51F's when they got a call from Cheyenne Mountain. The alien craft had recovered from the power loss and was back on its way to its previous orbit around the earth. Everyone at the mountain thought it strange that the alien craft re-engaged its camouflage device thinking they were sure the aliens knew they were being watched. However, when the ship returned to its original position and pose, they concluded that an eminent attack was not probable and the decision was made to stand down to condition orange. General Stephens called the ready-room at the Smithsonian bunker and arranged to have another video conference. Their orders had been clear. If the immediate threat to the nation's security were removed, they would stand down and allow for more time to gather intelligence. They remained resolved to their plan and course, and remained in a heightened condition, but they would not strike. It was essential to gain as much knowledge as possible on the craft and remain operational ready in the event of a change in status.

Bruce and James went to the conference room for the brief and waited for the others to arrive. Bruce was tired of the whole experience, physically drained of energy, and emotionally devastated, but more than anything else, he was frustrated with how little he or anyone else was able to do. He just wanted things to return to normal, but normal was something that Bruce could never experience again knowing what he now knew. He was sitting quietly thinking to himself over a cup of coffee when James spoke.

"Listen Bruce, I know it's been tough on you being away from home, but it has to be nearing an end."

"It does?" Bruce asked sarcastically, "Will it ever be over, now that we know that there are other species, other races of beings out there."

"We can only take one day at a time, Buddy. After all, I've known of their presence for the past fifteen years and have been able to lead a somewhat normal life."

"Normal—are you married, do you have children, take long walks in the park or go fishing or hunting on a regular basis? Do you sit around a fire, or lounge just visiting with friends, go to church and sleep in on Saturday mornings and complain about having to mow your lawn again? That's what normal people do, James."

"No, I guess I haven't found Miss Right yet."

"Is it really that, or is it your concern over the world in your less than normal life?"

"I didn't know you were such a philosopher, Bruce. Or is it just recently that you've become one?"

"Yeah, I guess I am. Its—uh, it just makes you think, that's all."

"Well, you won't have to think about it much after today."

"Why not?"

"Right after this briefing, I'm sending you home. You've done about as much as you can do here, and Lord knows you've been through enough lately."

"And, what about you, James, what will you do?"

"Keep on fighting for our nation's security, I guess, and maybe settle down when this is all over. Who knows? They might just be up there doing research." James said with a smile.

"What about Sean, if I leave, who will look out for his best interest. Will they wait to blow up the ship and Sean and Nancy with it as soon as I'm gone, or will they wait until I'm back home and too far away to know any different?"

"Hey, I resent that accusation. I'm as interested in saving Sean as you are."

"No, you're not, can't be. You've only known Sean from a distance. With you it was all business. You know—the big threat to national security."

James looked at Bruce seriously for just a couple of seconds, and then smiled. "You know Bruce, you're alright. No, I really mean it. I mean, you are the best friend a guy could ever have. I don't know maybe it's because you come from a more peaceful place than the big city, but I believe I'm seeing someone that really cares and would do anything, legal or not, to save a friend. It has really been a pleasure knowing you."

Bruce looked at James hard, trying to figure out if he was just patronizing him or really meant what he said. He sat quietly looking down at the floor for five minutes.

"James, did you really mean what you said about the aliens just wantin' to learn from us? Think about it. It doesn't make any sense. Why do we study other people during a time of war—we study our enemy to learn where they are vulnerable before we attack them don't we? We look for a chink in their armor. Maybe that's what they've been doing all this time; maybe their looking for our weaknesses, physically or even maybe mentally. They need to know as much as they can about us so they can ensure victory."

"But we're not at war with them, Bruce."

"Yet! They did make an offensive move when they destroyed those satellites didn't they? And, didn't the President pretty much declare war by making plans for an all out effort to destroy them?"

"Maybe you're right, yes, they did destroy our satellites and the President did agree to initiate a preemptive strike against them. But what are our alternatives, how do we do anything—but—make the first move and pray that it's good enough?

"I don't have the answers pal, but I know this; Sean is up there and unless he is already dead, he won't just sit around and let them observe him!"

"Point taken, that is why I was on your side before. That is the only reason we haven't attacked already isn't it?"

"No, I don't believe that for one minute. I might have a month ago, but I've already seen too much of our government in action. I've already heard how eager the military is to use everything at their disposal to shoot first and ask questions later. And one thing is for sure! They are not interested in saving Sean's life. He's expendable in their eyes."

"Bruce, I can't believe what I'm hearing. Aren't we all expendable during a time of war?" Don't you even think for one minute—that our leaders don't care about our military men and women dying on a battle field! They care, but they also know that it takes sacrifice sometimes to secure victory and ensure our freedom."

"Oh, you're right there. They know alright. That's why you never see the generals on the front lines with the soldiers. They believe in sacrifice for freedom, as long as it isn't their own."

Before they were able to continue their mildly heated debate the elevator announced its appearance with the ubiquitous ding, and several people got off. They were the same familiar faces that Bruce had seen the past week in one briefing after another. Only this time, the President himself stepped into the hallway. Those who were already waiting when he walked into the conference room stood up to greet him. He took the time to shake a few hands and made a point of making eye contact with every single man in the room then sat down at the head of the table. James and Bruce followed them in and Bruce took his seat while James walked to the center of the conference room and brought the meeting to order.

"Mr. President, it's an honor to have you with us today. Before we begin is there anything you would like to say?"

"Not just now, Agent Rose, perhaps when the meeting is over."

"Thank you, Mr. President. Ladies and gentlemen, we have the latest news of the alien craft moving back into their previous orbit. We can now safely assume two things. First, they have either repaired their ship or at the very least made enough repairs to maintain a stationary orbit, and secondly, they are hostile". James looked over at Bruce momentarily when he admitted that the aliens were hostile. "We are continuing with our plans to arm the two S51F's and bring the ISS into a position whereby they can assist by laser sighting the target for the missiles, and we must also add the fact that we have an ally onboard their ship. We need to assume that he is still alive, and until we see further aggressive action, we will study the craft to look for any weaknesses. However, once the craft re-established its orbit, it employed some type of stealth technology and disappeared. The good news in this regard is that Dr. Weiss, the professor that discovered the spacecraft at the inception of this dilemma, noticed a gaseous trail exiting the spacecraft. He believes that he can maintain a visual on the craft utilizing the same NASA software he used in his earlier exposure of the aliens. By applying the proper filters and running the profile through his computer, he can not only know precisely where it is at all times, but can get a clear image of the craft suitable for our intelligence gathering. I won't bore you with the details, but will explain that the computer can take the images of nothing more than radioactivity, gasses and heat readings and extrapolate that data into a normal looking image, much like those of the Hubble Space Telescope."

James stopped talking to the group for a moment to ask a technician if the parties at Cheyenne Mountain were online.

"I will now turn the meeting over to Cheyenne Mountain but before I do, I will say that Dr. Weiss has left the mountain for his observatory in Hawaii. He will be working from there from now on and has a satellite relay established to encrypt and relay everything he is able to gather the moment it is computed."

James sat down and allowed the meeting to progress. General Stephens gave everyone an update pertaining to the craft and their ability to trace its movements. He also made it known that they would be tracking each shuttle mission if used in the strategic plan, and added that all flights in North America had been grounded.

The meeting ended with everyone reporting his or her respective progress. This time not a single person was complaining about the impossibility of the mission. Just before James concluded the meeting, the President stood up and addressed the room.

"Ladies and gentlemen, we are at a crossroad that for many of us has been a long time coming. When I became President and learned about the alien spacecrafts we had, along with the thousands of square feet of related material, I was as shocked and dismayed as many of you were. To be completely frank, I thought that was all ancient history. I had pretty much concluded that we were alone in the universe, and it was something that I would not have to deal with as President. Now that we are at the precipice of taking life, regardless if it is human or not, we must adjudicate which direction we will take. Do we sit here and wait for the alien craft to make another aggressive move, or do we draw first blood?"

Even though it was a rhetorical question, several members of the President's staff and a couple of the heads of state for other countries replied in unison, "We draw first blood!"

"What we must do," he continued, "is continue our intelligence gathering and add resolve to our commitment while we prepare for the worst. In the history of the world at war, no country has ever engaged against an enemy so superior in size, strength or technology. The size of the craft alone suggests it is capable of carrying hundreds of thousands, perhaps millions of soldiers, if that is in fact their purpose. Furthermore, we have never fought an enemy about which we knew so little. I only pray that our history and the history of the world remember that we made the decisions we are making today with the interest and care of all humans at heart." The President saluted everyone in the room and said, "I honor your resolve and commitment to our nations and our nation's citizens." Then turned and left the room with his normal staff following closely behind.

James stood up and closed the meeting. "I trust that each of you will dwell on your part of this endeavor like never before. God Speed."

Bruce waited for everyone else to leave before standing and walking to the door. Leaning up against the door jamb, he watched as James gathered his materials. "I guess I'll be staying on a bit longer, huh?"

"Yes, whether you wanted to or not. I wasn't aware that they grounded all civilian flights, and since we can't spare anyone to debrief you right now anyway, it looks like you're in it for the long haul."

CHAPTER TWENTY-EIGHT

The Quod who had located Sean and the others was pounding at the wall that contained the secret closet so hard, that it appeared to the three hidden inside they would be found in a matter of seconds. Sean was not about to be taken prisoner again, because he felt that this time he would be killed for sure. The wall began to crumple as two additional Quod began to pound on the panel. Sean knew the moment to fight had come and reached out and pulled Gebel back against the wall inside the closet so he could have a clear shot. He pulled down his weapon, aimed for the spot in the wall that was beginning to open up and pulled the trigger. The resulting blast exploded through the wall and shred the three Quod.

Sean jumped through the opening first and fired again at the remaining Quod in the room. He continued to fire until nothing but Quod blood and pus like oil was spread over all the walls and floor, and nothing else moved. The stench was so repulsive that Sean had to fight the urge to vomit. Gebel and Rotusea came out of the room and looked around at all the carnage. Sean walked over to the door. As it opened to the Piiderk he saw thirty Quod heading his way.

"We've got to get out of here now, or we're all dead!" he yelled. "What is behind that wall?" He asked excitedly.

"I'm not sure, Rotusea replied. She asked Gebel but there was no reply.

"Get over here fast!" He yelled as he ran toward the center of the large room.

Gebel and Rotusea ran behind Sean. As soon as they were clear, Sean fired the weapon again blowing a huge hole into the wall that the bed had been placed against. They all ran toward the hole and jumped through. To everyone's surprise, they had blown a hole into the transportation chamber. The bodies of hundreds of Quod and Tahar soldiers were strewn everywhere. Sean waited for the thirty Quod to rush into the room with his back against the wall next to the hole he had just blown out. As soon as he heard them rushing in, he turned and fired, again blowing the Quod apart.

"Where can we go now?" Sean asked Rotusea in a stressful tone.

"Come this way!" she said as Gebel began to run through the great expanse of the transportation chamber. They ran to the far end of the hanger-like room and came to a small round room with glass walls next to the Zurostian Chamber that Rotusea had pointed out to Sean earlier.

"In here—quickly!" Gebel said holding the door open for them. As soon as they were inside, Gebel continued, "This is the Star Chamber. It is used to…" But before he could continue, Sean interrupted him.

"This is no good! They'll be able to see us! We've got to keep moving!"

"No," she said, "this battle is ours, and we can use the Star Chamber to send you back where you came from!"

"I'm not leaving without Nancy and the knowledge that Karna and, if need be this ship, is destroyed!"

Gebel and Rotusea were seemingly arguing over what he had said, and Sean was growing more impatient.

"Come on! We've got to move out of here!" he yelled.

Gebel opened a small panel in the wall and the three went to another maintenance passageway. "We'll be safe in here," he said. "Even if the Quod find our scent again, they are too big to get through the passageways."

Sean was the last to enter the access panel. As he closed the door, leaving just a small crack to look out of, he scanned the transportation chamber trying to make sense of what he was seeing. The room was as big as three football stadiums and had what looked like a window in the ceiling that opened out into space. The opening itself was three hundred feet wide and several hundred feet long. He studied the ships that were staged around the room and was dumbfounded by the mass of each ship. Each ship was a big as two cruise ships and was oblong. There were no visible windows in the ships but there were several areas of the surface that resembled polished copper. At one end, open to the main room in the center, were large ramps leading into each ship. The ramps alone were large enough to drive four semi trucks on side by side. He closed the door and crawled back further into the darkness.

While the maintenance passageways were completely dark to the Bilkegine, they did have enough ambient light for Sean to see once his eyes became adjusted to the low light conditions. Sean looked around him and noticed that Gebel was gone.

"Where is Gebel?" he asked.

"He has an idea to throw the Quod off our trail."

"What plan?"

"He is making his way back to the Star Chamber and will try to bypass the control panel from within the passageway. If he is successful he will activate the chamber and the immense light and high frequency it generates during operation will draw the Quod to it."

"He's going to bring them here?"

"No, the Quod will see the light and hear the sound and assume that we have all left the ship for the planet. You must remember that they are not great thinkers. When they see the chamber light they will not question the fact that we have used the Star Chamber to escape the ship."

Sean went back to the door and opened it slightly. He could barely see the edge of the Star Chamber. Suddenly a large group of Quod came into the transportation chamber and spread out in search of Sean and the other. The Star Chamber began to glow a brilliant blue light twenty times brighter than the cinbiote and produced an intensely high pitch squeal. Immediately, several Quod rushed toward the Star Chamber and Sean closed the door and waited.

The darkness of the passageway coupled with the ever growing fear inside Sean was taking its toll on his morale. He was getting tired of running and hiding and was just about to run out firing at the Quod when the sound stopped. He very cautiously cracked the door again in time to see the Quod leaving the transportation chamber.

"It worked!" he whispered to Rotusea.

Sean slumped down with his back against a control panel inside the passageway and tried to relax. A few seconds passed, and Gebel appeared from out of the darkness and crawled to where the two were sitting.

"Are you alright?" he asked

Rotusea responded to his question and the two spent several minutes talking to each other before Rotusea turned toward Sean and sat down in front of him.

"We cannot stay here." She started. "The lack of dighergant is making us too weak to move around. We must go back to a safe location and have a resting phase to recuperate."

"What should I do? Can you get me back to where Nancy is now?"

"I'm afraid that will not be possible until we have rested. The passageways are interconnected and do lead to the lower levels, but it would be too difficult with no light and in our weakened condition to go now."

"But the Tahar soldiers are still with Nancy, right? Do you have a way to communicate with them?"

Rotusea looked at Gebel for a sign to continue, and then looked back at Sean. "Sean," she spoke hesitantly, "Nancy is alone in the maintenance passageway. We could not stay with her due to the lack of dighergant. Our men would have surely died had they stayed with her during the whole time we were separated."

"How do you know she is alright then?"

"She will be fine as long as she stays inside on that level. Even if the Quod were to find her, they could not reach her. She is fine."

"What am I supposed to do while you are sleeping, sit here and do nothing?" Sean said angrily. "I've got to get us out of here and destroy this ship before I go, unless you can take control of it first."

Once again, Rotusea took a couple of moments to converse with Gebel.

"The Tahar has done considerable damage to the Spiruthun, and it is not a threat to the planet in its current condition. The only means of reaching the mid-ship has been closed by explosives. Only those warrior Quods, and others who were already on the Piiderk level or the two decks above and below it can reach the transportation chamber. We will now have several phases to accomplish our goals but we must have a rest first. You must use the time to rest as well. We will take the passageways back to our secure resting chamber and meet with you here afterwards."

Sean was finished talking and realized the logic of Gebel's decision. As he watched them disappear, he pulled open his pack and took out some of the food he had put inside. He leaned back and tried to relax but all he could think about was being back in the mountains in his hardware store and maybe having Nancy there with him.

He looked inside the pack and took inventory of his ammunition, then took another peek into the transportation chamber. When he was convinced that everything was quiet, he crawled deeper into his hideout and stretched out on the floor and fell asleep.

CHAPTER TWENTY-NINE

Dr. Weiss returned to his lab after stopping by his apartment for a short nap and began his work. Knowing that there would be people inside, he went in and made an announcement. It was a complete fabrication of the facts, but due to security he felt he had little choice in the matter. He took a campus guard along with him and posted him outside. He called all the students and staff who were working in the lab to a meeting and began his deception.

"As many of you are aware, I've been out of town the past two weeks. I had the privilege of speaking to a symposium on the advanced exploration of our solar system and was presented new information recently discovered about super black holes. Evidence has been produced, along with collaboration that a super black hole exists in the center of every galaxy including our own. We have never been able to see it because we didn't know what to look for. But it has become evident that dark matter, invisible to the naked eye, can be detected by observing light from distant stars as it is bent by the gravity of the giant black hole. Needless to say, I am very excited about the possibility of us taking part in this study; however, before we can go any further there are some modifications must be made to our equipment. And, because of our most recent find of the meteoroid, we have been selected to participate and present evidence at the next worldwide symposium." Dr. Weiss knew it was a safe lie because for the past twenty seven years he had never missed the annual symposium, and been a major contributor for the past seventeen years.

Every member of the student body and the staff in the lab cheered and clapped at the news. While the recent discovery of the super black holes was true, the reason for them attending was a complete fabrication. Nevertheless, the story was believed and everyone present began to ask questions among themselves.

"Please, please," the professor continued. "We must however make drastic changes to our system and to our security if we are to participate in the program. There are many grants being awarded for this endeavor and information gathered will be highly guarded. Therefore, it is imperative that we enlist the aid of our campus police to develop and provide manpower to a much tighter security protocol. Before we proceed, and while the changes are being made, each student wishing to participate must submit a thesis paper on the subject. Only the top five students will be awarded the necessary security clearance to enter the lab during the study. As far as the staff is concerned, they will form a committee to evaluate and judge each paper before presenting them to me. So, until further notice, the lab will remain closed to anyone without proper clearance."

"When will the study begin, Professor?" asked a member of the staff.

"I do not have the exact date yet, Avery; I must first receive bids for the conversion of our equipment. However, I will begin making changes to the computer database and programming immediately."

"What about class, professor? One student yelled from the back of the room.

"Ah, yes. My classes will be taken by Professor Van Shlive beginning Monday morning. Are there any more questions?"

"What about the projects we are currently working on, Professor? Some of us need the lab time to finish our degrees by this spring."

"Uh, yes, Rebecca, I understand completely." He replied, stalling for time to come up with a believable solution to his dilemma. "Each of you will submit your paper and equations on your hypothesis, and you will be graded on the work to date. If you have not completed enough study to finish your hypothesis as of today, you may submit your request for data in writing, and we will allow you to get the data from another lab at the University's expense."

Dr. Weiss was feeling very uncomfortable having to make up lies to cover his lies. He was also not comfortable speaking for the entire university administration by offering to pay tuition and lab fees at another university, but made a calculated guess that the government would offset any losses the college would incur during this national crisis. At any rate, he wanted to stop lying and cut the meeting short.

"If there are any more questions, please bring them up in your class time, and we will answer them at the earliest possible time. Thank you for your understanding. While the urgency cannot be avoided, this study truly is a once in a lifetime opportunity. Now, if you will all please excuse me, I would like to go over the security needs with the campus police chief."

Plans had already been made for tighter security, but Dr. Weiss took a few minutes to elaborate what the procedures were going to be with the guard posted at the door. After explaining that no one but himself would be allowed inside the building until further notice, he wasted no more time and got right to work on the computer programming. Since the telescope was to be down, he thought it would be prudent to move it into the best position to view the alien craft right away and leave it there to make it easier to conceal their deception.

At last the initial deceit was done and Dr. Weiss could continue his work. Although he had his doubts that the story that Agent Rose helped devise would be believable, it proved to be detailed enough to work. The professor brought the telescope into position and fired up the NASA computer. He tweaked the program to concentrate the search on the gaseous discharge and used the chemical trail to follow the craft into space. After several hours the first image was translated and for the first time, since the meteoroid collision, he was able to see the ship as it truly was.

Even though he had estimated its size fairly accurate, he was wrong about the shape. When the final analysis was complete, it wasn't a perfect sphere as he had presumed, it was oblong. He realized that the image he had before was one that was looking directly at the end of the craft and thereby giving it a spherical appearance. However upon closer examination and calculations he realized the ship to be twice as long as it was high. With this additional knowledge, he realized now how the meteoroid strike sent the ship spinning as violently as he had recorded. The star projection feature he thought was a cunning camouflage was nothing more than a series of bright lights created by some kind of gas exhaust. He could clearly see that they were able to arrange the glow of the lights in the pattern that most resembled the location of the stars that they were blocking. Furthermore, he discovered a huge hole large enough to fly the biggest commercial airliner through without the fear of coming close to the sides of the gargantuan spaceship.

"That is it!" he whispered to himself, "That is where the missiles will be able to penetrate the furthest. The laser pulse weapon they were so reserved about using may not need to be used at all. I must send this off to Cheyenne immediately."

Dr. Weiss sent the encrypted information to Cheyenne Mountain and began to program the computer to enhance every detail of the alien craft. Since it would take the computers hours to extrapolate the data for each sector, due to the enormous size, he wrote a quick program that would translate the data, encrypt the file and send them to Cheyenne Mountain after each section was completed. He then left the lab for a much needed rest.

He hadn't been sleeping very long when he was awakened by a banging on his apartment door. Wiping the sleep from his eyes, he got up, put his robe one and went to the door yelling as he walked, "I'm coming, I'm coming."

He opened the door. To his surprise it was the campus police. "You'd better come with me to the lab. Dr., there's been a break in."

"What! Are you joking? You couldn't even keep a building secure for one evening?" He yelled looking at his watch, "For four hours!"

"Wait a minute, Dr. Weiss, and I'll tell you what happened."

"I will change and meet you there. You can tell me then!" he yelled as he slammed the door in the cop's face.

"Ok, fine." The policeman mumbled under his breath.

The professor grumbled all the way to his bedroom. He put on some old wrinkled clothes he had thrown over the foot of his bed and walked up the hill to the lab. As he was coming up the hill, he noticed a window on the second floor fire escape broken out and figured that whoever had broken in probably had gone in there. He was very mad at security for not making sure the back fire escape ladder was stowed and secure. He thought that if they had done their jobs right, they would have been making rounds around the building and seen the ladder down and secured it. He made it to the top of the hill and went inside finding three campus police officers and the light on inside one of the offices.

"Okay. Someone had better tell me what's going on here!" he yelled angrily.

The chief of police walked up to him, pulled him aside and began to explain what happened and who broke into the lab.

"Dr. Weiss, I'm Chief Stickel, the night watch superintendant. Let me fill you in on what has transpired here tonight. At about 0300 the officer on watch heard a faint noise out back. He couldn't distinguish the sound at that time as breaking glass, but he called it in, and when we had shift change I had the replacement go and check it out before he relieved the man on watch."

"How much time elapsed between the time of the initial call and the time when his relief showed up?"

"Well, let's see," he said looking at his watch. "It would have been about forty-five minutes."

"You didn't think of sending someone out right away? Do you have a firm grasp on the meaning of security, Mr. Stickel?"

"It was a faint sound, Dr. Weiss. We don't have the manpower to check out every sound that is heard on campus. Anyway, like I was saying, the replacement showed up and made a sweep around the building and discovered the broken window. He called it in and stayed out back so the perpetrator couldn't escape the same way he entered, and I came to check it out. When I got inside, I saw those two female students working at the computers," he explained pointing to the girls sitting in the office.

Dr. Weiss cocked his head to the side to see who the girls were sitting behind the glass wall. When he recognized them he hung his head and sighed.

"I just knew something like this was going to happen." He mumbled.

"What was that Doctor?"

"Oh, uh it was just—nothing."

"So what do you want us to do with them, turn 'em loose till tomorrow?"

"No Mr. Stickel. I will take care of them personally. Give me a few minutes with them alone. And, while you're waiting, get someone from maintenance to patch the window and secure the fire escape with a padlock. And before you say anything about fire code, I know what they are, and I will accept all responsibility."

"Uh, Doctor, it's 0400. You want I should wake someone up in the middle of the night to patch a window?"

"If it's not too much trouble—Mr. Stickle," the professor replied sarcastically.

"You're the boss, Doctor."

The two girls waiting nervously inside the office were the two students who had been working on the meteoroid project when it had exploded. As he expected, his students and staff would be too smart to buy the story that Agent Rose cooked up and would think something was fishy. He guessed that they were more suspicious than the others, because of the way he ushered them out the night the meteoroid blew apart, then disappeared for two weeks afterward. Regardless, they had broken university rules and committed misdemeanor breaking and entering in the process. They knew that they could be expelled for what they had done and were more afraid of not finishing their degrees than paying the price of breaking the law. As Dr. Weiss pondered what he should do with them, he went inside the lab to discover how much they had been able to uncover. He sat down at the main terminal and reactivated the computer from hibernation mode. The first screen to appear was not the password entry window, and he was disappointed to see that they were able to hack the password he had set earlier that evening and gain access. While he was thinking of how to handle the situation he could hear the two girls arguing quietly inside his office but couldn't make out what they were saying.

"I knew we were going to get caught!" Cathy said weeping. "You're always getting me into trouble."

"I didn't have to twist your arm girlfriend. You know you wanted to know what was going on as much as I did. Don't try to deny it!" Rachel said right back.

"I might have wanted to know what was going on, but don't forget it was me who suggested we go back when we saw that cop at the front door. You just don't want to take the blame by yourself for breaking in."

"And you know I shouldn't have to. You were right behind me. You're just as guilty, so don't try to shift the blame on me!"

Cathy started to cry more intensely and began to tremble. "My dad is going to kill me when he finds out! I'll be lucky if he keeps paying for my tuition!"

"He's not going to cut you off, you're his charming little angel and you know it. Get a grip—will you. If the Professor comes in here and sees you blubbering like a little child, he'll think we're more guilty than we really are." Rachel said bitterly.

"Just shut up, Rachel, I'm through listening to you!"

"Fine, but like I said, you're not putting all of this on me. Just let me do the talking and we'll get out of this, okay?"

Cathy just ignored her and pulled a wrinkled up tissue from her pocket and dabbed her eyes and wiped her nose. She didn't believe that Rachel would be honest and figured her lies would probably get them in more trouble than they already were and she began to get angry. She stopped crying and just sat and stared at her roommate bound and determined to be the first one to say anything so she could tell the truth.

When Dr. Weiss couldn't hear them any longer, he slowly made his way to the office.

"Cathy, Rachel, I'm very disappointed to see you both here. What do you have to say in your defense?"

"Professor," Cathy said quickly, "it was our project that you were working on, and when you tossed us out two weeks ago we knew something was up. Then you came back with that story and everything. We're not stupid."

Rachel glared over at Cathy then looked back at the professor and nodded her agreement with what Cathy had said.

"What do you know about M46H that you didn't already know?"

"We know it didn't just fall apart like you said," Rachel said sarcastically.

"I would suggest you watch your tone with me, young lady. You are both inches away from expulsion and jail right now and I'm in no mood to tolerate any sarcasm! Now, for your own good, you'd better start talking and tell me everything you have discovered about the work I've been doing here."

Tears started running down Cathy's face again and she began to tell the professor what they had found.

"We just wanted to know the truth, Dr. Weiss. We figured that we had it coming to us, since we worked so hard on our project and everything."

"Just tell me what you know!" He yelled.

They both jumped back when he yelled at them. Neither had ever seen him angry before. He had always acted a little absent minded, but was always so polite.

"We know that you are spying on a military spacecraft, some top secret deal for the military probably," Rachel said sharply.

Dr. Weiss jumped to his feet and leaned into Rachel. "I have warned you once about your tone. One more facetious remark or smart answer and I will call the Sheriff."

"Sorry," she said quietly, sinking in her chair.

"How did you come up with that conclusion?" he asked, more calmly.

"We looked in the telescope and saw the outline of something that looked like another meteoroid but with a thick fog around it. Then we went to the computer to analyze it, but all we got was the message, 'Computing'." Cathy said still crying.

Rachel took up where Cathy left off and continued to explain. "Then I looked in the database computer for old files since we were here last. I saw a record of the meteoroid strike and saw a space station that it struck. But there was something wrong with the picture. The space station didn't look like the pictures I've seen on the NASA website, so we figured it was some new top secret military satellite or something." She said looking at Cathy.

"You are right! And you are in big trouble with the military for knowing about it! I will have to make a call to the National Security

Agency and find out what they want to do with you. Chances are they will throw you both in jail for snooping around a top-secret military project."

At first Rachel believed that the professor was trying to steal their work. They both thought of him as some old dried up professor that was beginning to lose his wits and hadn't had a discovery for so many years that he needed a boost in his career and was willing to steal to get one. Now that they saw him so mad, and they had been caught by campus security, and the NSA was involved, they really thought they were in big trouble and they both began to weep.

"Stay right here while I call the NSA agent I've been working with!" He ordered firmly as he stood up and walked out of the room. He slammed the door behind him to suggest he was really angrier than he really was. He walked out of the room and went into his office to call Agent Rose. While he was waiting for him to come to the phone he was wondering if they had made up the story to cover their butts. He wondered if they really knew that they had seen an alien spacecraft and were lying to protect themselves. Without having a means of knowing the truth he would have to rely on Agent Rose.

"Agent Rose" James said as he picked up the phone.

"Yes, Agent Rose, this is Dr. Weiss."

"Yes, Doctor. What can I do for you?"

"Unfortunately, I've had a break in at my lab by two of my students and they have seen the files and the spacecraft. I don't know how to proceed and need your input on the matter."

"Oh, I see. Who are the students?"

"They are both graduate students working on their Masters Degrees. The first one is Cathy Books, and the second is Rachel Zimmerman."

"Have you questioned them, Dr. Weiss?"

"Yes, but to be honest, I don't know if they are telling me the truth. They told me they think it's a top-secret military space station or huge satellite."

"You don't believe them?"

"I don't know how to tell. It's not really in my field of expertise. Would you like to talk to them?"

"Not over the phone, Doctor. Let me think for a minute."

Agent Rose thought quietly for a minute and finally came up with a solution. "I've got a solution, I think. Do you remember Bruce, the Sheriff from Morgan town, North Carolina?"

"Yes, I do. Rather large fellow?"

"That's him. He was planning on returning home today but all civilian flights were cancelled right after you got home. I will send him there on our jet. He can stop there to interrogate the two girls with a lie detector and go home from there. I'll have him pose as an agent with the NSA. I'll leave it up to him. If he thinks they are telling the truth you can deal with them, but if they are lying, then I will take care of them myself. How does that sound?"

"That sounds just fine to me. What will you do if the Sheriff thinks they are lying?"

"I will most likely lock them up until this nasty business is over, then, swear them to secrecy. If they ever speak a word of it to anyone and I find out, then they will die in prison."

"Very well, Agent Rose. I will look for the Sheriff tomorrow then. Thank you."

"Goodbye, Doctor."

The professor hung up and went back into the office where the girls were crying quietly with their heads hung low. He went inside, sat down facing them and sighed heavily.

"Girls, I'm afraid I have very bad news. I wish you had left well enough alone on this, but since you chose to snoop around where you didn't belong, I'm afraid you will have a high price to pay. There is an agent for the NSA coming later this morning to investigate your story. He will interrogate you both individually and give you both a lie detector test. If you are telling the truth about what you did and why, then you will be in my hands and will be expelled without your degrees. If you are lying, and I hope you are not, you will in all likelihood be imprisoned for an unspecified period of time. I hope and pray for your sake that you are telling me the truth."

"Dr. Weiss," Cathy said softly, "isn't there any way we can stay and finish our degree? We will do anything you say."

"Yes, we'll do anything," Rachel agreed, "We won't tell anyone anything!" She said excitedly.

"I'm sorry girls; it's out of my hands. We'll see tomorrow. Maybe, just maybe, if you are telling the truth I will cut you both a break! For tonight though, you will have to spend the night in the campus jail. Wait here. I'll go get the Chief."

Dr. Weiss left to get the chief. After the girls had been escorted to the campus jail for the rest of the night, the professor sat alone in his office and pondered. Why did those young girls have to be the ones to see the meteoroid strike the alien craft, and why am I, of all people, the one to be mixed up in this cover up?

CHAPTER THIRTY

Sean woke up inside the dark maintenance passageway in a panic and was completely disoriented. After a few moments, he remembered where he was and where the entrance panel was located and crawled out. He cracked the door slightly and peeked through the crack with one eye closed to make sure it was safe to leave. Just as he was beginning to open the door wider, to check in the direction behind the door, several warrior Quods walked beside the panel heading for one of the ships that was not destroyed in the earlier battle. It was now impossible to leave the way he came in and it infuriated him. It wasn't the fact that the door was no longer a usable means of egress; it was the fact that all he really wanted to do was get back to Nancy and get back home where he belonged. As before, during his war experience, he also was angry to be somewhere, doing something that he didn't want to do. Back then, he didn't desire to be in a foreign place, fighting foreign people and killing men he had never even met before but it was his duty and Sean never shirked his duties. It didn't matter back then, when he was ordered to go overseas and it didn't matter now. His duty, spoken or not, was to his fellow humans and while he did not enjoy killing anyone, he certainly knew that killing something that was pure evil would be justified when he reached his final resting place in heaven. At least that was how he was thinking. He had some serious conflicting thoughts going through his head regarding the slaughter of the Quod and the accidental killing of the Tahar soldier. He couldn't get the sight out of his head of the man who had given his life for a race of people, on a distant planet, who had never done anything that would deserve his sacrifice, and yet there he was bleeding on the floor after being shot by friendly fire. That thought brought back memories that he had nearly all but forgotten about from his youth in a Sunday school in the small town where he grew up. He remembered that Jesus was the first man to come to a distant place and gave his life for a people who didn't deserve his sacrifice, who had never done anything redeeming enough to deserve it, yet there he was nailed upon a Roman cross bleeding. Sean slipped into a meditative like trance while his daydream took him back to church and the cross of Christ. Suddenly he heard a loud crash that shook him out of his trance. His whole body jerked with surprise, but when he recognized there was no threat he went back to finish his thought. "Yes, I did not deserve what Jesus did for me on that cross. I did not do anything worthy of his dying and bleeding for me and I owe it to him to be thankful and repentant as much if not more than I owe it to this alien friend that has given his life for me to fight against evil in all its many forms," he whispered to himself.

Sean started to believe that for some unknown reason, God must have put him there on that alien spaceship to help as only he could. He began to think that God knew that Nancy would be involved and because of her past, knew that she would not be strong enough on her own. The more Sean examined the life he had lived and the people who had come into his life the more he realized that it couldn't have all been coincidence. There has to be a higher power behind all of this, he thought. I think that higher power is at work right here, right now.

He began to wonder how long he had been sleeping and where his Tahar comrades were. Recognizing the fact that he had become more dependent on them than he wanted to be, he went back inside and waited for them to show up. He grew angry waiting in the dark not out of fear or pride, but because he was worried about Nancy sitting alone in the dark on an alien spaceship, in the middle of space, with nothing but prayer to keep her company. That thought brought back another he had been pondering during quiet times in his life. He had thought it and even stated it out-loud: does God really exist? He even remembered asking or telling someone to pray for him before going someplace dangerous, and even remembered doing it since he had been there when talking to Nancy. "How or why would I do that unless down deep inside I know that there is a God and that He will look after me," he said, talking to himself in a low whispery voice. "Why do I think I have to be able to see, touch, hear and understand something before I can believe it? Sean, you're an idiot. You're a selfish, blind, close minded, narcissistic, egomaniac, who doesn't deserve anyone or anything! If someone had told me there were aliens in spaceships parked just off the planet who were here to destroy earth and make slaves of every human, I would have thought they were either crazy, deranged, insane, or just plain nutty, because I had never seen, touched, heard or understood how they could exist and travel such far distances. I would have told them they were idiots because if the greatest minds on the planet couldn't wrap their minds around that concept, and if they didn't understand how it was possible, who are you, or any other weak minded person to think anything otherwise."

Sean was lost in his thoughts when he heard a shuffling sound coming toward him from within the dark passageway. He quickly grabbed his weapon and braced himself mentally for another battle. Just as he was about to squeeze the firing mechanism he recognized Rotusea.

"Boy I am glad to see you two," He said excitedly as Rotusea and Gebel got within a few feet from him. "I was beginning to think I was on my own."

"Who were you speaking with?" Rotusea asked as they sat down beside each other.

"Oh that, I was just talking to myself."

"I do not understand. Why would you talk to yourself? It has no meaning. What good is it to talk to no one?"

"It's an earth thing I guess. It helps us think better sometimes, or maybe we do it when we need to hear another audible voice when we're alone or frightened. I don't know. It's just something humans do."

Gebel touched Rotusea indicating they didn't have time for idle chatter, and said, "There is little time, we must go now."

"Are we going to get Nancy?"

"Yes, then we are sending you both home."

Sean began shaking his head no, "No!" he proclaimed. "Not before I take care of Karna. I thought we were done arguing about this. It's my duty, my responsibility to take her out once and for all, and do what I can to save our planet!"

"First things first.Let's go retrieve your helpmate," Rotusea suggested. "Then we will discuss our options."

"My helpmate—huh, I like the sound of that," Sean said with a smile.

"She is not your helpmate?"

"Not yet, but who knows, anything is possible."

They headed down the shadowy passageways inside the mechanical corridors and through a few treacherous vertical maintenance shafts to reach Nancy's hiding place. They were all surprised to find nearly fifty dead Quod surrounding the area directly outside the access panel where Nancy was hiding. It appeared that they had in fact located Nancy and died trying to extract her. Unfortunately, the Tahar soldier who had accompanied her was found dead just outside the access panel as well. He had been crushed by one of the Quod and his body appeared to have been folded in half.

Sean ran to the access panel and yelled inside for Nancy. He called her name several times but could not hear a response. He was beginning to panic but could not open the access panel because it was crushed and twisted around a support post. Gebel and Rotusea, who were both much stronger then Sean began to help him pull the door open. When it was finally pulled back far enough for Sean to squeeze past, he crawled deep inside the corridor continuing to call out her name. He went farther back then stopped to listen but heard nothing. The tunnel was getting smaller and tighter and Sean was forced to lie down and pull himself through with his hands. Finally, after stopping to take a brief break to catch his breath, he heard Nancy's faint whispering voice calling his name. She had been calling out for Sean so long that her voice had dried out, and she was unable to speak above a whisper. She had also been crying and was afraid that Sean had been killed and she was all alone on the alien ship. When she heard Sean's voice calling out to her from the main corridor, she began crying heavily for both joy that she was not alone, and relief that Sean was alive.

"I'm so glad to see you," she said as she reached out and pulled Sean into her strong embrace.

"I told you I would come back for you, didn't I? I always do what I say I'm going to do."

Nancy had such a strong hold on Sean that he was finding it hard to catch his breath. Sean pulled her back so he could see her face and as her eyes met his, she looked up and kissed him. Then looking at him again, she said, "Sean, please tell me you will never leave me again."

He had been thinking of her as more than just a woman in distress. He had grown very fond of her and believed that, against all odds, he had fallen in love and that the feeling was mutual. He looked deep into her eyes as if trying to see her very soul, brushed some dirt from the top of her bald head, and wiped her tear away. Then in a quiet, tender voice, he said, "I love you Nancy, and I promise."

"No! Say the words!"

"Okay," he said laughing softly, "I will never leave you again. I promise."

They sat together holding hands in the dark and just looking at each other for five minutes before their moment together was interrupted by Rotusea's voice calling into the passageway. Sean leaned into Nancy and gave her a peck on the cheek. "I guess we better join them."

They got up together and crawled back out into the large corridor where Gebel and Rotusea were waiting. Gebel reached out and helped Nancy to her feet as she emerged. Wishing Gebel could understand what he was saying without everything being interpreted first, Sean asked, "What's the plan?"

"I had hoped the next step was going to be sending both you and Nancy home, but since you will not have anything to do with my plan, what would you suggest we do?"

"Give me a minute alone with Nancy first."

Sean took Nancy's hand and led her away from Gebel and Rotusea then sat down facing her. He looked directly into her eyes again while holding both hands. "Nancy, I've got to ask you something very important, well, several things actually."

She sat quietly looking intently at him and waited for him to begin.

"First, like I told you in the tunnel, I want you to know that I am falling in love with you and would like to continue to see you when this mess is over."

Nancy flashed a big smile and squeezed his hands. She began to say something but Sean reached up and touched her lips indicating her to wait and be quiet until he finished.

"Secondly, I need to ask you to do something that I believe you will not want to do."

A somber look came over her face as she leaned closer to Sean.

"Now, before you say anything, you need to hear me out completely. I would like to send you home. Gebel showed me the machine they used to bring us here and he knows how to use it. He can send you right back to where you were that morning, and you can get a message to Bruce for me. It is really important. Can you do that for me?"

Her somber look had turned completely into a frown. "Sean, I don't want to leave you. I'm scared that you won't come back, and I don't want to lose you."

"Listen, Honey. I'll be fine, but it's really important that you get a message to Bruce for me. It's our only chance to destroy this ship. If you do not go, the entire planet could be lost to the evil people trying to take it over. If I didn't think it was the only way I would never do it. Believe me when I say that I'm scared too, and I would rather have you right here beside me. But down deep in my heart, I would rather know that you were completely safe and I can't protect you the way I need to if you remain here with me. What do you say?"

She looked down at her hands as they were cradled by Sean's then back into his eyes. After thinking for quite some time, she finally agreed.

"Okay," she said tenderly, "I guess you know what is best."

"Good, there is one more thing. I want you to take the girl, Nakita with you. I don't think she even knows she is human, but I know she needs our help whether she knows it or not. Can you do that as well?"

"Sean, I believe I can do anything as long as you are with me and as long as I believe you will return safely."

Sean stood up then helped Nancy up. He gave her another hug and kissed her on the forehead. They went back to where Gebel and Rotusea had been waiting and watching and outlined the plan.

Looking at Gebel, but knowing Rotusea would automatically translate for him, he said, "Ok, Gebel, here is what we need to do. You take Nancy and the girl, Nakita and send them home in that transportation device you showed be earlier. Can you do that?"

He waited for Rotusea to finish the translation and reply.

"Yes, I can do that, it is a very good way to start. What will you do then?"

"I will take Rotusea and go to the dighergant rapitor chamber and try and destroy it."

"No, that will not work. Besides there is a back up reactor that would automatically come online. Leave that to us as a last resort. We still have enough Tahar soldiers to strike an offensive against the remaining Quod caught in the mid-ship sections. We will fight them from the Piiderk level and post men at every access point between the two levels above and below. When reinforcements try to reach the Piiderk, we will kill them immediately. Taking command of the Spiruthun should not be as difficult as it was before we cut off the Piiderk. Our only concern will be the warrior Quods inside the transportation chamber."

"Ok, but I'm not going to just sit around and do nothing. What would you suggest that I do while you send Nancy and the girl home?"

"You and Rotusea go to the new meeting place the Tahar have secured and coordinate a strategic attack someplace else. We still have to take the armory and cut off supplies from the warrior Quod. It is a stronghold that we must break if we are to take command of the vessel and hold it. Besides, as long as the Tahar are waging war on her ship, Karna will not begin her campaign against Earth."

"Good. Then let's get going!"

Sean gave Nancy one last kiss and made sure she completely understood the message she was to give the sheriff.

"You are clear on the message for Bruce?" Sean asked.

"Yes. As soon as I find him, I am to tell him what has happened and give him this as evidence," she said holding up the alien weapon Gebel had given Sean earlier. "Then I tell him what you plan on doing and ask him to contact the military so they can prepare to finish off the ship once they see some evidence that you were successful. The only thing I don't understand is what the evidence will be. What should they look for?"

"If they have been watching the spaceship, as I hope they are, they will know that something is drastically different."

"What if they don't even know it's up here. What then?"

"If what I plan on doing has the effect I think it will have, it will be obvious. Otherwise, tell them to scan space using the huge signal dishes I've read about. They listen for sounds in space. If they won't be able to see this thing, I'm sure they will be able to hear it."

"What about you? What should I tell them about you?"

"Oh yeah, I forgot. Tell Bruce that I will return home using the same transportation device you will use and don't forget to tell him not to worry."

Gebel left with Nancy and retrieved Nakita. Not knowing where they were going, Nakita went quietly along as she had been instructed by Karna. They traversed the dark maintenance passageways and vertical shafts to the transportation chamber. When they got inside they had to wait for several minutes for the Quod inside to leave the immediate area of the Star Chamber.

"What are we doing here?" asked Nakita.

"We're going home," Nancy replied excitedly.

"Home, no…"

"Yes home. Aren't you happy about it?"

Nakita did not know what to do or say. She had orders to stay with Sean and Nancy and not contact any Bilkegine, no matter what, but Karna didn't say anything about going anywhere. Nakita became nervous when the Quod began to leave because she was already in the Star Chamber, so just as Gebel had helped Nancy step into the Star Chamber, she jumped out and began to shout.

"They're over here! Come over here!"

The Quod turned to see what was going on and began to walk their way. Nancy was confused, especially since the two of them had spent so much time together talking in the warehouse and Nakita, although Nancy had been suspicious, never thought for a minute that she would turn them over to the Quod. Gebel didn't know exactly what to do, but had already activated the Star Chamber. The light had already begun to glow brilliantly, and tiny blue lightning strikes had begun to appear between the inside walls of the chamber as well. Nakita was outside the door jumping around and yelling in Bilkegine, "Come quickly they are escaping! Come! Come!" Gebel reached out and grabbed Nakita and pushed her inside the Chamber just as it was starting its final cycle. A brilliant light flashed inside the chamber walls in a dazzling display of electric wonder. They disappeared.

It was too late for Gebel. By the time the two had vanished in the Star Chamber, the Quod had arrived and had him by the back of the neck. Although he was a high ranking Bilkegine officer and of a higher class his orders to release him went unheard. It was obvious that they had orders to apprehend the female human subject and anyone seen with her.

The Quod leader took Gebel through the Piiderk and to the command chamber where Karna was waiting for information on her male subject's location. Gebel knew he would surely be tortured for information about Sean, and since he was displaying his Tahar crest, he knew there could be no way to explain and must find a way to take his own life before any interrogation could occur. The Quod arrived at the command center and just as they threw him onto the floor, Karna stepped into the room.

"Well, I am surprised to see you here, Gebel. You were the last person I would ever expect to be a traitor."

"I am no traitor!" he said firmly as he got to his feet. "Your Quod are so ignorant they wouldn't know you from a traitor. I was making adjustments to our transportation chamber, and they took me captive. If they had a mind between them, they would be dangerous!"

"So—I'm to understand that they made a mistake? If that is truth, why are you wearing this?" She asked hatefully as she ripped the Tahar crest away from his uniform.

"Do you not wear the crest of your Shem alliance during your ancestral celebration period? Besides that, what evidence do they have that I've done anything treasonous? I am attempting to maintain an extremely tight schedule to return the ship to full operational readiness, while they are running around harassing my crew."

"You deny your allegiance to the Tahar alliance regarding their recent attempt to mutiny?"

"It is true that I am a descendant of the Tahar alliance, but my clan has served the Shem alliance honorably for many generations. The Tahar alliance members of which you speak are despicable, loathsome and foot-hearty group of individuals that bring dishonor to the Tahar alliance. They are acting alone. I will let my record stand for me, Commander Nuubiya."

"You have not seen the human woman or male subject?"

"Commander, I have little time for anything but my duties."

"You have not answered my question Commander Gebel." Karna added angrily. "How am I to discern truth if you do not give me complete answers."

"No, Commander, I have no knowledge of your human subjects other than what I have heard. They do not concern me."

"Explain then, when he escaped from me earlier and attacked this station, I believe I saw someone who resembled you leading him away to safety. If that was you, your punishment will be severe."

"You will either take me at my word or you will not, but I testify that I have nothing to do with the humans."

"Will you swear on the name of the Tahar alliance?"

Gebel stood in silence because he had denied as much as his honor as a Tahar commander would allow. He would rather die than swear against his Tahar brethren that had died so valiantly.

"We will see, Commander Gebel," she said coldly. "Take him and interrogate him. If he has lied, tear out his heart and bring it to me."

Gebel stared at her as if to say he was not afraid of her and said, "Commander, I trust you will fail in your mission, as long as you treat your loyal officers with such disdain."

"Get him out of my face!" she screamed.

The Quod took Gebel out to the interrogation chamber, but before they could put him inside, he struck at the Quod and managed to escape. Since he had no knowledge of the ladder passages being blocked by a force-field, he first tried to avoid the pursuing Quod by leaving the Piiderk level, but after being thrown back by the electric shock of the energy wave he got to his feet and headed for the warehouse. As he was approaching the warehouse doorway, four more Quod appeared from inside and attempted to shoot him. He knocked a weapon free from the grip of the leading Quod, picked it up and ran the opposite direction. Realizing that he had no other route of escape, he crossed the Piiderk in sight of all the Quod and headed back to the command chamber. Taking his newly acquired weapon he ran into the control center screaming as he entered.

"Tahar Alliance! Tahar!"

He sprinted into the inner chamber where Karna sat in command of the Spiruthun and aimed his weapon directly at Karna, but before he could discharge the weapon, he was struck down and disarmed by three Quod guards. One of the Quod guards put his foot on Gebel's chest while the other two stood on his legs effectively pinning him to the floor. Karna walked slowly and methodically toward him, and while sneering down at him, she spat at him.

"You fool! Tahar alliance members are all fools, Gebel, and you are the biggest of them all! Did you actually believe you fooled me with your lies? That is absurd."

Then without saying another word, she reached down, picked up the weapon he had dropped, pointed it at his head and fired.

CHAPTER THIRTY-ONE

James left the conference room under the Smithsonian and went into the room that Bruce had been using as temporary quarters. Bruce was already packing for his trip home, hoping that the civilian flights would be allowed to operate soon.

"I guess you are anxious to get home huh, pal?" James asked as he leaned against the door jamb.

"Yeah, I'm just a simple mountain man," he replied humbly, "I ain't cut out for this cloak and dagger stuff."

"Do you think you could do one huge favor for me if I promise to get you home on our jet? I know I'm asking a lot, but I really don't have anyone else qualified but myself, and I just can't get away to do it right now. It's really important."

"You're not tryin' to buffalo me now are you? I'm the only one qualified, that's a laugh." Bruce said with a chuckle. "I'm the least qualified man around here to do any of this stuff, and for the life of me, can't even figure out why I'm even out here in the first place."

"Listen man, you've been a great asset to me, and I don't patronize anyone."

"If you say so," Bruce answered.

There was an awkward moment of silence as James waited for an answer from Bruce. Then Bruce looked up from his packing and asked about the favor.

"Ok, if I was to do this thing, this favor as you put it, what would it be?"

"You remember Dr. Weiss? He went back to his lab to study the ship, and was supposed to establish some tight security before he did anything else."

"Yeah and…"

"Someone broke into the lab and he thinks they discovered what he was working on but needs someone who knows how to interrogate prisoners to find out for sure."

"And that someone is me?"

"That's right."

"And I'm supposed to be the only one qualified for that huh?"

"As far as this is concerned, you are the only one I could trust with the knowledge of what is really going on here and I'd like to keep it that way. The two that you need to interrogate are students and they've stumbled on to what Dr. Weiss is working on."

"Didn't he just leave yesterday? How could he have gotten anything in that short of time frame?"

"I guess the doctor works faster that we thought. Anyway, the two who broke in saw everything, but claim to think it's a top-secret military weapon or craft of some kind. The professor and the NSA need to know for sure what they know."

"What do you want me to do, specifically?"

"I will give you NSA credentials, and you will pose as an agent and investigate the break in. You will interrogate the two students who broke in and give them a lie detector test. In the process, if you believe that they are telling the truth, and they think it is a military top-secret project, than you debrief them and make them take an oath of silence punishable by life imprisonment if they talk about it to anyone."

"And if they are lying?"

"If they really know what is out there, they will be taken to a secure site and held until this business is over."

"You can do that?" Bruce asked confused. "Without a trial of anything, just toss them in jail and throw away the key until whenever?"

"It's been done before, my friend, in the name of national security."

"Ok, I'll do it. Will they come here, or do I have to go to Hawaii?"

"You will go there, and the jet will wait for you to finish. I'll send two of our military security members with you in case they need to escort the two young ladies back here. Then the jet will take you home."

"Alright then, let's go."

Twenty minutes later, Bruce, two military police and the flight crew were airborne and on the way to Hawaii. It had been almost three weeks since Bruce had been home and more than a week since he had even talked to his wife. He would be glad when the whole business was over. He was tired, grumpy and just wanted for things to be normal again.

They landed and were picked up minutes later and immediately went to the campus police station where the two students were being held. Before the investigation was to begin, Bruce wanted to meet with everyone involved and get a complete story of everything that had transpired. He also wanted to set the mood for the meeting by acting the part of a no nonsense government agent. Although Bruce was a simple mountain man, he was having a lot of fun flashing his NSA badge around. If anyone had looked close enough, they would have noticed that it expired two days later. Nevertheless, it was official, and it gave Bruce more clout than he would ever have again in his life.

He asked everyone involved to meet in a conference room and requested them to bring all the reports and data that the suspects had seen.

Dr. Weiss was the first to arrive with a copy of the data. He was hesitant to release the data to anyone and hadn't let the campus police chief see it when he requested it for his report. When he recognized Bruce, he was relieved and gave the files to him. Bruce flashed his NSA badge for the doctor when he arrived and winked.

"It's quite a promotion huh, Doc?"

"Yes indeed," he replied, "then you are the investigator?"

"Yeah, that's me. Please refer to me as Agent Bruce, I don't want anyone to get confused or question my authority on this matter. I'm trying to be as convincing as I can that I'm a straight laced federal agent."

"No problem, Agent Bruce," the professor said smiling.

The three campus policemen came into the conference room and sat down after introducing themselves to Bruce.

"Let's begin," Bruce started as he paged through the report the campus police chief prepared. "You boys don't carry a sharp axe—do you?"

"I'm sorry, Agent Bruce. My man called in the faint sound, but could not distinguish the sound as that of breaking glass from his post in the front of the building."

"Why didn't your man on guard check it out?"

"He was told to stay at his post at the front door of the building."

"Was the door locked?"

"Yes, but..."

Bruce interrupted, "and did he have a car?"

"Yes, but he was..."

"How long would it have taken for him to drive around the building?"

"Uh, I'm not sure," the police chief said timidly. "A few minutes, I guess."

"In minutes chief, how long in minutes—specifically?"

"I'm not sure, maybe one or two at the most."

"He could have driven around the building in one minute, probably less, and checked it out then couldn't he?"

"I suppose he could have, yes."

"But he didn't. He sat on his butt and called it in."

"Yes he called it in," the chief said reluctantly.

"Then why didn't someone respond to his call that he heard something that needed checking out, especially after you were briefed on the importance of the security?"

"Look," the chief said getting angry, "we don't have the resources to check out every little, sound that..."

"Thanks, I've heard enough," Bruce said impatiently. "All you had to say was... 'because we're incompetent, sir, and we didn't think,' and that would have settled it, and I would have known exactly what happened! Because when it comes down to the truth, chief, that is what happened! You and your pretend-a-cop force here are incompetent and weren't thinking and allowed two teeny boppers to break in right under your noses and steal very sensitive government data! You had better pray to God that they don't know what they really saw, because if they do, all three of you are going to jail with them for gross negligence. How do I know you weren't on the take or in on the whole deal from the beginning?"

Bruce's attitude and tone was angering the police chief and every time Bruce had interrupted him he grew red in the face and his blood pressure went up. Finally he blew off.

"Now just hold it a minute Agent...Bruce is it? This is a college campus not some high level government office or military base. We make the calls the way we see them and my officer didn't just blow it off or those two girls wouldn't be locked up at all. He followed through!"

Bruce sat quietly allowing the chief to vent then responded accordingly.

"Oh, I understand. Pardon me I thought the guard was to blame and now I see that it was your decision to prioritize an out of control sorority party above that of a newly assigned high priority military security effort. So you're to blame and I was right from the beginning, you are incompetent and should be jailed or at the very least, fired!"

"You can't scare me with your federal badge and loud talk, I know my rights and this is my campus! I'm not the one that is on trial here. I'm not the one that broke in and stole your precious secrets!"

"Oh, you know your rights? Then you also know that the minute Dr. Weiss ordered the building to be locked down and kept secure by a twenty-four hour guard that he was giving you a direct order. You were also aware that the government was involved due to the sensitive nature of the data and that he even closed the lab to his own staff while these preparations were being made, indicating the seriousness of the security. And yet you just rolled along like it was another ordinary boring day on campus where you stay alert for any student writing in a book, spitting on the sidewalk or allowing a party to get out of hand. You must be a very brave man."

"Look pal, all I know is that we did our job right and you can't touch us!" the chief yelled.

"You think so!" Bruce said angrily. "Guards!" he yelled.

The two Marine guards came into the conference room quickly with their weapons drawn and aimed at the chief and two policemen.

"Until further notice, these three men are under arrest for treason. I have reason to believe that they allowed the break in to occur resulting in the leak of sensitive data. Furthermore, I believe that they are either co-conspires or have taken a bribe to allow the perpetrators access to the lab. Cuff them!"

One of the guards kept the campus police men covered while the other cuffed them with their own handcuffs, led them out of the conference room and put them into the jail cells right across from the two students. As soon as they were gone the professor asked what Bruce was doing.

"What was that all about, my friend?" asked the doctor.

"Two things doc. I sensed the chief was hiding something right off the bat. I don't know what, but I figured the two younger ones would spill their guts later on if they faced going to prison for treason. Since everyone fears the NSA, I figured that I would use that hold card against them to find out what he was hiding. I figure it was probably a bribe or something similar. You know as well as I do that most campus cops don't take their jobs seriously. They wouldn't be here if they could get a real job as a cop on the outside, so they take what they can get, and if they're offered something on the side for a key after hours, I think they'd take it, don't you?"

"I hope not, but I guess we'll see."

"There was one more reason I acted like I did right from the beginning though. I wanted to put the fear of God into the two girls. If they think the cops that arrested them are going to jail, what do you think they'll think their chances are of staying out?"

"Ah, very cleaver, Sherriff. I mean Agent."

Bruce took the information the professor brought and asked him to go over it. It was hard enough to understand under normal conditions, but being a simple mountain man made it that much harder. The professor broke it down to as simple terms as he was able.

"It's like this, Bruce. The two girls saw the craft's shape, but because of the gas surrounding it, they think it was cosmic dust. It looks like fog. As you may know, fog distorts things so one might only see parts of the whole. For instance, if you see a deer in the fog, you may see its tail, part of its head and one leg but you know it's a deer because you've seen a deer before and like a puzzle, your brain replaces the missing parts from memory and tells you it's a deer. You may have run upon this phenomenon before without knowing it. An accident happens, but because the witnesses are standing in different places and have different views, their brain replaces, from memory, what they cannot see and they draw their own conclusions to the truth. It is why you can have seven people see an accident or robbery and you can get six or seven different stories. These two young ladies have never seen an alien spaceship before, but they have seen a satellite, a space station and other things like asteroids, meteoroids, and etcetera. Because the gaseous cloud was shrouding parts of the alien craft, they could only see the top, a piece of the broken side sticking into space, and some sections of the bottom. Their brains filled in the missing parts like the puzzle pieces, and they concluded they were either seeing a satellite or unknown space station. They only assumed it to be a secret military device because of the position of its orbit. You see Bruce, normally, satellites and the ISS are in a much lower position in our atmosphere."

"Boy, you make this stuff sound simple. Ok, thanks doc. Go ahead and take the stuff back and lock it up some place safe. I'll talk to the two young ladies one at a time, and stop by and let you know what I think before I leave."

Bruce called for one of the girls and had them brought into the conference room where he had set up his lie detector. The first student brought in was Rachel. During the initial interrogations, she had been the tough one, but after spending the last two nights in jail, she didn't seem so tough any more. Bruce introduced himself to her as Agent Bruce and flashed his new credentials to her. At first he was playing it pretty light. He wanted to get to know her a little. He wanted to know what made her tick and where her weaknesses were. Bruce had done this type of interrogation so many times he could practically do one in his sleep. The first thing he needed to know was whose idea the break in actually was.

"So, tell me a little more about your project, and why you were in the lab the day the meteoroid blew up?"

"We were studying M46H as a part of our master's degree in astronomy. Cathy, my roommate, and I discovered the meteoroid long before it was close enough to see with the naked eye, and we got to name it. Anyway we were in the lab when it blew apart, and the professor was there as well. He told us that he had already studied it, and that it had fallen apart because of its huge size and the enormous stress it was under due to the gravitational pull between the sun and Earth. We knew that was a load of bull, but when he told us to leave, we didn't have a choice."

"And that made you mad, didn't it?"

"Yeah, it made us mad. We thought he was trying to steal our work."

"Was he?"

"I don't know, but when we snuck back to watch the meteoroid pieces that stayed in space to see where they were going, he was still there, and he stayed there all night. I know because I went back several times during the night, and every time he was still there. One time I snuck into the lab, and he was sleeping at his desk and one of the new computers that we're not allowed to use was running some complicated program. I tried to see what it was running, but the professor woke up and I had to run out."

"You didn't get to see what it was later on?"

No. I wish I did, but after he left, I went back and he had taken everything with him. I know it was about my meteoroid, somehow, and that's why, when he came back I knew all the bull about the symposium was a big fat lie."

"Is that why you broke into the lab? To see what he was working on?"

"Yes."

"What was it?"

"Near as I could tell, the meteoroid hit something, and it didn't just blow apart from stress like the professor told me. I thought it was a lie from the beginning."

"Why didn't you argue about it with him?"

"You don't know much about university life do you? If you want a good grade, you don't argue with your professor, especially when you're working for your master's degree."

"But you broke into the lab after you were told not to. Didn't you think that would hurt your grade?"

"I wasn't planning on getting caught!"

Bruce began to set up the lie detector and as he was pulling out the wires and cables, he explained what he was doing. "I'm going to administer a lie detector test on you and your classmate first. If you are both telling the truth, you will more than likely be dealt with from within the university, but if you lie to me, you will go with the military police officers and no doubt spend considerable time in a government facility. Do you understand?"

Rachel nodded and the Sheriff hooked up the machine, placed a new role of paper on the spool and placed the pulse indicator on her finger, wrapped the respiration meter around her chest, and attached a few leads that indicated the presence of sweat. He began to set the parameters for the test by asking her some basic questions like her name and if the address on the police report was accurate. He asked her if she was female and then told her to intentionally lie to the next few questions. When he had established his control limits, he began questioning her in detail with questions that could be answered yes or no.

"Did you break into the lab on Saturday morning between two and three a.m.? Is your classmate Cathy Books? Was it your idea to break and enter the lab? Were you the one to hack into the computer? Do you believe Dr. Weiss to be an honest man?"

To each question Rachel answered the question honestly and the machine verified that she was telling the truth. However, when he reached the questions about the police chief and the spacecraft, he got conflicting data indicating that she was not truthful.

"Did you bribe one or more of the campus security officers in order to gain access to the lab?"

"No."

"Did you actually see a military satellite in a geo-synchronous orbit around Earth?"

"Yes."

The lie detector began to scribble from side to side indicating a lie on both questions. Bruce took the leads off of Rachel and asked her to place her arms behind her back. She complied peacefully until Bruce put the handcuffs on her wrists.

"What are you doing? I told you the truth, honest!" She said distraughtly. A single tear began to flow down her cheek.

"No, you did not!" Bruce yelled directly into her face. "You don't know how to tell the truth!"

She had never been in any trouble before and it was probably why she was so tough and rebellious before. Her lack of discipline and respect for authority had probably been caused by her busy parents who thought their little girl was a precious child because she got good grades in school despite the fact that she began talking back at an early age. The fact that she was face to face with an authority figure that she couldn't intimidate or charm into letting her go was a new experience. That coupled with the fact that she had spent two nights in jail and had witnessed all three of the night shift campus police be placed in jail beside them caused her to break down.

"Ok, ok," she cried out as real tears began to flow, "Yes, it was me. I did bribe one of the officers! But I told the truth about seeing the satellite or whatever it was. I saw it, ok?"

Bruce instantly knew what she had lied about and why the machine indicated she was lying about the spaceship.

"I'm listening. Tell me about the bribe first. Why did you think you wouldn't be caught?"

"The police chief put his flunky officer on the front door because he was always falling asleep on duty. He told him if he left the front door he would be fired. Then he told me to use the ladder on the fire escape to get inside."

"I do not understand. Why would he tell you that?"

"Because the professor came down on him really hard when he came back from where ever he was and told him he had better be professional for a change and act like he knew what he was doing. Plus, I wanted to know what was inside and offered him something for getting inside for a peek at what the professor was working on."

"What did you offer him?"

"I'm ashamed to say."

"I'm not bargaining with you little girl. Tell me or you're off to jail for a very long time!"

"I told him I would invite him to our next sorority party, if he let us in for a couple of hours undisturbed."

"Why would he care about a party with a bunch of teenage girls? It doesn't make any sense."

"Because he's a sleazy looser, okay, just look at him!"

Bruce fought hard to keep from laughing out loud. When he regained his composure he asked about the satellite.

"Okay, you're doing fine. Tell me about the military satellite."

"I don't know what to say. I told you the truth. We're not sure exactly what we saw, but it looks like a satellite or something and I read somewhere that the military was spending a lot of money on a secret weapon."

"Where would you read something like that?"

"From my dad, he's like a conspiracy theorist or something. He's always online looking stuff up and talking about it non-stop at the supper table."

Bruce couldn't keep it in and let a smile form on his face. He was standing behind Rachel and didn't fear her seeing him and losing his credibility. He removed the handcuffs and told her if her classmate's story matched they would only have to answer to the professor. Bruce repeated the test on Cathy and found the same results. Not wanting to pursue the matter any further, he consulted with the professor.

"Dr. Weiss, the two girls believe they saw a military satellite or something but like you said they don't know what they really saw and have no idea what is really going on here. As far as the campus police, the chief is a disgruntled employee and was taking a bribe by Rachel to allow them access to the lab. She promised, are you ready for this, to invite him to a sorority party, but the other two clowns were actually doing their job. I would suggest you report him to your university authority and have him dismissed."

"Thank you, Sheriff, Oh, I mean, Agent Bruce."

"Ha, no, Sheriff is fine now, Dr. Weiss. I'm officially off duty as an agent of the NSA."

Bruce called Agent Rose and reported the breach of security then headed for home.

CHAPTER THIRTY-TWO

Most of the Tahar onboard heard of Gebel's death and gathered secretly to plan their strongest offensive against the Shem alliance and Karna, but now they added the specific goal to avenge the death of their leader. The second in command in the Tahar alliance was Hageze. He had grown up in battle and his mentor, Gebel, had prepared him for command. Although he did not wish to assume command under these conditions, he nevertheless was ready and willing to take the lead in this war and would take the battle to Karna personally.

Commander Hageze Biejur called his officers to the front of the room to issue the orders.

"Tahar officers, hear me now! The time has come for us to not only take this battle to the ruthless Karna, but to make it personal! She has struck down our leader, Gebel, as a coward and weakling needing an army of Quod to protect her at all times. When she killed the Tahar commander, she not only made the greatest mistake of her command while Supreme Commander of the Spiruthun, but as a Bilkegine citizen and will die a slow and painful death as her reward! We have watched her punish the weak, bully the meek and lie and cheat her way to the position of commander, but her time has come, and she must now die. We must take command of this vessel and save this planet and these people from her kind, now and forever, for we know it is not the true way. No battle has ever been as important as this one will prove to be. Never before have we seen the level of tyranny that we have witnessed with Karna in command. We must do everything in our power to stop her and those in her alliance. Join with me as we go into battle to defeat our enemy once and for all!"

The officers all saluted Hageze, then turned and gave the command for their troops to present arms to their new commander. When Hageze returned the salute of arms, he continued giving them their orders.

"As before, Gebel gave each of us our orders, and we carried them out with honor. As I give you your orders, I expect no less. We will fight with honor for our people. We will fight with honor and some of us will die. When we are victorious, those of us that survive will honor the fallen with memorials for all Bilkegine to remember for all time."

Hageze continued to outline the plan for the battle. "Before he died, Gebel and I spent many phases discussing strategic plans that might work against our enemy. In the battle that occurred just before his death, Gebel carried out one of the plans we had worked out together. It was his brilliant plan to detonate hidden explosives at all intersections of the ship above and below the mid-ship. The explosives used there were disguised as normal everyday equipment and placed by Gebel himself more than five earth years ago. I tell you this now so you can see how long and hard Gebel and I worked on our ultimate battle plans. These are not ideas thrown together in haste because we were losing ground in the battle. Gebel knew it better than most when he said, "you may have to fight a battle more than once to win" and I believe he had looked into the future and seen with his own eyes our most recent defeat, and at the same time, knew that a single battle never defines the outcome of the war. We may affirm that nothing great ever comes without perseverance. One of our plans may require the death of many innocent Bilkegine people. We do not wish to cause undeserved harm against our own, but with no other course of action available, it may be necessary in order to survive and succeed.

We will take control of the vessel by taking control of the Piiderk level and the command center, then shutting down all the life support systems on all the remaining decks. Before we can do that we must also take the transportation chamber and engineering levels. As you all know, this will not be an easy battle and the Quod are the most formidable foe we have ever fought against. On our last attempt we lost seven hundred Tahar soldiers, just trying to take the transportation chamber alone."

He pointed to the first three officers in the rank of fifteen and said, "You three take position in the main entrance to the engineering chamber with three thousand men. Your mission is to cut off any reinforcements who may try to assist those already posted in the engineering chamber." The next two officers in rank were appointed the task of terminating communication between the command center and both engineering and transportation chambers. It was the most critical task but the safest mission. Every other officer, who had previous knowledge of the overall plans, expected that mission to be appointed to Hageze' son, but to their surprise, when he did point to his son, Captain Corth, he told him to lead the strike against the transportation chamber, a mission that was sure to mean death. "Captain Corth, take three other officers of your choosing and lead the battle for the transportation chamber. Take five thousand troops and remember there is only one way into the Piiderk from the transportation chamber. Once you take it, that position will be easier to defend. One more thing, take these with you," he said as he reached down and opened a crate filled with a new and extremely powerful new weapon never before seen. "The human male discovered these along with the smaller weapon we are now referring to as the balzoi. This one is so much more powerful and much more accurate and makes our previous weapons resemble the chot."

"I will take the last three officers and nine hundred soldiers and secure the Piiderk. When the Piiderk is secure and engineering is secure, we will be able to take control of the command center and kill Karna. By that time, if the transportation chamber has not been taken, we will fall back to secure the Piiderk chamber doors and shut down life support for the entire ship. If we are forced to take this drastic measure, know this, only those inside the Piiderk will survive. Everyone else will die slowly as the dighergant expires. Let me be as truthful and open as possible right now. This is a plan that Gebel expressed to me in private that he would only use if the direction of the war meant the total destruction of the Spiruthun and everyone aboard."

With everyone clear of the battle plans the timing was established and the battle would start at the beginning of the next resting phase.

Restless anticipation was evident as each Tahar soldier readied himself for what would be their last battle. As each man studied their new weapon and understood the devastation it was capable of delivering, they found resolve in the fact that without them, the planet below and every human were sure to suffer at the hands of the Shem. Many recorded their last message to their clan members and secretly transmitted them by means of a secret Tahar transmitter hidden onboard that encrypted the transmissions and disguised them as normal radio waves coming from the planet below. Hageze took the time to reflect on his life as a Tahar soldier and later as an officer. He had been brought up through the ranks by Gebel because of his fearless devotion to the Tahar alliance and their cause. Because of the cast system of different classes of citizens, Hageze would have never been promoted beyond that of Chief, but due to the special relationship he had with Gebel, an exception was made. To that point, and to honor his mentor, Hageze would deny himself his one and only transmission for personal reasons and use his time to record a message to the clan of his leader, mentor and father figure, Gebel. It was a simple message and Hageze knew that Gebel would have done nothing different. It read, "To the clan of Gebel, of the house of Dectoron, Gebel has died honorably in battle."

✳✳✳

Sean and Rotusea had taken several hundred Tahar soldiers to the supply warehouse under the orders of Gebel and were making preparations to cut off the supply chain of the Quod. Unaware of either the major battle about to take place or Gebel's death, they were about to place themselves right in the middle of a hell storm. Sean was taking the lead role in the planning and Rotusea was acting as translator even though there were several others among them that had been trained and modified to speak the human language of English. Rotusea was also acting as second in command and had instructed each soldier in the event of Sean's death. They were expecting Gebel to join them at any moment but were planning on starting without him if he didn't show. Sean thought he had a brilliant idea, but needed some information to ensure its viability.

"Rotusea, I have a question."

"Yes, what is it?"

"The main warehouse on the Piiderk level has a large loading door that opens to space. Can that door be opened from inside the warehouse?"

"I am sure it can be, but without being inside a pressurized loading space facility, the entire warehouse will become depressurized and the entire contents will be sucked out into space."

"That's exactly what I want to happen."

"The problem is that whoever is inside operating the door will also be sucked into space. It will be a suicide mission."

"Yes, I know. It will have to be a volunteer mission."

Sean's plan was for several Tahar soldiers to sneak into the warehouse on the Piiderk level and take as many weapons as they could carry along with ammunition, with one person staying behind and blowing the door, effectively taking away the remaining supplies in that warehouse.

"One more question, Rotusea. Where is the armory that Gebel was speaking of, when he said we would have to defend in order to successfully win against the Quod?"

"It is on the Falkoe level. It is the second level below the Piiderk and the last level accessible after we closed all the intersections above and below mid-ship."

Sean went to the Tahar soldiers who were milling around waiting for their orders and asked if any spoke English. One Tahar came from the back of the crowd and proclaimed his ability to speak the language. Sean asked him to volunteer for a special mission because he would need someone able to communicate with and he agreed. Rotusea came over to learn what Sean was planning, but before he laid out his plans, she explained to the Tahar who he was and how he came to be leading them into battle.

"Tahar brothers, this human is called Sean. He has been taken by the Shem to study because it is believed that he possessed the greatest military mind on the planet earth. Gebel has confidence in him because he has proven himself so far in battle by killing a Quod with his bare hands. He escaped Karna and has been fighting and has joined the Tahar in the battle against Karna and the Shem alliance. In Gebel's absence, he will lead us in this battle to break the supply chain of the Quod, so we can later defeat the warrior Quods. Listen to his plan."

If Sean had been able to understand what she was telling them, he would have surely objected and set the record straight about killing the Quod bare handed. He would have explained that he was scared and in his fear, he accidently killed the Quod. But since he was not able to understand, he assumed their murmurs to be due to something else Rotusea had told them. He walked up to Rotusea and stood beside her and waited to begin as she finished her speech. "Tahar brothers, you are all brave and honorable warriors. I surrender my command of you to the human Sean."

When she finished and took a step behind Sean, the entire group struck the position of a Tahar salute to Sean. He looked back to Rotusea briefly and then back to the men who were still holding their salute. Sean mimicked what he saw and they all stood ready to go into battle.

"Tahar soldiers," he began, "you and I fight the same cause. We fight against a tyranny that would force itself on another people to take what does not belong to it. We fight for our right to freedom and our right to continue to live the way we have lived for thousands of years. Though we are few in numbers and smaller in size, we are mighty in our will to win and strong in our desire for freedom. For generation after generation my people have fought war after war to retain our rights, and there is no more powerful motivation than to fight to keep your liberty. You fight for a more noble cause. You fight for the rights of another people. Your people have fought and died to save another people's lives and way of life, and there can be no greater gift than to lay down one's life for another. For that I thank you in the name of all my people. Join with me now as we go into battle against the wicked leader of your enemy."

At the end of Sean's speech, the soldiers gave him their typical Tahar demonstration chant of agreement by stomping one foot repeatedly on the floor, making a drum like sound.

Sean continued outlining his plan.

"My plan is simple but it will require a volunteer to make the ultimate sacrifice of their life in a suicide mission."

Sean waited for Rotusea to translate and to see what the response would be. Almost before she was finished translating his words, seven Tahar soldiers stepped forward from all over the room. Rotusea spoke to each of them then all but one stepped back into ranks.

"Very well," Sean said. "Here is the plan. Ten of you will sneak into the forward warehouse on the Piiderk level and steal the weapons hidden here that look like this one." He held up his rifle like weapon. "They will take as many as they can carry along with ammunition. All but one will return here. When they are safely back, the lone man will operate the loading bay doors and open the warehouse to space, effectively sucking everything into space. This will serve to take away all the supplies, weapons and ammunition they have stowed there. Are there any questions so far?"

As before, Rotusea translated while Sean watched. When everyone nodded in understanding, Sean continued.

"After we have armed ourselves, the soldiers with the new weapons will take the point, and we will storm the armory. These weapons have a very effective and strong blast pattern that will give us the edge against a much stronger enemy. When we storm in, blowing everything up in front of us, the enemy will be forced into a corner. Unless they surrender, they will all die. It is my understanding that the Quod do not understand surrender, so if there are Quod warriors in the armory at the time of our attack, we must be prepared to destroy everything."

Sean waited for Rotusea to catch up and looked around the room to see the expression on everyone's face. What he saw was nothing short of complete resolve without fear of any kind. Sean felt an immense feeling of deep respect for their bravery. He had only fought out of fear and had never seen or even heard of anyone going into battle as fearless as these Tahar soldiers.

"The last thing you need to know before we start is that the armory is the most secure area on this ship. That means we must assume there is only one way in and one way out. Since we are few in number, it will be important not to get trapped inside once we siege the armory. To keep that from happening, only half of us will go inside, the other half will stay outside and secure the entrance. Each half will have an equal share of the new weapon so we each have an equal chance of winning our objective. Should either team encounter overwhelming opposition, we all pull back and leave immediately. We can always try again another time. Is everything clear?"

Rotusea finished translating and nodded to Sean that everyone understood, and Sean gave the go ahead for the ten-man team to leave for the warehouse.

Sean decided that he would lead the team to the warehouse against Rotusea's wishes. He wasn't about to let them do it alone. As they approached the warehouse, he remembered the door that he had blocked. Had he not gone, they would have lost valuable time and might have been detected trying to get inside. Because they had to use the door at the farthest end of the warehouse, they had to venture very close to the command center. They got inside and immediately gathered the weapons and ammunition. The volunteer who was to stay and open the loading bay door said his goodbyes and gave something to one of the Tahar soldiers, then walked to the loading door. Sean took the point leading the others out, but before they made it off the Piiderk they heard the crushing sound from the decompression of the warehouse.

Alarms sounded all around them, but it gave them an unexpected edge, as the security Quod were giving their attention to the Piiderk level. As Sean and his team made it to the falkoe level and toward the armory, they split into two teams. Sean took the point and assigned Rotusea the rear. Just as they reached the armory door, Sean called up the Tahar soldier able to speak English and issued his commands.

"Make sure they know what to do back there. I need you right beside me in case things change." Sean told his new translator. "Ok, let's do it!" Sean said.

He opened the door and there was a young Bilkegine crewman sitting at a desk just inside the door. When he saw the Tahar alliance running in, he jumped up and started running deep inside the armory screaming. Sean got off the first round with a loud explosion that brought Quod out from rooms on both sides of the corridor. As the Quod began shooting back with their much inferior weapons, the Tahar solders behind Sean opened fire. Quod soldiers flew apart with each successive round exploding around them. Sean was thinking how stupid they were for running out of the room into the barrage of fire when they should have known they would certainly die immediately. Sean remembered why he didn't like killing the Quod when the first hint of odor hit his nose. The smell was unbearable. They smelled bad enough when they weren't blown open, but once their bodies were opened up, it was like opening the lid from a week old garbage can sitting in a hot August sun full of chicken guts. Once again, Sean had to fight the urge to vomit and he was glad that he hadn't had much to eat since he arrived on the ship.

As they worked their way down the long corridor, they finally came to the Chief of Arms' office and a few more Bilkegine enlisted men but did not find any more Quod. Sean and the other Tahar men stopped firing and Sean yelled out for them to surrender, not realizing in the heat of battle that only one man there understood a word he said. From behind him, he heard one of the Tahar men yelling out and turned to discover it was his translator still following his orders to repeat everything he said in the Bilkegine language. The Chief of Arms came out of his office with his arms held out from his side.

"What's going on?" Sean asked the translator, but hearing nothing in reply, he turned briefly to find him dead at his feet. He had been hit with one of the Quod weapons and had finally succumbed to his injuries. "That's great!" Sean said to himself. "I've won the victory but can't communicate with my prisoners."

Just as Sean was about to shoot the remaining Bilkegine men inside the armory for lack of a better idea, Rotusea ran up from behind him yelling as she came. "Stop, Sean. He is giving up and has ordered his staff to do the same!"

Sean turned in surprise upon hearing Rotusea and wondered why she had joined them in battle when she was supposed to be protecting their rear.

"What are you doing here, and who is commanding our rear guard?" He asked impatiently.

"They are fine, the one we call Morgu is in command. He is a seasoned warrior."

"That doesn't answer the first part of my question. Why are you here?"

"I was able to tap into one of the communication panels to see if we were yet successful in cutting off communications between the command center and the last two strongholds and overhead a transmission calling for warrior Quods to reinforce the attack on the armory and came to warn you." She answered quickly.

No sooner had she finished explaining her presence, shots were heard coming from outside the armory. It was clear that the rear guard soldiers had come under attack from the warrior Quod.

"There is no way we can hold off an advancing warrior Quod attack. We must retreat and regroup now!" Rotusea explained.

"Okay, but we can't retreat back to the warehouse without being followed. We'll have to come up with another plan. Get those Tahar soldiers inside and close off the armory doors as quickly as you can."

Rotusea gave the orders to another Tahar soldier standing nearby and stayed with Sean to make other plans. As the rear guard came running into the armory corridor a strong bulkhead door more than two feet thick began to descend from overhead. Just before it came to rest on the floor, the last surviving Tahar soldier came sliding under, nearly getting his feet cut off. Sean quickly scanned the area around them to make sure they were safe for a while then became cognizant that they were trapped. He turned quickly and grabbed Rotusea's arm and began to walk toward the Chief of Arms' office.

"Tell him to go back into his office and meet with us." Sean ordered.

Rotusea translated the orders then ordered the Tahar soldiers to take the remaining Bilkegine armory workers into custody and secure the weapons lying around. With the armory secure, Sean and Rotusea went into the Chief's office to discuss his role in the siege.

"Chief Cremo, I know you have recently been promoted to Chief of Arms. Why should we trust that you would surrender and not turn around at first chance and try to escape, or worse?" Rotusea asked.

"I was promoted because the previous Chief was converted into a drone for failure to perform his duty. I was assigned the task of finding the male subject and have failed to do so myself and will no doubt receive the same punishment once the Commander learns of the armory being overrun."

"What did he say?" Sean asked while staring down the Chief.

"He said that we do not have anything to worry about because he fears for his life if Karna finds out he failed to protect the armory and deliver you to her."

"Ask him if he will join us then."

Rotusea turned to face the Chief and translated, "this is the male that the Commander had taken to study. He calls himself Sean. He wants to know if you would join us in our fight against the Commander and the Shem alliance."

Looking amazed at Sean's audacity, Cremo asked, "how many are you, and how do you judge your chances?"

Rotusea translated his questions to Sean.

"Tell him why Karna took me, and explain that our chances are better than hers because of our superior weapons and the fact that all but the middle levels of the ship are closed off to reinforcements."

"The Commander took this human because he is the most knowledgeable human about military strategy and needed to study him to learn how to defeat the human race. It is obvious that he is too intelligent for her to even keep prisoner, how do you think she will succeed against him? As far as our numbers are concerned, we are about twelve thousand strong and have these new weapons that you and the Quod do not have."

"Since I am dead if I do not join you and more than likely dead if I do not because of my failures, I will join you. You must know that I never agreed to this mission in the first place, but at the same time, I could not take the Tahar stand either, because my clan is from the house of Belsholzar which is of the Shem alliance. It put me in the middle, but since I am in this position, I might as well be on the winning side."

"How do we know you can be trusted? What is to keep you from using our trust to deceive us and turn on us when we drop our guard?"

"Beside my honor as a Bilkegine, you have in your possession two of my sons. They are the reason we surrendered when we did."

Rotusea stopped and turned to Sean and explained what was said. Sean thought for a few moments before he decided which direction to take, but thought he should get Rotusea's advice before he made his decision.

"I do not know for sure what direction to take. If what he says is true and we have his two sons, perhaps he is sincere and desires to help us. But on the other hand, his loyalties may lie with the Shem and Karna and he might be willing to sacrifice his sons to the will of the Shem. Would you trust him with your life?"

"Let us put him to the test. There are things that he could not do and survive regardless of the outcome of this war. If he violates any direct order from the Supreme Commander, he will be either killed or converted even if he claims his actions were necessary to obtain victory."

"What do you have in mind?"

"There are two things a Shem must never do. Wear the seal of another alliance and give aid and support to their enemies. If he does both, he will seal his own death and I do not believe he welcomes death as many Tahar warriors do."

Rotusea turned back to Cremo and gave him her Tahar crest to wear. Cremo immediately looked shocked when he realized that she was testing his resolve. He hesitated briefly then finally put the crest over his uniform and swore allegiance to the Tahar alliance. The first test was done but without a witness to his actions, he could always take it off and deny having ever worn it. Rotusea stepped out of the room and ordered the captive Bilkegine crewmen to be brought to the corridor just outside the chief's office. She then turned to Cremo and suggested he make his statement to his men to confirm his decision to join the Tahar. He stood up slowly and adjusted his uniform. Then, without any further hesitation, he walked to the doorway and announced his resolve to join the Tahar alliance in defense of the human planet and its people. Upon seeing their father make such a statement, his oldest son grabbed a weapon from the soldier guarding him and tried to kill his own father, but before he could advance more than two steps, Cremo produced a sharp knife like weapon and drove it into the chest of his son. His son dropped the weapon and looked into the eyes of his father in anger. All the armory workers present stood in disbelief as Cremo retuned the hateful stare and twisted the blade, immediately killing the young Bilkegine man. He released the grip he had on the young man and allowed him to slump to the floor, then turned and looked at Sean and Rotusea and said, "Is that proof enough of my resolve? How could I ever stand with any alliance that would cause a man's own son to want to kill his father?"

The three walked back into the office and Rotusea asked Cremo the best way to destroy the stockpile of weapons inside the armory. Cremo thought about it for a minute and then reached inside a compartment inside the wall and produced an explosive type weapon similar to a hand grenade. "This will effectively destroy all the weapons we have. We must pile every weapon not being used by the Tahar and detonate this device against the outer hull of the Spiruthun. It can be detonated remotely using this transmitter and the resulting explosion will not only destroy some of the weapons, but cause the outer bulkhead to disintegrate and eventually fail causing the entire area to decompress and be pulled into the vacuum of space."

Rotusea translated his plan to Sean and waited for him to reply. His only question was how they would escape being pulled into space along with the weapons since they were also trapped inside the armory. Cremo informed them of the additional closing bulkheads designed to protect the inner chamber of the Falkoe level from any damage to the outer hull and ensured that they would be safe inside. Rotusea thought that it would ensure his loyalty by assisting the enemy of the Shem but questioned how it would help in the long run since they would still be trapped. She relayed her concern to Sean and he asked her if Cremo knew another way out of the armory that may be hidden.

"No," Cremo replied to her question concerning another way out, "there is only the door you came through."

"There are no maintenance passageways accessible from inside the armory?"

"As I said, there is only one way in and one way out. And that is not an option any longer."

The whole time Rotusea and Cremo were discussing their options, he remembered how he and Gebel had escaped the Quod before when they were trapped inside Sean's room, and interrupted their conversation.

"I think I've got it," Sean declared. "We can blast through the inner walls like we did before. Do you remember, Rotusea?"

"Yes, but how will that help us when the warrior Quod are just outside

333

within the Falkoe level's main chamber? They will hear the explosive burst and investigate."

"Exactly, but what will they be looking for? They will be looking for an armed group, an army of soldiers."

"Is that not what we are? Do you suggest that we walk out of here unarmed?" She asked.

Remembering his military tour and the many drills in disassembling his M-16, he suggested an alternative. "We break down the weapons into its many individual parts and carry them out in our clothing. Then we just walk out through the wall four or five at a time and slowly make our way back to the lower warehouse. You said it yourself. They are stupid and un-capable of individual thought. I think it will work."

Everyone agreed in principle so they secured the remaining armory personnel behind a security bulkhead, gathered all the weapons and placed them against the outer hull of the ship and placed the explosives. Cremo thought it should be the biggest explosion possible to ensure a breech in the bulkhead and placed all but two of his grenades on top of the pile. They closed the inner security bulkhead door and began to break down the weapons into their individual components. The armory proved to be the perfect place to perform the tasks since it had all the necessary tools to achieve a total disassembly. Once all the Tahar soldiers had their weapons stowed inside their uniform, they all took off their Tahar crests and prepared to leave the armory. Chief Cremo placed the last two grenades against the inner bulkhead and they all retreated to the inner corridor.

"We must detonate both positions simultaneously if we desire to avoid drawing additional attention to ourselves. We won't have much time to escape because Karna or another officer will surely send someone to discover the cause of the explosion and we will be discovered. I suggest we leave in groups of five no more than a few seconds apart."

Sean and Rotusea agreed and they set the plan in motion. The explosion was much more intense than Cremo had anticipated and the ship shook violently when the outer bulkhead collapsed.

"Come on!" Sean yelled inside. "Let's get out of here!"

Just as expected, the warrior Quod still outside the armory were looking for a way inside when the explosion rocked through the ship, and they came over to investigate. Sean was just as anxious as he had been before when he saw the huge, bulking warrior Quod just outside the hole in the armory wall, but he stepped out in faith with Rotusea, Cremo and two other Tahar soldiers by his side. They avoided making any eye contact with the Quod and slowly walked across the Falkoe deck as if they were on their way to work; when they were thirty feet inside the main chamber, five more Tahar soldiers walked through following Sean and the others. As Sean and Rotusea reached the outer wall of the main chamber and turned toward the lower passageway leading to the warehouse, Sean turned to see how the Quod were reacting to the soldiers when he noticed Cremo heading back toward the armory. Not wanting to draw any attention Sean quietly called for Cremo to come back but he did not respond. Rotusea thought the Chief was trying to save his own life by returning to the armory, and was about to share her thoughts with Sean, when the Chief stepped back outside the armory carrying an extraordinarily large bundle, wrapped in the uniforms he had obviously taken from the dead Quod inside. He was walking faster than the others as he returned and Sean and Rotusea both thought he was going to draw too much attention but he was ignored just as everyone else had been. When he finally re-joined Sean and Rotusea, she turned toward him and angrily questioned him.

"What were you doing trying to get caught? Why did you go back and what are you carrying?"

"I forgot my newest weapon." He proclaimed. "If we're going to have a chance at defeating Karna, we're going to need this." He replied as he pulled back the material revealing another huge weapon.

"Did you see any more Tahar soldiers inside?" Sean asked.

"Yes, there are still two groups coming behind me."

Sean helped Cremo carry the bulky weapon and they headed for the meeting place in the lower warehouse. When they all returned, there were only thirty-two soldiers left alive. Sean ordered Rotusea and Cremo to go ahead of him and meet him later. Rotusea and Cremo had taken a shorter route because Cremo's weapon was too large to pass through the maintenance passageways. Since Cremo still had his remote transmitter and could operate the force-fields he had set earlier they were able to pass down the ladder ways and arrived before Sean, but on their way, they ran into one of the Tahar technicians that was assigned the safer task of disabling communications and Rotusea learned of the upcoming battle and Gebel's death.

Sean had hoped to meet up with Gebel once they returned to their hiding place, but when he arrived he was nowhere to be found. As Sean was heading over to where Nancy had been waiting, he noticed Rotusea sitting in a corner of the warehouse alone and distraught. Sean held up one finger indicating to Nancy that he would be another minute, and walked over to Rotusea.

"Are you alright, Rotusea? Did you get hurt?"

She turned slowly toward Sean and looked into his eyes as if trying to express her sadness without having to speak. "Come on," Sean insisted, "what's going on."

The Bilkegine race was unable to cry and rarely showed any emotion other than anger, but from her close observations and communications with humans, she was beginning to understand grief in a much different way. Sean could sense that something was dreadfully wrong but couldn't recognize the expression Rotusea was wearing. She finally explained.

"On our way back down here, I ran into a Tahar technician who was disabling communication lines. He informed me that Gebel is dead."

"What?" Sean asked surprised. "When, how?"

"He was caught by the Quod and they took him to Karna and she killed him. It happened right after we left him. I fear we are all doomed to fail without him."

"I'm sorry, Rotusea. Gebel was an honorable man. We will all grieve his loss."

"I am sure he died honorably but nevertheless, his death comes as a shock to me and although he informed his helpmate before we left Bilkegine that he would most likely die in battle, it will be difficult sending her the news."

"Were you close, Rotusea?"

"Yes, Sean. He was my only brother."

CHAPTER THIRTY-THREE

The military had accomplished the near impossible task of getting their plan initiated within the deadline. However, since the military leaders could not agree on a single weapon to use against the spacecraft, nearly the entire arsenal of specialized space crafts and weapons were included as alternative options and put on standby. The newly proven S51F fighter space planes, with their linear aerospike engines, were loaded with eight tactical nuclear missiles and were already fueled for takeoff. This latest space plane by Lockheed Martin was the personification of all the x-plane series and was capable of reaching speeds in excess of mach 25, or 25 times faster than the speed of sound. In the eyes of some, this feature coupled with the conventional takeoff made it the perfect military plane for the mission, but now, having the ability of carrying and launching the nuclear missiles from inside the airframe, not only gave the United States military superiority over any other nation but they believed it would prove lethal against this alien threat. It was considered by most to be the only weapon needed to destroy the alien spacecraft as long as they had use of the ISS to laser tag the target. Therefore, the ISS halted all experiments and facilitated an orbital burn of their main engines long enough to speed their way to the rendezvous point, and the team of astronauts readied the laser for use as a targeting device. However, for those who did not have absolute faith in the S51F's abilities, the Solar Pulse Laser satellite, the brain child of Alexis W. Linz was positioned in an orbit that would allow it to fire upon the alien craft. The Solar Pulse Laser was originally designed to protect the planet from meteoroids and other space debris that has the potential to strike the planet in heavily populated areas. However, due to failures in the guidance system and primary targeting computers, it was not considered reliable enough to continue funding and the project was abandoned. Seven years later, after resolving many of the satellites issues, the military picked up the project and funded Dr. Linz's project resulting in the Solar Pulse Laser or SPL. The primary operating principle is to capture the preferential scattering of gamma rays, protons and excited neutrinos from solar radiation and concentrate the accelerated fusion particles in a beam of energy released at 383 yottawatts per second at the target. A blast of pure energy, unadulterated by the earth's atmosphere, would annihilate the target leaving nothing but space dust and other innocuous particles orbiting the planet. Nonetheless, having never seen the device in actual use, those in the military who did not stand behind the SPL refused to put their trust in an unproven and highly controversial device. Therefore as an additional backup plan, four of the space shuttles were being staged for back to back launches, each now capable of carrying and launching four tactical, nuclear missiles each.

The Pentagon believed they were ready. The last image from Dr. Weiss showed extremely detailed images of the craft and an amazing, but puzzling situation had risen. Near the middle of the ship, on the opposite side from the meteoroid damage, a huge rectangular doorway had been opened, and all the contents of the craft had been evacuated into space. The door was calculated to be more than sixty feet tall and one hundred feet wide. It was a perfect alternate target for the missiles and all the military intelligence officers believed they would be able to penetrate deeper and produce more damage by utilizing it.

The President, Vice-President, Secretary of Defense and Chief of Staff along with leading members of the Senate were all taken to an undisclosed bunker to wait for the attack to begin. Due to Agent James Rose's experience and knowledge of the alien craft and other alien technology, President Fleming appointed him "Special Liaison and Commander of the operation. Agent Rose would be the last authority to give the go-ahead for the attack.

James had returned to Cheyenne Mountain and was coordinating everything from there. NASA had managed to speed-track two shuttles onto the launch pads in two different locations and was ready to launch. They had also placed the other two shuttles in the launch position on two platform shuttle carriers in order to expedite a second launch. All communications were being encrypted and monitored through the equipment on the mountain and reports were coming in from the ISS indicating they were ready to engage. Reports were now coming in on a regular basis and James knew his responsibilities were to save the planet at all costs, even if it meant killing Sean in the process. Pressure was coming from all sides and all governments to proceed with the preemptive strike against the aliens, but James had a bad feeling about rushing into it. It wasn't because he knew there were at least two humans onboard the craft. James knew that with every war came casualties, and that the potential loss of every human on the planet far outweighed the lives of two or even two hundred. He also knew that the aliens were hostile but since they hadn't made any other aggressive act against the United States, he didn't believe they should be taking action yet. He still thought it more prudent to wait and give Sean and anyone else up there on their side a chance to either fight or escape. For that reason alone, James was glad that the President gave him the final say on the mission, but knowing how the military mind operated, he would have to act soon or they might attempt to override his authority and go directly to the President.

Wanting to get a little peace of mind, James went outside the operations theatre and made a call to Bruce.

"Hello?" Maggie said as she picked up the phone.

"Hello, ma'am, this is Agent Rose. Is Bruce home?"

"No, he just called from the jet. He said he should be home in a few minutes. He is going to stop by the office first and pick up some things on his way home. Can I give him a message?"

"Yes ma'am. Will you have him call me the instant he walks through the door? It is very urgent."

"He won't have to leave again, will he, Agent Rose?"

"Oh, no, ma'am, I just need to talk to him."

"Okay, I'll let him know as soon as I see him."

"Thank you, ma'am," James said as he hung up the phone.

He walked back into the command theatre a little discouraged by not making contact. He needed to talk to Bruce to ease his conscience before he gave the go ahead to destroy the alien ship. It wasn't due to anything he could put his finger on, but more because he had become friends with Bruce and knew that he was counting on him to do everything he could for his friend Sean. He walked down the two levels of the theatre to the station General Stephens operated, all the while thinking of a way to stall just long enough to hear back from Bruce. "General Stephens, something has come to my attention about the aliens that I must check out immediately. Hold all operations as they are, and do not proceed until you hear from me directly. It shouldn't take more than thirty minutes, and it is very important."

"What! We're about to blow those alien scum into neverland, and you want me to drop my pants and wait thirty minutes? What happens if they find out we're out there and decide to attack like they did when they destroyed our satellites? What then?"

"General, let me worry about that! I have the last word on this, and I have to check this out. It's vital to national security!"

"No! I don't think so, Agent Rose. We haven't even launched the shuttles yet. What if things do go south with the S51F's and we need those shuttles? What do we do then, wait a while and give them more target practice while they launch? You think they'll just sit there and do nothing?"

"Fine, launch the shuttles, but do not, and let me reiterate again for clarity, do not, put them into position. If something does happen, and by that I mean, if and only if, the aliens attack before I return, you have authority to launch."

"I'll tell you this much, Agent, it goes against my better judgment, but as long as we are at least ready to fire, I'll play along with you for the time being."

James left the general, spewing something about spooks, aka any secret service agent, spy or agent with the CIA or NSA, and walked back into the corridor to wait for his call. As long as he was outside, they couldn't launch, at least not unless the aliens attacked, in which case it would have been too late for Sean anyway. He paced back and forth in the hallway, wishing he hadn't quit smoking years ago, when his phone rang. He quickly answered it, "Agent Rose!"

"Hey, Pal, I heard you needed to talk," Bruce said sounding tired.

"I'm glad you called me back quick enough, I've got to run a couple of things by you real quick."

"What is it? It isn't over yet is it?"

"No, that's why I called. We're about to launch the strike, and I need to know what you honestly think Sean's chances are. We haven't seen any evidence that he's even alive, let alone that he's done anything spectacular."

"Nothing? I would have figured he would have done something by now! It doesn't sound good for my buddy, does it?"

"We've seen some very detailed imagery on the ship and the only thing out of the ordinary is a large rectangular opening with a debris field around the craft."

"You don't call that a sign?" Bruce replied excited.

"How would that be a sign, Bruce?"

"Man, think about it. What kind of stuff is floating around, if it's not garbage, then why would they intentionally dump it, especially if they didn't want to draw attention to themselves?"

"We can't tell, but there is a lot of it whatever it is."

"I bet Sean blew that door open or something, and that's the stuff that was inside. That's the sign you're looking for that he's still up there fighting!"

"You may be right, but I don't know. I'll try to get a better look at the debris. You're at home right? I'll call you back as soon as I find out something."

"No, I'm at the office."

"How did you know to call me?"

"I called Mags and told her I changed my mind and decided to stay at work a while and catch up on a few things."

"Great! Stay there at least an hour and I'll call you back."

"You got it—hey—one more thing!" Bruce called out.

"Yeah, what is it?"

"Don't blow up Sean yet. I know he's still alive and kicking. Give him just a little more time."

"I'll do what I can, Bruce; but I can't promise anything."

Bruce hung up and settled down to his paperwork, hoping James would be able to see something that would prove that his friend Sean was alive and fighting for his life. He sat back in his chair and was trying to gather his thoughts about the last few weeks and trying to make sense of the whole thing, when the dispatch radio started squawking loudly.

"Dispatch—dispatch, come in anyone!"

Bruce nearly fell over in his chair surprised from the panic in the voice of one of his deputies. He jumped up and ran to the front desk where the radio was located and punched the transmit button. "This is the Sheriff, what is it Justin?"

"Sheriff, you've got to get down here right away!" Something weird is going on!"

"Calm down, keep your pants on and tell me what it is, Justin."

"Sheriff, are you coming?"

"Settle down! Where are you?"

"I'm down town between the bank and the hardware store! You better come quickly."

By now Bruce was freaking out. He didn't know what was going on, but when he heard hardware store, he figured it had something to do with Sean. He ran out and jumped into his car and sped down to the center of town. The fifteen minute trip under normal driving conditions only took him five since he took every shortcut and drove three times the legal limit. As he made the last turn onto Main Street, he could see that all traffic had stopped, and everyone was mesmerized by a brilliant light that was beaming down on the corner by the hardware store. He got out of the car and began to walk toward the center of the intersection but the light was so bright he couldn't see any details and turned quickly and retrieved his sun glasses. The light was nearly as bright as the sun and looking into it caused his eyes to burn. Just as he made it to the intersection and had pushed his way through the crowd, a shadow began to form inside the light. The light incrementally dimmed and eventually faded out completely, leaving two figures standing on the step of the hardware store in a state of shock. Bruce ran over to the two figures expecting to see Sean and Nancy, but when he reached them they turned slightly and he realized that Sean was not there. He took Nancy by the arms and slowly lowered her to the edge of the step and she sat down. He glanced up at the other girl standing on the steps to see if she was alright, but she was just standing and looking around as if she had never seen anything like it before, eyes wide and mouth hanging open. He turned his attention back to Nancy, noticed her shaking uncontrollably and yelled for Justin to bring him a blanket.

"Nancy," he said lightly shaking her arms, "Nancy, are you alright?"

"What?" she said dazed and confused, "Where am I?"

"Nancy, look honey, you've got to snap out of it, come on," once again shaking her gently by the arms. "Where is Sean?"

She began to be more cognizant and looking around recognized where she was and said, "Bruce, oh my God, Bruce, I'm home!" She began to cry tears of relief.

"Yes, you're home. Everything will be alright now. But, honey, where is Sean? I need to know what happened to Sean."

Nancy didn't respond immediately and Bruce was beginning to feel frustrated. He knew she was stressed beyond anything anyone could ever imagine, but desperately needed some answers. He yelled over to the deputy and instantly grew angry when he saw him trying to make time with one of the women that had been standing nearby. "What in the name of Pete is going on here?" He said quietly under his breath. "Why is everyone acting like nothing happened except me?" He got real angry and yelled again.

"Justin! Get your butt over here right now and bring me that blanket!"

Justin jumped when the Sheriff called his name and immediately ran to the car and grabbed a blanket from the truck then ran it over to the Sheriff. Bruce grabbed it from him while looking at him like he was ready to punch him. "What, what'd I do now?" Justin asked confused. "Jeeze, I was just trying to get a date."

Bruce draped the blanket over Nancy's shoulders and pulled it closed in front, then gently lifted her chin so he could see her face. "Nancy," he said softly and calmly, "where is Sean?"

A sudden look of terror came across her face as she finally came to realize what had happened. "Oh, Bruce," she said still weeping, "he's still up there fighting those horrible aliens! They are terrible, frightening monsters like you could never imagine!" She then began to cry very loudly and leaned into Bruce's chest.

Bruce held her and tried to console her as best he could while thinking of a way to get her someplace where she could be looked after. Morgantown didn't have a hospital, and the clinic wasn't open so he decided to take her with him. He looked around for someone to help out but as he turned to where the crowd had gathered, he noticed everyone had left. It was as if nothing out of the ordinary happened at all. Justin was leaning against the hood of his squad car acting bored when Bruce yelled for him again. It was as though Bruce was the only one who remembered anything happening. He thought that they must have been hypnotized by the light and somehow it caused them to blank it out of their memories. It must have been because my eyes were protected, he thought. Yeah, that has to be it. They were protected the first time by the hood of my car and this time by my sunglasses. There's no other explanation. "Justin! Come over here," Bruce yelled. As Justin got closer he instructed him. "Take this child to the office and hold her there until we can find out where she belongs. I don't recognize her as being from around here."

"What do you want me to do with her there?"

"Use your head for once, will you. Just put her in one of the cells and keep her company. Play cards with her or watch TV, just don't let her out of your sight for anything. Got it?"

"Sure Sheriff, whatever you want."

Bruce turned his attention back to Nancy. She had calmed down a little and was just staring at the ground with a blank look on her face and tears gently flowing down her face. Her eyes were red and puffy and she was so tired she could barely walk without help. "Come with me Nancy, I'm gonna take you home with me and my wife will take good care of you. Will that be alright, or is there someone else you want me to call?"

Nancy didn't respond at all verbally, she just went willingly where Bruce led her. Before Bruce could go anywhere else, he had to make a call first to let Agent Rose know what had just happened. He wanted to

ESCAPE SEQUENCE: THE ABDUCTION

believe that Sean was still alive and hoped that the two girls returning would be enough evidence to hold off the attack. He took Nancy by the arm and gently led her back toward the door to Sean's hardware store. He tried the door then remembered he had left the key in his desk, so he turned Nancy away from the door, stood sideways and smashed the glass out with his elbow. He reached inside, unlocked the door and stepped inside, bringing Nancy along side. When he let go of Nancy's arm, she began to slump to the floor, so he quickly grabbed her and sat her down in the chair next to the phone and made his call.

"Agent Rose," James said quickly into his phone.

"James, Bruce here. Hold everything!"

"What do you have, Bruce?"

"I've got Nancy and some girl! They just showed up in the middle of town right where Sean and Nancy disappeared!"

"What, how?"

"In the light, just like before!" he replied excitedly.

"What about Sean? Is he with them?"

"No, just Nancy and some other girl I've never seen before. What do you think? Is it enough?"

"I don't know what to think Bruce. Maybe he isn't back because he's dead, or maybe he's alive and still fighting. There's just no way to know and without something definitive, I'm afraid we'll have to go forward with our attack. I know that's not what you want to hear, but…"

"Oh come on! It's something! If he's not back with them; it's gotta mean he's still fighting!" Bruce was speaking loudly into the phone fighting for the life of his friend, when Nancy began to come to her senses and remembered what Sean had instructed her to do. She stood up and tried to tell Bruce, but he was talking so loud and was so focused on the call that he wasn't paying any attention to her. Out of frustration, Nancy began poking Bruce trying to interrupt him, and when that didn't get his attention she began beating on him with her fist.

"Bruce!" she screamed. "I remember something!"

"Hold on a minute, James, Nancy is yelling at me about something. What is it, Nancy? I'm on a very important call!"

"Sean gave me a message to give to you!"

"Oh! Hold everything James, Nancy says she has a message from Sean. Let me find out what it is!"

"Okay honey, you have my undivided attention. What is the message?"

"Let me think," she said pausing and looking to the ground. "Oh, yeah, he said to watch for a sign of smoke or some other sign that will indicate that the spaceship is in trouble. When you see the sign you can fire your missiles and blow it up! He also said," she paused another moment to remember the exact message, "oh yeah, don't worry about him because he would be safe by then. He gave me this and said I should give it to you as evidence that I'm telling the truth." She reached into her pocket and pulled out a very small device that was no bigger than a pocket-knife. It was much thinner and had a raised button on one side and a hole in one end.

"It's some kind of weapon, look," she said as she pointed the open end toward the wall and pressed the button. A flash of bright blue lightning flew from the weapon and with no more than a blue flash of light and a light buzzing sound it burned a four inch hole right through a parts bin and the brick wall behind it.

"Holy smokes girl, give me that thing! Bruce yelled, surprised and amazed. He took the device and examined it quickly. It resembled a pocket sized stun gun but instead of stunning the victim, it would burn a whole right through them. It was a remarkable device indeed, and was absolute evidence of a higher technology.

Bruce quickly grabbed the phone from the desk and relayed the message Sean had given him through Nancy then described the device Sean had given her to prove his story.

"That's all I need, Bruce. I'll get back with you as soon as I know anything!"

"What about the device?" Bruce asked. "Can I keep it?"

"Yeah right, just keep it someplace safe where no one else will see it. And don't use it!"

"Uh, it's too late."

"Well then, don't use it again. I'll pick it up myself when all of this is over."

James had gone over his allotted time but went inside to find everything still as he left it. He went to General Stephens and filled him in on what he had learned. Calling the President, James got approval for additional imagery to be studied for both more detail on the debris field and to look for the evidence that Sean had spoken of before they launched their attack. James didn't get the response he hoped for because of the potential threat to the nation, but was given fifteen minutes. James took what he could get and relayed the message to the general. If Sean didn't produce the evidence James needed within the time frame, he would be destroyed along with the ship.

James left the command theatre and explained everything that had happened to the technician operating the communication center. He then called Dr. Weiss and asked him for detailed imagery on the debris field, and was also instructed to scan the spaceship for anything that would indicate that the ship was in peril.

CHAPTER THIRTY-FOUR

The Tahar men had successfully cut the communication lines between the command chamber and engineering and were finishing the lines in the transportation chamber when the Tahar alliance started moving into position. As planned, the first team moved into the engineering chamber and set up a defensive position just outside the main entrance. When they secured a perimeter, the attack force moved in with the new heavy weapons blasting everything in sight. They knew that some of the Bilkegine crewmen were innocent workers, but this was war, and innocent people would die to end the tyranny. They caught the security Quod completely off guard, and while they scrambled for their inferior weapons, the Tahar soldiers advanced in far superior numbers. Quod, Bilkegine crewmen and equipment were all being blown apart and were burning. The three officers who were leading the attack inside the engineering chamber had split up and were each leading a separate advance down each of the three main corridors within the chamber. The team advancing down the middle corridor was taking the heaviest fire from the two Quod teams that, unknown to the Tahar, were placed there by Karna to protect the Piiderk level dighergant reactor core from possible attack.

The Piiderk level reactor was more vulnerable than the main dighergant reactor since it used highly unstable black matter as an accelerant matrix causing the dighergant radioactive particles to decay faster and provide an immediate burst of energy for emergency situations. While the end result would be like introducing nitrous oxide in a gasoline engine, it was substantially more volatile and if the core was ruptured, the radiated gas release would mix with the ambient dighergant material and explode in an atomic like explosion capable of rendering the mid-ship sections of the ship into a mass of molten metal. For this reason, the engineering section of the ship was equipped with anti-matter sensors that would initiate a core isolation protocol resulting in an immediate force-field containment designed to protect the control sections of the Spiruthun but allowing the complete decimation of anyone or anything inside the core chamber. Karna did not believe the Tahar would try to destroy the Piiderk dighergant reactor. She believed they would try to destroy the main reactor and use the smaller reactor to power and control the ship from inside engineering.

Regardless of the fact that the Tahar soldiers had superior firepower, the fearless advance of the Quod proved to be more difficult to overcome than they had predicted, and since they were advancing faster than the Tahar soldiers could reload their weapons, they were losing the battle. Although the Quod were not great thinkers, they did have enough sense to spread out far enough to keep more than one dying from each explosion, and this maneuver caused the Tahar to waste more ammunition and subsequently waste more time reloading. The officer leading the attack called for his men to close ranks and continue to fire, but before he could shout out another order, the Quod had reached them and one of them reached out and snapped his neck. Without a leader to give them direction, the remaining Tahar fought each man for himself as many were trying to retreat.

The other two teams were experiencing similar problems. The Quod were unlike any other Bilkegine army they had fought against. All the other battles they had fought were against other Bilkegine alliance, and they had little to no experience fighting against the Quod. Not only were they big and strong, but they were absolutely fearless. It didn't seem to matter how many were dying around them, each one kept coming as though they were an army of one.

Thinking he had an advantage being on the outside wall of the engineering chamber, the Tahar officer leading the attack on the south wing decided to fall back to the middle corridor to regroup. However, with the middle section now completely overrun by Quod, they got trapped in a cross fire and without recognizing what hit them the Tahar began to fall rapidly. As each Tahar soldier fell, the Quod picked up their new weapons and began to use them against the Tahar. The blood and other body fluids of both Quod and Tahar was so thick that the floor became extremely difficult to run on and many more fell to their death unable to stay on their feet. If all that had gone wrong wasn't enough, the sounds of the blasts from all the weapon fire had deafened them sufficient enough to prevent them from hearing the screams of the dying Tahar around them.

When it became evident that the battle had turned bad for the Tahar inside the engineering chamber, the officers outside ordered the men staged outside to rush to their brother's aid. Suddenly, three thousand Tahar men ran screaming into the chamber with their weapons destroying everything in their path. Not even taking the time to distinguish between Quod and Tahar, they fired blindly into the battleground. Like colonial fighting, the three thousand men lined up side by side in several ranks as they advanced either killing or destroying everything in the chamber. They continued to fire until they either fell dead or ran out of ammunition.

After thirty minutes of deadly, bloody battle, the war against the Quod in the engineering chamber was over. All that remained was two hundred fifty Tahar soldiers and one officer. Not one single piece of equipment was in working order and half of the room was in flames. The stench of the smoke, dead Quod and blood from the dead Tahar soldiers was intolerable but they had won their objective. The total body count was staggering. Four Tahar officers, five thousand, eight hundred Tahar soldiers, three hundred Bilkegine engineering crewmen and two thousand thirty Quod were all dead or dying. They had no reason to hold the ground since there was nothing left to defend, so the surviving officer ordered his men to join the Tahar brothers in the battle for the transportation chamber. Besides losing such large numbers of Tahar soldiers in the attempt to secure the engineering chamber, they also lost their original objective, which was to secure engineering in order to control the ship from outside the main command center. As the surviving Tahar regrouped outside engineering, waiting for the remaining soldiers from the North wing attack of engineering to report, the rear guard officer stepped into the doorway to the central corridor, took three dighergant grenades, and tossed them up against the Piiderk level dighergant reactor core and walked away. He knew that if they couldn't secure the reactor for their use, they would take the use of it away from Karna. Just as he was entering the main Piiderk corridor, the grenades exploded causing a crack in the reactor core's transparent shield and the escape of radiated gas. When the alarms sounded, the last remaining Tahar soldiers still fighting in the north engineering wing began to run for the exit leaving hundreds of Quod inside wondering what was happening. As the isolation force-field was activated, many Quod had made it to the doorway and were trying to fire upon the Tahar soldiers standing on the other side of the force-field when the core exploded. The horrifying screams and growls of the Quod inside could be heard all over the Piiderk as the radiated particles began to melt their flesh.

The Tahar who had survived the attack on engineering were exhausted and discouraged, but nevertheless were determined to reach their brothers in arms inside the transportation chamber. They now knew from first-hand experience how difficult it was going to be to defeat the warrior Quod inside. They regrouped, reloaded and mustered their resolve to proceed.

The battle for the transportation chamber was not going much better. While they did have the advantage of having only one way into the area, their one major disadvantage was the huge transport ships already loaded with massive numbers of warrior Quod in preparation for the attack of the planet below. Corth and his three officers decided to target each ship with a hundred men taking the entry ramp on each ship. The plan was simple. They would enter the transportation chamber slowly and infiltrate the Quod outside the ships by acting like they were joining the battle. They had removed their Tahar alliance banners that each had proudly displayed as part of their deception, and staged themselves to cover each ship in the transport bays closest to the Piiderk main corridor. Although they lacked the manpower to cover every ship in transportation, they did have enough to adequately cover the first two hundred ships closest to them. Their biggest advantage was the layout of the chamber itself. The area was one thousand feet long and divided into ten sections with air-tight bay doors between each section that could be closed off. They maneuvered into position and closed each door between the ten sections, and when the transportation crewmembers came out to investigate they were easily captured. Their plan was going smoothly and no shot had been fired. However, operators working inside who had witnessed the Tahar soldiers capturing other crewmembers, activated an alarm that brought the security Quod out of the operations center. When the firing began, the warrior Quod waiting inside the ships began to come out firing. The Tahar men who had been staged on either side of the loading ramps of the first hundred transport ships, couldn't fire fast enough to kill them all and they began to be overrun. Corth fell back and ordered his back-up plan, but because of the noise of the battle, most of the men staged by the transport ships did not respond. When Corth's plan was activated, and the outer door into space was opened, one thousand of his Tahar soldiers were sucked into space along with the warrior Quod that had come outside to fight. Those still inside the ships that were able to hold on managed to close the loading ramps of the ships and subsequently escaped their deaths. Corth regretted the loss of so many soldiers, but it had turned the tide in the battle to his favor. He gave the command to open the next series of bay doors to space to repeat the procedure, but before the door was opened enough to create a vacuum, the Quod outside, along with the crewmen operating equipment inside the bay ran into the ship and locked themselves inside. In one small way, Corth had won the battle, there were no Quod left in the transportation chamber to fight, but he failed miserably to secure the transportation chamber for use by the Tahar and he failed to stop the impending invasion.

Corth and two of his officers were discussing ways to disable the transport ships from lifting off, but they knew if they re-compressed the transportation bays long enough to disable the ships from the outside, the Quod would surely open the loading ramp doors and attack them again.

While the officers were discussing strategy, the men took the opportunity to reload their weapons and take a much needed rest. They were spread out all around the inside of the first loading bay section. While it was a huge expansive space capable of holding and supporting thousands of Quod warriors and two enormous transport ships, it was crowded with more than five thousand Tahar soldiers. Corth and his officers and several hundred soldiers were standing just outside the first loading bay section closest to the Piiderk level when an explosion unexpectedly ripped through the first loading bay section instantly killing more than half of the soldiers inside. The Tahar had never conceived the Quod using the onboard weapons to attack from inside the ship. As Captain Corth was screaming the order to retreat, a second and third explosion burst into the bay effectively killing the remaining soldiers inside. Corth and the Tahar men who had been outside the first bay were safe from the attack, but nevertheless, he had lost one officer and more than four thousand men in the short battle.

Hearing the explosion nearby, Hageze, who was on the same level taking position to overtake the Piiderk, and the command chamber where Karna was located, took his men to the transportation chamber in time to find his son Corth and a few hundred men retreating.

"What has happened?" Hageze asked Corth.

"The Quod fired on our position from inside the war ship and killed all my men. We thought we had them trapped inside, but it now looks as though I have completely failed."

"We must find a way to secure the transportation chamber or everything is for nothing. Without securing any future launch, they can still attack the planet."

"How, they are too many!"

"We must find a way. We will retreat to the Piiderk and come back with a plan. Go back inside and make sure that they cannot leave those ships. It will do them no good to launch with the launch doors only open half way, and they cannot leave their ships, but do something to ensure that no one else can come back and either open fully or close the launch portal."

Corth took fifty men back inside the transportation chamber to secure the control panel and the remainder surviving soldiers went to join the attack on the command center. Hageze was explaining his attack strategy to his men when another huge explosion rocked through the ship nearly throwing him to the floor. He immediately ran inside the transportation chamber and found his son lying dead beside his men. As he scanned the room, he saw one man attempting to crawl away and he ran over to him and picked him up and carried him to safety. He turned the man over and lowered him to the floor.

"What happened, did they fire upon you again?"

"No Sir, Commander," he whispered nearly dead, "we were shooting at the control panel with our new weapon and accidently punctured the fuel cell against the wall under the panel. The explosive release of the dighergant caused the cell to disintegrate."

The man died and Hageze bowed his head in honor of the dying soldier and his son, and let his head down gently. He glanced up to where the fuel cells had been resting against the wall and noticed a large expanse opened leading to a maintenance corridor that he was not aware existed. He slowly got up and walked over to his son and leaned over him. He stayed there many moments in silence than dropped to one knee and bowed his head in respect and honor as he did the other Tahar soldier.

"You too will be avenged, my son. You and all your brothers will be avenged."

He stood up and turned to the hole that was blown into the dark tunnel and stepped inside. The men who had gone with him to investigate the explosion stood outside and waited for several minutes before he returned. The accidental death of his son was not entirely in vain. In his death, he had provided a means to reach the Piiderk command center without being seen.

Sean, Rotusea and Chief Cremo reached the lower warehouse where they had been meeting to regroup and wait for the other Tahar men. They had managed to communicate directly with Hageze since hearing that Gebel was dead. Their attack on the armory had been a success and the mid-ship was now free from any weapons that could be used against them. Their only concern would be the Quod left on the Piiderk level and whatever weapons the crewmembers may be carrying. It has been some time since their narrow escape from the Quod on the Piiderk because of their slow descent and the weight of the new weapon that Cremo risked his life to retrieve. Sean was anxious to learn more about the weapon and stopped Cremo as he entered the warehouse.

"Rotusea," Sean said motioning her to come over to him, "I need you to translate for me." Sean turned to Cremo and began asking about the weapon.

"Chief Cremo what can you tell me about your weapon? How is it different than what we already have found?"

"It is great new." He said in broken and awkward English.

Rotusea looked to Sean surprised that Cremo was speaking in English and Sean walked until he was standing directly in front of Cremo. "So, what's up with the deceit of hiding the fact that you speak and understand my language?"

"I not positive you trustworthy, but now I trust more."

"When did you learn the language?"

"I was changed to speak while we travel here, to this tiny planet. I not speak your tongue but another. Before I learn your tongue, I speak what you call Spanish."

"Who taught you to speak English?"

Rotusea was interested in the answer to that question so she stepped closer.

"Before when I work power station, I learn English from female there, but when I move to weapons, she not teach more. Her called Zinont from house Brechtori. You know?" He replied looking at Rotusea.

"Okay, fine. Tell me about your new weapon. Why is it better than what we have now?" Sean asked impatiently.

"I will show." Cremo set the weapon up and activated a switch on the back side of the weapon. The weapon was extremely long and had a barrel that was tapered from one inch at the beginning where it was attached to a large box that Sean thought was a magazine, to more than five inches at the end. On the front of the box was a control panel that lit up when it was activated and began to make a quiet sizzling sound. When Sean heard it start up he took a quick step backward because it sounded like an electrical short. The box was sitting on the floor when Cremo activated it and once it was fully powered, it began to rise off the deck as if it were riding on a column of air. When it reached about four feet from the floor it stopped and floated silently. It hovered motionless while Cremo walked across the warehouse and began stacking the crate like boxes in the shape of a pyramid. When the stack was more than twelve feet tall, Cremo walked back to the back of the weapon and motioned Sean and Rotusea to stand back. He grabbed the weapon on either side like a machine gun and aimed the end of the barrel toward the stack of grates. He pulled the trigger and a whooshing sound exited the barrel forming concentric rings of white fog gradually increasing in size and speed until it silently hit the stack of crates. There was a long period of silence followed by the crashing sound of the crates as they fell down on the far end of the darkened warehouse more than one hundred feet away. Sean and Rotusea turned in amazement at what the weapon was capable of and Cremo nodded his head. "I show you more," he proclaimed as he left to stack more crates. This time he stacked crates only three high and more than twenty feet across. He slowly walked back behind the weapon and once again motioned for Sean and Rotusea to back away. He grabbed the sides of the weapon as he did before only this time he pulled back on the handles as it fired. The concentric rings formed but expanded to more than fifteen feet in diameter and once they reached the target, they continued to pulse from the weapon at the same size until he released the handles.

"This thing is awesome," Sean said excited. Rotusea agreed and asked him to explain how it worked. Cremo began to give them the details in English but it was too hard to follow because of his poor use of the language, so Sean stopped him and told him it would be easier if he explained it in his own language and let Rotusea translate. He agreed.

"This is the most powerful weapon that has ever been developed by the Bilkegine people. It has been in the making for more than forty months. As assistant engineering chief, I was assigned the task of working closely with Karna to develop, build and test new weapons. The beginning concept was her creation, but the design and modifications were the combined ideas of several key minds from our engineering, physics and armory divisions."

Cremo stopped to allow Rotusea time to catch up with the translation, then continued with the explanation and details of the weapons capabilities.

"Karna's original concept was to create a weapon that would utilize the power of our dighergant material to create a vacuum in space. Not in the sense of outer space, but in the sense of the dimensional space. The principle depended on our ability to take the dighergant material and accelerate it as it exited the weapon. We needed to accelerate it fast enough to create a miniature worm-hole effect that had the potential to draw anything in its opening into a different dimension. The weapon however was a failure from that approach, because we lacked the ability to create the worm-hole with such little power. In order to create a worm hole large enough and keep it open long enough to be effective we would need a dighergant reactor as large as the one on the main rapitor level. However, in the process, we discovered that by using the dighergant as the principle source of power for the weapon, we could generate a burst of energy that would grow exponentially as it left the weapon and displace anything in its path into pieces without harming the area around it. The most beneficial factor of the weapon, besides the immense burst of energy, is the fact that the dighergant energy source has a half life of three hundred phases and can be fired continually, thereby creating a vortex effect that could clear a path in front of the user large enough for a small army to pass through, unaffected by anything, including incoming fire from other weapons. Additionally, when the vortex is being generated, it also creates a force-field around the weapon preventing the operator to come under fire."

Seam walked around the weapon admiring the genius that went into creating it. "What do you call this thing?"

"It is called the Cyclonic Vortex Emitter," Cremo replied.

Before Sean went too far admiring the weapon, he realized that it was ultimately Karna. He knew it was designed to be used against humans and it made him mad. Suddenly he tried to grab the weapon and move it by himself, but it was too heavy. He had only been helping Cremo carry it before but when he tried to move it by himself he remembered how strong the Bilkegine people were. "How much does this thing weigh?" he asked.

Cremo studied the question in his mind trying to understand all the words but ultimately failed. He looked at Rotusea puzzled so she asked the question in his language.

"You will say maybe 158 kilograms," Cremo replied.

Sean did the math quickly in his head and converted it into pounds. "Three hundred and fifty pounds—holy smoke!"

Sean's last remark was something neither of them had ever heard before and they both looked at Sean with puzzled looks on their faces. "Holy smoke?" Rotusea repeated. "What does that mean?"

Sean laughed for the first time in a very long time and the thought of having breakfast with Bruce right before his capture came to his mind. His laugh quieted and became a diminishing smile. Then he looked at Rotusea and said, "Oh, it's nothing—just an expression. When are we going to use this thing on Karna and get this war over with once and for all?"

She realized that Sean had just remembered something from his past that made him happy but then he became angry again. She had never witnessed a human laughing before and since the Bilkegine never laughed, or cried for that matter, she was struggling to understand and wanted to ask more of Sean but refrained. She now had a better understanding of why Sean was so angry and why he hated Karna with such disdain. Sean was still looking at her expecting an answer so she walked up to him and touched his arm as she had seen Sean do to Nancy while trying to comfort her and said, "it will not be long. We have been preparing for this battle for many years and since it began, we have lost most of our Tahar brothers. But the time is coming to finish it as you said, once and for all."

Sean sat down and leaned against a wall to wait for the other Tahar to join them, and Rotusea and Cremo joined him.

CHAPTER THIRTY-FIVE

Sean and the other two Bilkegine people, Rotusea and Chief Cremo, had waited for more than an hour without hearing anything from Hageze. They had not even seen him since they learned of Gebel's death. Rotusea only knew that he was second in command of the Tahar alliance onboard the craft. In actuality, Rotusea outranked Hageze, but since Gebel was her brother, the Tahar Alliance leaders on Bilkegine thought it best to have her commissioned as an administrative and supply commander instead of a battle commander. Her role was to act as assistant but in the event of the death of both Gebel and Hageze then she would become the battle commander by default. As they sat in the warehouse waiting, that very thought was going through her head. What if Hageze has also met with death? Am I ready to assume command of the remaining Tahar soldiers? She thought. Since Gebel had officially named the earthling as a combat commander, who should lead, him or me? Sean noticed her looking at him while deep in thought and wondered what was going through her head.

"A penny for your thoughts." Sean said quietly.

"I do not understand, what is a penny? Do you require something of me?" she asked confused.

"No, it's another expression. It means I would give you a penny if you tell me what you are thinking."

"I am sorry, I still do not understand what a—penny is."

"It's the smallest denomination of our money. It is a coin of little value. I just wanted to know what you are thinking."

"Why not just ask me what I am thinking?"

"I did, that's the way we say it on Earth. It's just a saying, that's all."

"Your language is very difficult to understand. I thought I had a firm grasp of your language before I began speaking with you."

"Don't feel bad; Earth women say the same thing about understanding men. You're certainly not alone. So, Rotusea, what were you thinking?"

"Since we have been waiting here so long, the thought occurred to me that perhaps all the Tahar have met with their deaths. And if that is the case, I was wondering what we would do and who would lead us."

"That's easy isn't it? Who is next in command?"

"I am. But Gebel has also appointed you as combat commander, so perhaps it should be you."

"There is no question about who is more worthy to lead the Tahar in my mind. It is you. Perhaps we can do it together. We both have a good mind for battle. Don't you agree?"

"Yes, I do."

"Speaking of Hageze, how much longer should we wait until we do something?"

"That was the other thing I was thinking. I believe we should go and find out what has happened to the Tahar."

"Let's go!"

Sean stood up and helped Rotusea to her feet. He was somewhat amazed at how much she weighed compared to Nancy. He was surprised because they were both about the same build and looked lean and toned, but Rotusea felt like she weighed as much as a man. "You're not from Texas by any chance?" He smiled.

"Texas? What is a Texas?"

"Oh, never mind."

He then realized that their muscular build must be completely different than a human and it explained how Karna seemed so much stronger than he did and why Cremo was able to carry his weapon out of the armory by himself.

They walked over to Cremo and woke him up. He had fallen asleep waiting for the Tahar to return. But before Cremo stood up the Tahar rushed into the warehouse. As the first few soldiers ran inside they scanned the room quickly and noticed Cremo sitting against the wall. They immediately ran over to him and pointed their weapons directly at his head at point blank range.

"What is he doing here?" One of them asked in anger. "And why is he wearing the Tahar crest?"

Rotusea, who had walked over to the men as they were entering the room, heard them ask about Cremo and looked over at them to see one aiming at his head. She quickly turned to intervene when Sean pushed the weapons aside and stepped between Cremo and the Tahar soldiers. Rotusea began explaining from across the room, "He has come over to the Tahar side. He has proclaimed it in front of many Bilkegine witnesses and has given us aid and support. He has also given us much information that we can use against Karna."

The two Tahar lowered their weapons and sneered at Cremo in disgust. One of them stepped face to face with Cremo as he stood up and said in a low voice, in his own language, "I'll be watching you! If you make one false move, you will die!"

Now all the Tahar were inside the warehouse and Hageze found Rotusea and Sean standing beside Cremo. He came across the room and pulled Rotusea aside to inform her of her brother's death. When she reported that she had already heard and relayed the fact that Gebel had appointed Sean as combat commander, Hageze was surprised. Since he had been on another part of the ship when Gebel made the announcement he asked her to explain why. She recounted the story of Sean killing a Quod with his bare hands and proclaimed his bravery and quick thinking in the battle against the armory. He understood why Gebel would have made the decision but still had questions.

"Do you agree that he should lead the Tahar over one of us?"

"You are the only one to make that decision, Hageze. As you know, I am only commander in rank not battle commissioned, unless of course there is no other to lead. As far as the human is concerned, I will trust him with my life and believe we share the same goals and fight for the same cause. I believe the leadership of the Tahar Alliance on Bilkegine, who do not even know of his existence, would agree with Gebel if they had the opportunity to see him fight. He truly is a great warrior."

"I will give it some great thought, but meanwhile, we must prepare for our last battle."

"Where are the remaining Tahar hiding?"

"There are no more, these men are what remain of the Tahar onboard the Spiruthun."

Rotusea looked at the small number of men in the room and turned back to Hageze astonished and perplexed. "How can that be, the battles were that difficult, even with the new weapons?"

Hageze described the carnage that occurred both in the engineering chambers and transportation. He told her of the central engineering dighergant reactor core melt-down and the death of his son Corth.

Sean slowly walked over and joined Rotusea and Hageze. He didn't know if they were excluding him on purpose since Hageze had pulled Rotusea aside, but upon reaching them, Hageze welcomed him.

"So, we did not gain any ground at all?" Rotusea asked troubled.

"Not as we desired. But to answer specifically, we have gained ground but at a high cost of life on all sides. We were able to secure and close off engineering, but at the cost of the reactor core as I said. However, while that does alter our plans to operate the Spiruthun from there, we can still take control of the ship. We must take greater caution when we attack the Piiderk command chamber so no equipment is damaged. We did not succeed completely in the transportation chamber, but the warrior Quod are trapped inside the ships and are unable to launch against the planet below. In fact, the individual bays are locked closed and the launch portal is closed half way, and the control panel on the outside of the launch bay has been destroyed."

"Then we will not be able to launch either, will we?"

"Not in the present condition, but I believe we can find another way around the launch bay chambers and attack from the other side. I am trying to locate a working computation control monitor to learn the layout of that area."

Sean interrupted to find out what they were saying and Rotusea filled him in on everything that had happened. He then asked if Hageze knew of their success in the armory and the destruction of the weapons in the warehouse. Rotusea informed Hageze of Gebel's plan to take the armory and included what Sean had ordered concerning the supply and weapons stores in the forward warehouse on the Piiderk level.

When everyone was current on what had been accomplished, the only thing left to do was seize the Piiderk level and the command center.

"Let's get moving on the Piiderk level before Karna has a chance to regroup," Sean said. "We've been waiting around doing nothing for nearly two hours."

"When Corth was killed by the explosion, a large hole was opened to a large passageway and maintenance area that I am not familiar with. I am trying to discover what is in there and what areas would be impacted if we could access the control panels inside," said Hageze.

Rotusea translated what was said, and Sean got excited. He turned and motioned Chief Cremo to join them then said, "I understand that you do not trust the chief, but he has done much already to help us defeat the armory and escape. He told us that he was assistant chief of engineering before he was promoted to the armory. He just may be the one to get the information you need on the new maintenance area."

As Chief Cremo got closer to the group, he slowed down and bowed his head showing his respect and honor for Hageze. He was holding his arms out in the gesture of surrender when he stopped beside Hageze and Rotusea. Hageze glanced at Rotusea to see her reaction and recognizing that she had already accepted him as trustworthy he reached out and gently pushed Cremo's arms down and said, "I am told you were beneficial in giving aid to the destruction of the armory and weapons. Thank you for your assistance. I also understand that you have proclaimed your allegiance to the Tahar while being a member of the Shem. You realize that by wearing our crest and proclaiming publically your allegiance, you will be considered a traitor and if caught, you will be killed?"

"As I have told Rotusea and the human, I never agreed with the Shem and the way they have ruled. I have served because I am from a clan whose house descended from the Shem and no other reason. When faced with death, I turned to the Tahar and I have killed my son with these two hands because of the Shem. I have no allegiance to them any longer, whether I die or not."

"Rotusea has also informed me that you were chief of engineering before you were made Chief of the Armory. How long were you an engineering crewman?" Hageze asked.

"I have been in engineering my entire life. My father was of engineering and was the architect of many Bilkegine space transportation vessels. I have known this ship since it was conceived and know it as well if not better than the Chief of engineering himself. What do you need to know?"

"I have discovered a large maintenance area that runs beside the Piiderk main corridor just outside transportation. When a large explosion caused the wall to open, I ventured inside to try and ascertain any possible use but the area was black to me. I need to know where I can find a working computation monitor where I can learn what the area controls."

"I know of the area you speak of," Cremo said excited to help. "It is known as the Piiderk support chamber. You do not need a computation monitor to learn what you need. I have a complete knowledge of everything within."

Sean asked Rotusea what was happening and she responded, "I will educate you after I know everything, it will be faster." She then turned her attention back to Cremo and asked, "What is in the chamber? Is it something we can use?"

"Yes, most helpful. Within the chamber are many controls, it is the primary dighergant reactor distributor for the entire Piiderk level including the command center, transportation and living chambers as well as a secondary maintenance corridor that leads to the Piiderk Command Center, the Transportation Systems Controller, and the Primary Life Support controller for all living quarters."

"Do you mean to tell me that we can control the entire ship from inside that chamber?" Hageze asked as excited as Bilkegine people get.

"No, I do not mean to misinform you. You cannot operate the Spiruthun from there, but you can operate the life support systems, the transportation control monitors and you can discontinue power to most of the Piiderk level."

"Can we operate all the chamber apertures individually from there?" Rotusea asked.

Cremo thought about it for a few moments, going through each control panel in his head and pointing into the space in front of him as though he was actually pushing buttons. Then looking up at the ceiling, one last time, he replied, "Yes, I believe we could close and disable all apertures except the primary portal aperture entering the Command Center itself. All others, within the Piiderk level, including transportation can be operated from within the support chamber."

"No one will be able to unlock or override them from anywhere else?" Hageze added.

"Not unless they posses one of these," Cremo answered holding up a crystal key. "And I have the only one."

"It looks like an ordinary energy collimation crystal. How is it different?" Hageze asked puzzled.

"As an engineering master, it was necessary to design an energy collimation crystal that would work on any and all devices onboard this vessel. Instead of needing hundreds of individual arrays, this crystal was designed to work on all of them by adjusting the frequency fluctuation modules, which in turn realigns the crystal particles and modifies the placement of each crystal held within."

Sean interrupted again and asked Rotusea what he was holding up. When she explained what it was and how it worked, he said in amazement, "We've got a pass key, a master that will work on any door?"

"Exactly." Rotusea replied.

Hageze finally stopped asking questions and began to formulate a plan. He stated that he needed a few minutes to think alone and would return to explain what they needed to do. One of the things he had to ponder was the role that Sean would play in the next and final attack. As he formulated his plan, he made a mental note of what they must secure before they could effectively call their war a victory.

While Hageze was away, Rotusea took the time to explain everything that had been discussed and theorized how Cremo could benefit them.

Hageze returned as she was concluding her explanation. He had decided that Sean would play a vital role in the operation.

"Here is what I believe to be the best plan of attack." He said as he returned to the group. "As I see it there are still three major objectives we must accomplish if we are to be victorious. The first thing we need to do is isolate the Piiderk level from all other levels. Gebel has already taken care of isolating the mid-ship from all other levels above and below. By doing this, he provided protection from not only the Quod on those levels, but any other crewman who could defend against our attack. If we are able to effectively close and lock all other means of entry, we need only strike against the Quod that are presently on the Piiderk level. To that end, we must take and secure the central command center including the war chamber and weapons stations. To that we must also add the isolation and destruction of every attack ship inside the transportation chamber, leaving only the individual landing shuttles. We must not destroy that section or we will be trapped on a dying vessel as well. And we must also destroy the main dighergant reactor core on the rapitor level. I believe if we take each one in a specific order, we will be able to accomplish these tasks with the remaining Tahar soldiers. Once we have secured the central command center and killed Commander Nuubiya we will be able to destroy the dighergant reactor core remotely by overloading the reactor and closing the exhaust aperture. The ship will eventually be decimated but I believe we will have ample time to escape in the shuttles that remain. We will transmit our victory from the shuttles and proclaim our authority to rule to Bilkegine. Once the word of truth is verified, all the other alliances will rally together and overthrow the Shem Alliance. They know that their failure to seize this planet will result in their losing the trust that the other clans and alliances have in them and they should abdicate their seat of authority willingly. However, given the fact that all Quod are currently located on this vessel, they would be easily overthrown should they resist."

Hageze watched for any disagreement while he explained his plan. The only one that seemed to have a problem with the plan was Sean, but Hageze realized that he had not yet heard everything since Rotusea was still translating. As she finished, Sean shook his head in agreement but added one thing.

"Let me begin by saying that I believe the plan to be an excellent idea. However, I would like to make one request. I would like the honor of killing Karna, Commander Nuubiya personally."

Hageze and Rotusea nodded in agreement and Cremo asked what his role would be.

"Chief Cremo," Hageze began, "you have so far proven faithful to your pledge to join the Tahar. I have no reason to doubt your loyalty, and before I explain your role, please accept a position of rank as a Captain of the Tahar Alliance. Promoting a lower classman to a position of honor as a Tahar officer is a privilege reserved for those holding a commission of battle commander or higher. I too was promoted from within the lower classes by Commander Gebel. It is a rare promotion, and one that should be taken in all seriousness. Should you die in battle, a memorial will be erected in your honor and your descendents will be elevated to the class of Delnori under the house of Tahar."

Then Hageze turned and faced Sean. "While it is impossible for me to officially welcome you to the house of Tahar, you will be honored by our people as a brother for your efforts in this war. I know that while we have come to defend your people from the Shem Alliance, you too have fought to defend the lives of the Tahar. For your continued support and willingness to die in battle, I give you this, a token of the honor we owe to you." He said as he passed his own Tahar crest to Sean. "I also will grant your wish to personally kill Commander Karna Nuubiya."

The time had come to put their plans into action but Sean still wasn't sure he understood the entire plan. Since he couldn't understand anything Hageze had said, he only had the brief summation that Rotusea had given him to go on. The Tahar were getting their weapons prepared, and each man was gathering as much ammunition as they could carry and placing it in some type of bag designed to carry their rations and other supplies. Everything had been dumped out on the floor of the warehouse to make room for the ammunition. Sean reached down to grab one of the bags but could not even lift it off the ground. It was another reminder of how strong these people were. He had never thought much beyond the battle on the ship but he was beginning to wonder what would happen if Karna was able to launch her attack. The superior weaponry of the Bilkegine would outmatch any conventional weapon that the military had so badly it would be like comparing a water pistol to a howitzer.

Since the hole entering the Piiderk support chamber was located inside the transportation chamber, it meant they would have to move very quickly and in small groups through the Piiderk level where there was sure to be many Quod warriors. This was another step that Hageze had not counted on with his plan and Sean was going to have to talk about it before they were caught off guard.

Sean found Hageze standing with his men giving them some last minute details of the plan. Sean walked up to him with Rotusea beside him as interpreter and explained some of his concerns.

"Hageze, could we have a word with you in private?"

"Yes, let us go there," he said pointing to one of the corners of the warehouse that was empty.

"I am not trying to usurp your authority Hageze, but I'm not completely sure I understand everything and would like to go over it with you in detail before we continue."

"You do not think it is a good plan?"

"No, it's not that, I just think it would be better if I understood every detail. Plus there are a couple of things I think you might have overlooked."

"Very well, we can discuss it in detail once we reach the support chamber beside the Piiderk main corridor."

"I guess that will be ok, but before we go that far there is one thing."

"What is this, 'one thing' you speak of?"

"Well, for starters, when we attacked the armory, we believe Karna called for Quod back-up and we were nearly beaten. When we escaped through a hole in the wall, we had to walk slowly out in small groups in order to avoid drawing attention to ourselves. Those warrior Quods are more than likely still on the Piiderk level in the main corridor."

"That is not a problem we can do the same thing. We will advance slowly in small groups."

"That's not good enough. If they see anyone with a weapon, they will assume we are an army and open fire on us. The only way around it is to take these off," he explained pulling on the crest he was wearing, "and, we will have to break down the weapons into small parts that we can conceal under our clothing."

Hageze thought about what Sean was saying and agreed, "the only problem is we will be unarmed if we do run into resistance. What do you suggest if that happens?"

"I don't know, but it didn't happen before and it will likely not happen again. We'll have to take that chance. Once we get inside the support chamber, we can re-assemble our weapons and proceed. Rotusea and I can go over my other concerns while the Tahar soldiers work on their weapons."

"That is a good plan. I will spread the orders. You can take the lead when we venture out onto the Piiderk from below."

The time had come for them to leave the safety of the lower warehouse. As before, Sean took the lead stepping onto the Piiderk level and was not surprised when he saw hundreds of Quod milling around the main corridor in search of an enemy target. Sean cautiously walked across the Piiderk level fighting the urge to run. He headed toward the outside wall that separated the Piiderk from the transportation chamber and as he turned around a corner, he saw at least three hundred more Quod standing at the portal waiting to enter the transportation chamber. They had not yet figured out how to re-pressurize the loading bays and the inside section of the transportation chamber just before the first loading bay was filled with Quod as well. Sean stopped dead in his tracks and turned to signal the others following behind him to turn back. The group that was traveling with him slowly turned and walked back to the ladder-way and returned to the warehouse.

Upon returning, Sean was greeted by Hageze and Rotusea.

"We have to figure out another way into that room," Sean said. "If we can't, we'll be stuck here too long to do any good. Eventually the Quod will break through the debris that is closing off the upper and lower decks and if that happens before we take the ship, we're all dead."

"Let's consult with Cremo. He will know the Spiruthun better than all of us." Rotusea suggested.

"Cremo," Rotusea called. "The passage to the transportation chamber has many Quod outside waiting to enter the attack vessels but the chamber is not pressurized and they cannot enter. Is there another way into the transportation chamber or into the Piiderk support chamber?"

Cremo thought for a minute before he began to explain their options. "There is another way into the transportation chamber but it will be of no use to you since it will undoubtedly be full of Quod as well. The only way into the Piiderk support chamber, besides the new hole in the wall, is through the War chamber. There is a maintenance passageway that connects the War chamber to the support chamber, but without first seizing control of the command center we would not have access. I am sorry but I can be no help to you in this matter."

Sean listened closely as Rotusea relayed what Cremo had said. He thought about it some more but couldn't come up with an idea either. Finally he said, "We can at least get a little closer. If we go back to the Piiderk level and walk in small groups as before, we can make it to the forward warehouse."

"What can we do there that we cannot do here?" Hageze asked impatiently.

"I guess it would just get us closer to our objective, and it would give us the opportunity to advance more quickly if needed. If we re-assemble our weapons in the…"

Rotusea interrupted with information that Sean had forgotten. "Sean, do you not remember, we de-pressurized the forward warehouse. We cannot go inside or we will die instantly."

"Dog gone it!" Sean said loudly as he threw his weapon to the ground and kicked it across the floor.

"What does that mean?" Rotusea asked puzzled again with Sean's confusing sayings. "Is not a dog a small furry animal you call a canine? How does that help us?"

"It's just another saying, Rotusea, something we say when we are angry and frustrated. I don't know what it means or even where the saying came from. I'm just mad as a wet hen that's all."

Cremo, who had been thinking the whole time Sean was shouting off, turned abruptly, "I believe I have a solution. There is one other place we can go but the room will only hold—half of our number." He said looking around the room. "There is another place that is used as a utility corridor for the forward weapons controller. The room was used previously as a weapons storage facility before we converted them to the dighergant disruptors. There is a small vertical conveyance system that goes from the smaller forward warehouse on the falkoe level below us, directly to the weapons storage corridor. Inside it is a small maintenance passageway that travels underneath the Piiderk level and goes directly into the Piiderk support chamber. It is a very small passageway and has many dighergant venting tubes inside. It will be extremely hot inside, but we can go unseen. Once the first group is cleared of the weapons storage corridor, the vertical conveyance can be returned and the remaining group can go through."

Rotusea translated it for Sean's sake and the plan was put to action. Sean and Cremo would be the first to lead so Cremo could begin working on the panels and control right away. Just before Cremo got on the elevator, he turned and instructed them on one more important note. "You must remember that the weapons storage corridor is immediately beside the command center's main control chamber. If any sound is made it will be heard and it is more than likely that Quod will be sent to investigate. There is a portal that connects the two chambers."

Sean suddenly recalled the room Cremo was speaking of from the tour of the ship that Karna had given him. He remembered that the control room was void of any staff working and also remembered looking back into the room as he was leaving and seeing the workers coming back into the room from a small door he had not seen earlier. He now knew exactly where he was and how close he would be to Karna. They continued up the elevator two at a time until they had all reached the Piiderk support chamber.

Sean and Cremo were the first to reach the chamber and as they stood up, and as Sean stretched his back out, Cremo began padding his way into the darkness. This was the darkest place Sean had been on the ship and he was even having a difficult time seeing where he was going. As Cremo walked deeper and deeper into the darkness, Sean stopped not wanting to get lost. Rotusea had come up behind him followed shortly by Hageze. Sean ventured toward the direction Cremo had gone and finally caught up with him. Sean could hear Cremo patting the sides of the wall lightly and wondered what he was doing.

"What are you doing, Cremo?"

"I look for control panel to brighten room." Cremo said in his broken English.

Rotusea had followed Sean silently and as Sean turned around to pat the wall behind him in search for a panel, he ran right into Rotusea knocking her to the floor with Sean falling down on top of her. "Who is there?" Sean asked quietly as he began to push himself off.

"It is I, Rotusea." She replied. "I am sorry I did not know you were there. What is Cremo looking for; perhaps I can help him find it?"

"He's looking for a control panel that will brighten the room."

"We were not aware that the rooms could be brightened in the dark places."

Sean got back to his feet and began walking back toward Cremo. By the time he joined him again, his eyes had adjusted to the darkness and he could distinguish between the shadows and the darkness behind them. Cremo stopped tapping the walls and said in a very soft voice, "I find the panel."

"Well that's great, but how are you going to see good enough to do anything about it?"

"I no need see to change. I feel with hands as eyes."

"I feel with hands as eyes?" Sean whispered to himself. "This guy's got to get with the program and learn to talk before he drives me crazy."

Doing exactly what he said he was doing, Cremo used his hands as eyes like a blind man and found the switches and panels he needed to change. Sean thought it was amazing how in total darkness, he was able to slide out some kind of crystal and switch them around without getting them mixed up. As good as Sean could see, he couldn't even tell them apart, but Cremo shuffled the crystals in his hands then slipped them into their proper slots in the panel. When he activated the panel again, the light became bright enough for them to see.

"How well can you see now?" Sean asked.

Rotusea had come up behind Sean again was the first to answer, "It would be like your dusk."

"Good," Sean declared. "I can see like it is daylight without having to squint like on the Püderk level, very good."

Having seen Sean in action for himself, and with Sean pointing out some of the problems that Hageze had not prepared for in his planning, Hageze had come to the conclusion that Sean may be a better warrior than himself. It was not a problem for him to admit that someone was better than he was and the Bilkegine for the most part did not have huge egos that needed to be exercised on a regular basis like humans, so Hageze decided to relinquish leadership to Sean as Gebel had done. He figured if Gebel, who was far more intelligent than he was, had seen the merit in making Sean a battle commander, who was he to challenge it.

When all the remaining Tahar soldiers had made it through the tunnel and were re-assembling their weapons, he stepped to the middle of the chamber and quietly called them around. In a very soft spoken voice, he explained his intentions.

"Listen my Tahar brothers, we must be extraordinarily quiet so the Quod, on the other side of this wall, do not hear us, but I have something very important to say."

When Hageze began to speak, Sean turned away from watching Cremo work and listened. Hageze motioned for Sean to join him and waited until he stood beside him.

"I will follow the human, called Sean, to our victory. He is a great warrior and is fighting for the same thing we are, and for the same thing my son Corth died to protect. We have had many trials on our long mission, and have lost many of our Tahar brothers, and now we must find the strength in our small numbers to defeat Karna, no matter the cost."

He stopped talking for a moment and looked around the room. There was complete silence except for the tinkling of the crystals that Cremo was working with, and then he continued.

"Who is with me? Who among you will follow this human?

He waited and watched for a sign of support then one by one his men began to stand up in show of their willingness to fight with the human as their leader.

CHAPTER THIRTY-SIX

Agent Rose had Dr. Weiss watching for any sign from the alien craft that would demonstrate that Sean had been successful. Time was running out, and if he didn't see a sign in the next ten minutes, he would have no choice but to give the go-ahead on the strike. The pilots of the S51F's were very nervous sitting in the orbit out of visual sight but no doubt within some kind of radar or other more sophisticated early warning system. General Stephens called for condition red, and all personnel took their positions.

"We are at defcon one General," said one of the officers at a large control station in front of the big board, "ten minute countdown commencing in five, four, three, two, one mark."

"All hands to their ready stations!" commanded the general.

Agent Rose paced the floor just outside the war room waiting for the call from Dr. Weiss that would give Sean a little more time to evacuate the ship before they launched their missiles. As if time were racing by exponentially, every second passing by faster than the second before, James was beginning to worry about Bruce's friend. It was as though he knew Sean as well as anyone now, and he wanted him to succeed more than he wanted anything before. It wasn't that he didn't want to blow the aliens into cosmic dust, it was just a pity that someone as brave as Sean was going to die trying to win a war single-handedly, and his heart went out to him. His phone began to ring, and he looked quickly at his watch to see how much time he had, and discovered that he only had two minutes and forty-six seconds and counting. It wasn't very much time, but he hoped it would be enough.

"Yes! Agent Rose! He said hurriedly into the phone.

"Agent Rose, this is Dr. Weiss. I'm afraid I do not have the news you were looking for, but I do have some interesting images that may persuade your people to delay the launch." The doctor said calmly.

"What is it Dr. Weiss?"

"I have sent the image through already, you should have it available in thirty seconds."

"Great, doctor, thanks. I will get back to you."

"You're quite welcome. Good luck."

James ran inside the war room and spoke into the general's ear. General Stephens ordered a delay in the count-down, and the Captain on the control desk repeated the order.

"Count-down delayed at minus two minutes, twenty seconds, sir."

"Okay Agent Rose, Let's see the image, and if it's not what we need, we're going ahead with the launch! Agreed?"

"Yes, sir, agreed."

The general and James left the war room for the briefing room where the NASA computer imaging computer had been set up. The image had already been received and processed, and the technician was standing by to run the program.

"Run the program," said General Stephens.

The computer screen came up completely black. The stars came up blurry then focused sharp. At first they didn't know what they were supposed to be looking at. Then on the far top left of the screen, they could make out the ship and around the ship the debris field.

"I've already seen this footage!" the general stated frustrated.

Before James could say anything, the image pulled back and focused on the debris field. There were hundreds upon hundreds of huge green/gray skinned aliens floating among the debris. Some of them still grasping weapons. The image zoomed in on one of the dead aliens, and it was clear that he had a huge hole burned right through the center of his chest.

"Now, this is something new!" James exclaimed.

"Yes, I'd have to agree, but how does it change the fact that the ship is still a threat to us Agent Rose?"

"Oh, come on, general. Isn't it clear from that image that a war is going on inside the craft? That's our boy up there and from the look of it, he's got help and he's doing a great job without our help!"

"I don't know. I just don't see anything that is definitive. I'll have to call it in."

"Fine, call it in, but they've got to see the image to get the full picture! I'll have to insist!" James stated emphatically.

"You know that will slow things down, and that's just what you want!" General Stephens said, pointing his boney finger at James.

"I don't care what you think, general. I still have the last say on this mission, and I think that image tells me that Sean is waging war on the alien ship and doesn't need us screwing things up right now! Unless you want to be pulled from the project all together, I would suggest you get the image off right away!"

"You know, that's great, but I'm going over your head on this one, pal, and I'm done taking my orders from you as well!"

"Please yourself, general, but unless I hear it from the President, we don't advance."

"Send the file to the Pentagon now!" The general yelled to the technician as he was stomping out of the room.

James didn't care who he made mad, as long as the right decision was made. He knew the military mindset all too well. He knows that all they ever want to do is shoot first and ask questions later. Their favorite saying, when faced with a decision of knowing the good guys from the bad guys, was to "shoot them all and let God sort them out" and that wasn't going to happen on James' watch.

✵✵✵

The military strike from earth was coming, but Sean didn't know it. He had come up with a plan to kill Karna and take command of the ship. His plan was to use the new weapon to gain access to the command center and kill Karna, then load all the Tahar survivors onto one of the transport shuttles inside the transportation chamber, again using the new weapon as a means of gaining access then let the Tahar destroy the parent ship.

Sean believed his plan was simple but had all the essential elements that a successful plan must have in order to bring victory. First it had an element of surprise. He believed that Karna and the Quod would think that they had seen the last of the Tahar, because of the horrendous losses they had incurred during the last battle. The second element a good plan had to have is speed. Every battle ever fought in earth's history where speed was used as a way to overrun and overpower the enemy was successful. With the new weapon they had, they could easily run in blasting away and keep running until they reached their destination. It would not only destroy everything in front of them, but they would be able to move so quickly that the enemy could not form a defense or regroup against them for another battle.

The third element they must have was resolve. He believed more than any other time or with any other group, that these Tahar soldiers had the resolve to fight until the last man was standing. Their tenacity went beyond mere courage or dedication, it bordered on spiritual. Sean remembered reading about some of the ancient races on earth and how they motivated the soldiers to fight. One Spanish commander burned his ship so his men wouldn't want to give up and go home. Vikings believed that if they didn't die in battle, they couldn't get into Valhalla, the hall of Odin, in which the souls of heroes slain in battle were received. The Tahar didn't need that kind of motivation to keep fighting. They fought for honor. They knew that the alliance in power was evil and was taking a planet and killing a people selfishly, and they couldn't live with the knowledge that their lives were at the expense of another entire species.

Hageze was sitting against a wall and pondering the battles that were coming when Sean approached him with his plan. He had Rotusea and Cremo with him as he outlined where and when they would strike. Rotusea and Cremo took turns translating as Sean explained the details of the plan to him.

"The plan is rather simple, Hageze. Since we are so few in number, we can't afford another traditional combat against Karna or her army of

Quod. Although we have reduced that number significantly, we have but one thousand soldiers left to fight with. Instead of taking a large number of men, I suggest we take only twenty men and strike against the command center hard and fast, using the new weapon that Cremo calls the Cyclonic Vortex Emitter."

Sean waited for Rotusea to catch up translating and Hageze to question anything. When he nodded without saying anything, Sean continued.

"I figure that I will take the point, and the rest of our small team will fall behind me. We will move very quickly across the Piiderk level toward the control chamber itself, we blast everything in the room killing everyone and take control of the ship. Cremo will operate the equipment left unharmed with the new weapon and open and close the necessary doors that we will need to access. And since all of the doors leading to the Quod will be locked, he will not come under attack."

Hageze sat back and thought about it for a minute then asked a couple of questions.

"What about the balance of the Tahar onboard?"

"Okay, everyone else who will be saved will muster in the Piiderk once we have control of the ship and again, using the CVE, we will make a pathway to the transportation chamber where they will be loaded onto one of the shuttles."

"What about the Quod still remaining in the Piiderk immediately outside the transportation chamber? How will you overpower them?"

"Cremo will have complete control over all the systems inside the transportation chamber. We will blast the CVE and those who are not killed or blown inside transportation, will no doubt run inside and lock the door to save themselves and try to secure the transportation chamber. Once they are all inside, Cremo will open every loading bay, and since the ships inside loaded with warrior Quods are still physically connected to all the system controls, he will remotely open the rear hatches and simultaneously open the outer launch bay doors effectively sucking every last Quod into space. The Quod who are able to remain inside the ships will die from the cold or lack of oxygen. After several minutes, he will close the doors and allow the Tahar to enter the transportation chamber and board the ship like I said before."

Without hesitation Hageze stood up and proclaimed that it was an excellent plan and began passing the word among the Tahar to allow them to make preparations. At the same time, Rotusea and Sean went around the room and began telling each volunteer exactly what they would do and told them what they would need for the last mission.

CHAPTER THIRTY-SEVEN

The Pentagon received the image of the debris field and dead Quod. The President, along with his chief council and the heads of all the military branches reviewed the file and immediately went into locked chambers to discuss their options and make the final decision. General Stephens had made several calls to other generals at the Pentagon and verbalized his objections and frustrations of having to take orders from a non-military spook. He had attempted to get as many of them in his corner as possible and knew that military men stuck together and should have control over the Government in times like they were currently under. The politicians were always worried what people would think and their political carriers should they make a bad judgment. The President stood up to address everyone in the room.

"Gentlemen, we have to make a decision, and we must make it for all the right reasons. The shoot first and ask questions later mentality of your predecessors cannot and will not be allowed to continue. I know that I have given the approval to make this mission possible, but given the most recent intelligence from the alien craft, I would say that we definitely have someone on our side up there, and it looks like they are doing a good job without us. I will give you each two minutes to state your case, if you disagree with my observations, but I warn you that only logical and reasonable objections will be considered. Furthermore, I urge each of you to consider your continued service in your current capacity, because this administration does not have room for any cowboys."

General Montgomery Stelle, the United States Army Commanding General, was the first to speak. "Mr. President, what I see in that image is intelligence that is at least two hours old. Since we don't have the capability of having live data, I would suggest that we proceed with the mission as it has been planned from the beginning. We don't really have any significant intelligence pertaining to the military capacity of the alien craft other than what we saw when it destroyed our satellites like they were toys. For all we know, that was just a firecracker put under a bucket, and they haven't even broken out their big guns yet. I say we move on as planned."

As soon as he finished, General Louis Watson, Commander of the Air Force, spoke up. "Mr. President, Sir, I must agree with General Stelle. I have no doubt that everyone in this room believes that the aliens are hostile and have every intention of invading this planet in one way or another. I for one do not wish to stand idly by and put all my hope and trust in one man. God knows that he is doing a remarkable job, based on the image we all just viewed, but he is still just one man against what appears to be an army of giants. If it had not been for the fact that the aliens were armed heavily, also indicated on the image, I might be inclined to wait a while longer for no other reason than we have no idea of how long they have been up there. But that is not the case. They are heavily armed. Eventually, no matter how good this one man is, Mr. President, he will fall. When he does, how long will we wait before we decide to take action? For all we know he could already have died in the battle that produced all those bodies. Like I said, I agree with General Stelle. We should fire now, while we still can."

The Secretary of Defense stood up and addressed the room. "Mr. President, I'm sure each man in this room would have something to say about the image and the alien craft for the record, but since time is of the essence, we should stop at this juncture and take a vote on whether we proceed or not. It will give you the thoughts of everyone here without having to hear each one argue his point first."

"Let me remind you all that while we are a democracy, a majority vote in this room means nothing. I still have the final word and the decision is mine alone." The President said firmly.

The Secretary of Defense walked to the center of the room and asked for a show of hands from those who thought that the mission should continue, as planned, at the earliest possible time. He counted and of the fifteen men present, not counting himself or the President, he counted twelve. Wanting to make sure the others still thought that the plan was needed, but the timing was the issue he asked for another vote.

"Of those who did not cast their vote to go ahead as planned immediately, how many believe that the actions we proposed are warranted but should be executed after we get further intelligence?"

The remaining men all raised their hands and the secretary nodded at the President and sat down. Agent Rose was listening in on the meeting, along with General Stephens and wished he was able to see the numbers of men who had voted. Somehow he knew that things hadn't gone his way. As he sat quietly waiting to hear what the count was, the President addressed the room again.

"Those of you who presented your points had credible issues and I thank you. Unfortunately, I must make this decision by myself, and the safety and security of every American must be behind my decision. It is with great appreciation and pride that I say, job well done to that lone soldier in that alien craft, but one soldier does not make an army, and it takes an army to defeat an army. With immense sadness I must agree that the time has come to put this threat to our country down. I vow to remember that lone soldier, to make a memorial to his memory, should he fall, for Americans everywhere to remember the day that he laid down his life for us all."

The President left the room, and the Secretary of Defense picked up the line to Cheyenne Mountain and General Stephens.

"General Stephens, You heard everything, I presume?"

"Yes sir."

"You have authorization to launch; we are go to resume count-down."

"What about Agent Rose? The general questioned.

"Is he there with you now?"

"Yes sir."

"Put him on."

The general took the phone and handed it to James, then left the room to continue his count down. James reluctantly put the receiver to his ear.

"Agent Rose."

"Rose, you are to step down immediately. General Stephens is now in command of this mission."

"Understood sir," James replied without a challenge.

He laid the phone back on the receiver and walked toward the door without going back through the war room. Once outside, he looked up toward the sky and whispered, "Good luck, Sean."

✳ ✳ ✳

Karna had been so preoccupied with the rebellion on her ship that Sean had become of little significance to her. The reality of so many thousands of Tahar Alliance members being able to get through the security screening and crew selection process before they left their home planet of Bilkegine was staggering to her. The Tahar Alliance had to be far more imbedded into the Bilkegine system of Government than she or any of her alliance would be willing to admit. The proof was right in front of her, as more than half of her crew lay dead. Another hard fact for Karna to admit was that she didn't have the reign of terror that she thought she had over her crew. They weren't really afraid of her or what she was able to do to them, as evidenced by the mutiny.

She was sitting in the dimmed light of the War Chamber with nothing but the intense spot light of dighergant radiation pouring down over her. She calculated her next move. She knew that the Tahar had to be defeated; that, they were so little in numbers that they dare not attempt another siege, but something inside her was telling her to launch the attack on earth without the knowledge she had hoped to gain from Sean. There was a knock on the chamber portal but lost in thought, she ignored the knock completely. Not wanting to pay the consequences of disturbing the Commander and knock a second time, the messenger who was bringing news of the space planes just out of sight on their horizon, decided to wait and give her the news at the end of the resting phase.

Hageze had agreed with Sean's plan but made one last suggestion before they initiated. He suggested that they wait a few more hours until the beginning of the resting phase. Despite being under attack before, he knew that the automatic initiation of the resting phase would calm things down, and unless they were under direct fire at the time, many of the crewmen, especially the Quod would automatically return to their quarters to rest. Sean agreed and decided to use the time to better prepare for any surprises that may present themselves after the battle started. When the lights began to dim, indicating the start of the resting phase, Sean knew the time had come. He called Rotusea and Hageze over to him he informed Hageze that he and Rotusea would go scout out the Piiderk level to see if his suggestion was working.

Sean and Rotusea left the way they had arrived inside the Piiderk support chamber and went back through the tunnel and came up inside the weapons supply area just inside the control chamber. As he passed the door that led inside the chamber, he couldn't resist the opportunity to sneak a peek inside. Against Rotusea's objections, he pushed the control button just to the side of the portal and the revolving metal panels began to slide open. He opened the portal just enough to open a small hole in the center of the portal and bend down far enough o peer inside. It was dark and with the exception of the spot lights over each working station, he could see nothing. He thought the room was empty and was just about to open the portal wider when one of the seats swiveled around and a crew member wearing the dark hooded uniforms stood up and walked across the room. They were headed right for the door and Sean thought they might have heard the slight sound of the portal opening and he turned to run into the darkened corner of the room. He waited a few moments expecting the door to open and the worker to come inside, but it never happened.

"Wow! That was too close for comfort!" He whispered to Rotusea. "Let's keep going. I want to get to the Piiderk main corridor and get a look around."

They continued down the elevator, got inside the lower warehouse, and advanced into the Piiderk main corridor. As they were sneaking around trying to gather more intelligence, he noticed an over abundance of drones gathering and cleaning dead bodies form the ship. There were no other signs of any other crew members around and just as Sean was beginning to believe the plan would be easy, they turned the corner around the cinbiote and saw a massive build up of Quod just outside the transportation chamber. His worse fears were realized when he deduced that Karna was beginning her attack.

"Dear God," he said. "She's launching the attack now!"

"What?" Rotusea asked surprised.

"We've got to get the plan going! She's going to attack the planet now!"

Rotusea called Hageze on their secret transmitter and informed him on what they had witnesses. She told him to prepare his men and muster in the forward lower warehouse and wait for them there. She turned to head for the warehouse but Sean reached out and stopped her.

Cremo and Hageze jumped to their feet and Hageze called out for their men to head for the warehouse. As they were making their way through the tunnel, Sean and Rotusea had stopped and were waiting behind the cinbiote to continue to watch the Quod. He was having some difficulty seeing into the transportation chamber and wanted to get closer to see what they were doing. He stepped out from behind the cinbiote but Rotusea grabbed him.

"What are you doing? You will be seen and they will attack." She warned.

"No, look, they are not armed. They are waiting to go inside the transportation chamber. Their weapons must be on board one of those ships but since they cannot operate the loading bay doors from there, they are confused. Somehow we've got to get them inside."

"Now is not the time. We only have these small weapons and they will not deter them from attacking us. Some of them are security Quod and they will detect your presence and attack. We must wait until we are many before we try anything like that." She insisted.

Sean agreed and they turned and went back to the warehouse to wait for the others. As the men came through the tunnels and proceeded down the elevator one at a time, Rotusea was giving them their instructions. Once everyone was inside and they had their instructions, they were ready to go. Sean stepped up and gave the order to advance and told them what to expect once they were outside on the Piiderk.

The Tahar soldiers began to leave in small groups of five men and were hiding their weapons behind them as they left. The plan was to get as close as possible to the transportation portal before displaying any aggressive movement. Just as Sean was about to leave, Cremo called him and motioned for him to come to him.

"Sean, I have problem to solve. When we have Spiruthun control, you leave me to stay." He said in his badly spoken English.

"No, what do you mean leave you? Why?"

"Someone must be behind to overload the dighergant reactor core from the controls in command center. The escaping shuttles not powerful enough to escape before Spiruthun destroyed and they will be caught in explosion. If I be behind, I can make overload after you gone."

"Is there another way you can get off the ship before the ship explodes?" Sean asked concerned.

"Yes, I can, use Star Chamber and transport to escaping shuttle before explosion of ship. I have two crystals." He explained as he handed the master control crystal to Sean.

"Why are you giving me this crystal? Isn't this the crystal that can control every device on the ship? Won't you need it to operate the control panels?"

"No this all I need. You take. You might need emergency."

"Okay my friend. You know more than I do how everything works. God speed!"

"Yes, your God, does he help?"

"Yes, He does Cremo. Yes, he certainly does!"

"Good. Then God speed you as well."

The men were all on the Piiderk level in the main corridor just outside the transportation chamber. They were standing in groups of five, spread across a seventy foot wide hallway looking directly at the Quod standing just outside the transportation chamber. Sean was coming up behind them and wanting to stay out of view in case the security Quod present caught his scent. He gave the order to slowly advance on their position and keep their weapons hidden until the last possible moment. Sean had set up the new weapon Cremo had built and was pushing it along behind the Tahar on its column of air. The plan was to get half way toward them before they moved to the side and let Sean blast a hole for them to travel through, but as they began to reach their position, one of the Tahar men got jumpy and pulled his weapon out from behind his back too early. One of the warrior Quods caught a glimpse of the weapon and immediately signaled an attack.

All they had to do was isolate the warrior Quods in the transportation chamber and their objective to take control of the command center would have been realized without much trouble, but now with the Quod on the alert and beginning to attack, there plans would have to change. Sean immediately screamed for everyone to get behind him and he fired the vortex emitter directly into the oncoming Quod. The rings began to display and grow into an immense ring of energy and by the time it hit the Quod it was at full power. Some of them were so close when it struck them that they were instantly blown to pieces, while the others were picked up and slammed against the wall between the transportation chamber and the Piiderk. Since the blast was so silent, the Quod that were inside the transportation chamber didn't hear anything and did not attack. However, one of the Quod that had been slammed against the wall fell down and landed in the portal effectively blocking the automatic door to remain open. Sean quickly fired again blowing the giant corpse further into the transportation chamber and into the crowd of Quod inside, knocking several to the floor. The portal slid closed and Sean saw the opportunity that he had wanted from the beginning. He ordered everyone to fire on the portal to disable it. Rotusea translated his order so quickly that before Sean didn't have a change his mind. The second he gave the command he regretted it because the noise of the weapon fire would surely alert Karna and those inside the command center. It was too late. Sean hadn't thought far enough ahead when he gave the order to disable the portal, and his rash decision had effectively trapped everyone on the ship. Since that portal was the only way inside the transportation chamber from the Piiderk or any other level, they would have to come up with an alternative plan.

"Okay, never mind that problem for now." He said to himself. "Lock and load my Tahar brothers, everyone to the command center!" He ordered as he turned the Cyclonic Vortex Emitter around to face the primary command center and control chamber.

As they began to run across the huge expanse of the Piiderk, several security Quods came out of the command center heading straight for them. They had either come because of the noise from the attack on the transportation chamber, or they had seen or smelt Sean coming and immediately came rushing toward the advancing Tahar army. Two of the Quod went back inside for reinforcements, but by the time they came out of the chamber, the original Quod had been blown back against the farthest wall more than forty feet away. Being more brawn than brain, the back-up Quod were not discouraged by the other Quods lying dead around the room and continued to rush toward Sean. Once again, Sean pulled the trigger on the Cyclonic Vortex Emitter. This time, because they were so close to the weapon when it discharged it's tremendous energy wave, they were not only blown back against the stone like wall, but struck it with so much intensity that their bones were all broken and their heads were caved inward, causing those that didn't die instantly to fall to the ground twitching and convulsing horribly.

When the Tahar army made it to the command center main chamber they rushed inside shooting everything that moved. However, due to their earlier mishap in engineering, they took more careful aim leaving the controls for the ship intact. The crewmembers inside displayed little resistance to the Tahar and it looked as though everything was going as planned. Once the command center was secure, Sean rushed into the side chamber with five Tahar soldiers but found it empty. He figured they had escaped through the portal he had peeked through earlier and went to investigate, finding a pile of dead crewmembers just inside the weapons supply chamber. As he stepped into the room and over the bodies, a figure came out of the dark recesses of the room holding his weapon high. Unknown to Sean, Rotusea had the forethought of leaving a few men behind at different stations to guard their retreat had it been necessary. Sean nodded at the Tahar man and gave him thumbs up even though he knew it wouldn't mean anything to him. Sean quickly turned around and went back into the main command center and saw that Cremo was already at work closing and locking different areas of the ship. Sean went to the room to the left of the main chamber and stopped at a huge portal. It was locked. Sean turned and asked Cremo what was behind the door.

"It is the War Chamber. It is from where the Commander watches battles and gives her orders." Cremo replied in his native tongue.

Sean looked at him with a bewildered look on his face, and Cremo realized Sean didn't understand him. Before he could explain in English, Rotusea had come in and having heard the question, translated Cremo's explanation. He was reluctant to just barge in thinking that surely Karna had barricaded herself inside and was just waiting for him to come inside so she could kill him. However, at the same time her death was one of his prime objectives, and he wanted to be the one to kill her for what she had put him and Nancy through. Sean turned back toward Rotusea and Cremo and said, "Is there any other way in or out of the room?"

No one answered.

"Come on!" He said loudly. "I've got to know! Is there another way in or out?"

"I do not know." Cremo answered.

Hageze had joined them in the command center right behind Rotusea. "I will go inside! Unlock the door!" he ordered. Cremo went to the proper control station and unlocked the door but it wouldn't open. Hageze kicked at the door and as it slid open, he jumped through the middle section and rolled inside with Sean right on his heels firing around the room.

"It's empty! Where is she?" Sean asked angrily.

"She has escaped," Rotusea said from behind, pointing to a panel behind the large seat in the center of the room.

"Forget her! She'll get hers when we blow the ship!" Sean exclaimed.

They all turned and left the War Chamber, and Sean gave the word for Hageze to go lead the rest of the Tahar to the transportation chamber and onto the ship.

"How will we get inside with the Quods there, and the portal damaged?"

Sean had forgotten about both of them in the heat of battle. He turned to Cremo and instructed him to close and lock every doorway, passageway, maintenance tunnel or any other means of reaching the Piiderk level. "I've got to think a minute and I don't want to have to worry that someone will attack. One more thing," He said to Rotusea. "Post guards around this command center, it is the only way anyone can operate the ship or open the doors."

Sean sat in one of the operator seats at the control panels and thought for a couple of minutes. Then, in a quiet and controlled voice, he told Cremo what to do.

"Cremo, here is what I want you to do. First open all loading bay doors so that every loading bay is open to the space inside the transportation chamber. Then open the entry doors of each ship at the loading ramp. You can do that remotely, yes? Okay, once all the bays and ships are open, close the launch window in the ceiling of the chamber."

Hageze and Rotusea were listening carefully as Sean gave directions to Cremo, and were both confused with what he was doing.

They talked quietly among themselves for a few moments and Rotusea called Sean from across the room.

"Sean, we do not understand. Why are you re-pressurizing the transportation chamber and each launch bay? Will not the Quod inside and the crewmen think it is safe to exit the ships and begin to operate the control panels on the other side of the launching bays?"

"Yes, you're right. That's what I am counting on. Once Cremo closes the launch window and re-pressurizes the room, everyone will assume that Karna has taken control over the ship again and resume their ordinary tasks. I plan on giving them two minutes only before I open the launch window again, sucking everyone in the whole transportation chamber into space and leaving it easy for us to get onboard. Then once the bay is completely empty or those who were able to remain inside are dead and frozen, we will re-pressurize the chamber. We will only leave the launch window open for one minute. That should be ample time to kill everything inside the transportation chamber."

"Again, that is a brilliant plan, Sean. But how do you suggest we get inside the chamber. The portal is still not working and we have no way to repair it from the Piiderk." Rotusea asked.

"Can that door be destroyed with any of the weapons we have available to us?" Sean asked looking at each of the three with him.

"No, it is too strong. It is designed to hold back against the pressure of our ship in the event of a launch. As you will see, when the number one launch bay is open to space."

"Let me think about it some more." Sean replied quietly.

Everyone stood around the room quietly waiting and thinking of a possible solution to the problem. More than twenty minutes passed in silence and the Tahar men outside began to wonder what was happening and asked if it was secure enough for them to leave the Piiderk and re-enter the warehouse where they had their bags and could get something to eat. Sean was a little hungry himself now that the adrenaline was not coursing through his body, so he allowed them to leave. "Open the door for them, will you Cremo? Just leave one man to guard the door."

A few more minutes passed quietly. Suddenly Sean jumped up and screamed, "Eureka!"

His sudden movement and screaming startled everyone around him, especially Hageze and Rotusea. Hageze was startled so much that he fell backward against the wall and slid down on his back with a scared look on his face.

"I'm sorry," Sean said with a big smile on his face. "It's just that I thought of the answer. It was in front of me the whole time and I just plain forgot about it."

"What is it?" Rotusea asked.

"Cremo, Rotusea, you remember when we were in the armory and I blasted a hold in the wall to escape?"

They both nodded in silence.

"Well, it wasn't the first time I had done it. The first time was in the quarters where Karna had put Nancy and me when we first got here. When Gebel was with us we had to escape the Quod, and I blasted a hole in the wall to get away from them. I just remembered that the hole opened into the first bay inside the transportation chamber. I didn't know what it was at the time, but that's our answer. Since the Quod are all gone, we should be able to just stroll onto a ship and escape. Have you been able to get all the loading bays open and open the launch window to space yet?"

"Yes, everything is as planned except for one ship. There was one ship that had disconnected the umbilical and they were preparing to launch when the first attack occurred. Perhaps they are trapped inside or just being safe, but either way, the ship is damaged and cannot launch." Rotusea was standing with her back to the door and was translating everything to Sean. Just as he turned to face Rotusea to discuss the issue, Sean yelled out, "Look out!"

It was too late, Karna had managed to kill the guard posted outside the door and had slipped in during their conversation unnoticed. As she ran toward them, Karna lunged in an attempt to stab Sean with a razor sharp dagger, but when Rotusea turned to see what he was warning them about, she stepped right into the blade. Sean punched Karna in the face with all the strength he had in his body. To his surprise, she fell back and slammed hard against the floor. He quickly took the dagger out of Rotusea's chest and dove for Karna. Coming down hard on top of her, he sank the dagger hard into her neck and pulled it down across her right shoulder. She screamed so loud and at such a high pitch that it caused extreme pain in Sean's ears. As he rolled over in pain, Karna got up and began to run away. Hageze, who had been sitting on the floor against the wall, didn't even have time to get up before it was all over. Thinking that he had given her a mortal wound, Sean decided to let her go and die alone. He sat down beside Rotusea and gently pulled her into his arms. She looked up at Sean with her large black eyes and painfully reached up and touched the side of his face.

"Come on, Rotusea. You'll be alright. We'll take care of you. Just hold on." Sean whispered to her. Then he turned and yelled, "Go get someone to help!"

Sean knew she wasn't going to be alright based on the amount of blood pouring out of her open chest, but didn't know what else to say, so he held her close to him and gently rocked her.

Rotusea let her arm drop to her side and whispered, "You have fought bravely, Sean Daniels. Remember me."

"I will Rotusea. I promise."

Her head dropped to one side and she was dead. Sean raised his face to the ceiling and screamed as loudly as he could, "Karna!—I'm—coming for—you!"

Cremo had managed to open the outside bay doors and decompress the transportation chamber. The entire army of thousands of warrior Quods were now floating lifelessly in space and the launch window was closed and the chamber re-pressurized.

"It will be two minutes more, and the Tahar can board." Cremo said, but when he turned to see if Sean heard what he said, he was gone and Hageze with him.

CHAPTER THIRTY-EIGHT

The countdown had resumed at two minutes, twenty-one seconds when the special meeting at the Pentagon had ended, and Dr. Weiss was prepared to capture everything for the record. General Stephens was anxious for the mission to be over and the lien threat to be obliterated and the crewmen aboard the S51F space planes were glad to finally launch their missiles and head for safety. Everyone seemed to be happy to be back on schedule for the launch except Bruce and Agent James Rose.

The atmosphere inside the War Room on Cheyenne Mountain was all business as the countdown continued.

"Launch minus six, five, four, three, two, one, launch, again I say launch." The operations officer said into the microphone. The S51F pilots all received the launch codes and final launch sequences simultaneously, and the missiles were all souring toward their designated targets from two directions. If nothing else, they thought the sheer force of being caught between the two blast forces created by so many nuclear explosions should disable the craft enough to cause it to drift further into space, but if they were able to penetrate the targets as believed, the ship should be vaporized.

The reports came back to the War Room almost immediately.

"Red seven, to mission control, missiles away!"

"White five-o to mission control, missiles away!

The control technician in charge of the Solar Pulse Laser reported, "Blue seventy-six, firing initiated."

"Stars and Stripes to mission control, laser targeting activated and missiles are inbound." The International Space Station reported.

"All eagles away, General," the watch commander reported, "Impact in four miles, three, two, one mile and closing, Sir."

"It's all or nothing now!" General Stephens said loudly.

The watch commander switched to time till impact, "impact in three, two, one, impact!"

They could only wait for a call from Dr. Weiss, now. They knew it would take several minutes before all the data could be processed through the computers and the NASA imager. While it really didn't matter what the outcome was since they had thrown everything they had at them, the room was still anxiously waiting for the call from Dr. Weiss.

Dr. Weiss was watching the entire operation unfold through the eye of his telescope. He was one of the scientists who feared the unknown effect a nuclear explosion of that magnitude might have on earth's upper atmosphere, but realized that it was the only course of action the planet had against the alien spacecraft. The explosion was so powerful that all he could see in the telescope when the missiles exploded was a brilliant light that mirrored the intensity of the sun. He knew he would have to wait for the computer to calculate the readings from the release of gasses and other radiation before he would be able to see and image and was anxious to see what, if any, negative effects the explosion caused.

✳✳✳

The Tahar were in the middle of boarding their escape ship when the blast ripped through the Spiruthun. The vessel shook so violently that the bay doors that had been closed between them and the one remaining attack ship full of Quod was shaken open, and the Quod that had come out of their ship to investigate saw the Tahar soldiers and began to attack. Several Tahar soldiers took positions around the opening and were blasting the Quod as they attempted to clear the bay door. Ammunition was running low, and if they didn't get loaded quickly, they would be overrun.

Although the actual hull of the ship was not breeched by the explosions, several areas of the vessel were on fire, and explosions were going off on every level. Sean was on the Piiderk trying to find Karna when the attack occurred. He came to the cinbiote and thought he should use it one more time to rid himself of any radiation poisoning he may have from the long term exposure of the dighergant material on the ship. As he approached the cinbiote, Karna sprang out of a doorway that led to the chamber beside the transportation chamber and struck him across the upper body throwing him twenty feet across the floor. Without a weapon, Sean thought he stood little chance against Karna because of her physical strength, but he was not about to lie down and die now. He got back to his feet and ran at her with everything he had inside him. The adrenaline was once again coursing through his body and he could feel his strength growing exponentially. Screaming as he ran, he jumped toward her the last five feet, came down on top of her he grabbed her around the neck and spun her to the ground. As he landed he heard bones cracking in her shoulder, and she let out another high-pitched scream as the pain shot through her body.

"You—are—going—to—die—now! You black hearted witch!" Sean screamed in her face.

He scrambled to his feet while holding her in a choke-hold. If he hadn't wounded her with the dagger, Sean wouldn't have had a chance against her, but in her weakened state, and since Sean had broken her collar bone and was bearing down on it with all his strength, she had little choice but to go with him as he dragged her along walking backward.

Sean was wondering what he was going to do with her since he lacked the physical strength to either choke her or snap her neck. Then he got an idea. He started backing toward the cinbiote, remembering that Karna had never entered to retrieve Nancy or him from it before, and figured it must not be good for them. Step by step, against her struggling to free herself, Sean dragged her into the cinbiote.

"You're—coming—with—me!" Sean seethed.

Once they made it to the brilliant light of the cinbiote, Sean began to feel stronger and a sense of peace began to come over him. He could feel himself getting stronger and at the same time felt Karna get weaker.

"Are we having fun yet?" He whispered into Karna's ear.

"You are—killing me," she said weakly.

She finally stopped struggling and her entire body began to shutter, then went limp. Karna was finally dead.

Sean lay there for a few minutes soaking up the light and warm feelings and would have stayed inside the cinbiote indefinitely, but suddenly was shaken back into the reality that the ship was being destroyed by another violent eruption deep inside the belly of the vessel. As he was rolling out from under the lifeless body of his enemy, the light of the cinbiote went out. Sean jumped to his feet and ran to his previous living quarters and the hole in the wall leading to the transportation chamber.

Cremo had completed the final sequence of commands that would bring the dighergant central core to a sudden melt down and catastrophic explosion that would destroy the ship and everyone on it. He had initiated the sequence just before the missiles had struck the Spiruthun and began to leave the command center for the Star Chamber when he heard a transmission from the ship the Tahar were escaping with.

"Cremo, come in are you there?" Hageze called into the communication transmitter onboard the escape shuttle. "Cremo, come in."

Cremo ran back to the control panel and replied.

"Yes Hageze, I am here. You must leave now; the dighergant reactor core will fail at any moment."

"We cannot lift off, the launching bay door was opened between our ship and the last remaining attack ship that had disconnected their umbilical. Their bay is pressurized and they are firing upon us. We are all onboard, but they managed to get to the remote control panel and have closed the launch window. Can you open it again?"

Cremo ran to the other control panel on the other side of the ship and took his last crystal and used it to bypass the remote control panel in the number two launch bay. Then we ran back to the original panel and opened the launch window.

"Cremo, come in. It is opening and the Quod are being sucked into space. Well done. Get to the transportation chamber immediately and use the Star Chamber to time-shift into our ship. Here is the tracking coordinates."

Hageze read a series of number quickly into the communicator and ended transmission.

Assuming that Sean was onboard the escape shuttle, Cremo took the crystal out of the nearest control device and sprinted to the Star Chamber. Unknown to him, the crystal allowed a portal to open onto the Piiderk level and several Quod came rushing in. Just as he was entering the room where Sean and Nancy had been held captive, two Quod caught up with him and picked him up and threw him across the corridor. The Quod headed toward him again and Cremo scrambled to his feet and grabbed a weapon lying nearby on the floor of the Piiderk main corridor. He picked it up to fire, but as he pointed the weapon one of the Quod grabbed him and broke his back with his bare hands and dropped him to the floor. Sean was nearing the door to his chamber and hadn't seen the battle between the Quod and Cremo due to the brilliant light inside the main corridor and was surprised to see the Quod as they headed toward him.

The ship was erupting in a chain reaction of one explosion after another, and Sean was trapped on the ship. He did not have a weapon, and the ones lying around on the floor were out of ammunition. He was running out of time and energy but most of all patience. He had been through more than he would ever be able to forget and he was not going to put up with one more thing, but deep down he knew he was no match against two giant Quod bare handed despite what had been reported otherwise. His only option was to stop and pray.

"God," he began, "I know now like never before that you exist. I know that what I have heard on Sunday mornings the past few months is more than superstition. I also know that you are aware of everything that is going on and when you are needed, but I've got to ask, will you help me survive? I know it's up to you Lord. Only you know if I was ever meant to survive this trial, so I guess it's now or never. Before I die on this alien craft, please forgive me for my many sins against you. I didn't know. I thank you for giving me your Son to die for my sins and now put my life into your hands. Amen."

As he opened his eyes and looked up, the two Quod were gone. He quickly looked around the room as far as he could see but saw no sign that they were there. He saw Cremo lying on the floor crumpled up in a strange way and ran over to him.

"Cremo," he said sadly, "Oh, man, I'm sorry."

Cremo cringed in pain as Sean turned him onto his back.

"Oh my Lord, Cremo, is there anything I can do for you?"

"Your Lord, He is a good God?"

"Yes Cremo, he is more than that. He is a loving and caring God who takes care of his people."

"Are you his people, Sean?"

"I am now, Cremo, I am now."

"Can he be my…"

Cremo died but Sean knew what he was going to ask. He wasn't sure he knew the answer and didn't even have the knowledge to guess, but he thought the answer would have been 'yes, Cremo, He can be your God too'.

CHAPTER THIRTY-NINE

The NASA computer and imager finally completed the calculations and Dr. Weiss viewed the image to see if the outcome of the attack was successful. With utter shock and disbelief, he sat in the dark room and picked up the phone to call the general at Cheyenne Mountain.

"General Stephens, this is Dr. Weiss." He said quietly. "The images have been compiled and are on their way to you now. You will have them available in two minutes."

"What do they show, Dr. Weiss." The general asked anxiously.

"You had better wait and see for yourself general. I am not qualified to make any assessment in these matters."

"You can tell if it's still there or not can't you?" The general asked frustrated.

"It is still there general. The missiles failed to penetrate the ship and the Solar Pulse Laser simply bounced off the surface as if it was a mirror."

After he hung up the phone, the general went to the launch commander's station and ordered him to break radio silence with the S51F pilots and put him through.

Moments later the space planes reported in.

"Mission control, this is Red seven. Confirm."

"Mission control, White five-o. Confirm."

The operations officer confirmed their transmission and coordinates, and then reported to the general. "General Stephens, I have Red seven on the box, he is the closest to the spacecraft."

"Put him through to me, Captain." General Stephens ordered. "Mike, do you read?"

"Roger, Cheyenne, this is Red seven, is that you John?"

"Listen carefully, Mike. I need confirmation on the condition of the alien spacecraft, repeat, confirmation on the condition of the spacecraft, copy?"

"Copy that general, give me five minutes to get into range, over."

While he was waiting the general stormed out of the War Room and into the briefing room to watch the image on the NASA computer. He bolted into the room shouting, "Run the file!"

Just as the file began to run and the first images were coming into focus, James walked into the room. He saw the missiles clearly approach the alien craft and then the brilliant light and subsequent cloud of dust. Two minutes later, as the cloud cleared, the ship was there, and while it was clear that some damage did occur, it was not destroyed and continued to display it's camouflage pattern. The general turned to leave. When he saw James standing there he stopped momentarily and asked him to join him in the War Room.

"Come with me. I've got Red seven doing a fly-by."

They walked together back to the War Room. By the time they arrived the S51F was just transmitting.

"Repeat—the craft is still intact but there are…"

A huge explosion ripped through space in the middle of the transmission. The percussion was so immense that it vaporized the space plane and all aboard instantaneously.

"They're gone general!" said the launch commander.

"What do you mean they're gone? You mean we've lost communication? Get them back!" He shouted.

"No general, I mean they are gone; disappeared from our scanners!"

"What's going on?" The general screamed.

"White five-o to mission control, come in mission control!"

"Go White five-o!"

"Red seven has been vaporized along with the alien spacecraft. Repeat, Red seven vaporized with alien craft."

James walked slowly out of the War Room with his head hanging down. He walked out of the mountain and took out his phone and dialed a number.

"Sheriff Faulkner, please." James said.

A few seconds later Bruce answered the call.

"Sheriff Faulkner."

"Bruce, James. I'm afraid I have bad news."

"My buddy didn't make it did he?"

"I'm afraid not. I did everything I could to give him more time but in the end we felt we had to act if we were to have a chance against the aliens."

"So, what you're saying is that we blew him up?"

"No, but we tried. We were not able to penetrate their defenses."

"I don't understand, James. How do you know it's over?"

"A few minutes after we learned that the missiles and pulse laser failed, the ship just blew up."

"Well maybe Sean won after all," Bruce said.

"Yeah, maybe he did at that."

Cheyenne Mountain stepped back down to normal security level, defcon five. They hailed their mission a success, and life began to return to normal. The files began to be collected for storage in some obscure location, and Agent Rose went back to Washington within an hour of the alien craft's destruction.

Bruce was divided by what had happened to Sean. On one hand, he was happy that Sean was the hero, that he had single-handedly defeated an alien invader that had originally abducted him. On the other hand, he had lost a very close friend who he had known a very long time and who would be missed by everyone who ever had the privilege of knowing him. He would be sorely missed.

Bruce decided to go down to Sean's hardware store and walk around for a while to help him get a grip on the reality that he was gone. He parked his squad car in front of the store, took out the key that he had forgotten earlier, opened the door, and stepped inside. He was standing admiring the perfection in every parts bin and remembered Sean's love for the old building when he stepped on a spot on the floor that always produced a loud squeak. Suddenly a brilliant light came out of nowhere and illuminated the hardware store. He thought he recognized the light as that which the aliens had used to take Sean at the beginning of the horrific nightmare and from when Nancy and the girl, Nakita, were returned. This couldn't be the same thing, he thought as he walked toward the door and pulled back the cardboard that had been put in the door to cover the broken glass. I was just told that the alien craft was destroyed with Sean in it.

Bruce tried to pull back the cardboard a little further to see if it was just a play of lights caused by the street lights coming on or the setting sun coming through but it wouldn't move any further. He reached for the knob and as soon as he grabbed it he dramatically pulled back his hand due to an intense burning. "What in the name of Sam hill is going on here?" He mumbled.

He stepped back a few steps because of the immense heat coming through the old wooden door and expected it to burst into flames any second. He turned quickly around, and with some difficulty, climbed up onto the counter by the cash register so he could see over the window display. The light was so bright he had to hold his hand over his eyes to shade them from the brilliance. Then several small blue lightning bolts began to strike the ground and light poles all around the area. Bruce was closer to the light than he had ever been and his face was actually getting burned. He looked down at his squad car parked just outside the door and saw the paint begin to bubble and smoke.

As Bruce turned to shield his face from burning any more, he saw the back door that lead to the alley behind the store. Bruce knew that the alley was blocked by a large fence by the sidewalk, but he ran out of the store and into the alley. He hit the fence running and threw one leg over the fence and finally managed to climb over just in time to see the light begin to dim slightly. Then he heard a loud clapping sound and when the light went out, he saw Sean standing in the same spot he had disappeared from so many weeks earlier.

Sean slumped slightly after the light dimmed, and Bruce was there to catch him before he hit the ground.

"I've got you buddy!" Bruce said, as he gently lowered Sean to the step. "I thought you were dead! Great Caesar's Ghost it's good to see you!"

"Sean looked up at his large friend and said, "Oh, you know you can't keep a mountain man down."

"You know you're right, but I got a call from the government just ten minutes ago, and they told me the alien ship was destroyed and you along with it."

"It did?" Sean asked excited.

"That's what they told me."

"I didn't know. We had set the spaceships reactor core to overload. As I was running to the escape ship, I ran into a bunch of really big and really ugly alien guys."

"How did you get away from them?"

"You know what I did, Bruce. I prayed."

"You—You prayed?"

"As a matter of fact I've been doing a lot of that lately. And you know what? God does care and there is no doubt in my mind that He's out there looking out for us."

"Well, Maggie will be glad to hear you say that. But, if the escape ship left without you, how did you get home?"

"I thought I was a goner for sure. Until I remembered this," he said taking a crystal key about the size of a credit card out of his pocket and holding it up.

"What does it do?"

"It allowed me to operate the, uh, transport device they called the Star Chamber. It's what they used to bring me and Nancy to their ship."

"Well buddy, I for one am glad to see you made it back in one piece, and I know of one other that will be happy to see you." Bruce said with a huge smile.

"Oh, Yeah, Where is Nancy?"

"She's at my place. Want a ride?"

"Uh, sure, but there is something I need to do on our way."

"What's that?"

"You know the old silver mine outside of town?"

"Uh, yeah sure I do, I played there all the time when I was a kid. What about it?"

"How deep does it go?"

"Oh, man, that thing probably goes down more than three hundred feet, maybe more. Nobody I know has ever been to the bottom. Why all the interest in that old place all of a sudden. Isn't there something else you want to do first?"

"No. This is important."

"What gives?"

"Let's just say I may need a home for some special new friends."

✳ ✳ ✳

Life went on as usual for most of the citizens of the world. Oblivious to the fact that they were ever in any danger of being terminated by an alien species, they carried on with their usual chores, daily jobs and boring commutes, but for some, like Sean and Nancy, life is a gift designed to be treasured, and they treasured every day together from that day on.

Sean has several new routines added to his daily regime. Every morning after he showers with lukewarm water, he picks up his lucky Army medallion, pocket-knife and crystal key, then walks down to eat a full home cooked breakfast and kisses his wife goodbye before he walks to the store. Yes, a lot has changed and Sean figures that he has the aliens and God to thank for all of it.

Every now and then the Sheriff's office gets a strange call to investigate weird noises heard down by the old silver mine, and every now and then, he tells them it's probably the ghosts of the old miners swinging their picks and leaves it alone because he knows the truth and he's finally learned that the truth can really set you free.

The End